About the Author

After studying Russian political, social, and economic history, and the United Nations Human Rights Treaties in the Graduate programme at York University Toronto, Josie Mounsey conducted extensive research into human trafficking networks and the lives of ordinary Russians in the late twentieth century. She again brings this knowledge to life in her second novel, a suspenseful, moving narrative. After over thirty years living and working in Canada, Josie now lives in the UK with her husband, Joe Mounsey.

Dedications

To the millions of victims of sex trafficking throughout the world, and to the brave souls who risk their own lives to help them and to try to bring traffickers to justice.

To my husband, Joe Mounsey, who has not only tramped around Russia with me but has been a continuing source of love and support, even in the midst of our recent chaotic Trans-Atlantic move.

Josie Mounsey

I Must Remember

Austin Macauley Publishers™
London • Cambridge • New York • Sharjah

A CIP catalogue record for this title is available from the British Library.

ISBN 9781035852819 (Paperback)
ISBN 9781035852826 (Hardback)
ISBN 9781035852833 (ePub e-book)

www.austinmacauley.com

First Published 2024
Austin Macauley Publishers Ltd®
1 Canada Square
Canary Wharf
London
E14 5AA

Acknowledgements

My thanks go to the many people who encouraged me in my writing career. Parts of the early draft of this novel were read and commented on by Prim Pemberton and the individuals who participated in her writing workshops, Creative Writing in Cabbagetown, Toronto: Ann Bjorseth, Ilene Cummings, Sylvia Daigneault, Philip Jessup, Gobnait McAnoy, Barb Nahwegahbow, Steve Thompson, and Andy Webster. I miss our Wednesday afternoon get-togethers.

Alan Cumyn, my mentor in the Creative Writing program at the Humber School for Writers, Toronto, provided much-needed encouragement and advice in the formative stages of this story.

Writing can be a lonely pursuit, and I have to thank my family and friends for grounding me in reality from time to time.

Table of Contents

If I were to remain silent,
I'd be guilty of complicity.
Albert Einstein

The past is not a bad witness.
Russian Proverb

Ignore the past—you lose an eye.
Forget the past—you lose two eyes.
Russian Proverb

1
A Village Somewhere in Siberia
October 1991

Anja buried her face in the pillow. The words stung. "Forget him! Your father doesn't want you!" her mother had said in the horrid voice she used now. Her voice had been nice when they had lived in Leningrad. But here, Anja must never tell anyone that was where they came from. Here, her name was Yelena Borisovna Zubova, the daughter of Boris Zubov. That is what the papers said—the papers Boris got for them. But she wanted to be Anja Yelena Galichina again. When she was Anja, her papa loved her, wanted her. They all lived together—Anja, Mama and Papa—in the apartment in Leningrad.

Here, she had to call Boris 'Papa'. She tried not to call him anything. Boris had driven them from Leningrad, the place where they didn't come from. He wasn't really her papa. Her papa didn't have a bald head and horrid pictures on his arms. Her papa had brown curly hair like hers. His face was nice. When he cuddled her, he sometimes ran his whiskers around her face. She giggled now thinking about it, then froze, remembering: *Your father doesn't want you!* She must have done something really bad. Hadn't he always told her that, however naughty she was, he would always love her?

She sat up and ran a finger along the lines of stitching on the quilt covering her bed, tracing the strips of different fabrics from the small square in the middle as they wrapped around and around. She liked the bright colours, the pretty flowers, but today they looked dirty, as if they had been washed in the muddy river where the old women did their laundry. She liked to listen to their gossip as they worked. One day, when they didn't know she was there, she heard Dotnara Vektorova tell Gertruda Delezhova that she didn't think Yelena could be Boris's daughter as she didn't look a bit like him.

Now, Anja picked up the rag doll and hugged him. Mama had forbidden her from taking him to bed with her. "He smells, Yelena." Anja liked the smell. *Tyotya* Yevdokia Marlenova, Boris's aunt in whose house they now lived, told her the doll was a character from a fable, but *Tyotya* couldn't remember which one. He had always lived in this house and had taken on the smell of the wooden walls. He had a brown face, black hair and bushy eyebrows—really, one bushy eyebrow, the other had lost most of its wool. He wore brown *valenki*, like the felt boots Anja wore. His pants were mustard colour and his blue checked shirt had a red and blue collar which draped over his shoulders like the shawls the old women wear here. *The old women Mama doesn't want to end up like.* Anja heard her telling Boris that early one morning when they hadn't known she was awake in her bed behind the curtain in the kitchen.

Anja wished she could see Katya, her best friend. But Katya lives in that other place. She would have started school now; the school where they had hoped to sit side by side as they had in kindergarten. Anja had missed the start of school in the village and was made to sit in the only spare seat. It was next to Stepan, a nasty boy with bright red hair. He made fun of her unruly curls, saying she looked like the mop his mother used to wash the floor. At the end of her first day, he waited for her outside the school and pinched her until she cried. Laryssa Kirillova Polzina, their teacher, took him by one ear and led him home to his mother. The very next day, Stepan was moved to a desk in the front row and a girl called Kalisa came to sit with Anja. She wasn't as nice as Katya, but had the same blonde braid hanging down her back.

One day, Laryssa Kirillova told them that Leningrad was now called St Petersburg and asked if anyone in the class could point to the city on the map on the wall. Anja jumped to her feet, rushed to the front and put the tip of one of her fingers on the edge of the Gulf of Finland.

"When Mama and I lived …" She clapped a hand over her mouth, remembering Boris's warning: *The bad men will come and take you away if you tell anyone where you used to live.* She scurried back to her desk, cheeks burning, swallowing back tears, the laughter of the other children ringing in her ears.

Now, Anja lay back on her bed thinking about the day they left Leningrad. *The place you don't come from,* she quickly reminded herself. That day, she was very excited. Mama had told her that Boris would drive her to the home of Eugenia, one of Mama's friends. Mama would join them later. Boris drove her in *Dyadya* Mikhail's big black car—it had a little cupboard with real drinks.

Dyadya Mikhail wasn't really her uncle, not like *Dyadya* Pyotr, but Mama said that was what she should call him. He was Mama's friend, and Mama was always smiling when she was with *Dyadya* Mikhail. Eugenia had big dangly earrings and let Anja play with the make-up on her dressing table.

It was fun, but not as much fun as going to *Dyadya* Mikhail's *dacha*, where there was a dollhouse just for Anja. It had miniature furniture, even a kitchen fitted with a stove. She pretended she was cooking meals for the family of little dolls perched on chairs around the table. The stove didn't really work but she imagined steam coming from the pan of *kasha* as she ladled it into tiny bowls.

When Mama and Boris arrived at Eugenia's that day, they bundled Anja into the car and Boris drove very fast, swinging around bends, narrowly avoiding cars travelling the other way. She was very scared, but Mama hugged her close and told her it was going to be all right. "We're going on a trip … just for a while." Eventually, Anja fell asleep, her head on Mama's lap.

She awoke in a strange bed in a strange house. She had looked around. *Where's Mama? Where is she?* Anja got out of bed, pulled the door open a crack and listened. There were voices.

Papa's here! The thought propelled her onto the landing and down the stairs, where she came to a halt at the kitchen door. Anja's eyes scanned the room. Her papa wasn't there; it was just Mama, Boris, and a woman who was taking something out of the oven. It smelled nice, like the special treats *Babushka* Sophia used to make. Before she died.

Boris said they had to wait at the house until he heard from the Boss, which was what he always called *Dyadya* Mikhail. On the second day, Mama got angry and picked up the telephone and called the *dacha*. She put the receiver down quickly and she and Boris went outside. Anja had stood on tiptoe, trying to see over the profusion of plants on the window-ledge. Mama was walking around the garden, running her hands through her hair then waving her arms about. Boris grabbed her, pinning her arms to her sides. He said something to her, his face close to hers and, after a little while, they came inside. Boris picked up the car keys and left. Mama sat at the kitchen table. She didn't answer when Anja spoke.

When Boris came back, the big black car had gone. In its place a smaller one. "A Zhiguli! You expect me to travel in that old thing?" Mama had yelled. He said it was '*less conspicuous*', whatever that meant. Then he loaded the bags into the car. Anja's excited "Are we going to see *Dyadya* Mikhail?" brought a scowl from Boris and tears from her mother. As they travelled, Anja buried her head in the corner of the seat and imagined she could hear Papa reading her favourite story, The Firebird: ... *The mischievous wind covered the feathers with grass and leaves, but nothing could rob them of their glowing rainbow colours.*

Later, they came to this village and to this house, the home of *Tyotya* Yevdokia Marlenova. It is a small house, but *Tyotya* said they could stay as long as they liked. Her husband died a few months ago and she liked the company and help around the house. Anja had run from room to room calling Papa's name. Mama grabbed her by an arm, telling her that Papa had done a very bad thing and was never coming back. Anja had struggled free and run outside, kicking at a pile of wood at the side of the house. It was *Tyotya* who tempted her back inside with a *pryaniki* fresh from the oven, telling Anja she could have the warmest bed—the one behind the curtain just off the kitchen, where the stove burnt night and day. Mama and Boris had to share a room at the back of the house.

Now, in the dim light, Anja sat up and ran a finger along the wooden wall at the side of her bed, tracing the faded pink and blue painted flowers. *Tyotya* said her husband decorated the wall when they were married many years ago. Some of the flowers were upside down, and the old woman laughed when Anja asked if he had stood on his head to paint those.

Voices came from the other side of the curtain, and Anja swung her legs to the floor and hid the rag doll under the quilt. She tugged off her woollen dress and put on the white dress with the sailor collar, the one her father bought her before he went away. It was her favourite, and she had been wearing it the day they left the place she isn't allowed to mention. Thin red ribbons hung from the waist and swirled around when she turned a circle. She perched on the side of the bed and closed her eyes, imagining that when she opened the curtain Papa would be there with the other people from the village who were coming to share the special cake with pink icing *Tyotya* made. She hoped he had brought her a gift. Then she remembered: *Your father doesn't want you*! But maybe, on her seventh birthday, he would forgive whatever she had done.

2

A Place South-East of St Petersburg, Russia October 1991

Heel to toe … heel to toe … fifteen measured steps then the tips of the toes of Sergei Dmitrievich Galichin's left foot touched the wall. He disentangled his feet and turned to the right. Five, six, seven steps … another wall. Always the same. The steps never changed. Sometimes, he gave up counting, slid down to the fetid floor and closed his eyes, shutting out the overhead light that burnt night and day. When he first came here—wherever here was—he tried to keep count of the times daylight seeped through the barred window high above. He had scratched the plaster wall with his fingernails. A downward stroke for each of six daylights—on the seventh a diagonal line. Then one day as he scratched the wall, he wondered if he had already made the mark. He had paced around trying to remember, studying his jagged fingernails for telltale plaster. But how could he distinguish one day's plaster scratchings from another?

Now, he sat in a corner of the floor, knees tucked into his body, and ran a hand up and down the rough cloth of his dark blue pants, scratching first one leg then the other. Harder now until it hurt. Raising his right arm, he twisted his fingers through his matted hair and picked at scabs in his scalp. He pulled his hand away, carefully gathered together the pieces of grey hair and skin caught in his fingernails and put them in the pocket of his jacket. When he came here, they had shaved his head. After he stopped making his marks on the wall, he began to check the length of his hair. The sides now reached half-way down his ears. How many days, weeks, months, did that mean?

The clang of an iron door slamming reverberated through his head and down his spine, intensifying the now-familiar stabs of hunger which seemed to be with him even in sleep. He looked across at the tray with the metal bowl and mug sitting by the flap in the bottom of the door—he had licked both utensils clean several times, so there was nothing to be had from them. He picked at his teeth, hoping to find a globule of fat, a remnant of bread. Nothing. He listened for the squeak of wheels in the corridor, for that was when the flap in the door would open, a hand reach in to retrieve the tray and return it with its offering of bread and lukewarm soup. *Maybe today there will be a strand of meat in the bottom of the bowl or a sliver of cabbage floating in the grease on top.* Sergei licked his lips now, imagining how he would break off a small piece of bread, dip it into the soup and move it slowly around his mouth. One day there was a chunk of potato skin floating in the soup. He had pulled it out quickly and secreted it under the grey blanket on the cot on which he slept in case the guard came back to claim it. Later, he huddled under the blanket, facing the wall, and sucked the potato skin clean before pulling off piece after piece and chewing them slowly. Every day now, he examined the soup carefully. *That potato skin tasted good.*

He tapped on the wall. No answering tap came. It had been like that for a while. He knew not what happened to the man who used to be there, the man whose words had bolstered Sergei's spirits. One day he was there. The next gone. He hadn't heard them take him. Sergei liked to think he was spirited away. It gave him hope that one day his turn would come and he would again be sitting at the kitchen table with Mitch, his son, discussing some aspect of a case or a finer point of law. *Law?* He shook his head.

One night he heard Sophia's voice: "Seryozha … Seryozha … is it you?" He sat up and looked around, heart pounding. "Seryozha …" A smell of perfume wafted in the air. "I'm here, I'm here, Sophia," he called. She was there in the corner. He rose unsteadily to his feet and went towards her but, as he reached out to take her hands, his fingers found only the damp wall. He staggered around the cell, waving his hands in front, searching for her. "Sophia! Sophia! Where are you?" His voice louder, more frantic. *"Zatknis'! Zatknis'!"* the guard yelled and rapped on the door with his nightstick.

That was the night his mug had been filled with *Chifir*, the bitter, concentrated brew of tea. He had at first enjoyed the sense of release the narcotic-high gave him. Lying on the floor, he imagined he was floating above himself, looking down. He saw a child with brown curls sitting on a chair. His granddaughter. It was her. His Anja. She was sewing pink stitches in the corner of a piece of white cloth. She held it up to him. "See *Deda*. It is for *Babushka's* birthday." He tried to speak, to tell Anja she must come home, but she faded, then was gone. Sometime later, he had slumped onto his cot, willing the room to stop spinning. It was then he heard her, his dear Sophia. But how could it be? Hadn't he held her hands—the hands he felt getting colder and colder as her life drained away? He and Mitch had stood by her grave as the Rebbe intoned the words of The Mourner's Kaddish: "May His great name grow exalted and sanctified …" He had stared at the coffin as it was lowered into the ground, thinking how his beloved wife was denied the comfort of her religion in life. All he could do for her was bury her in the ground sacred to Jews, returning her to her rightful spiritual place; the place she sacrificed to marry him. Long after the Rebbe and mourners had left, he and his son kept silent vigil over the grave, each lost in his own memories, his own regrets for things said and not said. They walked away together, two lonely souls.

When he first came here, the thought of his son comforted him. What did it matter that he was in this filthy hole where every last vestige of self-respect was stripped from him, and where he would sell his own soul for an extra hunk of bread? At least his son was safe, somewhere far away. To walk away from Mitch in the Cathedral undercroft was the hardest thing he had ever done. Outside, he wandered aimlessly, the chants of the crowds all around him lauding their new hero: "Yeltsin! Yeltsin! Dissolve the Party! Axe the KGB!" Sergei's head had been full of his son's voice, pleading with him not to go. But he had to. It was the only way to keep Mitch from harm.

As time passed in this place, he willed himself not to think about his son. *If you do, they'll know where he is. They'll get into your brain and find him.* He told himself so many times he didn't have a son, he began to believe it. When he tried to picture him, all he saw was a shadowy figure without a face. Maybe it was better that way. When he first came here, he dreaded the cell door opening. He knew what awaited him in the room with the blinding light, the beam of which penetrated even tightly closed eyelids. The voice behind the light always asked the same question, "Where is your son? Where is he?" The questioning started gently. The soft voice wove into his brain until he could not even tell them who he was. When the voice became loud, he tried to shut out the words, scared he would blurt something out. Staring into the light, he no longer knew whether he was sitting, standing, or lying down; his body weightless. "I don't have a son … I don't have a son …" he whispered. Sharp blows across his face jerked him back to reality. Fear came back. Fear they would find his son. In that room, when he was at his lowest ebb, he thought of his beloved Sophia. No one could hurt her anymore. Snatches of her favourite poem came to him. At first jumbled words floated around in his head, but if he blocked everything out and went into the world only he and his wife shared, the words assembled into order. Then he would begin to intone to himself the haunting words of Anna Akhmatova's poem:

Black and enduring separation
I share equally with you.
Why weep? Give me your hand.
Promise me you will come again ...[1]

Now, the clomp of boots jolted him from his reverie. He shifted back farther into the corner, fearing they had come for him again. The flap in the bottom of the door opened and a hand retrieved the tray, then replaced it with another. He stared at it for some minutes, recalling how on his first day here he only managed to swallow two spoonsful of the greasy liquid before throwing up over the floor. He had looked around, but there was nothing with which to wipe up the mess. The smell mingled with the stench of the bucket which he used as a latrine. As time passed, he had watched the vomit harden, then disintegrate into dust.

In the early days when the grim-faced guards threw open the door and ordered him to pick up the latrine bucket, he walked quickly out of the cell, trying not to let the bucket slop on to his bare feet. As he moved along the stone-flagged corridor his head twisted from side to side, eager to catch a glimpse of another human being. He knew they were there; he heard their cries.

One day, he was sure it was Mitch's voice he heard. "Who's that?" he shouted. The bucket clattered to the floor, its contents spilled over his feet as hands gripped his arms and dragged him back to his cell.

Since then, he walked silently with the latrine bucket. He counted his steps on the way back, quickening his pace as the open door to his cell beckoned. A sigh of relief would escape his lips as he lowered the empty bucket into the corner and heard the door slam. Then panic gripped him. The room had got smaller in his absence. It was then he started measuring his floor space. Fifteen steps; seven steps.

There was a time he had hope, foolish hope—the time before they brought him here. They came for him just hours after he parted from his son. He had been

---

[1] *From 'In Dream', by Anna Akhmatova (1889–1966)*

toying with the food on his plate at the kitchen table. Since then, he had tried many times to remember what the room looked like. *Why can't you remember?* he berated himself. *It was your home.* The word *'home'* now seemed strange. What was home? Was this now his home, where he would spend the rest of his life? He shuddered. And why had they brought him here? He had not done anything wrong—nothing they could know about. His mind went back to the feeling of helplessness as they dragged him into the street. Anastasia, who cooked for him, cried out as they forced him into the back of a van. He shouted to her: "Tell Vera Aleksandrovna! Tell her …" The clang of metal doors on the van obliterated the rest of his words and shut out the world he had known. He scrambled to his knees in the darkness and felt for a handle on the doors. Nothing. He banged on the doors with his fists. The floor juddered and the vehicle began to move as he crawled across the metal ridges in the floor and braced himself against the side. What seemed like hours later, the engine noise stilled and the doors opened. As he climbed out he screwed up his eyes against the white lights that pierced the darkness. A dog barked. *You should have shouted out,* he told himself many times since then. But who would have heard? Who would have cared?

For the first few days, he convinced himself today was the day. The day the door would open and they would tell him it was all a mistake. He had gone over in his mind what he would do. He would put on his own clothes, button his shirt—he thought he had been wearing the cream and brown check that Sophia gave him the Christmas before she died. His pants would be next, followed by his jacket. *Were you wearing a jacket, an overcoat? Where are my clothes?*

These thoughts troubled him for days.

Now, he swallowed the last drop of soup, ran a crust of bread around the bowl, put the bread in his mouth and sucked it until there was nothing left. Then he lay on his cot, facing the wall, and pulled the blanket over his shoulders. He closed his eyes and thought of Sophia; her body warm against his, his arm over her waist, his face nestled into her back. He breathed in the smell of perfume and drifted off to sleep.

3
Halifax, Canada
October 1991

Jacko thrust a wad of dollars into Mitch Galichin's hand. "That's it for the season," he said. "We'll see you next year?"

Mitch shook his head and tucked the money into the inside pocket of his jacket. "Thanks, but I need to find regular work."

Jacko locked the ticket booth and with a cheery wave sauntered off. Mitch turned and stared at the boats; their rhythmic bobbing at the moorings calmed the sense of unease in his stomach. Under different circumstances, he might have enjoyed the six weeks he spent selling tickets for trips on Jacko's boat, 'Atlantic Rose'. Behind the small sliding glass window in the wooden hut, he felt relatively safe. But, from time to time, Jacko's shouts of: "Lapitsky! You're supposed to be encouraging people to take a trip!" forced him out onto the boardwalk.

Mitch found it difficult to respond to his assumed name, 'Andrei Lapitsky'; the name on the papers that gained him entry into Canada. He spoke as little as possible, trying not to slip into the Russian that sprang into his head and almost made it to his lips. His English—the English *Babushka* taught him in Leningrad, to the chagrin of his father—sounded fractured to his own ears. "You never know when you might need it. It is our secret!" *Babushka* had whispered. The young Mitch loved secrets. Now, he wasn't so sure.

It's time to move on. Try somewhere else, he told himself and set out at a brisk pace. Apart from an elderly couple walking arm-in-arm and a woman and child coming towards him, the waterfront was deserted. The wind whipped leaves into spirals and whirled them into the air.

For as long as Mitch could remember, he felt caught in a whirlwind over which he didn't have any control. On the cargo ship from Vyborg, he had stared at the walls of his cabin, the throb of the engines his only companion. He felt empty, alone in the world, ripped away from everyone and everything he knew. One night, he stood on the deserted deck and watched moonlight dancing on the water. His gaze followed the white tips of the wash from the ship until they vanished from view. *What good is life without my family, the people I love?* he asked himself, gripping the rail with his bare hands, struggling against the urge to climb over and launch himself into oblivion beneath the waves. How long he stood there, he didn't know. A blast from the ship's horn jolted him back to reality and he thrust his hands into his coat pockets and turned away. *Anja. I must stay alive for her sake ...*

Now, as he walked, a shiver ran through his body. *How could you have thought of killing yourself? You can't abandon Anja and Papa.* His thoughts went back to an evening when he and his father had shared dinner and a bottle of wine in his father's kitchen. It was the night before they had gone to pick up Anja for the first time after Natasha relented and let Mitch see his daughter. That evening, they had been so happy planning where they would take her, what they would do, sharing reminiscences, and had even spoken openly of Mitch's mother, Sophia, for the first time since her death. Since then, Mitch had cursed himself for not taking Anja somewhere safe when he had the chance. But that was all in the past. *The only thing now is to earn money—big money—fast. Then, when it's safe to return to Russia, I'll be able to pay people for information as to Anja's whereabouts.* He daren't let his thoughts go further than that.

"Emily! Emily! Wait! Wait for me!" Mitch stopped in his tracks. His heart skipped several beats as he watched the child running up a pathway towards the road, her mother in pursuit. The voice more urgent: "Emily! Wait there!" The woman grabbed the child. Mitch let out his pent-up breath and walked on quickly, trying to swallow the lump in his throat which threatened to choke him as he wondered who would keep his Anja safe now that he wasn't there to watch over her.

Twenty minutes later he opened the door of the blue-painted house on a side street off Spring Garden Road and climbed the stairs to his rented room on the second floor. He filled the kettle from the tap over the washbasin, ignited one of the gas rings, and flopped onto the bed. His mind drifted back to the last few hours he spent with his precious daughter. He knew every detail of that day six months ago. Her voice was clear in his head. His car had broken down and Anja innocently suggested, "Why don't we call Boris, Papa? He's *Dyadya* Mikhail's driver. His car never breaks down. It's fun." The reference to Mikhail Victorovich Yagudin, his ex-wife's lover, had tipped Mitch over the top. "I'm sick of hearing about fucking *Dyadya* Mikhail," he barked.

There was a tremor in Anja's voice when she spoke: "Mama says it's bad to say those words."

Mitch had watched as his father took Anja's hand and walked with her to a nearby *kafe-konditerskaya. Why do I let my temper get the better of me?* Mitch had berated himself as he waited for the car to be towed away. *Will you ever learn? It was losing your temper that got you into this mess in the first place.* Later, he tried to make it up to Anja by buying her a new dress for her friend Polya's birthday party. He remembered now how she spun around in the white dress with the sailor collar, thin red ribbons twirling from her waist. When it was time to take her back to her mother, she had struggled out of Mitch's embrace and run to catch up with her grandfather, the bag containing the dress flapping behind.

If only I knew where she is. For the first few weeks after arriving in Canada, he convinced himself she was dead. The whole world was cloaked in black. Then the letter from his father's friend Vera Aleksandrovna Kishinevskaya arrived, via Kirill, Vera's contact in Halifax. She wrote that information from her sources led her to believe that Anja and Natasha were no longer in St Petersburg (as Leningrad was now known) and were thought to have fled to somewhere in Siberia. Mitch had paused in his reading of the letter, the tension in his shoulders dissipating, as realisation washed through him. There was hope his beloved daughter was alive.

He had closed his eyes for a few moments, allowing the vision of Anja—the happy little girl whose dimples in her cheeks deepened when she laughed—back into his mind. The muscles in his cheeks had relaxed, painting his face with the first glimmer of a smile for months. He thought about his high-spending, high-living ex-wife. *Siberia? She wouldn't go to a place like that willingly. Maybe she didn't have a choice.*

'Gangland wars are rife,' Vera wrote, 'and Mikhail Yagudin and his henchmen haven't been heard of for weeks. There is nothing to suggest he is with Natasha.' Mitch had read those words over and over again, trying to convince himself his daughter was no longer in danger. But how could he be sure? Vera ended the letter with a plea for Mitch to stay where he was for now.

He had sat for some time holding the letter in his hands. *Papa? She didn't mention Papa. Why hasn't he written to me?*

Now, the kettle spewed steam and spat water. Mitch didn't move, concentrating instead on the picture of Anja in his mind: her unruly corkscrew curls, the pinpoint freckles across her nose and cheeks, the dimples. He needed to fix her in his head. That way she was still real, alive. After a few moments, he got to his feet, made himself a mug of instant coffee, stirred two spoonsful of sugar into it, and lit a cigarette. He closed the shutter on the window. When he first came here, the light through the window was filtered by the dense foliage of a tree. He liked the sense of security, hidden from the world. Last night, the last of the leaves were stripped off in the wind, exposing the one place he felt safe. *Time to move on.*

In the chair by the small round table, he sipped his coffee. A wave of longing washed through him as he wondered what Anja was doing on this her seventh birthday. His thoughts drifted back to the *kafe-konditerskaya* she had chosen for a treat on her third or fourth birthday.

His parents were there, and Anja's eyes sparkled as the waitress placed the plate of pastries in front of them. Long tails of the white ribbon which held her hair in place trailed on the table as she knelt on her chair and tried to decide which cake to eat first. Mitch had reached out his hand to take the one with pink icing, the one he guessed she coveted. Her bottom lip trembled, her brow puckered into a frown. He had laughed and moved his hand away slowly to select an uninspiring looking cake from the other side of the plate. Anja giggled, her fingers already grasping the pink-festooned prize. Now, a vision of his daughter, pink icing smeared around her lips, filled his mind. He hoped, wherever she was, someone cared enough about her to celebrate her birthday. *Maybe Papa? Maybe Papa has found her. But he would have written.* Mitch leaned forward and held his head in his hands, choking back tears.

Perhaps I should have made more of an effort to get to know people here. There were other ethnic Russians in the city. Kirill had urged Mitch to try to blend in with the local population. "That way, you're less likely to be noticed as an outsider. Act as though you've lived here for years, have a history here." Mitch wasn't convinced, still wary of talking to fellow Russians. "You don't know what their connections are back there. It only takes one person who knows a member of the *vory v zakone* ..." Even to say the name brought back visions of the smouldering wreckage of his car, the poor old man Slava who died when the bomb meant for Mitch exploded. The smell of burnt flesh. No, he was better off on his own.

But Kirill persisted and, late one Saturday afternoon, took Mitch to a friend's home where a group of congregants were celebrating the Sabbath. "There is no church in which to worship, so it's very informal. Open to all." The room was hot, lit by candles. A table at the front, covered in a gold-coloured cloth, held three icons propped against the wall. The elongated eyes of the Saints depicted in the icons seemed to bore right into Mitch's soul, threatening to reveal his innermost secrets. He moved to a shadowy corner at the back of the room, from where he watched the mostly elderly congregation making the sign of the cross and kissing the icons. What little he knew of Russian Orthodox services was gleaned from a brief visit to a church in Leningrad as a small boy.

His father had told him it was their secret: "You must never tell anyone." He had gone on to explain that religion wasn't allowed in the Soviet Union. "Like being a *zhid*?" His father's face set in a grimace after Mitch asked that question. Years later, Mitch came to realise that his own mother had been forced to renounce Judaism when they came to Russia.

On that long ago day in the church, Sergei told Mitch that if he prayed hard his prayers would rise with the incense all the way to the very top of the dome and then to heaven. But in the crowded room in Halifax, as Mitch looked up at the low ceiling, he could only imagine the blue-painted dome and the window where light streamed through. For an instant, his thoughts travelled to the church in which his marriage to Natasha was blessed. *Don't think of it,* he told himself as a young man at the front of the room began to sing. Mitch was soon lost in the words:

My sinful soul, why don't you cry?
Cry, my soul, always weep.
Through this consolation will come to you ...
They sing the song of the archangels.
Hallelujah ... Hallelujah ... Hallelujah.[2]

The words pierced the brittle façade he had built around his emotions, and he wiped his eyes with the back of his hand and stared at the floor.

---

[2] *My Sinful Soul*: Traditional Russian Orthodox spiritual chant.

Sometime later on that Sabbath, fluorescent light flooded the room. There was movement around him. Folding tables and chairs were brought into the room and a smell of once-familiar dishes blotted out the aroma of candle wax. He had stood to one side as people took their places at laden tables. “Come on, Andrei!” Kirill steered him to adjacent chairs and began heaping food onto plates. The hot *pelmeni*, drizzled with butter, were good. *Not as good as Babushka’s*, Mitch told himself as he garnished his with lemon juice and vinegar. “When was the last time you had a decent meal?” Kirill joked as Mitch dug into the salad of chopped tomatoes and cucumbers in sour cream. It wasn’t just hunger that made him fill his mouth with food. It had been the only way to avoid answering probing questions from the people sitting near him. He hadn’t felt like talking, and what did he care about their trivial concerns, their ailments and groans about how much better life had been in the Soviet Union under Stalin?

4
Halifax and Moncton
Early November 1991

Mitch cradled his mother's *Samizdat* copy of the poems of Anna Akhmatova in his hands. It was the only tangible thing he had of his previous life, and he now understood how his mother had found comfort in the tragic verses which flowed out of grief for the poet's son's imprisonment during the Yezhov terror. He placed it carefully in the bag with the rest of his meagre belongings, then shrugged into the seaman's jacket the Captain had given him on the ship. The coat looked okay in Halifax, but anywhere else would mark him as not belonging. His shoes, the ones borrowed from Maxim Vladimirovich, the man in whose house he sought refuge in Leningrad, now had holes in them. He fingered the wad of notes in his coat pocket. Before he left town, he would buy warm clothes and boots.

Bag in hand, he opened the door, left the key in the lock and descended the stairs. In the hallway, he peered through the small window at the side of the front door. It was a habit he started when he first came here, convinced the *vory v zakone* knew where he was and were out there waiting for him. He had never seen anyone watching the house, nor did he think he was being followed. The habit lingered.

There were a few people on the street; some smiled or said "Hi!" as they scurried past clutching take-away cups of coffee. At a used clothing store, he bought a thick coat, gloves, hat, sweater, winter pants and boots. He changed into them in a public washroom, crammed the seaman's coat into his bag and left his cast-offs in a heap in a corner. *Someone might need them.*

Watery sun broke through grey clouds as he walked past what had become familiar sights in the city. Apart from the fear of discovery, he liked it here. Maybe, this was the place he would bring Anja and his father when this nightmare ended. From a telephone kiosk he called Kirill, promising to let him have an address when he had one. As he put the receiver down, Mitch felt a sense of loss. Thirty-something Kirill had an air of trustworthiness, something that was lacking in so many people nowadays, particularly in the Soviet Union, where children were encouraged to inform on parents, and neighbour informed on neighbour. Mitch had come to rely on Kirill's advice, his guidance on how things are done in this country, whose customs and way of life were very different from his own. He had expected to feel at least a slight sense of belonging to this country of his birth, the country where he had lived for the first four years of his life. He may have landed on Mars, for all the difference that made.

He lit a cigarette. *Better keep moving,* he told himself and hurried down the hill. With a bit of luck, he could get a job in a bar somewhere to tide him over. Christmas was coming. It was too painful to think of Christmas without his daughter, but at least there might be seasonal work.

If not, he'd move on again. There still felt something illicit about being able to move from place to place without having to obtain permission from someone in authority. In Russia, despite theoretical protection for freedom of movement, citizens had to carry internal passports tying the holder to their area of residence.

Mitch made it to Moncton in two days. Hitching rides mostly with truck drivers, he avoided probing questions by feigning sleep. As the kilometres clicked by, it felt good; weaving a haphazard path across the country would make it more difficult for anyone to find him. But, the threatening presence of those nameless, faceless, heavily tattooed spectres, travelled with him, impossible to shake from his mind.

His last ride was with a driver for a haulage company based in Moncton. With a whoosh of air brakes, the truck stopped on the edge of town. The driver pointed down a side street. "The big white house on the corner. Tell them Andy sent you," he yelled as Mitch climbed down from the cab. Mitch watched the vehicle lumber away and pondered whether to take Andy's advice.

What if someone asks him if he's seen a man with dark brown curly hair and a foreign accent? Someone like me. Maybe I should look for somewhere else to stay. But, where? He walked slowly along the sidewalk, stopped outside the house, pulled off his gloves and lit a cigarette.

The cigarette was almost down to the butt and he still hadn't made a decision. A door slammed and he turned around to see a short, red-faced man, carrying a small suitcase. "If you're looking for somewhere to stay, you won't do better than here," the man assured, pointing towards the house. "The breakfasts … well, what can I say?" Mitch noticed the buttons on the man's overcoat strained across the bulge of his stomach. *Maybe just one night,* he thought to himself, threw the cigarette butt into the road and walked up the front path.

The doorbell was answered by a slim woman wearing a floral-sprigged apron over a dark blue, long-sleeved dress. She wiped her hands down the apron, tucked a strand of hair behind her right ear and said something which Mitch didn't understand. She hesitated, then urged in English, "Come in out of the cold." Mitch stepped into the hallway. Through the open door of the dining room he glimpsed the remnants of breakfast. The smell of coffee … bacon … lingered in the air, and he realised how hungry he was.

"Lise Le Juge." She held a hand out to him.

"Andy sent me," Mitch mumbled and clasped her hand.

"Ah, Andy. Bit of a rogue, but a big heart," Lise responded. "He was at school with my husband, George. We run this place together." She waved a hand around. "We let out rooms by the night, week or month. Whatever suits."

There was an awkward silence.

"You don't have to commit to anything longer than one night," she cajoled. "You look as though you could do with something to eat, some rest."

A faint trace of a smile creased Mitch's face.

"I'll show you to your room. Then, when you're ready, come down to the dining room and I'll see what the hungry hordes have left!" Mitch followed her up the stairs. "Our guests, they're mostly salesmen in town for a few days, a week."

A transient population—the thought ran through Mitch's mind as they entered a large room. It overlooked the garden, beyond which was a blank wall. "The bathroom … it's along the corridor," Lise explained. "Come down when you're ready." Her hand on the doorknob, she turned and said, "I don't think you told me your name."

"Lapitsky," Mitch answered. "Andrei Lapitsky."

"I need it for the records." She smiled and closed the door softly behind her.

Damn! I should have used another name, Mitch cursed. *Too late now.* He yawned as he sat on the bed and fingered the plump coverlet. It was tempting, but he unpacked his belongings and, after a quick wash in the bathroom, tucked some money into the pocket of his pants and went downstairs. A vacuum cleaner hummed in the distance. In the dining room, an enticing smell of coffee drifted through the serving hatch, through which he glimpsed Lise busy at the stove. Seated at the table, he helped himself to a chunk of doughy white bread from the basket and spread butter on it. He was on his third piece when Lise set before him a plate on which several rashers of bacon and two fried eggs sizzled. Mitch stared at the plate thinking how his Jewish mother would have disapproved. But even her religious beliefs had been severely tested in the last years of her life when food was more and more difficult to come by in Leningrad. He took up his knife and fork and began to eat. From time to time, Lise bustled past. Mitch noticed grey flecks in her dark hair; like his mother, she seemed to be one of those women of indeterminate age. She met his glance, and he put down his knife and fork and wiped his mouth with the napkin. "Thank you," he muttered, gulped the last of his coffee and pushed back his chair.

"Lapitsky … Andrei Lapitsky? Is that what you said?"

Mitch nodded. A flush crept up his neck, into his cheeks.

"I've not heard that name before. You're not from here?"

"I was born here, in Canada." He got to his feet.

"Sorry. George says I'm too nosy. But it's not that," she shrugged. "I'm interested in people, what they do, where they come from."

"You wouldn't find me interesting. Quite boring." Mitch feigned a laugh.

"You don't speak French. When I first spoke to you …"

"I used to. My mother. She was French."

"We're Acadian. Even French-speaking people often don't understand us," she laughed as she gathered up crockery from the table.

It was past noon when Mitch came back downstairs. A couple of hours sleep and a long soak in the bath had revived him.

"Off out?" Lise called from the kitchen.

Mitch peered around the edge of the door. "I thought I'd look for work … bars, cafés, those sort of places. Just to tide me over."

"If you hang on, I'll give you a ride downtown. I have to go to the grocery store."

"It's okay. I need the walk. If you could tell me …"

"No questions. That's a promise!" She raised her hands in mock surrender. When he still hesitated, she added, "It's quite a way."

Fifteen minutes or so later she dropped him off outside a bar. The owner was friendly enough, but there weren't any vacancies. Mitch was tempted to have a drink, but it wouldn't do to turn up looking for work smelling as though he was going to drink the profits. Besides, he needed to save money. Outside, he stood for a while looking at the river; already a thin film of ice edged the bank. His thoughts went back to walks along the side of the Neva with Anja, the tassel on her pink hat bobbing along in front as he tried to keep up with her.

Two hours later, he had exhausted most of the likely places to find work. The biting wind was finding its way through his coat and sweater. He'd give it another half an hour and then get the bus back—Lise had pointed out the bus terminal before she dropped him off. Outside a small café, he drew on his cigarette, ground out the butt with the sole of his boot and stepped inside. A dark-haired woman peered out from an alcove. "Be with you in a moment," she called.

Mitch looked around, relishing the warmth. It wasn't a bad place. Red checked oilcloth covered the tables. *Probably a family business. Not much chance of anything here,* he thought to himself and sat down on a chair close to the counter. The woman talked rapidly on the telephone; he guessed she was from Spain or maybe Portugal.

"Now, what can I get you?" She wound the strings of an apron around her waist and tied them firmly in a bow at the front. "There's not much left. I was going to close up."

"I'm sorry," Mitch blurted. "I … I'm looking for work."

"You are?" The woman's eyes opened wide and she threw her arms in the air. "Saints be praised … it's a miracle!"

"It is?"

"That … that was my husband on the phone. Stupid man!" she spluttered. "Hurt his back, he has. Playing the curling. I tell him. Will he listen? No! No!" She shook her head. "And now, you come through my door. A miracle. That's what it is." She laughed loudly and Mitch couldn't help joining in.

"I can't cook," he said tentatively, "at least, not very well."

"Cook? Ahh, we don't do much cooking around here. I make the soup. You can stir that can't you? Wash dishes?"

Mitch nodded enthusiastically. The woman was better than a shot of vodka.

"And sandwiches? I show you how. No worry. You manage. You look like a dependable type."

He swallowed hard.

"You hungry?" she asked and, without waiting for an answer, suggested, "There's a drop of soup left. I get you a bowl while we talk. Coffee? You like the coffee?"

Mitch ate hungrily. Maria talked. She needed someone to help until a few days before Christmas, when she and her husband Angelo—she paused to again curse his stupidity, while Mitch secretly blessed the unfortunate man—would leave for their annual visit to their family in Mexico. “You and me, we get on fine,” she said and patted Mitch’s hand.

5
Moncton
December 1991

Although it was early, Main Street was crowded with shoppers as Mitch made his way to work on this the last Saturday before Christmas. The chatter of people buzzed in his ears as they called to friends, exchanged greetings, exclaimed over festive shop windows. It was all so different here. Back home, Christmas celebrations are prohibited by the atheist Soviet state, but Russians do what they have always done: circumvent the official doctrine and celebrate in their own homes. Festivities take place the first week of the New Year, culminating on Christmas Day, January 7. He thrust his hands into his pockets and stepped into the road, making way for three children running haphazardly; he thought they were girls, but who could tell, bundled as they were in hats, scarves, and heavy coats.

As he walked, he remembered previous Christmas celebrations with Anja … his Annushka. Like most children, Christmas held a special magic for her, a world where everything is possible, where dreams come true. Her excitement built as Christmas Eve approached and with it the arrival of *Ded Moroz*, Grandfather Frost, on his horse-drawn *troika* loaded with toys. He pictured her last Christmas, nibbling on one of her favourite *Archangel Kozulya* cookies while reciting a poem she and her cousins Dasha and Gena had learnt. The rendition ended when the children collapsed onto the floor in fits of giggles. He sighed, wondering what Christmas would be like there now. The country was in turmoil, the president expected to resign. What would happen next? *Annushka? Papa? What will happen to them?*

Think positively, he told himself as he stepped back on to the sidewalk. *It's the only way to keep them safe.* A vision of Anja came into his mind. He saw her clearly as she offered him a painted wooden tree ornament—a doll dressed in brightly coloured traditional costume, headdress decorated with yellow flowers. He heard his daughter's voice: "They're sunflowers Papa. They come out when the sun shines." She looked up at him, a smile deepening the dimples in her cheeks. Now, he swallowed back a lump in his throat and said a silent prayer for her. His words matched each step he took.

Five minutes later, he stamped snow off his boots and stepped inside the café. He paused, breathing in the warm, pungent smell of vegetable soup, his thoughts travelling back to when as a young child he would rush into the kitchen trying to guess what *Babushka* was cooking. She would yell at him, tell him to take off his shoes, and point at the telltale smears of mud, water, snow, marking his route from the front door. She never stayed cross for long and would soon produce a *pryaniki* or two—his favourite honey spiced cookies.

"Sorry I'm late," he called to Maria, as he hung up his coat and wrapped the ties of the long white apron around his waist. He looked around the room. The chairs, tables with their bright red check oilcloths, coloured ornaments decorating the windowsills, plants still awaiting their Christmas blooms, were all part of his life now. For the first time in years, he looked forward to going to work. Although there was only a handful of customers now, soon the café would be buzzing, Maria and Mitch working seamlessly around each other serving sandwiches whose generous fillings spilled onto plates, and bowls of piping hot soup which were quickly devoured by a loyal band of customers. Each day, for a few hours at least, his anxiety about Anja and his father was pushed to the recess of his mind. On his way back to the guest house, his fears would return. Then he would calm himself, convinced that today was the day; the day there would be a letter awaiting him from his father or from Vera. It would tell him all was well.

Diners today were in festive mood, some wearing red and white hats redolent of the images of Papa Noël Mitch had come to recognise as symbolising the spirit of Christmas in this part of the world. He found himself joining in their conversations; the strange mix of French and English came easily to him now. Maria never questioned Mitch about his past, his strange accent, what he was doing in a city where he obviously didn't belong. Once, when they were busy, he had slipped up and spoken to her in Russian. She looked at him quizzically, then squeezed his arm gently, shook her head and said: "The two of us … far from home."

As he did at noon every day, Maria's husband, Angelo, hobbled into the café and sat at a small table by the entrance to the kitchen. While he devoured his soup and sandwich, he moaned in a loud voice about his aches and pains, how no one suffered like him. In the background, Maria kept up a diatribe telling Mitch not to listen to any of her husband's stories. "He'll be okay when we get on the plane home to Mexico on Christmas Eve. He'll make a miraculous recovery!" She waved a knife around in the air. "Then, when we're on the way back here, he'll have a relapse. Mark my words!" She jabbed a knife in Angelo's direction.

"Listen to her, eh! Talking rubbish, as usual." Angelo winked as Mitch hurried past.

"The useless article!" came from the kitchen.

Despite the bickering, Mitch sensed a deep closeness between them. One he had never experienced with Natasha.

On his way to the bus stop after he finished work, Mitch stopped at a phone booth and dialled Kirill's number in Halifax. "I forwarded a letter to you yesterday," Kirill began.

"From my father?" Mitch cut in anxiously.

"No, Vera."

"Did she say anything about …?"

"She just asked me to make sure you got the letter," Kirill cut in. "You should get it on Monday or Christmas Eve, if the mail isn't snarled up." When Mitch didn't respond, Kirill went on: "You heard what happened over there?"

"*Nyet.* Not recently."

"Yeltsin … he's claimed Gorbachev's office in the Kremlin. Not that any of this will make any difference. Nothing will change. Like always!"

Mitch let out a loud sigh. "Kirill, I'm going to be moving on again after Christmas. My job's finishing on Monday. There's nothing much here and I need to earn money to go back to Russia, find my daughter."

"Mitch, that would be stupid. It's not safe for you there."

"I have to find her. With all that's going on over there …"

"And what good will you be to her lying on a slab in a mortuary?"

Mitch shuddered. After promising to delay any decision until he had seen Vera's letter, Mitch put down the receiver. He stared at the phone. *Kirill's right. But I can't go on like this, not knowing. It's eating away at me.*

Through the windows of the bus back to the guesthouse, Christmas lights blinked red, green, blue, white, in the darkness. They were mere flashes to Mitch as his mind went over the reasons that might have kept his father from writing to him. *It must be Anja. Something's happened and he doesn't want to tell me.* "Please God, don't let it be her." Passengers on the bus turned as one to stare at him; the words had escaped from his lips. He slid down further in his seat. A moment later, he felt a touch on his left arm. He turned and looked into the face of a woman sitting across the aisle. She smiled. "Don't worry about it. It's this crazy time of year. Nothing comes out right!" she chuckled.

* * *

Mitch's job at the café finished on Monday. He was sad to part company with Maria, who had become a comforting presence in his life, someone he knew would be there, apron wrapped around her ample waist, when he arrived for work. Today, as he put his coat on to leave, she bundled the leftover food into a plastic bag and insisted he take it home. "You were a gift from Heaven," she said, pressed an envelope into his hand, and kissed him on both cheeks. "And whatever it is you're worrying about, it will sort itself out. Have faith," were her parting words.

Faith? Mitch thought as he stepped out onto the ice-encrusted sidewalk.

He saw his bus pull away just as he reached the terminal. The lights of a bar beckoned.

What the hell! It's another twenty minutes until the next bus, he reasoned as he crossed the street. Inside, he was met by a cacophony of noise. Settled in a corner with a shot of brandy, he lit a cigarette, adding to the fug already floating above the crowd. His eyes followed the curl of smoke; he saw nothing. Christmas celebrations loomed like a death sentence. After Anja was born, there had been joy at Christmas, New Year, watching her face light up as she pulled the wrapping paper off one gift, then another. He had watched the expressions on his parents' faces; if he had ever done anything right, it was to give them the happiness which their only grandchild brought. *How has it come to this? When did joy turn to misery?* He needed another drink.

* * *

The next morning, Mitch pulled the bed covers over his head, shutting out the chink of daylight creeping through the gap in the drapes. How long he lay there he did not know, but the next thing he was aware of was tapping on the door. He surfaced from beneath the bed covers and murmured, "Come in."

Lise put her head around the side of the door. "You okay, Andrei?"

"Just tired," he yawned.

"Do you want me to save you any breakfast?" When he didn't answer, she went on, "There's bacon and eggs and—"

"No! No, thank you." He raised himself up in the bed, holding his head, trying to stop the room from spinning. "I'm not hungry."

"We're off to pick up last minute things for the meal this evening. I'll leave some cereal and a baguette … you might fancy something later. And there's fresh coffee in …"

"Has the mail come yet?" Mitch interrupted.

She shook her head. "It's been getting later every day."

After she left, it took a while for Mitch to gather the strength to get to his feet and stagger to the bathroom. The house was quiet, quieter than he had known it. The last of the paying guests left on Saturday morning, and Mitch had watched as they scurried off, anxious to be home to celebrate with family and friends.

Downstairs, he poured a cup of coffee and was just lighting a cigarette when he heard a sound on the doorstep. In the hallway, he pulled the front door open, startling the mailman who had just raised the flap of the mailbox on the wall of the porch. "I'll take it!" Mitch snapped and held out a hand. The man shrugged and handed the bundle over. Mitch sifted through the assortment of envelopes, some sporting labels with the sender's name and address adorned with colourful baubles, reindeer, ornamental trees. He sorted through them again. "*Der'mo!*" he cursed aloud. Now he would have to wait until the end of the week before hearing Vera's news.

He shivered, went inside and slammed the door.

Late afternoon, he was lying on his bed trying to read a book that Lise's husband, George, had lent him. After reading one paragraph three times, still not taking in the words, he put the book down, got to his feet, plucked his cigarette from the ashtray, and stared out of the window. Snow had been falling all afternoon coating everything and bringing a strange brightness to the gathering dusk. The colours of the brown hat and striped scarf decorating the snowman Lise and George's grandchildren built last weekend were now almost obliterated.

As he watched, the wind whipped the hat off the snowman's head. It was then he saw her. *Anja! It's her. She's there, playing in the snow.* She picked up the snowman's hat and reached to put it back on its head. Mitch pressed his nose to the glass. She turned and waved to him. Heart pounding, he raised a hand. "Annush …" her name died in his throat. All that was left was the snowman. The hat was still on the snow-covered ground. He closed the drapes and sank down into the armchair. Cigarette ash dropped on to his pants.

* * *

That evening, Mitch looked around the table where George and Lise's extended family gathered for the celebration meal. He would rather have stayed in his room, but Lise brushed off his objections: "No one should be alone on Christmas Eve. It isn't right." Mitch had begged a few minutes to change his clothes, comb his hair. In reality, he needed to steel himself for what he knew would be a happy family gathering. "We're eating early, so there will be time to open gifts before Midnight Mass," Lise told him. Mitch had hurriedly explained that he didn't share their faith but would be happy to clear things away while they were all at church.

The noise level around the table reached crescendo as George, Lise, and their son, daughters, partners, and grandchildren, recounted family stories and teased each other good naturedly. Mitch was lost in his own thoughts and it was a few moments before he realised that Béatrice, who sat on his right side, was speaking to him. "Do you like my new dress?" she demanded, shaking his arm. He looked into her innocent young face, struggling to find his voice. Undeterred, she told him that her other *grand-maman* bought it for her in Toronto. "She lives there, you know. I have to call her Granny."

"That's nice," Mitch blurted.

"Do you have a little girl?" Brilliant blue eyes stared at him.

"Yes," he mumbled.

"Why isn't she here with you?"

"She … she lives somewhere else."

"I'm sorry," Béatrice's mother, sitting the other side of the child, apologised. "She's always asking questions. Drives me crazy." She grabbed her daughter's napkin and wiped remnants of trifle from around her mouth.

"What's your little girl's name? Does she like trifle?"

"Béatrice! It's rude to keep asking questions," her mother scolded.

"It's okay." Mitch took a deep breath. "Her name is Anja, and she likes a sort of trifle. Not the same as you have here." Strangely, talking about his daughter comforted him, brought her to life, at least in his thoughts.

An hour or so later, fiddle music and laughter drifted through from the sitting room as Mitch worked methodically in the kitchen, stacking the dishwasher and piling the next load on the counter. That done, he rolled up his sleeves and plunged his hands and forearms into the sink of hot bubbly water. The monotony of the job suited his mood, dulled his senses. He had just stowed the last saucepan in the cupboard when Lise came into the kitchen. "We're going now," she said, adjusting her hat and pulling gloves from her coat pockets. "Sure you won't come with us? It's a beautiful service and …"

"No. No thank you," Mitch cut in. "I'm a lost cause where religion's concerned."

"I'm sure you're not. You're an absolute angel doing all this. Thank you." She hugged him. "Help yourself to drinks. Whatever you want," she called as she walked into the hallway.

He listened to the noise of their departure. Lise called to George to hurry. "What have you done with my scarf?" George countered. Mitch plucked the scarf from under the kitchen table. "Is this what you're looking for?" he asked. George grabbed the errant article, slapped Mitch on the shoulder and gave a mock salute. The front door slammed in his wake.

In the sitting room, logs crackled in the fireplace. Crumpled wrapping paper overflowed from a plastic sack in a corner. Mitch picked up a doll from a side table, stared at it for a few moments before setting it down where he had found it. Then, glass of brandy in hand, he sank into an armchair by the fire and watched flames flicker and dance. Leaning back, he looked around the room. The arms of the sofas and armchairs were worn in places. The wide floorboards bore the patterns of decades of feet tramping across them and stains of long-forgotten provenance. The hand-hooked rugs spoke of another time. In the glow of the firelight and lights from the Christmas tree, it was warm and friendly, lived in, the kind of home he loved. He thought of his parents' apartment in Leningrad—the one they shared with *Babushka* when he was young. By modern-day standards, it was shabby. He sighed loudly. Oh how he wished he was there now, behind the door with peeling paint, the cracked linoleum, chairs that creaked if you so much as moved a muscle, voices of neighbours drifting through paper-thin walls. And, most of all, the unquestioning love of his family.

He drained his glass, got to his feet and poured another. *What should I have done differently?* He knew the answer to that: he should have ignored the information about those trafficked girls, never have exposed those behind the racket. He'd known he was playing with fire. *Papa warned you, but you knew better! Thought you could change the world. This rotten stinking world.* He leaned back in the chair and stared at the flames in the fire; they were blurred by tears welling behind his eyes.

After a while, he gulped back another mouthful of brandy, picked up the TV remote control from where it had fallen on the floor, and pressed the power button. It was a few moments before he made sense of the jumble of noise coming from the TV. The screen flickered, but what he heard was now distinct. He got to his feet and moved closer to the TV. The inevitable had happened. The Soviet Union was no longer! Mitch was open-mouthed as he watched footage of the Soviet flag being lowered from the Kremlin. The ideological experiment begun by Lenin's Bolshevik Revolution was over. This is what he had hoped for, for so many years. *Govno! It can't be happening now! Anja? Papa? What will happen?* He gripped the back of a chair as the world he had known spun out of control.

6
Moncton
December 1991

In the days between Christmas and New Year, Mitch checked television broadcasts for the latest news from Russia. He paced around, smoked cigarette after cigarette, as each day he waited for the mailman to appear. He finally convinced himself that Vera's letter was lost in the jumble of Christmas mail. Until, on New Year's Eve as he came down the stairs to breakfast, Lise waved an envelope triumphantly above her head. "It's here! Your letter's here!"

Mitch stumbled down the last few steps and grabbed the envelope.

"Go on in," she urged. "There's toast and coffee on the table. I'll bring the rest in a few minutes."

Seated at the table, Mitch slit the envelopes open and extracted Vera's letter. Her words jumped out at him:

My Dear,

I know you are anxious for news of Anja, but there is still no positive information as to the whereabouts of her or Natasha. There haven't been any sightings of them in St Petersburg and, as I told you before, they are thought to have fled to Siberia to avoid the violence around Yagudin. One of my contacts reports that a man, reputed to have been Yagudin's driver, is living in a village near Omsk. In the same house, there are also two women—one much older than the other—and a young girl.

Mitch gripped the letter between his fingers. *Anja? Could it be Anja? She's alive?* He let out a pent-up breath. *If it is them, why are they with Yagudin's driver?* Mitch's mind went back to the fateful day on Nevsky Prospekt when Anja had suddenly called out her mother's name. He felt again the horror of seeing his wife on the other side of the street, Mikhail Yagudin's arm wrapped around her shoulders, her head pulled into his neck. He heard again Anja's voice exclaiming excitedly as she pointed to the driver getting out of the big black car: *"That's Boris, Papa. He's nice. He took me to Katya's when you were away."* Now, Mitch pushed his chair back and paced around the dining room. *I can't leave Anja with a man like that, a man with connections to the vory. I have to go back there.* He looked at the letter in his hands.

I'm trying to check it out. But please don't get your hopes up. It's too soon to know for certain. And, Mitch. On no account are you to come back here. It isn't safe for you.

He sank down onto a chair and skimmed through the rest of Vera's letter, searching for news of his father. There it was:

Your Papa, he asked me to explain that he has hurt his hand. A silly accident. You know he isn't good at doing jobs around the house. Don't ask me what he was doing, but a chisel or something slipped and took a piece out of his right hand.

Mitch sat down, trying to imagine how the accident had happened. *His right hand?* It didn't make sense. He checked the date on Vera's letter. *October. Over two months ago. Surely his hand has healed now. Maybe he'll write when there is definite news of Anja.* He glanced through the rest of the letter. Tales of people who Mitch knew vaguely, and comment on the political crisis in the country, most of which had been overtaken by recent events.

"Everything okay?" Lise asked as she put a plate of bacon and scrambled eggs in front of him. She refilled his empty cup.

"I don't know," was all Mitch could say.

"Anything we can do to help?"

He shook his head. *If only it was that simple.*

In late afternoon, Mitch joined Lise and George in the sitting room where they were drinking tea.

A partially-eaten fruit cake sat on a plate on a side table. "You'll have some tea?" Lise said, getting to her feet to fetch another cup and saucer from the hutch.

"Sit here by the fire." George rubbed his calves. "My legs are scorched."

Lise put Mitch's cup of tea on the table by the side of the chair vacated by her husband.

"What about a piece of cake?"

"I'm not hungry, thanks," Mitch said as he sat down.

"George and I, we're going to our daughter's home this evening," Lise went on. "Yvette said you are very welcome to come along. You made quite a hit with Béatrice, her daughter."

"She's a lovely child." Mitch stared at the flames in the fireplace. "If it's okay with you, I'll stay here."

Her forehead creased in a frown. "You'll be okay by yourself?"

"I'm used to that," Mitch murmured. "But thank your daughter. I appreciate the offer."

"I'll go and get some logs in," George said, rubbing his hands together. "It's going to be a wild night. They're forecasting more snow."

Sometime later, Mitch watched their car slither down the road, headlights illuminating a curtain of snow. He went upstairs and pulled down his bag from on top of the armoire. As he packed, his thoughts drifted back to the first New Year's Eve after Anja was born. She would have been two months old. He had cradled his sleeping daughter in his arms as they listened with Natasha's family to the Kremlin clock bell ringing twelve times on the TV, each making secret wishes for the next year. The *Zakuska* table was laden with savoury and sweet delicacies. *Natasha and I were happy then ... weren't we?* he asked himself now. He let out a long sigh. *You're deluding yourself.* There had always been a thread of tension running through their relationship, and the ever-present figure of her father looming in the background, waiting to step in and pay for whatever extravagancies Natasha demanded—luxuries Mitch couldn't afford. Now, as he tucked the last of his possessions into his bag, he made the same secret wish he had made every year since Anja was born.

A glance at his watch told him it was nearly nine o'clock. *Time to leave.* After a quick check around the room to make sure he hadn't left anything, he picked up his bag and went down the stairs. He felt bad not telling Lise and George he was leaving. He knew they would try to dissuade him. It was their kindness he couldn't take, the way they had welcomed him into their family. To be part of a happy family emphasised all he had lost. In the sitting room, he piled more logs on the fire, then secured the fireguard in place.

The street seemed clothed in blue light as he closed the front door for the last time. In the kitchen, he had left a note thanking Lise and George for their many kindnesses and enclosed enough money to compensate for leaving without notice. It was no longer snowing, but the drifts on the sidewalk were deep and his progress slow. As he headed towards the downtown district, noises from parties drifted from houses. Through windows he glimpsed happy people around dining tables, groups with glasses in hand. On the street, he passed only a solitary man carrying a dog. Snow sparkled, untouched by any footsteps but his own. In this perfectly still world, he found himself listening … listening for the crackling and howling of the snow. In a trembling voice, he started to sing one of the songs he and Anja made up as they tramped through the snow together. After the first few lines, he stopped in his tracks. *The words? I can't remember the words!*

He knew there wouldn't be much traffic at this time on New Year's Eve, but hoped that once he reached the main road someone would take pity on him and offer him a ride. He stopped at a Tim Hortons and bought a coffee and a Boston Crème doughnut—the sugar would give him energy for the journey ahead. As Mitch got up to leave, a young man seated at the next table asked, "Where you headed? I saw you walking, carrying your bag."

"I'm trying to get to Newcastle or somewhere up that way."

"Want a ride? I'm going as far as Canaan," he said getting to his feet. "I've been working and I'm late for the family party. Expect they'll all be in bed before midnight, though. The doughnuts will do for breakfast." He laughed and held a box aloft.

And so began another journey.

7
Village Near Omsk, Siberia
Monday, 6 January 1992

Anja breathed on the kitchen window … once, twice … rubbed her fingers across the circle of melted ice crystals and looked out. In the gathering dusk a figure, bent into the wind, picked its way along the ice-encrusted track. With her face pressed to the glass, Anja squinted, trying to see who it was. The figure looked much like all the old women in the village: fat, wrapped in a woollen coat, scarf wound around head and neck, feet planted in boots.

Anja rubbed the tip of her nose. It was ice-cold. She listened. The only sound was the howling of the wind. Mama, Boris, and *Tyotya* Yevdokia Marlenova, were resting. For tonight, no one would sleep. Tonight was *Sochelnik.* Christmas Eve. The night they would decorate the tree Boris cut. She danced around the room, faster and faster as she thought of all the fun they would have. She wobbled. Her foot knocked against one of the legs of the table on which she and Mama had placed the Christmas tree ornaments. A glass ornament slid to the floor. It shattered!

A gasp escaped Anja's lips. She stood still, holding her breath, waiting for one of the bedroom doors to open. No one came. A sob caught in her throat. The ornament was her favourite: the ballerina dressed in sparkling white. She carefully picked up one severed foot, its ballet slipper still intact, and cradled it in her hand for a moment. Then she lifted the edge of the tablecloth where it brushed the floor and pushed the pieces out of sight.

Anja wondered if *Ded Moroz* would leave her any gifts tonight. She had worried he didn't know where she was now, but Mama said she was sure he did and that maybe he would leave a parcel of clothes. "They'll keep you nice and warm. The ones you have aren't thick enough for the cold winters here." Anja had pouted. She didn't want horrid clothes. She wanted a doll. Or maybe the dollhouse from *Dyadya* Mikhail's *dacha.* That would be fun. Mama said she was too old for dolls, but surely it couldn't hurt to have just one. Stepan, the nasty boy at school, told her *Ded Moroz* didn't exist; it was a story adults made up to make sure children behaved themselves. She bit her lip now, thinking of the shards of glass. But she knew *Ded Moroz* was real. Papa said he came all the way from *Veliki Ustiuk*, in Northern Russia. On his journey, he had to avoid *Baba Yaga*, who chased his horse-drawn *troika* and tried to steal the sacks of toys. Anja hoped tonight that *Snegurochka*, the Snow Maiden, would be with him. Anja had seen pictures of her dressed in white boots and blue coat trimmed with ermine—Mama said ermine was very expensive—and she helped *Ded Moroz* work his magic and make children's dreams come true. Anja was sure *Snegurochka* knew what she wanted most in the whole world.

Maybe she could also send her grandparents to see her. And Babushka Sophia from Heaven. *Papa will like that. We will all be together again.*

She leaned her elbows on the shelf of the *krasnyy ugol,* the traditional corner where *Tyotya* says her prayers every day. She believes in someone called Jesus, whoever that is. Tomorrow is his birthday, and next year *Tyotya* said they would go to his house in the village. It has a big wooden cross on top. Anja wondered if it would smell of the cabbages *Tyotya* said were stored there during the time when religion was forbidden. Now, she looked warily at the elongated eyes of the saint, whose name she couldn't remember. She took two steps to the right. The eyes followed her. She skipped to the other side of the room. The saint watched. *Tyotya* said that, wherever she was, the saint would know what she did. She should always be kind to people, then the saint would smile at her. Anja looked at him again and hoped he hadn't seen her break the glass ballerina. Maybe he would smile tomorrow, on Jesus's birthday.

All morning, *Tyotya* had been preparing food for the feast they would have this evening. Standing on a chair in front of the stove, Anja had stirred the *kutya,* the porridge made from wheatberries, honey and poppy seeds. She knew how to do this. *Babushka* Sophia had shown her, telling her that the grains symbolise hope. Anja knew all about hope. Maybe if she ate a big bowlful of *kutya,* Papa would find her. She hoped for that every day.

She thought of the Christmas feast at *Dyadya* Pyotr and *Tyotya* Mila's apartment. *Before Papa went away. Dyadya* Pyotr is Mama's brother and he and *Tyotya* Mila have two children—Dasha and Gena. Anja and her cousins had recited a poem *Dyadya* Pyotr taught them. She whispered the words to herself now:

"With my goat, so small and funny;

I go walking every day.

In our garden green and sunny ..."

She remembered Papa taking her hands in his and dancing her around the room, singing loudly. She twirled around and around now, careful not to go near the table again, recalling the swishing noise the skirt of her party dress made. Then they had all hurried into the dining room and dug spoons into the big dish of *kutya. Dedushka* Lyosha told her that in the olden days peasants fasted for thirty-nine days and then on *Sochelnik* they would sit down to a twelve-course supper—one course for each of the Apostles. Anja didn't know what they were but thought they must be something nice.

Today, while stirring the *kutya,* she had asked *Tyotya* if they were going to have twelve courses tonight. *Tyotya* shook her head, saying that was an old tale. Peasants never had that much food to spare. They didn't fast either, as they needed strength to work the land. Tonight, the villagers would do as they had always done and throw a spoonful of *kutya* up to the ceiling.

"If it sticks, the honey harvest will be plentiful," she said. Anja thought she must remember to tell Papa that when he comes for her. *It will be fun to do that with him. He will laugh his funny laugh as we send spoonsful of kutya soaring to the ceiling. Afterwards, he will lift me high in the air so I can wipe it off,* she giggled.

Then she remembered what Mama said yesterday: *"He isn't coming to take you home. He did a very bad thing and has gone away. Maybe to another country."* Mama had tucked in Anja's bedcovers, telling her, "It's time you were asleep."

Snuggled down in bed, Anja whispered, *"Spokoynoy nochi,* Papa."

Now, she knelt on her chair at the table, which was already set for the feast. She had helped *Tyotya* spread the big white cloth, in the centre of which was a tall white candle. She patted the *bobal'ki*, the Lenten bread; later, they would break off pieces and dip them in honey. Mama made the *bobal'ki* herself at the *bulachnaya* where she worked in the village. When she came home today, she smiled as she unwrapped the cloth from the bread.

Mama looked different here from when they lived in the other place. There, she had pretty clothes, shoes with big high heels, dangly earrings and smelled of perfume. Here, she wore woollen stockings, long skirts and dresses under the grey coat which brushed the top of her *valenki*—the felt boots which everyone here wore—over which, when it was wet, she wore rubber boots. She smelled nice, though, of freshly-baked bread. Sometimes, Anja would go to meet her from the *bulachnaya,* pulling the little sledge along the frozen tracks crisscrossing the village. On the way home, they collected logs in the forest, piled them on to the sledge and stacked them in the shed at the back of the house ready for Boris to chop with his axe.

Boris made Mama a secret Christmas gift: a wooden tray, which he polished and wrapped in special paper. Anja made her a little cloth; it is a bit crooked but almost fits on the tray. While Mama was at the *bulachnaya, Tyotya* taught Anja how to sew the pattern of red stitches. The cloth was now folded, tied with red ribbon and hidden under Anja's bed.

At the table, her eyes strayed to the glass dish filled with chocolates in brightly coloured wrappers. Boris brought them from Omsk, where he went to work every day. He sometimes brought Anja treats and gifts for Mama. *He is nice, but not as nice as Papa ... my real Papa. Maybe they can both live here and I'll have two Papas.* Her hand reached out towards the chocolates. *Tyotya*'s voice hummed in her head: *"Not even a little morsel, Yelena. We must not eat until the Bethlehem Star appears in the sky."*

She climbed off the chair, ran to the window and gazed upwards, searching the sky. Undaunted, she crept back to the table and wrapped her fingers around her favourite chocolate—the one in crinkly blue paper with the picture of the brown bears, *Mishka Kosolapy*. With the chocolate held firmly in a hand behind her back, she edged past the saint, lay down on her bed behind the curtains, unwrapped the sweet and sucked it slowly. As the chocolate melted, she worried Boris or *Tyotya* would notice one of the sweets was missing. *And the glass ballerina.*

8

A Place South-East of St Petersburg, Russia February 1992

A pain in the small of Sergei's back jolted him into consciousness. He rolled over. A figure towered above him. The nightstick found its mark again, connecting with his hip bone. He shielded his face with his arms as the guard pulled him from his cot and shoved him through the open doorway of his cell. Clasping the loose waistband of his pants, he tried to keep up with the man's long strides. At the end of the corridor, the guard threw open a door and pushed him inside. "Okay, Igor. He's all yours." The door slammed.

Grey light streaked through a barred window. Sergei hunched his shoulders, his back against a wall.

"Get your clothes off!"

Sergei looked into a pock-marked face, topped with faded red hair. *O Bozhe!* He shuffled back towards the door. *What's he going to do to me?*

"You heard me!" the man growled. "Clothes off!"

Sergei let his pants drop to the floor, fumbled with the buttons of his jacket and shrugged out of it. He shivered, and wrapped his arms around his body. Then he noticed the bath of water.

The barked "Get in!" startled him. "You want me to throw you in?" mobilised Sergei's limbs and he stumbled over to the bath, held on to one side and put his left foot into the water. It was barely warm. As he lifted his other leg, the guard knocked him sideways. His foot slid from under him and his head hit the edge of the bath. He went under the water and struggled to take a gulp of air, arms flailing. Then he gripped the sides of the bath and spluttered, bracing himself for the inevitable shove which would send him into oblivion.

The guard grabbed Sergei by his hair, poured liquid from a bottle on to his head then put the bottle on the floor. "This should delouse you," he laughed loudly as he rubbed in the strong-smelling substance. Sergei's scalp was on fire. He watched as the man took a bar of dark green soap from the side of the bath. He flinched as rough hands scraped across his neck and back, piercing painful boils. After a few moments, Sergei slid slowly down in the bath and rinsed his head and upper body. On the snapped command, he got unsteadily to his feet, never losing sight of the guard's hands as he soaped them again. The guard rubbed the small of Sergei's back with widening circular movements. Fingers slid down between his buttocks before moving slowly round to his stomach. The soap back in its place, Sergei splashed water over his body, watching the guard as he dried his hands and picked up a small bottle from the counter.

He lifted Sergei's limp penis. "Not much of a man are you?" Sergei looked away, trying to ignore the hand sliding back and forth. "Oh, so you like the boys," the guard said as, against his will, Sergei's penis stiffened. "They all like that!"

Sergei shrank back against the tiled surface of the wall.

"You think I'd soil myself with a *durák* like you?"

Sergei shook his head quickly.

"It's the big tough ones I like." He let go of Sergei's penis and laughed. "They cry for their Mamas when I'm finished with them!"

Sergei shivered.

The guard walked over to a counter, turned and barked, "Out!"

Water dripped from Sergei's body, adding to the puddles already on the floor. He walked carefully towards a chair, grabbed a towel from where it was draped over the seat and dried himself quickly. With the towel wrapped around his body, he looked for his clothes. They had gone.

The guard unlocked a drawer, pulled out scissors and motioned towards the chair. It was some moments before Sergei could galvanise his legs into action. He sank down onto the seat, limbs twitching. A hand gripped a lock of his hair. The scissors bit through. Soon, piece after piece of matted hair was strewn over the floor.

"Now the whiskers." The blades of the scissors opened again and hovered in front of Sergei's wide-eyed gaze. He pulled the edges of the towel around his chest and shrank back in the chair, as still as his quaking limbs allowed. He held his breath and closed his eyes as he felt the blades close to his chin, steeling himself for the moment they pierced his throat. *Get it over quickly,* he begged silently. The man's fingers dug into Sergei's head, pushing it from side to side until he feared his neck would break. His head dropped forward. He took a gulp of air and opened his eyes.

"This is going to be fun," the guard laughed. "I hope my hand is steady!" He waved the open blades of a razor in front of Sergei, nicking his nose. The man's foul breath was warm. From a bowl, he produced a brush and lathered the front of Sergei's neck and lower part of his face. Sergei felt the blade of the razor scraping downwards from under his left ear; it caught his chin. "Sit still, damn you!" the guard spat, and wiped the blade on an edge of the towel. Sergei pressed his body into the back of the chair. The frame bit into his shoulders. His head jerked back again. He held his breath, hoping this was the end. The blade moved over his top lip, across his chin and down to his throat. It rested above his Adam's Apple. Sergei willed himself not to move. It seemed an age before the blade slid down his neck. Then the grip on his chin was released. Sergei ran the fingers of one hand around his neck then touched his nose, feeling the stickiness of blood.

The guard rummaged in a cupboard and pulled out a pile of clothes; a pair of shoes balanced on top. "Put these on!" he barked.

Why? Why do I need these? Sergei clutched the bundle to his chest. *Am I going home?*

Then his hand went to his mouth. *They're going to kill me! That's what they're going to do. Is this what they did to the man in the next cell? He wasn't spirited away, they brought him here and killed him!* He sank down onto the chair again, hunched away from the window, blotting out the outside world. He thought of his cell, the world he had made for himself. He was safe there.

"My cell? I want ..."

"*Naden' etu grebanuyu odezhdu!*" the guard barked.

Sergei gripped the back of the chair with one trembling hand, then the other, as he struggled into the underwear. The cotton felt soft against his skin. The pants were loose. Did he have a belt? Seated on the chair, he fumbled with the shirt buttons. The socks caught on jagged toenails as he pulled them on. "Move!" the guard hissed from behind him. Sergei's fingers were clumsy as he tied the shoelaces. Then he reached for the jacket from where it had slid to the floor, stood up and put it on.

"What are you waiting for?" the guard yelled. A stream of spittle hit Sergei in the face.

"Can't I go back?" he pleaded.

"Out!"

Sergei turned. He saw now that the door was open. "Where am I going?" he asked. "My son …?"

"Shut your mouth! You don't have a son."

What does he mean? Mitch is dead? They found him? Sergei opened his mouth to speak.

His inner voice cautioned, *Nyet! Remember ... you don't have a son. Don't think about him or they'll find him.* But from somewhere deep in his memory, a shadowy figure emerged. He willed it to go away, but it came into focus. Brown curly hair, the face he knew so well—the one he had watched change from the chubbiness of youth to the furrowed countenance of manhood, the once sparkling brown eyes dulled with disillusionment. *Don't think about him. He went away. Mitch went away. Or did I imagine that?* He pinched his lips between the thumb and forefinger of his right hand and looked around. *Perhaps I imagined it all.*

"Move!" The guard shoved Sergei in the small of his back.

His head hit the door jamb. He looked around, dazed. Took a step back. "I want … I want to go back to …" He didn't finish the sentence. The guard's next blow propelled him into the corridor. He bounced off the wall and, before he could steady himself, hands gripped his arms.

"Take him away!" the guard yelled and slammed the door.

Sergei tried to free himself from the two men who held his arms, managing to grab the waist of his pants with one hand to stop them slipping further down. "I want to go back … back to my cell," he whimpered as he was marched along a corridor. First one locked door then a second opened as they approached. They passed through. *"Verni menya, pazhalusta,"* Sergei pleaded. His words echoed in the silence.

As they approached the third door, one of the men produced a folded paper from his overcoat pocket and handed it to the guard. *What is it? What does it say? What are they going to do with me?* He held his breath. *They're going to kill me!* His legs buckled. The man on his left hauled him upright. The other man took the paper from the guard, put it in his pocket and gripped Sergei's upper arm. The door opened. "No! Not there! I can't go out there!" Sergei yelled as they propelled him forward. He blinked rapidly and tried to raise a hand to shield his eyes from the floodlights. His arms were in a vice. He squinted. A thick layer of ice covered the ground. They were in a courtyard, enclosed on three sides by a high brick wall topped with curls of what looked like razor wire. *The wall! They're going to shoot me!*

Sergei twisted his neck to look back. The door was closed. There was nowhere for him to go. He cringed. Everything was so big here. Towering above him. A dog barked. Sergei flinched. The handler struggled to restrain the animal on its leash as it lurched towards them across the compound. *Is this it? They're going to let the dog get me. Tear me to pieces! "Nyet! Nyet!"* he pleaded. "Don't let it get me!" The man on Sergei's left warned the handler to keep the dog away. It was only a few feet from them now, and curled its lips, snarling, revealing yellow teeth. The men hustled Sergei towards a car in front of big wooden gates and, as they approached, the driver got out and opened the rear doors. Sergei was wedged into the back of the car between the two escorts. Doors slammed and the men either side of him lit cigarettes; Sergei breathed in the smell of another world. The car pulled forward and the gates began to open. He shrank down in his seat. They passed slowly through the gateway, made a left turn and, with a roar of the engine, picked up speed.

The road was straight; wasteland shrouded in dim light on either side. Sergei looked at the horizon, realising that for so long for him the horizon hadn't existed. Blood pulsed through his temples. *Where are they taking me? And Mitch ... what's happened to him?* Tears welled in his eyes. *The guard said I don't have a son. What did he mean? How did he know? Was Mitch there in that place?* He tried to look back. The man on his right snarled at him. Sergei's thoughts went back to the times the bright light shone in his eyes. *Did I tell them? Did I tell them where Mitch is?* He chewed at the fingernails on his right hand, searching for a speck of familiar plaster, as he tried to unravel the muddle in his mind.

He could now see a cluster of buildings in the distance. Then more buildings. Above them the gilded onion domes of a church. Houses and shops flashed past. Blurred figures hovered at the side of the road as the car sped through the streets. Sergei shrank back. *Why are these people here? What are they doing?* "Where are we going?" His voice sounded small and he wondered if it was his voice. He looked at the men on either side. Their arms were folded across their torsos; they stared ahead, unsmiling, cigarettes dangling from lips.

Cars seemed to come at them from all directions, headlights flickering. Sergei gripped his hands together, eyes fixed on the line at the back of the driver's neck where it met severely trimmed grey hair. When he looked up, he saw the black pinpoints of the driver's eyes in the rear-view mirror. They turned a corner; the man shifted his head slightly. Now, red-rimmed eyes in black-smudged sockets stared back in the mirror. *Who is that? Is there someone else here?* He ran the fingers of his right hand around an eye. *What's happened to me?*

At a clogged intersection, the car inched forward. Sergei craned his neck searching for clues on shops, street signs—anything that might tell him where he was. There was nothing … nothing he could see without his spectacles, which had disappeared long ago. He caught the curious gaze of a young boy in the back seat of the car on their right. It was driven by a man, a woman by his side. Ordinary people going about their ordinary lives. *Sophia, Mitch, and I, were once ordinary people. Weren't we? Once?*

They sped across a bridge over a frozen river. There were fewer buildings, fewer people. He willed himself not to think about where they might be going. Thoughts crept in. *A forest clearing? A shallow grave?* He wrapped his arms around his body. *If they wanted to kill me, wouldn't it have been easier behind those walls where no one could see?*

Ice-encrusted trees flashed past. The man on Sergei's left lit another cigarette and passed the packet and lighter to the other man. The smoke was hypnotic. *I'm imagining this. It's a dream and I'll wake up in my cell, lying on the cot. Fifteen steps ... seven steps.* For a moment, he was comforted. Then another thought came into his mind. *I'm already dead. That's what it is.*

The idea didn't frighten him. He thought of Sophia as she lay in her coffin. Her face bore the faint trace of a smile, as if she was trying to tell him something.

The car slowed. The driver inclined his head towards the forest. Sergei's body stiffened as the vehicle pulled into a clearing at the side of the road and stopped. "You need a piss, old man?" the man on his right growled.

Every nerve in Sergei's body was taut. *It's a trick. It's a trick to get me out there. "Nyet ... Ya ne."*

"You piss in the car, we'll kill you!"

Sergei shrank into himself.

The driver made his way through the snow between a row of trees, followed by one of the other men.

"Want to walk around?" the man next to him asked, getting out of the car. Sergei shook his head. The door slammed, then the man reached in and removed the keys from the ignition. Sergei watched him pacing around, puffing at a cigarette. He was soon joined by the other two men and took his turn going into the forest. Sergei's muscles relaxed. *If they were going to kill me, they would have pulled me out, dragged me in there.* There were cars speeding past, but no one would want to get involved. No one would care. The three men were now deep in conversation. *What are they talking about?* They walked slowly back to the car, knocked snow off their boots, and climbed in. Sergei breathed more easily as the driver started the engine and pulled into a gap in the traffic.

They soon slowed at a checkpoint. The driver handed a document to the uniformed officer. The young man looked at it, leaned into the car, fixed his gaze on Sergei for a moment, then handed the paper back to the driver. As they accelerated, Sergei tried to read the road signs. *St Petersburg? Is that what it said? Nyet. It can't be. Unless I've gone back in time. Can they do that ... in that place?* Then he remembered. *We voted. The city ... it's no longer called Leningrad.* A glimmer of hope stirred. *I'm going back ... back home. It's Vera. She's persuaded them.* He leaned back in his seat and closed his eyes, as exhaustion overtook him.

Sometime later, he jolted awake and was startled to see they were in the city … his city. The roof of the Moskovsky Station was stark against its faded green façade. He leaned forward. Throngs of people surged through archways onto the sidewalk. Some darted between vehicles to join others waiting for trams in the centre of the road. *So much traffic. So many people. It's all still here. Life went on as usual while I was locked away.*

The man on Sergei's right snapped at the driver, asking why he was taking such a circuitous route. A heated discussion started between the driver and escorts, each man propounding his own view about the best roads to use to avoid traffic snarl-ups. Sergei listened, trying to pick up clues as to where they were going. They gave nothing away.

The Vostanija metro station was now in sight. Sergei swallowed hard, thinking of the first time he had brought Sophia and Mitch to this part of the city. He had waited so long for that day. Now, in his mind's eye, he saw the white lights of the Christmas tree dancing against the night sky, felt a small gloved hand in his, Mitch's young face alive with wonder as he gazed up at the tree. *If only I knew he was alive, safe. And Anja? I should be out there looking for her.* He scanned the sidewalk, searching for his granddaughter.

Further along the Nevsky, his hopes of going home faded. The bronze stallions on the Anichkov Bridge came into view, beneath it the frozen Fontanka. It was snowing now. The windshield wipers beat a methodical rhythm. The car slowed, indicators clicked, then the driver accelerated across oncoming traffic.

Sergei tried not to think of the times he had driven this same stretch of road, on his way to participate in the farce of a trial, defending the accused—the innocent, the guilty, not that that had any bearing on a verdict. The car slowed as it entered the forecourt of the building. It was all so familiar. People hurried towards the entrance, some carrying briefcases, hugging files close to their chests. He knew what they were thinking, going over their opening arguments or rehearsing the words they would use in summing up a case. *A lifetime ago.*

The car swung around the side of the building, turned again then stopped in front of the gate in the high wire-fenced enclosure. Sergei stared at the windshield wipers, following, but not following, their movement. The gate opened and the car slid forward. Strength seeped from his body as the gate clanged shut.

9
Montréal
February 1992

On this early Monday evening, Mitch slid spaghetti into a pan of boiling water then tipped tomato sauce out of a screw-top jar into a saucepan to heat. He had the night off from the bar where he worked. As he stirred the sauce, he watched the parade of boots pass by on the sidewalk which, if deep-banked snow or ice didn't block his view, he could just see through the high shallow window in this basement where he now lived. He sometimes tried to imagine what the owners of the boots looked like. There were the stiletto-heeled ankle boots, stocking-clad legs; these took some time to pass by as fashion-conscious wearers picked their way along the slippery sidewalk. Then there were the black boots with an inch or two of grey, black, or sometimes navy, pants visible; these belonged to the formal-suited men working in banks, insurance companies, and the like. The ones Mitch liked best were the small boots belonging to children. He had seen most colours pass by, some with brightly-hued toggles or tassels. Sometimes they ran or slid. Mitch imagined these children with bookbags bouncing on their backs. They were often accompanied by larger, sensible boots with fur poking out of the top, maybe belonging to a proud grandmother.

At first, he was surprised he could look at the feet of these children without feeling a pang of loss for Anja. Strangely, the sight of these children doing the things children have done for generations, made him feel close to her, gave him hope that she was doing the same … somewhere.

Two weeks ago, Vera reported that the woman and child in the village in Siberia had been positively identified from photographs as Natasha and Anja. A surge of relief washed through Mitch's body. *She's alive! Annushka ... she's alive!* The muscles in his shoulders had relaxed for what seemed like the first time in months. *They are using false names, Natasha posing as the wife of Boris, who was Yagudin's driver.* As Vera's words sank in, a chilling thought struck him: *If Natasha is passing herself off as Boris's wife, then Anja ... Anja must be calling Boris 'Papa'!* His precious daughter was calling another man by the name which was rightfully his. *Nyet! She can't be! I'm her Papa, not him.* Then another thought hit him: *If she believes Boris is her papa, they must have told her I'm dead.* He had paced around the room, trying not to let his mind conjure up visions of Anja crying … crying for him, her papa, the papa who was dead. *Maybe she's forgotten me already. Nyet! Not my Annushka. I must tell her ... tell her I'm alive and will come for her soon. But how? Send a letter to Vera and ask her to get it to Anja somehow? But, they'll know. Even if she can read the letter herself, she's bound to tell. That's what children do. And what if anyone else reads the letter? Finds out she's my daughter? She'll be in more danger.*

His head buzzed, and it had been some minutes before he picked up Vera's letter again. *Boris seems to have severed his ties with the vory,* she wrote. *She doesn't know that,* Mitch scoffed. *How can anyone be certain a mobster like him won't revert to his criminal ways? I have to get Anja out of there, bring her here. And Papa?* Vera hadn't mentioned him.

In the early days in the basement here in Montréal, he had tried to ignore the stories in the newspaper—stories of mafia gangs running their nefarious empires in this city. He panicked when anyone knocked on the door, scarcely breathing as he pressed his body flat against the wall, where he hoped he could not be seen. His heart thumped loudly until he heard footsteps recede up the area steps. As time wore on, he began to relax. On his journey from Moncton, he had woven such a haphazard path that at times he felt lost in a maze himself. It was ludicrous to think he might have been followed here by someone acting for Yagudin's mob. *Wasn't it?*

Lately, he had ventured further into the city, searching for places he knew as a child. As he wandered around the neighbourhoods, he began to feel he belonged here. The language was his, the people were his—at least half his. When speaking French, the softness of the language moulded his attitude to life, enabling him to see things in a diffused glow. It crossed his mind that he should try to locate his childhood friends. *Jean-Pierre, Sebastian ... what were the names of the others?* The friends he missed so much when he first moved to Leningrad, but to whom he now found it difficult to attach names or faces. *They will have changed, probably have their own children, maybe of a similar age to Anja.* He had promised to bring her here one day. *I wonder if she remembers.*

Now, he drained the spaghetti, tipped it into a bowl and poured sauce on top. As he mixed it together, his mind worked to formulate a plan. He couldn't drift aimlessly any longer. He had to get a grip on his life, do something about a better job. First, he needed to find out what he had to do to regularise his status in the country. Tomorrow, he would make enquiries about obtaining a copy of his birth certificate and that of his mother. The originals, together with other documents, were destroyed in the bomb which exploded under his car. *Slava!* A shiver ran through his body as he thought of the old man—toothless grin, head clad in a knitted hat—the caretaker from the apartment building in Leningrad where Mitch, Natasha, and Anja, had lived.

Since that terrible day when Slava was blown up by the bomb meant for Mitch, the old man's face came back to him many times. Sometimes it was the first thing he saw when he opened his eyes in the morning. He tried to ignore it, but that made him feel worse, as though denying the poor man ever existed. He must allow him to live on, if only in his thoughts. He dug a fork into the spaghetti. "Glory!" he scoffed, remembering the meaning of Slava's name.

* * *

The next morning, he awoke early—for once, his sleep had been undisturbed. He craned his neck. The occasional person passed by on the sidewalk, but it was too early for the cavalcade of scurrying boots which signalled the rush to work and school. He inched open the door to see what the weather was like. An icy blast hit him, and he closed the door quickly. He didn't have to be at work until six this evening, so had time to take his washing to the laundromat and, while that swished around, pick up provisions from the nearby grocery store. He would cook a light lunch and then go to a Services Québec office to find out how he could get copies of the birth certificates he needed. That would be the first step in proving his Canadian citizenship. It wouldn't be without risk, as he had entered the country with a Russian passport in a false name, but hopefully he could establish his real identity before anyone found out. He often wondered whether his alias, Andrei Lapitsky, really existed. *There's a tombstone engraved with his name in a silent graveyard?* He shuddered.

He was late arriving for work at the bar that evening. As he served drinks, his mind raked over his visit to the government office. It had seemed a simple procedure. He obtained the appropriate form at the counter but, as he began to fill in the boxes and read the notes, it was clear he needed a photocopy of a valid photo ID and proof of his home address, in his real name.

He had tried to explain to the clerk but was met with a shrug of the shoulders and, "*Ce sont les régles.*" He countered with a plea that there must be exceptions to the rules in special cases, and was told it might be better if he consulted a lawyer. His shout of, "For Christ's sake, I am a lawyer!" brought a security officer to his side. "*D'Accord! Je pars!*" Mitch uttered, shaking the hand from his arm.

Now, he put down the cloth with which he had been drying glasses, and took the form out of the back pocket of his pants. Another glance told him what he already knew: without proof of identity, he couldn't establish he was the Mitchell Sergeivich Galichin born in Montréal on October 6th, 1962. He folded the form again, stuffed it into his pocket and began stacking clean glasses on the shelves. As he worked, he went over options in his mind. He could get a lawyer experienced in dealing with situations like his. *Refugees must have similar problems,* he reasoned. He had to do something. His work permit was a forgery and he couldn't risk being deported back to Russia before he was able to prove his real identity.

If he could find his mother's only sibling—a brother who lived in the city years ago—maybe this *Oncle* could help him get a copy of the documentation he needed. Mitch had already tried calling all the people by the name of 'Weitz' listed in the telephone directory. *The synagogue? Someone there might know him. But which synagogue? Where to start? Would a non-Jew (or half-Jew) be welcome in one of those places?* He leaned on the counter. *Surely there's someone in this city who remembers Maman, her family.* His mind drifted back to his early childhood here in Montréal. He was four years old. He and Maman sat at a big table. There was a woman—blonde hair, pulled back from her face on one side. A dark-haired man. Her husband? A large brood of children. *The boy? We went to the same daycare.* Mitch closed his eyes. *Mathieu! That was his name. Maman would sometimes collect us when she left work and hurry us along the streets until we reached the house. It was always such fun there. Freshly-baked cakes or cookies. What the hell was her name ... the woman ... Mathieu's mother?*

Tante ...? He went through the alphabet in his mind, trying to dredge up her name. "Simone! That's it! *Tante* Simone!" he uttered somewhat louder than intended.

Micky, his boss, turned from pouring a glass of beer, a puzzled look on his face. "It's a name I was trying to remember," Mitch muttered, headed around the counter and began to collect used glasses. *Tante Simone. Simone what? What the hell was her surname?* Without that he was sunk. *She could be dead by now ... like Maman. You have to try, it's the only chance you have,* he told himself as he loaded glasses into the dishwasher. *Maman? Didn't she say Mathieu's father was a lawyer? "Like your Papa."* It hadn't meant much to the young Mitch—his Papa had been a shadowy figure in a photograph Maman kept by her bed.

Simone. She's the key. On his next day off, he would scour the city and see if he recognised anywhere. *She must have lived close to the daycare.* It was a bit of a longshot, as the odds of the daycare or the house still being there nearly thirty years later were remote. *She's probably moved away.*

"Andrei!" Micky's voice snapped him out of his trance. "Bee Jesus, man. What the hell's wrong with you?"

The background chatter in the bar hushed. Mitch stared at the broken glass at his feet.

"You going to stand there all night looking at it?"

* * *

Two weeks later, Mitch stood at the end of a street. For a moment, he couldn't take it in. This place—the place he had stumbled upon at the end of yet another day tramping around the city—looked familiar. His mother's voice from all those years ago urged him on: *"On y est presque. Non loin maintenant."* He felt her warm hand in his as he took a few tentative steps along the sidewalk. He stopped. All the houses looked alike. Steep steps leading up to front doors. *Which one was it? Which house did Simone live in?* He heard again Maman's voice: *"A quelques pas de plus."* He shuffled on. Stopped. Stared at the house in front of him. *Is this it? Is this where Simone lived?* "Maman?" She had gone. No voice, no comforting hand to guide him. There was a light shining through the transom above the green-painted door. As Mitch watched, a ginger cat jumped down from the wall at the side of the porch. It walked sedately down the steps and rubbed itself around Mitch's right pant leg, purring softly. He lit a cigarette, inhaled, and watched as the cat picked its way across the icy ruts in the road and disappeared down an alleyway. Mitch turned and looked up at the house. *What if it isn't the right place? Even if it is, they've probably moved ... died ... divorced. They won't even remember me or Maman.*

He took another drag on the cigarette, threw it into the road and climbed the steps.

10
St Petersburg, Russia
February 1992

The gate clanged shut. Sergei sat with his eyes closed, head bowed. The blackness behind his eyes penetrated his very being. The men on either side of him threw open the car doors and heaved themselves out. The one on Sergei's right, yanked Sergei's arm. *"Vyyti!"* he barked. Sergei opened his eyes, took a deep breath, moved across the seat, swung his legs around and got unsteadily to his feet. The wind spat needles of snow into his face. It was eerily quiet here. His escorts gripped his arms as they walked him towards a door. He stumbled. Their grip tightened. The men held identification badges up to a side window and the door opened. Inside, Sergei stood back against the wall, the outside world shut out. In the narrow corridor, he walked behind one of his escorts; the other man followed closely.

Downwards now. His hands grazed rough walls as he missed his footing on one of the dimly lit steps. Their footsteps were loud, like drumbeats in the low-ceilinged passageway. They were now in a room with open-barred cells on either side. He knew this place. Before, he entered through a door at the other end of the room. He wore a dark suit, commanded an air of authority, his position as *Yurist* setting him apart from the guards, or the prisoners awaiting trial or transportation to previously unimaginable places. His shoulders slumped.

A guard opened the door of a cell and one of the escorts pushed Sergei inside. The door clanged shut. The key ground in the lock. Sergei gripped the bars, telling himself this couldn't be happening. *"Eto nepravilno,"* he pleaded. "I've not been charged with anything." His two escorts exchanged noisy banter with the guards then the sound of their footsteps faded in the passageway.

The only sound now was the muffled conversation of two guards who sat at a table in the middle of the room. The other cells were empty. Sergei sank down onto the stone bench along the wall, head cradled in his hands. His eyes followed cracks in the rough-hewn floor as he tried to make sense of what was happening. *If I'm here in court, they must have charged me with something.* He thought back to when they first took him to that place. There was a piece of paper. A pen. A finger jabbed at a place on the page. A shouted order telling him to sign. The overhead light reflected on the single sheet of paper. He squinted. The words ran together; they had taken his spectacles. "I haven't done anything. Why won't you believe me?" he had pleaded. They told him if he admitted his guilt he would be moved to another place. "There'll be other people, you'll walk outside, eat good food, fresh bread." Sometime later, a hand gripped his head and slammed it against the metal desk again and again. The ringing in his ears stayed with him for days.

One day or night—he knew not which—he had stared at another sheet of paper. There were fewer words. A guard stood by the table, slapping a fist into his other hand again and again. The beat pounded through Sergei's head. Another man entered. A kinder face. He spoke softly, explaining that the piece of paper was unimportant. Sergei's hand reached for the pen.

Now, a loud voice broke into his thoughts. "You can't do this! A ten-year stretch! I didn't do anything! I've been set up!" Two guards dragged a man down the steps from the courtroom and bundled him into a cell. The door slammed shut. The man yelled: "I'll get you lot for this!" and kicked at the bars. *"Blyad! Blyad!"*

Sergei leaned back against the wall and tried to block out the loud expletives from the other cell. *Think, man, think.* It was so long since he'd had to think, he'd forgotten how. *They'll be calling you soon. You have to know what you're going to say.*

"Would you like some coffee?"

Sergei met the gaze of a guard.

"You may be here some time. They've adjourned for lunch."

Coffee? He tried to recall the taste. His mouth was dry. He nodded his head.

The guard stared at him. "I remember you."

Sergei's hands shook as he took the paper cup the guard pushed between the bars.

"Doesn't seem right, a man like you … here."

"Can you …" Sergei ventured, "… can you tell me why I'm here? What the charges are?"

The guard shook his head. "They don't tell us."

"If they've charged me with something, I should have a lawyer. Someone handling my defence."

"Don't ask me. I just do as I'm told, like the rest of us here." The guard gave Sergei a sympathetic look. "The whole system's crazy!"

"What time is it?"

The guard shifted the left sleeve of his jacket slightly. "Just after one. Should be an hour or so, then we'll get you in there."

"What month is it?"

"February."

"Is it still …?" Sergei scratched the back of his head.

"1992." The sympathy in the guard's eyes increased, then he turned and yelled at the man in the other cell to quieten down.

Sergei slumped onto the bench. *What year did they take me? What month?* He sipped his coffee. It was strong and sweet. As he sat there, he tried to retrieve memories from where he had hidden them. *Sophia died—when? Was it 1989 … 1990? Has she been gone so long?* Fragments began to emerge. There was a lake, a boat, the laughter of a child. Anja. It was her. His granddaughter. For a moment, his heart lightened. *Maybe it's better not to remember.*

He had to find a way out of this. Work out what to do. If only he could think clearly. Visions flashed through his mind like frames in a movie—doors opening, slamming, a razor dangling in front of his face, his head hitting the metal desk. He jolted upright in an attempt to dislodge the images. *It doesn't matter what happens to me. As long as Mitch and Anja are safe.*

Voices approached along the corridor, and two men in dark overcoats came into view. They looked like the men who brought him here. But how could he tell? On the journey, he hardly looked at their faces. They stopped outside the other occupied cell. A chair scraped back and a guard got to his feet. The prisoner walked slowly to the door of the cell; the men led him away, supporting him on either side, his feet dragging. In the short time the man had been here, he seemed to have shrunk.

Pain gnawed at Sergei's stomach. Familiar pain. In the place where he was before, he had been unable to control his bodily functions. He ate little, but still the pain came like a blunt knife slowly twisting inside him. A thin stream of mucus would run down his legs. Nothing mattered there. *Not here, please,* he begged silently, put his coffee cup on the floor and clenched an arm across his stomach. He rose unsteadily to his feet gripping the top of his pants with one hand.

"Toilet! I need the toilet!" he shouted to the guard. A key ground in the lock. The door swung open, then the guard clasped one of Sergei's arms and guided him to the door behind the desk.

He was hardly through the doorway when he slid his pants down. He breathed again.

In the cell, he paced back and forth for what seemed an eternity. Then the door at the top of the stairs to the courtroom opened and the head of a guard appeared. He called to the guard behind the desk: *"Privedi ego s soboy."* Sergei stepped back as the guard approached. "Come on. Make it easier for yourself," the man cajoled, unlocked the door, pulled Sergei's arms behind his back and snapped on handcuffs.

Sergei's steps were slow as he emerged from the cell. With a foot on the first stair, he hesitated, strength draining from him. His feet felt like lead weights. His mouth was dry, his stomach an icy chill. He was now at the top of the stairs. The cage was in front of him. He tried to pull back. The guard inside the courtroom yanked on his arm and pulled him inside. Sergei took small steps, neck bent, staring at his shoes.

From his seat on a bench, it was some moments before he raised his head and looked around, hesitantly at first. The room was a blur of faces, a murmur of voices and shifting of seats as more people filed in. He caught the flicker of a hand. *Mitch?* He mouthed his son's name. The hand waved again. *Vera Alexandrovna Kishinevskaya.* His long-time friend smiled across the room. Their eyes met. Sergei bent forward, trying to hide his emaciated body. Next to Vera, Leonid who, together with his wife, shared Vera's apartment. *Leonid? Wasn't he supposed to take Mitch somewhere? Oh God! Please don't let anything have happened to Mitch.*

At that moment, a door opened. Everyone rose to their feet. Sergei saw a blur of blue uniform. He took a sharp intake of breath. Hope drained away. *The judge. It's him! Arkady Soukharnikov!* His fate was now in the hands of this man known to be on the take, in the pay of regional bosses or anyone willing to finance his lifestyle. Sergei also knew it was no use relying on the two citizens, known as 'nodders', who always agree with the judge's decision. The room tipped at an odd angle.

The charges were read out: "Illicit transfer and trafficking of children for sexual exploitation … procuring of minors for pecuniary gain …"

"Nyet! Nyet!" Sergei yelled. "That's not true! You're lying!" Sergei lurched forward.

"Order! Order!" Soukharnikov rapped. "The accused will be quiet!"

Another voice pealed out: "He is innocent! It's not him you should have in the dock," Vera was on her feet, shouting and waving her arms, "it's those …" A gavel pounded. The rest of her words were lost.

"Silence! I will not tolerate interference from the public!"

A hush went around the room. Leonid pulled Vera back into her seat.

"This is wrong! Wrong! I haven't done anything!" Sergei yelled as the guard manhandled him on to the bench. His legs were numb. Pins and needles ran up his arms from where the cuffs chafed his wrists. "I haven't done anything," he murmured.

The clamour in the courtroom buzzed in his head. *If only Mitch was here, he'd know what to do.* He dismissed the thought quickly. *Whatever happens, Mitch must be free to make a new life for himself and Anja. Nothing else matters.* He squirmed in his seat. The scabs on his body itched; there was no way he could reach them. Tears pricked his eyes. How had he come to this? He had not done anything wrong. But that was irrelevant in the corrupt system that passed for justice. Energy drained from him as the irony of what was happening sank in. The crimes they were accusing him of were the ones for which Mitch had risked his life exposing the real perpetrators. *The same crimes.* He no longer wondered who they would make pay.

He glanced up. Vera smiled at him. He shook his head at her then stared at the floorboards in front of his feet, white in parts, pounded by prisoners' shoes. Prisoners like him. As he sat there, his mother's voice from long ago came back to him: *"You can't let the system win. Don't let them get the better of you. Fight back. It's the only way to survive."* How many times had she said that when he was growing up and whined about some injustice? Sergei got to his feet. "You can't do this! I demand legal representation!"

"Quiet!" Soukharnikov snapped.

"A lawyer! I demand a lawyer!" The guard grabbed Sergei by his shoulders. "It's my right!" he yelled as he was forced down onto the bench.

The judge leaned towards the prosecutor. "Proceed."

The prosecutor read from a document. Sergei gasped. In his head, he heard again a quiet voice, saw a kind face, a piece of paper, felt his hand reaching for the pen. He, Sergei Dmitrievich Galichin, had pleaded guilty to the charges and waived his right to be represented.

"They made me sign it! They forced me!"

"If the accused doesn't keep quiet, he will be removed from the courtroom!"

Sergei twisted his hands in the handcuffs in a futile attempt to be free. His shoulders slumped. *How can I prove it? Prove I'm innocent? I was made to confess under duress.* Without a lawyer, he didn't stand a chance. *What's wrong with you?* he berated himself. *You've spent your life defending people. Why can't you think straight now when it matters most?* In truth, he had seen too much. Too much to believe he could win.

His eyes met those of Vera Alexandrovna. She held his gaze. Sergei tried to smile, to reassure her. His lips felt set, the muscles in his cheeks rigid, as though *rigor mortis* had already set in.

He heard, but didn't take in, the voices in the room. A strident call went out: "Umida Hudaberganova. Call Umida Hudaberganova." A door opened. A girl was led in by a court official. She wore a pale blue dress and the fingers of her right hand held together the edges of a grey cardigan. Her other arm was wrapped across her waist. The room was quiet as she took the witness stand.

Who is she? Sergei craned his neck to get a better look.

She began to speak hesitantly, her voice low. In answer to the prosecutor's questions, she told the court that she was fifteen, from Uzbekistan. "My parents, they were Ashkenazi Jews. They died. I was on my own." She scanned the onlookers as though searching for someone. Sergei noticed that a man seated in the second row looked directly at her and nodded his head almost imperceptibly. She continued: "I worked in the market in Tashkent. One day, the man who owned the stall said he could get me a job … a good job in Leningrad. He said I would be looking after the children of his friend." She gulped and opened her mouth to continue. No sound came out. She gripped the cardigan tighter and shook her head.

"Take your time, my dear." Soukharnikov's tone was kindly. A murmur of approval swept around the room.

"There were no children," she said in a shaky voice. "His friend in Leningrad he … he locked us up. Me and the other girls." She broke down and sobbed loudly.

Sergei's heart went out to the girl. She was so thin, so pale. A child. Her whole body shook. *It's girls like her that Mitch was trying to protect.* His son's voice ran through his head: *"I have to do something, Papa. I can't stand by and let them get away with it. Someone has to stop them. In a few years, it could be Anja."*

"What happened then? Can you tell the court what happened?" the prosecutor prompted.

"He sold us to some men. They took us to another place, a long way away." The girl looked at the man in the second row. He leaned forward, and she took a deep breath and spoke again. "The men who came to that place, they ch … chose a girl. The man who chose me … that was the first time … he said he had paid more for me. I hadn't been with a man before." She hunched her shoulders and stared down at her feet.

"I think we have heard enough." Soukharnikov dragged the words out. The girl wiped her eyes with the back of her hand. "We just need you to tell us who did this. Who sold you to those men?"

Why are they doing this if they say I have already confessed? Sergei knew the answer. It was all part of the theatre, the farce that was the Soviet version of justice. One he had seen played out many times. This time was different.

"Him!" The girl pointed at Sergei, then dropped her arm to her side. Her next words were almost inaudible: "He sold me."

Sergei got to his feet. His breath came in loud gasps as he struggled to get air into his lungs. With a supreme effort, he rasped, "You're lying! Tell them!" He stared at the girl in the witness box. She turned away from him.

"Silence!"

"I've never met her!"

The judge rose to his feet. "Remove him!"

"They've told her to say this. Threatened her!" Sergei twisted his body out of the guard's grasp. Another guard appeared and grabbed him. "Can't you see how frightened she is?" Sergei yelled.

"My witness. She's bound to be frightened in the presence of this man." The prosecutor turned towards Sergei, a satisfied look on his face. "The man who made a sex slave out of an innocent young girl."

"There are people who can help you," Sergei yelled and tried in vain to wrestle free of the guards. "They'll find a place for you. They won't find you. The ones making you do this!"

“Get him out!” the judge rapped.

Sergei was now on the floor. One of the guards grabbed his legs. For the briefest moment, the girl’s eyes met his. She looked away.

As they pulled him from the court, he twisted his head trying to see Vera. “Don’t forget your promise!” he yelled to her as loudly as he could.

Vera was on her feet. Her fingers gripped the back of the seat in front. The door at the back of the cage slammed shut. Every nerve in her body jangled. She stood for some moments, staring at the space where her dearest friend had been. “I won’t forget,” she whispered.

11
St Petersburg, Russia
February 1992

Vera Alexandrovna Kishinevskaya sat motionless in her chair. The whispered words of Leonid and his wife, Lyuba, washed around her: "She has to eat something. She won't do him any good sitting there like that," came from Lyuba as she tucked a blanket around Vera's legs.

"No one can help him now. The man's finished," Leonid rasped. "His age. In one of those places." He shook his head and followed his wife out of the room. The door closed softly behind them.

Vera heard nothing. In the hours since she watched her dear Seryozha dragged from the court, she couldn't get his voice out of her head, crying out to her. It whirled around faster and faster until she felt the only way to let it out was to pull her hair from her head strand by strand.

When they first brought him into the court, Vera hardly recognised the man with the sunken cheeks, the haunted look in his eyes. He tried to hide his emaciated body, but she saw. And the cage. She had shuddered, steeling herself to look at him through the bars, forcing a smile onto her face, hoping shock wasn't reflected in her eyes.

Fifteen years. Hard labour. That's what the judge said, but everyone knows what work camps are. How can a man Seryozha's age survive in a place like that? He is innocent, like multitudes before him.

As people filed out of the court, she and Leonid had remained standing, locked in shock and disbelief. Then, ignoring Leonid's protests, she walked purposefully towards a clerk who was gathering together documents from a desk in front of the judge's bench. "I wish to see Sergei Dmitrievich Galichin … the man who has just been taken away." She drew herself up, straightened her shoulders.

"Eto nevozmozhno," the clerk replied, adding more papers to the bundle in his arms.

"Nonsense! I demand to see him."

"I have already told you. It is not possible," he hissed.

"Prisoners are allowed visitors. Even those who are guilty. Which he is not!"

"You're not helping him," Leonid cautioned.

She brushed his hand from her arm.

"The court has given its verdict and the prisoner has already been taken away."

"Where? Where have they taken him? I demand to know!"

"You will have to submit a written request."

"Written request?"

"Requests have to be in writing. That's the procedure." The clerk clutched his stack of papers close to his chest and turned to walk away.

"Listen to me! I haven't finished yet!" Vera demanded of the clerk's receding back. She raised her voice: "I thought the Stalinist era was over … long ago!" The door to the inner sanctum slammed behind him.

Now, Vera gave a long sigh and sat up in her armchair. Her eyes strayed to the chair in which Sergei had sat so many times, glass of brandy at his side, lost in the music of Shostakovich. She stared hard at the chair, wishing she could somehow spirit him back from whatever awful place they had taken him. She chewed on the knuckles of her right hand remembering a man she had once known. He was incarcerated in the camps for five years. When he came home, his shoulder bones protruded like wings. His eyes? She could see them now. Blank. Devoid of emotion. *Don't think about it,* she admonished herself, pushed the blanket to one side, struggled out of the chair, and went to the cabinet where she kept her gramophone records. She ran her fingers over the sleeve of the well-worn record: the maestro's Second Piano Trio. She hugged it to her breast, remembering how Seryozha always teased her, asking when she was going to join the modern world. "The music wouldn't be the same without the familiar scratches," she would laugh as the eerily high notes of the cello began to fill the room. Then, somewhat lower, the piano and violin came in, creating a strangely comforting sense of abject mourning. As the last notes of the tragic finale—the bitter-sweet Jewish-themed *totentanz*—faded, they would both be lost in thoughts of the fragility of life.

The fragility of life—why am I always surprised by it? Vera asked herself now. She whose secure childhood came to an abrupt halt that night in 1917 as she and her elder sister, Olga, clung together under their coverlet of straw in the stables of their parents' country estate in Vyborg. In the rising tide of violence sweeping across Russia, previously loyal servants turned into assassins. The tumult over, the newly-orphaned girls ran to the house of the local doctor, their hands entwined as their lives were until Olga died some thirty years ago.

And now, my dearest Seryozha. Lost, like everyone I love. She choked back tears, took the record out of its sleeve and placed it on the turntable. Her fingers hovered above the arm which held the stylus. She couldn't bear to put it on. At the window, she looked out at the lights of the city, wondering where he was now. In the weeks following that day in August, the day they took him, she had tried frantically to find him, uncover any information about his whereabouts. But even her most trusted contacts were scared. Scared they might be seen talking to her or that their phone lines were tapped. She began to fear he was dead. That is, until early this morning. A note was slipped under the door. It was brief, giving only the date and the name of the court. Leonid had driven her there. Hours later, the shadow of her dearest Seryozha was hauled into that cage.

She shivered now. *What if he thinks I too have abandoned him? Nyet ... he will know,* she comforted herself. They had always been close, often reminiscing that it was not luck but fate that brought them together that freezing night during the *Blokada.*

Vera had been prising scraps of floorboards from a derelict house in the city and carefully stowing them in a canvas sack which she would tie around her waist and hide under her coat. It was too dangerous to walk through the streets carrying anything; she had seen a woman beaten to death for a crust of bread. It was then she heard it. The scuffling sound. *A rat!* She salivated at the thought of meat—like most of the starving population, she had tried to forget what the taste was like. But the memory was there, below the surface. Hammer in hand, she had gone in search of the rodent. In a sliver of moonlight she saw a figure. It was scraping paper from a wall. She stood stock still, cursing herself for not having noticed the precious scraps of wallpaper, the glue from which Olga could have made into soup. As she backed away, her boot caught on something. She overbalanced. The hammer dropped onto the frozen earth; the earth which had once been covered with floorboards. In the shadows, she groped around searching for the hammer. Her fingers touched something. It was cold as ice. She leaned forward. The eyes of a frozen corpse stared at her. Stifling a scream, she turned and ran. Straight into him. He clamped a hand over her mouth and gripped her arm with his other hand as she tried to break free. He was strong. Before easing his hand from her mouth, he whispered, "*Militsya.* Two of them just passed by." His beard was frosted with ice, the skin around his cheekbones white in the moonlight. Was he an old man? She couldn't tell. Everyone in the city had aged beyond their years. Children looked like wizened crones. Her heart thumped loudly in her chest as she looked around for a way out. She could take a chance. *If he's really old, I might outrun him.* Then he released his hold on her arm and smiled. She stared at him. It was so long since she had seen anyone smile.

She struggled with her sack of wood as he walked behind her through the streets. "Let me take it," he urged. She gripped it tighter through her coat willing herself not to give in to the dizziness that threatened to overwhelm her. "You don't have to worry. I won't steal it." His voice far away.

When she came to, she was lying on a mattress on a floor. She heard the murmur of voices, felt the rough wool of a blanket covering her. She tried to sit up, but sank back down.

Olga! She'll be wondering where I am.

"You're awake. We were worried about you." It was him, the man. Vera turned away. It was then she saw the old woman. Her eyes were sad as she looked down at Vera, but she had the smile—the same smile as the man.

"Where?" was the only word Vera's lips could form.

"You're safe here with us," the woman murmured.

"Olga. I must …"

The man pulled Vera into a sitting position and supported her while the woman held a cup of warm liquid to her lips. "Drink a little of this."

An hour or so later, Vera leaned heavily on the man—who she now knew was called Sergei Dmitrievich Galichin—as he walked her home through the ice-cold streets of Leningrad, her sack of firewood tied beneath his coat. They wove a haphazard path around bodies frozen where they had dropped. The sight no longer seemed strange in this city whose inhabitants were little more than walking dead.

After the war, she harboured hopes the two of them would marry. She did her best to hide her feelings, fearing that to declare them would mean the loss of her trusted friend. At times, she felt she could no longer stand being so close to, but so far from, this man who made every part of her body tingle. Then, she would retreat into herself, hide in her bedroom while Olga made excuses when he came to the door. Time passed and with it any romantic notions she harboured. She came to appreciate his finer qualities: his inner strength, his sense of fairness, and his innate ability to always put others before himself. Running the clandestine network, helping the persecuted establish new lives far from here, had given them both the shared fulfilment they might never have found in marriage. His marriage to Sophia? Well, what could she say? It was as if Sergei had been waiting, knowing Sophia was there all the time.

Now, as Vera stared out of the window, she heard again Seryozha's shouts when they dragged him from the court. *"Don't forget your promise!"* His words echoed in her head. She had been foolish to make that promise. It was on the morning before the newspaper article exposing the members of the trafficking ring was published in England. Sergei appeared at the apartment and brushed away her offer of a cup of coffee, a glass of brandy. He had closed the door to the kitchen where Leonid and Lyuba were seated at the table finishing their breakfast.

His fingers dug into the tops of her arms, his face inches from hers. "You have to promise me," he urged, his tone agitated. She had tried to wriggle free of his grasp, but he held tight. "They will come for me. You must tell Mitch I am dead. He must not come back here."

Since then, she had agonised over whether she should honour her promise. Until today, she had hope. Hope that he would come home and that one day he and Mitch would be together again. But now? Whatever she did would have terrible consequences. How could she decide without Seryozha's wise counsel to guide her? His sharp legal brain, tinged with compassion, had always been there, helping her pick her way through the labyrinth of obstacles she and Olga had overcome in their fight to cover up their privileged past—a past that could have meant death to the sisters. She gripped the windowsill and leaned her forehead against the glass. The cold numbed her brain.

Sometime later, she sank back into the armchair, and twisted her now sodden handkerchief around and around in her fingers. How could she find the words that would break Mitch's heart? *If Mitch finds out I lied, he will never forgive me for denying him the chance to help his father, get him out of whatever hellhole he is in now. Whatever I do, how can I live with myself and the knowledge of what I did?*

"Seryozha?" she whispered. *"Pomogí mne!"* No answer came.

12
Montréal
February 1992

At the top of the steps, Mitch looked for a name, something familiar, anything that would tell him this was the right house. He took a deep breath and pressed the doorbell. He waited.

Footsteps approached from inside. Mitch drew back. "It's bound to be for you, Mathieu!" a female voice called. *Mathieu? Could it be?* The door opened. Mitch gaped at the woman before him. Her hair was grey, not the blonde he remembered. But it was her. The facial features, the green eyes.

"Vous cherchez Mathieu?" she asked.

Mitch struggled to find his voice. "Simone?"

She nodded. A puzzled frown creased her face.

"Mitch. *Je suis Mitch* … Mitch Galichin."

Her right hand went to her mouth.

"My mother. Sophia Weitz. You were friends before …"

"Sophia's boy?" she gasped.

Mitch's face relaxed into a smile.

"Mon Dieu!" She touched his arm, tentatively. Her other hand flew to the side of her head. "I don't believe it! After all these years …" She stepped out onto the front porch. "Sophia? Your mother," she scanned the street, "she's here?"

He shook his head. "Maman died."

She looked at him uncomprehendingly. "No. No. She can't have. Not Sophia." Tears pooled in her eyes. "When … what …?"

"Two years ago." Mitch gulped down a lump in his throat. "There wasn't anything they could do. She had cancer."

“I’m so sorry.” Simone guided him into the hallway gently, as if fearing he would disappear under a firmer touch. “Sophia’s son,” she exhaled, and closed the door behind them.

“Luc! Mathieu! Come see who it is. You’ll never believe who’s here.”

Mitch breathed in a slightly musty smell, overlaid by furniture polish applied by generations of inhabitants. It stirred in him a faint memory … long ago.

An hour or so later, Mitch leaned back in his chair at the big dining table. Over cups of tea, he had related some of the story of their lives in Leningrad.

“I wrote to your mother several times but, when she didn’t reply, I gave up.” Simone sighed.

“She wanted to write, but contact with anyone outside the Soviet Union … well, it’s frowned upon. Punished.” He saw again his mother’s face, twisted in anguish, as she tore a letter into small pieces. “She had to do it for our sakes, mine and Papa’s.”

“How could you bear to live somewhere like that, where you can’t even write to a friend?” It was Mathieu who spoke. Mitch couldn’t get over the fact that this well-built, bearded man was the child he had known. He and Mitch had a lot in common, though. Both were lawyers, both divorced.

“Maman, she never liked it there. She was forced to give up her religion, everything she loved about her old life.”

“Not everything, Mitch,” Simone murmured. “Your mother and father. Theirs was a real love match. She would have done anything to be with him.”

Mitch swallowed hard. “She did.”

“It was difficult for her here too, shunned by her family and friends. Bad enough for anyone, but for your mother, with her Jewish upbringing … family, traditions, they were her life. Without them she was like a lost soul, searching for something she could never have.”

In the silence that followed Simone’s words, an image came into Mitch’s mind. His mother’s face, the flicker of candlelight. She was singing softly, words he didn’t understand. He remembered now how when she sang, she shuffled her feet. As he got older, he began to understand that this was the time, the time she went back to her past, the only way she could connect with the people and traditions she loved. She was in another place, another time, her face reflecting the beauty of what she saw.

“When you were a few weeks old, she stood outside their house … your grandparents … when she knew they would be walking to the synagogue.”

Simone took a gulp of tea. "She thought that if they saw you, they would at least want to get to know you."

"What happened?"

"She hid behind a tree. It was bad enough them shunning her, but she couldn't bear to have them turn away from you." Simone gripped the edge of the table with her fingers. "I didn't tell her I had already been to see them, pleaded with them." She shook her head. "It was no use. The old man. He was stubborn!"

"She went there again. Just before we went to Russia." Mitch paused, his mind going back to that day. "She left me in the car, but I followed her up the driveway, hiding behind trees, pretending I was stalking an Indian."

"Sounds about right for a four-year-old boy," Luc said.

"A big man. He came out onto the doorstep. I couldn't understand what he said, but he was really angry, shouting at her, shaking her."

"That was him!" Simone muttered.

Mitch remembered how steep the steps had seemed as he ran to his mother's aid. Before he got to the top, he fell and cut his knee. Maman had hauled him to his feet as the door of the house slammed. "Later, she told me he was my grandfather. She'd led me to believe they were both dead. In heaven, she'd said."

"That was the kindest thing to tell you, Mitch. How would a young child cope with rejection? It could have screwed you up for life," Simone said.

More screwed up than I am now? Mitch asked himself.

"Your grandmother. She came here to see me after your grandfather died. I gave her your mother's address."

"She wrote to Maman. Maman wanted to bring me here to Canada … just for a visit … but the authorities wouldn't let her. At least, they would have let us go, but Maman wouldn't have been allowed back into the Soviet Union." He remembered the defeated look on her face when she came back on the last of many days standing in line at the Office of Visas and Registration.

"Barbaric!" Simone pushed her chair back and picked up the teapot. "I'll make another pot."

"It would have been too late anyway. Maman found out Grandmére died before her letter arrived."

"Years ago, when she lived here, your mother was to come on a visit I was arranging to Russia. A delegation from a charity," Luc began. "Simone and I, we thought it was the only way she would be happy if she could see him again."

"When was that?"

"You were about two, I think. You were going to stay here with Simone and the rest of the gang."

"Did she go?"

"No. None of us went. The authorities there, they wouldn't sanction our visit."

Mitch thought then of the numerous disappointments peppering his mother's life. *If only I'd been a better son.* He took the cup of tea Simone offered him. He looked around, remembering he and his mother sitting at this table, the fun during mealtimes, raucous guessing games, which he was sometimes allowed to win.

"Your father?" Luc cut into his thoughts. "Is he still there?"

"Papa? I think so, but I haven't heard from him since I left. I can't get any answers, not that make any sense. One of his friends, she wrote and told me he had injured his hand, was unable to write."

"Couldn't someone write his words down?"

"That's what I thought." Mitch paused before going on. "He … he wasn't doing too well the last time I saw him. That was six months ago." His voice trailed off as he thought of the slump in his father's shoulders as he climbed the steps in the Cathedral in Leningrad. "He's lost without her."

Luc drained his cup. "I think we could all do with something stronger." He got to his feet, opened the hutch and took out four glasses and a bottle. "Are things any better over there now?" He held the bottle up to the light then began to pour.

"For ordinary people … no." Mitch took the glass from Luc. "Yeltsin says he's going to privatise companies, shops. But, it will only be a few who benefit. Those who know the right people, or have enough muscle to bully and coerce others. There's so much corruption it's …"

"Here too!" Mathieu interjected.

"Not on the same scale as there," Mitch replied. "It's a way of life for most people. They have to find a way around the system, otherwise they can't exist, can't feed their families." Mitch took a gulp of his drink. "Prices have risen by something like four hundred percent in the last few weeks. God knows how people are coping." *If only I could be there to help Papa.* Every time he sat down to eat a meal, he worried that his father might not have enough to eat. Anja too. Money wouldn't go far now. "I hated the Party, but now," he took a deep breath, "people will be floundering. They're not used to thinking for themselves."

"Your daughter … Anja, you said?" Simone asked. "She's with her mother in Russia?"

"She is, but I want to bring her here."

"Can you do that?"

"It's complicated." Mitch grimaced.

Simone leaned towards Mitch. "Her mother? She would let her come?"

"That's part of the problem, but," Mitch paused, wondering how much to tell them, "I need to get a copy of my birth certificate, Maman's too. Then—"

"That should be easy enough," Luc interjected.

"Thing is, I entered Canada with a passport in someone else's name."

"Why would you do that when you're a Canadian citizen? You were born here, for heaven's sake."

"It happens a lot," Luc patted Simone's hand. "I see it all the time. For various reasons, immigrants, refugees, sometimes it's better to leave their previous identity behind for a while."

"But surely?" Simone looked quizzically at Mitch.

"It's a long, complicated story," was all Mitch said.

In the silence, Luc replenished their glasses.

Mitch twirled his glass around and around on the table before taking a gulp. "What I really need is to find Maman's brother."

"Yaakov?" Simone grimaced. "You won't get much out of him. He didn't do anything to help your mother. Wouldn't even acknowledge her."

"All I need is for him to help me get the birth certificates, then I can regularise my status here, bring Anja."

"He's a lawyer, but I don't think he's practising now," Luc began. "There was a fire. His wife and sons perished. I think there's just him and a daughter."

"Do you know where he lives? I've tried calling all the Weitz's in the telephone book."

"The last I heard he was more or less a recluse."

"Is there anyone who might know where I can find him?"

"I'll ask around. The legal community here is pretty tightly knit. Someone will know where he is, what he's doing."

"I'd really appreciate it." Mitch breathed somewhat more easily now.

"The legal system over there?" Luc asked. "When I was there years ago there was a lot of corruption."

Before Mitch could comment, a door slammed. “*Quelqu’un à la maison?*” a female voice called from the hallway.

Luc pushed his chair back. “That’ll be Sophia.”

Mitch jerked upright. “Sophia?”

Simone gasped. “*Mon Dieu!* We should have told you. Sophia. Our youngest. We named her after your mother. After four boys, we were blessed with a girl.”

“She was a late addition! Their last fling!”

“Take no notice of him!” Simone brushed off her son’s comments. “Before she even arrived, I was determined she would be called Sophia.”

“Bit of luck it wasn’t another boy.” Luc beamed at them from where he now stood in the doorway. “Imagine what his life would have been like in the schoolyard with a name like that!”

Mitch smiled.

“She’s so much like your mother, Mitch. Not a bit like any of us. Just the sweetest, gentlest young woman.” Simone’s eyes shone. “I can’t tell you what a relief it was that she didn’t turn into a tomboy. The boys did their best, but she wasn’t having any of it.”

Mitch got to his feet, steeling himself to meet the young woman who bore his mother’s name.

13
Western Siberia
March 1992

Sergei lay on the wooden cot and stared at the roof timbers. He listened for the howling of the wind as it pitched and turned through the *taiga* and whistled through the spaces between the huts. An eerie quiet had descended. In the deep, bitter cold of this harsh land, even the wind died. He shivered, thinking of the hours ahead. Hours cutting logs in the forest, when each breath felt like steel in his lungs.

Moonlight flickered over the mosaic of rags and scraps of paper stuffed in the cracks and knots in the timber walls. He raised his head from the pillow, pulled his woollen hat further down over his ears and forehead, and listened to the gentle snores coming from the cots either side of the iron stove. The two men who slept there were lucky, their beds warmed by heat from the fire. But he and Pavel were luckier than most. They each had an extra blanket. Five days ago, they watched silently as two guards carried out the corpse of the man who had occupied a cot on the far side of the shack. They never knew his name; he had not spoken to anyone. The blankets fell to one side as they dragged the stiff form out of the cot. Pavel held the door open while the guards—one holding the arms and one the legs—struggled outside with their burden. Sergei and Pavel peered through one of the small windows as the ungainly procession wove its way across the yard and disappeared inside the medical hut. Then, while Sergei kept watch, Pavel quickly stuffed the blankets out of sight high in the angle where the roof timbers met the wall above his own cot. Only he could reach them there. Each night since then, they hurried back to the hut after the meagre meal which passed for supper. Pavel would retrieve the blankets from their hiding place, warm them on top of the stove, and secrete one in each of their cots. They hoped the dead man's cot remained empty; they needed the warmth of the blankets.

"Seryozha?" Pavel's voice came to him softly through the silence. *"Ty ne spish', Seryozha?"*

"It's too cold to sleep." Sergei reached out a gloved hand and made sure his overcoat was still on top of the blankets. His legs twitched as he tried to ignore the burning and itching of the chilblains which had spread over his feet.

His thoughts drifted back to the day he was hauled from the courtroom, dragged into the courtyard, and thrown into a van where four other prisoners were already sitting on metal benches. At Moskovsky Station, armed guards escorted them through corridors, strangely empty of people. Soviet music blared out over the loudspeaker system as they walked along the platform to the rear compartment of the train. At first, he scanned the faces at the windows of the carriages, hoping to see someone he knew. Someone who would know he had been taken. Then he looked down at his soiled clothing and averted his eyes from curious stares. A few minutes after they climbed on board, the train pulled out of the station. The dimly lit compartment was a haphazard mix of thinly upholstered seats and wooden crates. The guards spread themselves out on the seats; the prisoners sat in a slumped line, linked together by handcuffs, on long wooden crates along one side of the carriage. Through the grime-streaked window opposite, Sergei watched the city slip past. Then they were in open marshlands. The train slowed and a yellow and white painted station house slid into view, triggering a memory of when he travelled these tracks with Sophia and Mitch. Sophia had kept young Mitch occupied by telling fantastic tales of the people who lived in the station house. As Sergei sat on the crate on his journey to he knew not where, his beloved Sophia came to him: she was dressed in a yellow-sprigged summer dress, her beautiful face framed with locks of brown wavy hair. Sergei wiped her image from his mind, unwilling to risk his wife being tainted by the squalor his life had become.

The train rattled on for what seemed an eternity. All the while, he looked for a way to escape—anything would be better than what he now suspected awaited him. Siberia. The name sent a shiver through his body. He and the other prisoners were handcuffed most of the time. A younger man, when released from the handcuffs, might have squeezed through the window in the toilet compartment, but the guards always kept the door open. Maybe they got some sort of perverted pleasure watching prisoners urinate or squat on the filthy toilet.

At station stops, the platform their end of the train was always deserted. No one came to try to sell them anything—people knew who occupied the rear carriage. While the prisoners made do with lukewarm slops that came from a kitchen somewhere further up the train, the guards swilled vodka and ate small oranges. The smell of the oranges filled Sergei's senses until he felt he would kill for just one segment. At dusk that first day, three young women ventured into the carriage. Sergei watched the guards' hands wandering over the curves of the women's breasts, buttocks. Later, noises came from the darkness.

As kilometre after kilometre of track spread out behind the train, he had squirmed on the crate in an effort to minimise the chafing of the handcuffs on his wrists, as the men either side of him shifted position. He hoped Vera had kept her promise. *Better Mitch thinks I'm dead than come back here and risk his life. And Anja?* Some days, he imagined he could hear her excited voice telling him about her friend Polya's forthcoming birthday party as she skipped along by his side on that last day, the day he took her back to Natasha. He hugged the hope that she was safe.

Now, he huddled further down in his cot. Each day outside, biting cold scalded exposed flesh, bringing fear of frostbite; faces disfigured, a finger lost, a toe, a hand, a foot, an ear. It happened—so far to others, not to Sergei or Pavel. When they could no longer feel their feet or hands and the only sound in the forest was the grinding of heavy metal saws, they longed for the heat of summer. But Pavel warned him: "When summer comes and swarms of black flies feast on your face, neck, arms, you'll yearn for cold days."

He learnt from Pavel and other prisoners that the camp was near Perm and was part of the old Gulag system—the system the government said was no longer used after Stalin's death.

Who but a fool would believe the propaganda? Some of Sergei's clients must have ended up in places like this. He felt ashamed he had never given more than a passing thought to the hapless souls transported to the camps, many of whom were destined to die from overwork, malnutrition, sickness. Was he to become one of the nameless statistics whose deaths are covered up? Numbers without faces. No families or friends to mourn.

Within days of his arrival at the camp, his every waking hour was focused on trying to avoid the group of men led by the man they called Gosha. Sergei never knew, and didn't want to know, Gosha's other name. What he learnt quickly, although not quickly enough, was that the camp was split into several main elements. Among them were prisoners, like himself and Pavel, who were detained for political reasons or for no reason at all. There were the North

Koreans, easily identified by their striped shirts and blue pants, whose labour was used by the government of their country to pay off its debt to Russia. The group more feared than any other—the *blatniyeh*—were the criminal element who obeyed the informal code of criminals, and of which Gosha was a leading member. On his first day working in the *taiga*, Sergei made the mistake of refusing to saw logs for Gosha. Two guards sat on a pile of timber and smoked cigarettes while Gosha's men punched Sergei and kicked his legs from under him. He lay in the snow and watched as Gosha walked over to one of the guards and took the lighted cigarette from the guard's hand. After two or three puffs on the cigarette, Gosha leaned down and held it over Sergei's face. Sergei's eyes zeroed in on the glowing red tip. He felt the pain as it seared first one cheek then the other. "I heard that in Tsarist times, outcasts like you had their tongues cut out!" Gosha's laughter echoed through the forest.

*"Dostatochno!"*A big man towered over Sergei. *"Pozvol'te mne pomoch' vam."* Pavel murmured as he reached down, grabbed Sergei's arms and hauled him to his feet.

From that day, the warmth of their friendship sustained Sergei. And their friendship with Jakob, the quiet Jew, who made up stories to entertain them while they worked. In the times when Jakob's quietness turned to melancholy, he was silent, writing stories in his head. Later, he would tell his tales of love and loyalty that nothing could destroy. Like the tale of the man whose wife sang to him and cradled him in her arms as he lay dying in the smouldering ruins of his shop, torched during the time of unrest before the Bolshevik Revolution when Jews were unfairly blamed for the country's woes. Jakob's lyrical voice told of the woman's undying love for the man whose child she was carrying. "It's just a story," he muttered when Pavel asked if it was true. The tears in his eyes said otherwise. For Sergei, the story brought back memories of his own father's death at that same time in Russia's violent history. His mother's voice had always held a softness when she spoke of the young husband she lost … the father Sergei never knew. Some days in the forest he thought he heard her voice floating down on a shaft of light.

For days, a rumour circulated that the new president, Boris Yeltsin, had announced the release of Russia's 'last ten' political prisoners. From a camp near Perm, it was said. As the men lined up behind the big wooden gates in the mornings before work began, a snigger trickled along the lines. *"Desyat'?"* they laughed, each looking around at the rows of men spread out across the yard.

Early yesterday, Sergei joined in mumbles of disbelief at a new arrival's tale. The Soviet Union is no longer. *That cannot be. He lies. "Nevoz, nevoz,"* was the verdict.

What does it matter? I have Pavel and Jakob. They are still here, Sergei told himself now as he lay watching the moonlight. He rubbed one foot over the other. He rubbed until the chilblains hurt.

14
Montréal
April 1992

Mitch opened the door and stepped inside the hallway. He looked around for an elevator then began to climb the staircase. Luc had told him that Uncle Yaakov lived on the third floor of the four-story building, and was almost a recluse since his wife and two sons died in a fire in the family home some years ago. His only remaining child, a daughter, did what she could for her father, but found him difficult to deal with and now had an apartment of her own in another part of the city.

If Yaakov's own daughter finds him difficult, what chance do I stand? Mitch asked himself as he paused on the first landing. *What sort of man wouldn't help his own sister when she needed him?* Simone had tried to explain how things were when his mother left home: "Her father was stubborn, but it wasn't only the shame or the religious thing. It was because your father is Russian," she began. "You have to understand. It was the height of the Cold War, people were paranoid about spies and traitors. Not that anyone could have described your poor mother as a traitor …"

"Nor my father as a spy!" Mitch interjected.

"She was a young woman, very much in love," Simone had sighed. "Back then, particularly in the strict Hasidic sect, that didn't matter. She was promised to someone else. Children, even adults," she fixed Mathieu with a meaningful look, "were expected to obey their parents."

On this Sunday morning, Mitch had called in to see Simone's family on his way to his uncle's home. "At least he's agreed to see you," she had smiled encouragingly, brushing a speck off his overcoat.

Now, on the landing of the third floor, Mitch paused and took a last drag on his cigarette. He looked back down the staircase. *Maybe it's best to let things be, leave them alone. So many years have passed, so what does it matter?* As he ground the cigarette butt under his shoe, a voice in his head urged, *You owe it to them. Someone has to explain their side of the story, show what a good woman Maman was, tell them they misjudged Papa.* He reached down, picked up the cigarette butt and tossed it into a bin in the corner. *And you need his help with the birth certificates.* He took a deep breath and headed along the corridor.

Outside his uncle's apartment, Mitch stared at the name on the door: Yaakov Yosef Weitz. The metal door knocker felt cold in his hand. The thump it made pierced the silence and reverberated along the corridor. He heard a bolt being drawn back, and willed his hands to stop trembling. Then he was face-to-face with an older version of himself; the likeness was uncanny.

Uncle Yaakov looked Mitch up and down. "You can't be anyone but a member of the Weitz family," he said in French. There was sadness in his eyes. "Come in."

In the hallway, Yaakov took Mitch's overcoat and hung it in the closet. Music played; a liturgical dirge. The room they stepped into was clothed in sunlight. The furniture was shabby; some of it looked as if it had come from a charity shop, or maybe hand-me-downs from friends after the fire. The room was tidy, not the muddled mess in which Mitch assumed most people of a reclusive nature dwelt. "Let me turn this off." Uncle Yaakov raised the arm of the old-fashioned record player. "The old music. It is comforting." The trace of a smile lifted the corners of his mouth as he looked at Mitch. "Well, young man. Just looking at you confirms you are who you say you are."

Mitch struggled to find his voice. It was like looking into the future and seeing himself in twenty or thirty years' time. He couldn't imagine wearing the black pants, waistcoat and collarless white shirt, nor having long *payot* dangling either side of his face—he remembered his mother explaining that most Hasidim men follow a Biblical commandment not to shave the sides of their face. But the thick unruly curly hair (now a mixture of faded brown and grey), facial features, deep brown eyes, the tilt of his head. It was all there. Mitch wondered now whether when his mother looked at him, she had been reminded of her brother. He had often caught her staring at him, a sad look on her face. Perhaps that was it.

"So, Sophia's son." Yaakov indicated one of the armchairs.

"Do you mind?" Mitch asked, slipping one arm out of his jacket. "It's hot in here."

"Mwḫl myr. I'm always cold. Blood, it's not circulating well. *Nyt zynt ...*"

"Climbing the stairs made me overheat." Mitch laughed nervously, draped his jacket over the back of the armchair and sat down.

Yaakov lowered himself into the armchair the other side of the small fireplace, and put his hands out, warming them in front of the glowing bars of the electric heater. "I often wondered about you. A friend told me, soon after you were born, Sophia had a boy." Yaakov spoke in a soft, reverent tone, mostly in French but with the occasional words Mitch assumed to be Yiddish.

"*Dyyn b'áb* ... Your grandmother. She was heartbroken she never got to see Sophia again or to meet you. *T'at'* he forbade us to contact her."

"Surely you could ..." Mitch swallowed the rest of his words.

"To my shame, I crossed to the other side of the street one day when I saw her coming towards me. She was pushing a stroller." Yaakov stared at the fireplace.

Mitch winced, imagining the pain his mother must have felt that day. He looked at the man sitting opposite him. *What sort of person could do that? His own sister.*

"I thought about contacting her after *T'at'* was gone."

"Why didn't you?" Mitch's tone was brusque.

"I was embarrassed. I hadn't been there for her when she needed me." The flickering glow of the fake flames danced across Yakov's cheeks. "I failed her, and now it's too late," he sighed.

Mitch's voice cut into the silence that followed Yaakov's words: "Maman, she tried ... tried to get permission for the two of us to visit Montréal when she heard he had died." His thoughts went back to the taunts of his friends at school, calling him a traitor when it was known his mother was seeking permission to go to Canada. "It was no good. They said if she left she wouldn't be allowed to go back to Russia. Even seeking permission made it difficult for all of us."

"Being Jewish couldn't have helped in a place like that."

"She could never admit it ... to being a Jew. I know it saddened her, denying her faith."

He heard again his mother muttering the words of the *Amidah,* the blessings recited by Hasidims at the start of each day. She had sworn him to secrecy. At age ten, swept along on the Soviet patriotic fervour fed into his childish brain, and fiercely proud of being in the first batch of his Young Pioneer group to take the Solemn Promise, he came close to blurting it out. He wanted to be like his friends who were praised for telling tales about their parents, grandparents, friends, neighbours. But before the words formed in his mouth, something blocked them.

"Forgive me, I should have offered you something to drink. I usually only imbibe on the Sabbath or holidays, but today … I think I can make an exception. Not every day my nephew comes to visit." The old man's face relaxed into a smile. *"Wwyyan? Rwyt?"* Mitch nodded, hoping it was what he thought it was.

"And then you must tell me about your life," Yaakov called over his shoulder as he shuffled into the kitchen.

Mitch got to his feet and looked around the room. *No family photographs? Were they all destroyed in the fire?* It was one of Mitch's deepest regrets that he was forced to leave his personal possessions in Leningrad. He remembered the feeling of desolation as he handed over his wallet containing photographs, Anja's scribblings … he had hidden away a tiny picture of her, but the people who helped him escape found it, took it from him along with every trace of the person he used to be. The only thing he had left from his previous life was his mother's *Samizdat* copy of the poems of Anna Akhmatova.

He stared out of the window. Sunlight flickered through the trees in the park on the other side of the street. A couple strolled in the morning sunlight, arms around each other. A man chased a young toddler, reached out and hoisted the child into the air, turning around and around. Mitch remembered doing the same with Anja on the banks of the Neva. The story … she loved him to tell her the story of the people stranded on an ice flow, the helicopter that rescued them. He could still see her face as she looked up at him, arms aloft, waiting for him to lift her into the air and whirl her around and around. Now, he gripped the back of a chair trying to dispel the sound of her laughter as they whirled faster and faster.

Several glasses of wine later, he finished relating the story of their lives in Leningrad, or as much as he could bring himself to put into words.

Yaakov leaned forward in his chair. "*Dyyn mwt'r …* I remember the day they brought her home from the hospital. I was three years old and used to being the only one. *'yk h't nyt wwy 'yr.* Wanted them to take the baby back. But it wasn't long before she had us all under her spell." The expression on his face softened. "You know, Mitch, when I came home from my first day at school, she had put some of her favourite candies in my slippers. The sweetest soul …" His voice trailed off.

"She always was. Always putting everyone else first." They sat in silence, lost in memories.

"They were happy? Sophia and your father?"

"Very. Looking back on it now, I realise they were so much happier than most couples. Happier than anyone I've ever met."

"That is good. *T'aq' gwt.*"

Mitch looked at his watch.

"Won't you stay and have lunch with me? Something light," Yaakov offered.

"I should be getting back. I have to work this evening."

"But you haven't told me how it is you came back to Montréal, to Canada. Your wife? She is with you?"

"Natasha and I … we're divorced."

"It is not good, but sometimes necessary." He clasped his hands together. "She is of the faith?"

"Jewish? No."

"Your daughter … Anja?"

"She is with her mother."

"In Russia? You left her?"

Mitch avoided meeting Yaakov's gaze. "It's complicated," he muttered.

"I'd like to hear about her." When Mitch hesitated, Yaakov added, "Not if it's too painful."

"She brought me nothing but joy," Mitch whispered, almost to himself. "Talking about her," he shook his head, "it's still difficult."

The furrows in Yaakov's brow deepened. "It's ten years now. *Ẕ'n y'r zynt myyn b'alybt prwy* … my Rachel, my sons, Yosef and Eli … ten years since they died. The grief is as raw as it was that day."

Mitch tried to imagine the horror of losing loved ones in a fire, the images with which Yaakov must now live, the feeling of helplessness. His mind replayed his own nightmares that started after he passed details of the trafficking network to the journalist in England. Plagued by fear of what might happen when the exposé was published and reports filtered through to the Soviet Union, he hoped fervently that the newspaper offices would burn down, taking the evidence with it. At night, his paranoia had taken a terrifying twist. Bright orange flames licked around the building and rose into the London sky, filling the air with choking smoke. A figure at one of the windows tossed the squirming body of a girl towards the ground. The girl's skirt billowed out like a parachute and for a moment was suspended in mid-air. Mitch rushed forward, arms open to receive her. As he touched her, she melted in the heat. When he awoke, his hands felt as though they were burnt.

Now, as he stared at the palms of his hands, an involuntary shudder ran through his body.

"Don't keep it inside too long, Mitch," Yaakov's voice penetrated his thoughts. "Or you'll end up *'a trwy'ryq 'alt m'nṭṣ* like me."

Mitch searched for words.

"I can't even bear to look at pictures of them. Their eyes. They reproach me, asking why I wasn't there when they needed me. I've hidden them away, the photographs."

"But you think of them?"

Blood seemed to have drained from Yaakov's face. "*Zyy'r n'm'n.* Rachel, Yosef, Eli ... the first words I utter every morning and last thing at night. I try to convince myself that doing so means they haven't gone."

"I know what you mean. I'm the same. An old man. Slava. I was responsible for his death ..." While he helped Uncle Yaakov put together a simple lunch, Mitch related the terrible story of how the caretaker of the building where Mitch, Natasha, and Anja, lived was blown to pieces by the car bomb meant for Mitch. He could still smell the stench of burnt flesh.

"It wasn't you. You weren't responsible for the old man's death."

"Neither were you. Not for what happened to your wife, your sons."

"Oy-yoy-yoy!" Yaakov shook his head. "What are we like?"

Before Mitch left, Yaakov opened a cupboard and brought out a canvas bag. "I want you to have this. It's a photograph album. Pictures of Sophia as a young woman, you as a baby, and some which I think were taken just before you went to Russia. *Dyyn mwt'r 'wyk.*" Mitch took the bag and clasped it to his chest.

"Sophia, she left it on the porch at my parents' home."

"I was with her. I think I was four." He remembered rushing up the steep steps to try to stop the man, he later learnt was his grandfather, shaking his mother.

"*Mwt'r.* She daren't let *T'at'* know she had it, so she kept it at a friend's home. After he died, she told me about it. She was going to show it to me, but," he shook his head, "it wasn't to be. After she died, her friend brought it here."

Mitch sat back in the chair and opened the album. Yaakov hovered by his elbow and pointed his finger at a photograph which was loose inside the front cover. “That one. *Mwt’r must have put it there.* It was taken in my grandparents’ garden … your great-grandparents.”

“Great-grandparents?” Mitch echoed his words. He had never thought about great-grandparents. He looked at the mostly black-clad figures. The only one wearing white was a young girl who was undoubtedly his mother.

“Sophia. She was twelve. It was after her *Bat Mitzvah*.”

“I thought only boys had that sort of ceremony.”

“Girls too. When they’re twelve. They become daughters of the commandment.”

Looking at the smiling face of his mother as a young girl, reinforced all she had given up.

“She was brave,” he whispered. “I can’t imagine what it must have been like leaving everyone she loved. Never seeing them again.” As the words left his mouth, he realised he knew exactly how it felt. History had repeated itself.

“It was painful for all of us. The days after she left, the house seemed shrouded in grey, as though even the walls were missing her.” Yaakov sat down in the other armchair, pulled out a handkerchief and wiped his eyes. “For weeks *Mwt’r* waited for her to come home. She used to stand at the front windows at the time Sophia usually arrived back from college.”

“Did no one challenge your father’s decision, get him to relent?”

“*Mwt’r* and I, we tried.” Yaakov shook his head. “He was stubborn. What he said went …”

Mitch closed the album and put it back in the canvas bag. “I’ll enjoy looking at it later,” he said as he got to his feet.

Yaakov rose from his chair and gripped both of Mitch’s arms. “Thank you. Thank you for coming to see me, sad old man that I am.”

“I’m glad I came,” Mitch said with genuine feeling as the old man kissed his cheeks.

“Thursday, you said.” Yaakov drew back. “I’ll be ready when you come by. It’s the least I can do to help my sister’s child.”

* * *

It was late afternoon when Mitch let himself into Simone’s house using the key she had given him. Being with the Belleau family was the closest he had come to a real home for a long time. Mathieu was now sharing an apartment with his girlfriend, and Simone wanted Mitch to move into the family home. "There's all this space. The three of us, we're rattling around. Why don't you, Mitch?" Simone's offer was tempting, but not yet.

"We were wondering where you'd got to." Simone emerged from the kitchen now, wiped her hands on her apron and kissed Mitch on both cheeks. "Began to think he'd locked you in there," she laughed. "If you're hungry, we saved you some lunch."

"Uncle Yaakov. He made lunch for us."

"What did he have to say for himself? Did he explain why he didn't help his only sister when she needed him?"

"I didn't ask. He seems distraught still … his wife and sons."

"He needs to think of others, not just himself. Does he ever think of the true meaning of religion?" Simone was off on a familiar track. "Whatever faith you subscribe to, surely concern for your fellow human beings is the basis of everything?"

"It didn't seem right to ask him today. Not when I'm just getting to know him."

Simone clucked her tongue. "You're too kind. Like your poor mother. Always seeing the best in people."

Mitch pulled out a chair and leaned the bag containing the photograph album against a leg of the table.

"I've just boiled the kettle, and there's a batch of almond cakes still warm from the oven," Simone tempted.

Mitch smiled at her. He enjoyed the friendly rapport with Simone and her family. He was becoming fond—too fond—of their daughter, Sophia, which was part of the reason he resisted moving in. He was too old for her, and he didn't need distractions. All his effort must go into getting Anja back.

"He said he'd help me get copies of the birth certificates. Mine and Maman's. I've got a day off on Thursday, and he's going with me."

Simone set the teapot on the dining room table and pushed a plate of almond cakes towards him. "It'll be good for him to get out into the world again."

15
Montréal
April 1992

Pale shafts of light streaked the room as Mitch struggled awake. He blinked hard trying to focus on his watch. *"Govno!"* he exclaimed. *It's almost midday.* His mouth was parched and he reached for the glass of water on the floor by his bed. It was some minutes before he roused himself enough to sit up properly and longer still before he got out of bed and shuffled to the table, feet entangled in yesterday's clothes littering the floor. *You have to pull yourself together, get out of this twilight world,* he admonished as he broke free from a T-shirt twisted around both feet. He looked around, shook his head. *How can you hope to make a home for Anja in this dump?*

He sat down, leaned his elbows on the table and cradled his head in his hands trying to ease the pain in his temples. He was sick of waking with a hangover every morning. Each evening, as he set out for his job at the bar, he resolved not to touch a drop. His good intentions lasted barely an hour. He told himself it wasn't good for business if he kept refusing when customers wanted to buy him a drink. That was his excuse.

Maybe if you hadn't drunk so much you might have been a better father to Anja, realised earlier what was going on with Natasha and that thug, he thought now as he got to his feet and picked up the empty brandy bottle from the counter. He flinched as the bottle hit the bottom of the kitchen bin.

He put the kettle on the stove and rummaged in the cupboard in which he kept his meagre stock of food. There were a couple of slices of bread. He took them out of the packet, examined them for mould, and dropped them into the toaster. He had used the last of the butter yesterday, but there was still a scrape of red jam.

Footsteps sounded on the entrance steps. He stood stock still. The mail slot opened and he breathed again as several flyers fluttered to the floor. He leafed through the coupon books and other so-called bargain offers he rarely bothered to use, and when he did it was only to be told at the check-out that the coupon had expired. It was then he saw it … the envelope bearing Kirill's distinctive script. Mitch tore it open, his fingers feeling for the letter inside. *Papa? Has Papa written?* His shoulders slumped. The letter was from Vera. *Maybe she has news of Papa, Anja,* he comforted himself and sank down on to his bed in the corner of the room. Her words jumped out at him:

My Dear,

This is the hardest letter I have ever had to write. But much as it pains me, write I must. Oh, how I wish things were different.

Mitch gasped. The palm of his right hand flew to his chest. *Anja! Something's happened to Anja!* He was scared to read what he knew Vera had written. *You have to know,* he told himself as he retrieved the letter from where it had fallen on the floor.

There was nothing we could do. It was your father's heart. The doctor said it just gave out.

It's Papa! Papa's dead! For a fleeting second, a shiver of relief ran through him. *It isn't Anja.* Then guilt. *How can you think like that?* he asked himself. "Papa?" he murmured into the silence. "You can't have gone." A vision flashed before his eyes. His father's care-worn face, tears rolling down his cheeks. He heard again the last words Papa said to him: *We'll have plenty of time later, when all this is over and we're together again. You, Anja and me.* Those words had kept Mitch going through the months since he watched his father walk away. The loneliness Mitch felt then was nothing to the emptiness now. There was to be no later. His father had gone. He gulped back the huge lump in his throat.

There was no warning. No one could have known. He seemed fine when I saw him the previous evening. It must have happened that night while he was asleep. Be comforted he knew nothing about it. The funeral. It was in a fenced off section in the Jewish cemetery. A special dispensation so that he could be close to your mother. I laid flowers on their graves. It was all I could do.

Mitch gulped back tears, unable to take in anymore. How long he sat there he didn't know. When he eventually roused himself and got to his feet, a pall of steam hung in the air.

There was a burning smell. The kettle was jumping around on the stove. Mitch grabbed it. *"Durák!"* he yelled, flung the kettle into the sink and ran cold water over his hand. "I can't do this," he sobbed as he staggered to the bed, cradling his right hand. "Papa? Why didn't I know … know you'd gone?" He lay down and stared at the ceiling, trying to block out the chill in his stomach, the throbbing of his hand. "You can't even boil a fucking kettle without fucking it up!" he cursed and turned his head to the wall.

* * *

It was early evening when Mitch took a final drag on his cigarette and ground it out with the sole of his shoe on the sidewalk in front of Simone and Luc's home. On the way here, he had called them to make sure they would be in. Then he called Micky, telling him he couldn't work this evening as he had hurt his hand. The palm and fingers now sported blisters. He was sure Simone would have some concoction with which to soothe and heal. He just wished the rest of his troubles could be solved as easily. He climbed the steps and, with his left hand, turned the key awkwardly in the lock and let himself in.

Simone came into the hallway to greet him. Seeing his handkerchief-wrapped hand, she helped him off with his coat and hung it up. "What happened?" she asked, ushering him into the kitchen, where Luc was seated at the table. "Did you hurt it at work?"

"No. It was this morning, at home. The kettle boiled dry on the stove. I picked it up." He shook his head. "I wasn't thinking straight."

"Too much of the grog?" Luc raised his eyebrows.

"That may have had something to do with it."

"You shouldn't be working in that bar. It's too easy to think drink is the way to forget everything … everything you've been through." Simone pulled a chair out for Mitch to sit on, then unwrapped his hand carefully. She looked at the blisters, and pronounced, "I don't think you've done any lasting damage."

"That's the only good news I've had today," Mitch said as he sat down.

"What's wrong? Micky fire you?"

"No such luck."

Simone pulled the First Aid box out of a cupboard, set it down on the table and extracted a tube of ointment. Mitch grimaced as she spread it on the blisters. "I'll put a bandage on. You don't want to risk getting an infection," she cautioned, pulling the wrapping off a bandage. "Is something wrong?" she asked again as she wound the bandage around his hand.

"Papa. Papa's dead." Mitch's words fell into the empty space in the kitchen.

"Dead?" came from Luc.

"Are you sure?" from Simone.

"I had a letter from Vera, his friend in St Petersburg."

Simone put a hand on his shoulder and squeezed. "Oh, Mitch. I'm so sorry. After everything you've been through."

Tears ran down his cheeks and splashed on his pants.

Simone cut the end of the bandage and tied it neatly around his hand. She pressed a handkerchief into Mitch's left hand.

"What happened?" Luc ventured.

Mitch wiped his eyes and cleared his throat. "His heart. She said it was his heart."

"Did he have a problem with his heart? Before?"

"If he did, he didn't tell me."

"When? When did he die?"

"Two months ago." He reached into his jacket pocket and placed Vera's letter on the table. "It took all that time for the letter to reach me. He's been dead for weeks and I didn't know."

Simone patted his arm. "Your father's friend? Did she say anything else?"

"Read it. There's nothing personal." Mitch pushed the letter towards Luc, who he knew could read Russian.

Translating, Luc read Vera's letter aloud, helped by Mitch when he stumbled over a word or phrase. "I'm so sorry, Mitch." Luc tucked the letter into the envelope. "That's an awful thing to happen, especially with you so far away. If there's anything ..."

"It's my fault," Mitch cut in. "The strain, the worry, I put them both through."

"That's what kids do, Mitch. You should hear some of the things ours did. Makes my hair stand on end to think of it!" Luc smoothed down what hair he had left on the top of his head.

"Bet they didn't get mixed up with the *vory v zakone,*" Mitch mumbled.

"Believe me, they got close!"

"I don't think I even took on the *vory* for the right reasons. Those girls, the ones who were trafficked, I felt sorry for them, was outraged by what was happening. But it was Yagudin. When I found out that *ublyudok* was running the network, I wanted him to suffer. Suffer like—"

"That's nonsense, Mitch," Simone cut in. "What about those girls you knew? Their parents, your friend's sister? That's why you got involved in the first place, wasn't it?" When Mitch didn't answer, she went on, "I'm sure your father was proud of what you did. Not many people would have had the guts."

"Look where it got me. My father's dead. Anja's God knows where!"

"You have to stop this." Simone's tone was harsh. "All this blaming yourself, feeling sorry for yourself." She took both Mitch's hands gently in hers. "Mitch, there's a young child out there, your daughter. You have to pull yourself together for her sake."

Mitch stared at the floor.

"Why don't you write to her? Tell her you love her and will come for her soon. There must be some way to get a letter to her without anyone else seeing it."

"What if the letter gets into the wrong hands," he looked up and met her gaze, "and they find Anja?"

"Listen to me! You're the only chance that little girl has for a decent life. What hope is there for her in Russia? You've said yourself that the poverty is terrible, prices have gone sky high. Far worse than when you left."

"Simone's right, Mitch. You can't condemn her to that sort of life."

"Is that what you want for her?" Simone mocked.

Mitch struggled in vain to find his voice.

"You have to have some sort of plan for her future and yours," Luc went on. "You've already made a start with the birth certificates and, when you've sorted out your citizenship, you need to establish your law qualifications in Canada and get a permanent job. Then you'll be in a position to make a proper home for her."

"You could make a start by coming to live here. We've asked you so many times, and we'd love to have you," Simone tempted. "You can cut down on expenses, study full-time, and before long you'll be some high-flying lawyer sorting out other people's problems."

"Never again, Simone. Anja's all I care about."

"Then get off your backside and do something about it. She deserves better than what you can offer her at the moment."

"I know you're right, but …"

"No buts, Mitch," Luc interjected.

"Now that's settled, I'll get you something to eat. I'll cut your food up like I used to for the kids!"

* * *

Two hours or so later, Mitch climbed into the bed he had slept in several times in Simone and Luc's home. It felt increasingly like his home. The only home he was likely to have for a while. As he pulled the bedclothes up, thoughts of his father flooded through him. His father, who had been such an influence in his life. The one who tried to guide him, protect him. He would never see him again. Never hear his voice. Mitch shifted uncomfortably as he went over the times he had made life bad for his parents. Even before he met Natasha, he caused problems with his loud criticism of the Soviet system. Then there was Natasha's pregnancy and their determination to be married, despite objections from both sets of parents. The money problems, the divorce, his drinking. And then his stupid attempt to stop the trafficking of those young girls. Had he really thought he could beat the *vory?* He must have been mad. His father had begged him not to get involved.

An image stuck in his mind—the day he and his mother arrived at the airport in Leningrad. He was four and, shy at first, had pulled away from the father who, until that day, was a photograph on his mother's nightstand. His father bent down, Mitch climbed on to his back and looped his arms around Sergei's neck, just as he had seen other boys do with their fathers. That felt so good. "Oh, Papa," he sobbed now. "Why wasn't I a better son? The son you and Maman deserved."

16
Western Siberia
April 1992

Sergei unbuttoned his coat and loosened his scarf. He was sweating. Yesterday, he needed two pairs of gloves and had to stamp his feet to bring his freezing toes back to life. Today, as the early-morning chill evaporated in the *taiga,* a warm wind blew through. Soon, there would be ticks burrowing into skin, causing fever and rashes—it was rumoured that men had been known to go mad from it, but Pavel said in the years he had been here, he had not seen anything like that. "It is a tale that Gosha and his gang spread around to frighten newcomers, make them scared to expose skin," the big man sneered. "They laugh when sweat runs down faces and heat causes comrades to sink to their knees from exhaustion, wrapped as they are in layers of clothes."

Sergei unwound his scarf from his neck and stuffed it in his coat pocket. He looked around. *Where is Gosha?* Sergei had watched him and two of his men slink off into the forest. *That must have been an hour ago.* But, who knew how time passed here? Sergei had stopped trying to keep track of days, weeks, let alone hours. Each day was punctuated by mealtimes, work, sleep. That was the sum of life. *Maybe that's what life is meant to be. Nothing more, nothing less.*

"What do you think they're doing in there?" Pavel whispered. Rumours had circulated that Gosha was a homosexual. Sergei didn't care what Gosha did with other men, as long as he kept away from Pavel, Jakob, and himself. The three of them were like a family, or the closest they could get to a family in this place. Their friendship was the only thing that kept Sergei from ending his life. *Without them, what is life?*

Pavel and Sergei took either end of a saw and began to grind through one of the felled trees. They paused briefly as laughter floated towards them. "Keep your head down," Pavel hissed. "They're coming back."

Sergei watched as the blade ground through the timber. There was something comforting about the rhythm of the saw as it hummed; the noise varied from tree to tree, or maybe it was their cutting action that caused the different sounds. Some time ago, his sleep was punctuated by nightmares. Nightmares in which the timber screamed and writhed as saws cut through it. It was a living thing, with feelings, hopes for the future. Just like his own future had been cut short, felling the tree stopped it existing as it was meant to exist. One night, trees towered above him, screaming out one word over and over: *"Palach! Palach! ..."* Their branches and roots wrapped around him. He had awoken, struggling desperately to free himself, get air into his lungs. The bedclothes were tangled in a knot around his body.

Now, as he worked, he whispered to the timber, placating it, saying it would go on living, albeit in a different form. "You will get out of here soon, go out into the world." He piled a cut log on top of the stack.

"Come, my friend," Pavel murmured sometime later. "Time to go."

Sergei looked around. "Where is Jakob?"

Pavel raised himself to his full height and scanned the forest above the heads of the assembled work gang waiting for the order to march back to the camp, although march was a grand word for their shambling gait. "I don't see him. Maybe he went back to the camp earlier." A guard walked along the line of men, counting. He came back, counting again. Then another guard walked along the line. He shook his head when he got back to the front. "One short," he shouted. "Anyone know who is missing?"

Sergei and Pavel kept quiet. It wouldn't do to throw suspicion on their friend. They couldn't keep worried frowns from their faces, though. *Maybe he made a break for it.* Sergei's thoughts drifted back to a story Jakob told them a few days ago. He had gone over his friend's words many times in his head since then: *One day, a warm wind blew through the shtetl. It got stronger and stronger, whistling around the wooden homes, picking people up and whipping them around like leaves. Savtas and Sabas rushed to grab their grandchildren, hanging on to them as they struggled against the fierce wind ...* Jakob's voice had trailed off and, despite pleas for him to finish the story, he sat in silence, staring into the forest. Later, as Sergei and Pavel took his arms and began to lead him back to his hut, he whispered, "The next morning, there was nothing left of the *shtetl.* The people ... those good people ... they were suspended from the trees."

“I don’t see the *Jid*!” Gosha’s vile tones jerked Sergei from his reverie. Those words were followed by laughter from Gosha’s acolytes.

“He won’t get far,” one of the guards promised. “Not when we let the dogs out!” Sergei and Pavel stepped to one side as the men began to shuffle forward along the path to the camp. One of the guards slapped his nightstick in his hand. “Get a move on!” he yelled and struck Pavel’s arm with the stick. The big man didn’t flinch.

“We’ll look for him. Bring him back,” Pavel said. “He had a problem with his gut.”

The guard sneered. “You expect me to believe that?”

“Give us ten minutes. That’s all we need. You have a cigarette while we look, the three of us.” Pavel took two steps into the forest. “If we find him, you will be a hero.” The guard looked towards the receding column of men.

Pavel turned and forced an encouraging grin on to his face. “Better than losing a prisoner.”

“Desyat’ minut.” He lit a cigarette, then bellowed to the guard at the rear of the line that he was going to carry out a quick search of the area. “Don’t let the dogs out before I’m back!”

Light was fading as the three tramped through the *taiga.* The ten minutes was almost up when they heard a noise. “Jakob? Is that you, Jakob?”

The three stopped in their tracks. A wolverine was tearing at the carcass of a lynx. Its small eyes fixed on them for a moment, then turned back to concentrate on pulling a large lump of flesh from the kill.

The guard aimed his gun as they backed away, eyes focused on the animal. Despite its relatively small size, the wolverine is the most feared of animals in the *taiga.* Sergei held his saw in front of his body; his other hand gripped his own throat, the area the wolverine was most likely to attack to bring down its prey.

It wasn’t until they were some distance from the animal that they relaxed. Sergei wiped sweat from his brow. It was then he saw them. Boots. Jakob’s boots swung in the breeze. Sergei steeled himself to look up. He gasped. The noose around Jakob’s neck. His friend’s words came back to him: *The people ... those good people ... they were suspended from the trees.*

17
Montréal
May 1992

The stairs creaked as Mitch made his way downstairs. He looked around. *Where is everyone?* The house was strangely quiet; quieter than he had known it since moving in three weeks ago. At this time on Saturday mornings, Simone was usually clattering around in the kitchen, brewing coffee, making pancakes, frying eggs, while Luc caught up with the weekend newspapers. *They must all have had a late night,* Mitch mused, remembering that yesterday they had all been to the game between the Montréal Canadiens and the Hartford Whalers—everyone, that is, except Mitch. He could never work up enthusiasm for ice hockey, something he had come to regret since the death of his father whenever his thoughts drifted back to the times Papa had tried to interest him in the game. Seeing Luc and his sons dissecting each game, arguing over whether a goal should have been disallowed, had reinforced in Mitch how much his father must have longed to have similar conversations with him. Conversations that would never now take place.

He heaped ground coffee into the filter, filled the machine with water, pressed the switch, then stepped out into the garden. After living in apartments all his life, he really appreciated this oasis where he could breathe in the early-morning air. Already the gentle breeze carried a hint of summer to come. Since moving in with the Belleau family, his life had taken on a more positive tone. Being part of a family again had changed his outlook. He still felt indescribably sad when he thought of his father dying alone, his daughter living in that freezing, inhospitable place—he shivered now at the thought.

Simone seemed to sense his bleak moments; her tales of his early childhood and her friendship with his mother usually lifted him out of sorrowful moods. At least now he had a link to his past, and happy memories were beginning to replace dark ones. Living in this chaotic household, with people drifting in and out, it was impossible to wallow in misery for long.

As he wandered along the garden path, he realised how much better he felt since he had cut down on his drinking. He was no longer working at the bar, and most days helped Simone's friend Mireille in her patisserie. It was only casual work, filling in when staff took time off, serving coffee, clearing tables, washing dishes, but it was more sociable hours than in the bar.

The money wasn't bad, although he suspected Simone had persuaded Mireille to pay him more than the minimum wage. His outgoings were small, as he no longer had rent to pay, so he was able to put a bit aside for the time when he could make a home for Anja.

He stopped, lit a cigarette and gazed around the garden. His thoughts returned to another morning. Was it only eight months ago he stood in that other garden, the garden of the house in Lyuban to which he fled fearing for his life when his exposé of the gang running the trafficking network appeared in the British newspaper? That same evening, he had listened with a growing sense of dread to the story coming over the airwaves—a story bearing all the horror of former Stalinist times. President Gorbachev was held under house arrest at his *dacha* in the Crimea by members of his own staff, who demanded he declare a state of emergency and authorise reform measures. Russia's flirtation with democracy was over.

As Mitch had feared, the next day a publication ban was put in place, ending his hopes that news of the atrocities committed by Yagudin and his henchmen would be made public in the Soviet Union. By the time the ban was lifted, the country would be in chaos; no one would be interested in what would be old news. Later, after discovering Natasha had whisked Anja away from her friend Katya's grandparents' house, he had raced back to the city, forced his way into Natasha's apartment, searching for his daughter. It was then the explosion rocked the building. His breath caught in his throat now as he pictured the flaming wreck of his car on the street outside, the cloying smell of burning flesh.

Don't think of it, he told himself, and sat down on the rusty iron bench at the end of the garden. He remembered his mother and Simone sitting here all those years ago, or was his memory deceiving him? There used to be a sandpit by the fence—he and Mathieu played there while Maman and Simone drank tea and chatted? He wondered now whether Maman had ever thought back to those days or whether she blotted out her previous life in an effort to be accepted in the more rigid environment in the Soviet Union. He realised now that in Leningrad she had very few friends and almost never laughed. Not the way she had with Simone.

Maybe one day I'll sit here with Annushka, he thought, stubbed out his cigarette in the ashtray on the garden table and made his way back into the house. Inside, he poured coffee and sat at the kitchen table, wondering when he would hear from his daughter. Before he left his basement apartment, he had written to Vera in St Petersburg giving his new address and asking her to try to get his enclosed letter to Anja without Natasha or anyone else seeing it. He was impatient to hear from her, to know Anja was okay and knew he loved her. Maybe he should risk a telephone call to Vera.

"Good morning!"

Mitch looked up, startled at the sound of English in this Francophone household. A young woman stood before him. Her blue pyjamas were sprinkled with white polar bears.

"You must be …" She rubbed her eyes.

"Mitch," he breathed.

"You're the Russian Sophia told me about?"

Mitch nodded. "That's me."

"Odd name for a Russian," she yawned.

"It's a long story."

"At least you speak English. My French is appalling."

"And you are?"

"Sorry. I'm Lucy. Sophia's friend."

Mitch vaguely recalled talk of someone coming to stay.

"My grandparents … my mother's parents … they used to live in the house next door, and Sophia and I played together when my family visited. We live in Toronto."

She reached into a cupboard above where Mitch was sitting, exposing an expanse of flat stomach, her belly button; Mitch was transfixed. She stepped back, mug in hand, and closed the cupboard door. "Let me get you some coffee," he babbled and pushed his chair back.

"It's okay. I'll help myself." She poured coffee and put the mug on the table before grabbing the milk jug from the fridge. The two sat in silence while she ladled sugar into her mug and stirred it around.

Mitch noticed how tufts of blonde hair protruded at odd angles from her head, the way a longer strand hung over one side of her face. She looked up and met his gaze. Her eyes were almost turquoise, edged with deep blue. Her elfin face relaxed into a smile, revealing dimples in her cheeks.

He gulped. *Anja. Anja has dimples like that.* He had loved to tease her and watch them deepen as she laughed. "What … what do you do in Toronto?"

"I've just finished my second year of law school." Her eyes met his again and he looked away.

That would make her twenty-three, four? She looks younger. Too young for you, he told himself sternly. *You don't need to complicate your life.*

"Do you know where they keep the Tylenol? My head's thumping."

He got up and rummaged in the cupboard where Simone kept pill bottles. "There's aspirin," he said placing the bottle on the table in front of Lucy.

She tipped two tablets into her left hand. "Too much wine last night."

"Did you go to the game?"

She nodded. "But, I'm not much of a one for hockey."

Mitch smiled. "Me neither."

"They won, though. Beat the Whalers three-two." She put an aspirin into her mouth and sipped the coffee before taking the second pill. "They're on a winning streak. Apparently." She shrugged her shoulders and laughed. There were the dimples again.

"So have you decided what area of law you'll specialise in?"

She grimaced. "I've been doing a combined degree. Law and Social Work. Now, I'm not so sure."

"That often happens," Mitch commiserated, remembering the fine ideals which had led him to study law in the Soviet Union. Ideals he soon found were unachievable in the corrupt system that passed for justice there.

"Oh, of course. I remember now. Sophia, she said you were a lawyer in Russia. Is that right?"

He nodded, got to his feet and refilled his coffee mug.

"What sort of people did you represent?"

"All sorts," he mumbled into his mug.

"You must have had some specialty, something you were interested in," she persisted.

"Over there, you take the cases you're given," he said, turning his head at the sound of footsteps on the stairs.

"Oh, I see you two have met," Simone said as she breezed into the kitchen. "Pancakes or eggs and bacon?" She looked from one to the other. "What's it to be?"

"Pancakes would be nice." Lucy's face relaxed into a smile.

"Me too." Mitch filled a mug with coffee for Simone.

"Now, why aren't my kids as helpful as you?" she remarked as she donned her apron.

18
St Petersburg and Montréal
July 1992

Vera Alexandrovna shifted in the armchair. Her hands went to her ears in an effort to block out the raucous bleep pulsing through her brain. *It's only the telephone,* she told herself. *One of Lyuba's friends.* The noise stopped and she felt herself drifting off again.

"Eto dla vas," Lyuba called from the doorway. "*Syn Sergey Dmitrievich.*"

Vera gripped the arms of the chair and pulled herself upright. "You told him I was here?" Lyuba wrung her hands and nodded.

"Tell him … tell him I won't be a moment." Vera closed her eyes, trying to compose herself—it was one thing telling lies on paper, but how was she to keep deceit from her voice when speaking to Mitch? *Tell him exactly what you said in the letter.* She went over it again in her mind: *heart attack ... doctor said he would not have known anything ... buried close to your mother's grave.* She got to her feet and walked slowly into the hallway. *You have to do it, you promised Seryozha.* The telephone receiver lay on the table and she took a deep breath before picking it up. "Mitch?" Her voice trembled as she spoke.

"Is that you, Vera?" he breathed.

"Da ... eto."

"Your voice sounds odd. *Ty v poryadke?"*

"I'm getting over a cold." The lie tripped off her tongue.

"Did you manage to get my letter to Anja?" Mitch blurted.

"Not yet. My contact in the village, she's still trying to get it to her, but she's always with Natasha, Boris or the person in whose house they are living."

"Surely there must be some way," he sighed, trying to hide his exasperation. "I need her to know I haven't abandoned her, forgotten her."

"I know."

"And Papa?"

Vera gripped the edge of the table with her free hand.

"Can you tell me more about how he died? It was such a shock ..." his voice trailed off.

"It was a shock for us all." Vera sought for the words she had so carefully rehearsed. "A heart attack, the doctor said."

"Had he seemed unwell before?"

"*Nyet.* Not that anyone noticed."

"Anastasia? Was it Anastasia who found him?"

Vera shifted uneasily. *"Da."*

"It must have been awful for her." When Vera didn't comment, he continued: "Maybe I should write to her. Is she still there ... in the apartment?"

"*Nyet.* I think she went to live with a relative somewhere."

"What about Papa's belongings, his papers, furniture? There were Maman's things. Mine too. Family photos."

"We stored most of it in a warehouse Leonid's friend owns outside the city." *At least that isn't a lie.*

"Spasiba."

"I didn't know what else to do."

"I should have been there."

"You couldn't have done anything, Mitch. No one could." *No one could have stopped them sending him to that terrible place.* She shivered.

There was an awkward silence before Mitch asked, "How are things there?"

"Difficult. Shortages of almost everything."

"Nothing changes then."

"Will it ever?" Vera sighed. "How are you getting on."

"I'm making progress. Sorting things out gradually."

"That's good."

"I'm thinking of applying to law school. I need to upgrade my legal qualifications to practise here."

"Your father ... he would have liked that." The muscles in Vera's face relaxed.

"Any news of Yagudin?"

She took a sharp intake of breath. What should she do? She'd been over this scenario again and again in her mind. How could she let Mitch spend the rest of his life in fear of the *vory*? She cautioned herself: *If he knows, he'll want to come back.*

"Vera? Is something wrong?"

He has to know. He'll never forgive me, but he has to know. "There's something," she began. "Something I should have told you."

"What? Is it Anja? Something's happened to Anja?"

"Nyet. Eto nay Anja!"

Mitch let out a breath.

"If I tell you, you must promise not to come back. It still isn't safe."

"Tell me! Tell me what it is!"

"Whatever happens, Mitch. You mustn't come back here. Your father, he wanted you to make a new life in Canada for you and Anja."

"Vera! For Christ's sake tell me!"

"Yagudin. Yagudin's dead."

"Dead?" Mitch gasped. "How? When?"

"A rival gang. A gunfight."

"When? When was this?"

"A few months ago." Her voice was little more than a whisper.

"A few months ago? And you didn't tell me?"

Vera began to sob.

"I can't believe you let me go on … I've been petrified!"

"I'm so sorry."

"Sorry!" Mitch snapped. "Did Papa know?"

"*Nyet.* It was after he went…" Vera gulped and corrected herself quickly, "after he died."

"What about the others? The thugs who worked for him?"

"They're dead too."

"All this time I've been scared out of my life, frightened the bastards would find me, do something to Anja."

"Mne thuck zhal," she cried. The noise brought Lyuba into the hallway. Vera shook her head and shooed Lyuba away. "Mitch. Yagudin's death. It doesn't change things. There are other people … violent people … they know what you did."

"The other gangs, *militsiya*. I know."

"They don't forget."

"I can't stay away forever, Vera. I have to be with Anja. She's my daughter, for Christ's sake."

"She's safe, Mitch. Yagudin's no longer a threat to her."

Mitch breathed a sigh of relief. *If I've achieved nothing else, at least there's that.*

"Natasha? What will she do now? Go back to St Petersburg?"

"I don't know." Vera paused. "Whether she does or not, *you* mustn't come back here, Mitch. What's happened doesn't change things. It's still not safe."

"I don't know what I'm going to do. I can't think straight."

"Your father. He had such high hopes for you." Vera gulped back the lump in her throat, pulled a handkerchief out of the pocket of her dress and wiped her eyes. "He was adamant you should stay where you are, Mitch. He wanted a better life for you and Anja. It was his dearest wish."

"I know."

"I'll write and let you know when we've been able to get the letter to Anja. Then …" The line went dead.

* * *

Mitch stared at the phone for a few moments. *Stupid woman! She should have told me! All these months …* As his anger began to dissipate, he cursed himself for hanging up on her. *What if she won't help anymore? There's no one else. No one to keep an eye on Anja.* He picked up the receiver, cradled it in his hands. *You have to apologise,* he told himself, looking around for the scrap of paper on which he had written Vera's number.

"Mitch?" Simone put her head around the door of Luc's study. "Is everything okay?"

He replaced the receiver, slid the chair back from the desk and got to his feet. "Vera. I was talking to Vera."

"How is she?"

"Sounded as though she has a cold."

"Any news of Anja?"

He shook his head. "She told me … Christ! What the hell was she thinking?" He ran the fingers of his hands through his hair.

"What is it?"

“She told me Yagudin’s dead. Him and the rest of his gang. They’re all dead.”

“That’s good news. Isn’t it?” Simone looked enquiringly into his troubled face. “What happened?”

“Gangland fight. A couple of months ago. And she didn’t tell me!” He slammed his fist down on the desk. “Can you believe that?”

“She must have had her reasons.”

“It’s still not safe. That’s what she said. Not safe for me to go back.” He paced around the room.

“You’re not thinking of going there?”

“I don’t know.” He pulled a packet of cigarettes out of his pocket. “There are others. Others who know what I did.” He took out a cigarette. “Do you mind?”

“You look as though you need it.” Simone opened a drawer in the desk and pulled out an ashtray. “Luc and the boys smoke in here, though they always deny it.”

“If I could just see Anja,” he mumbled as he lit the cigarette. “See for myself that she’s okay.”

“And what good would that do?” Simone asked. “You’d only unsettle her.”

He walked over to the window and looked out. There were children playing in the street below … two boys kicked a ball … a young girl chalked on the sidewalk. He wondered what games Anja played, there in Siberia. Her friends? She was growing up and he didn’t know anything of her life now.

“The best thing you can do for Anja is to sort out your citizenship, get started on a proper career.”

He turned to face Simone. “And how long will that take?”

“She’ll still be there. She’ll still know you’re her father, you love her.”

“She’ll forget me. Probably has already.” His words sent a tremor through his body.

“You know that’s not true,” Simone countered. “If you go there now, Mitch, you’ll run into trouble. What good will you be to her …?” She couldn’t bring herself to say the last word.

“Write to her again,” she suggested.

“You can’t imagine how it feels to write to my own daughter in a name that isn’t hers … or mine.” He leaned against a bookcase, head bent, staring at his feet.

“Why don’t I make us some tea?” Simone suggested.

"I'm going for a walk." Mitch ground his cigarette out in the ashtray. "I need to clear my head."

"Want me to come with you?" Simone offered. "Might help to talk things through."

"I'm not very good company!" he snapped and headed to the door.

"You haven't had lunch," she called over the banisters as he clattered down the stairs.

"I'll get something."

* * *

Sometime later, Mitch sank gratefully into a seat on the patio of a café and ordered a black coffee. His feet hurt. He must have walked miles but remembered nothing of where he had been or what he might have seen. He had gone over and over things in his head, one moment vowing to go back to Russia, to Siberia to find Anja. *Then what?* he had asked himself. How was he to get her away from Natasha, out of the country? She would be frightened. The further he walked, the more he came to acknowledge Vera was right. *It would be suicide to go back. If they come after me, Anja will be in danger.* He needed to plan more long-term. Sort out his citizenship, apply to law school, find a job and a permanent home. A home with a garden for Anja. *She will like that.*

He realised now that to him Anja was still the six-year-old he last saw fifteen months ago as she walked away, hand-in-hand with his father. In her other hand, she swung the bag holding the new party dress he bought her. In her excitement, she had twirled around the store, white sailor collar covering her narrow shoulders, thin red ribbons swirling from the waistband. He could still hear her giggle, see her dimples deepening. *I wonder what she looks like now.* He took a gulp of water from the glass the waiter placed on the table. Try as he might, he couldn't imagine her any different from the daughter he left behind. Unruly brown curls held back from her face with long ribbons—sometimes red, sometimes blue—eyes just like his, nose sprinkled with freckles. In October, she would have another birthday. Without him. *Eight. How old will she be before I see her again?* He stared into the distance, seeing nothing.

After a few minutes, he stirred sugar into his coffee, picked up the small almond cookie resting on the saucer and dunked it in. *I shouldn't have lashed out at Vera,* he berated himself as the cookie melted in his mouth. *She didn't deserve that. Not after all she's done for me.* Vera, who with his father planned Mitch's escape from Russia, as they had secretly done for so many persecuted people over the years. He felt ashamed that his words had reduced her to tears. Tears which he now realised were as much grief for the death of her long-time friend, his father. The two had known each other since the terrible days of the *Blokada,* when the inhabitants of Leningrad were cut off from the rest of the world by the Nazis, when corpses on the streets became so commonplace that everyone walked around them.

Mitch drained the last dregs of coffee, put some coins on the table and walked out on to the sidewalk. *You have to forget what happened. Look to the future. Figure out how to get Anja out of Russia,* he resolved and checked his watch. *Time to get back home. Simone will be worried. I'll write to Vera. Maybe she can get someone to go through Papa's belongings and find some family photographs ... pictures of Anja.*

He arrived at the bus station in time to see his bus pulling out of the bay. Cursing under his breath, he flopped onto a bench. A young girl, her short blonde hair streaked with mauve, rested her backpack on the end of the bench. She looked around, seemed uncertain what to do.

Can't be more than fourteen, Mitch thought to himself. She met his gaze for a moment then grabbed the backpack and scurried to the end of a line of people waiting in the section reserved for long-distance buses. As Mitch watched, a man walked towards her. He was dark-haired, dressed in black pants and green shirt. He paused beside the girl and seemed to be saying something to her. She shook her head and took a step away from him. Mitch got to his feet and dashed towards them. "You'll earn good money. Nice clothes, jewellery," the man said and gripped the girl's arm with one hand. She shook her head again and tried to wriggle free. "With looks like yours ..."

Mitch lunged at the man, grabbed his arm and pulled him away from the girl. "I know what you're up to. You creep!"

"Stay out of this!" the man growled at Mitch.

"Leave her alone!" Mitch yelled and ducked to avoid the fist aimed at his chin. As he regained his balance, he kicked out hard with his right foot, missed the target for which he was aiming and connected with the man's knee. Mitch turned quickly, meeting the startled looks of bystanders as he scanned the crowd. The girl had gone. He ran, dodging between people waiting in bus lines. He couldn't see her anywhere. Looking back, he glimpsed the man hobbling away, helped by another man. Mitch sped out of the bus station, searching possible places the girl might have gone. It was several minutes before he spotted her running along a side street. He was out of breath when he drew level. "I mean you no harm," he panted. She quickened her pace. "You have to stay away from men like that. Women too." He took a gulp of air. "Whatever they tell you, don't go with them. You'll never be able to break free." She stopped running and hunched her shoulders. He could see she was crying. "Listen to me for a moment." His voice was soft. "You're obviously in some sort of trouble. Running away from home?" She turned away.

"You're not from Montréal, are you?"

"No," she snuffled.

"I bet your mom and dad are worried about you."

His words opened the floodgates. Mitch passed her his handkerchief and sat on a low brick wall while she composed herself. "Want to tell me about it?"

She shook her head. "You wouldn't understand. No one does."

An hour or so later, he bought her a one-way ticket and put her on the bus to her hometown. She had told him her story—not an uncommon one for a young teenager—while she ate a sandwich and they both drank coffee at the café he had been in earlier. She had used the telephone there to call her parents. "Dad's going to meet me when the bus gets in," she told him, smiling for the first time.

Now, as he waited for her bus to pull away, he looked around. There was no sign of the man who tried to accost her, nor of his accomplice. He wondered how many victims they had lured into the sex trade from this one spot. It happened everywhere. Even in relatively safe countries like Canada. He forced a smile and waved to the girl as the bus passed where he was standing at the kerbside. He hoped she would heed his parting words to her: "Never speak to strangers. Not even someone like me." It was all he could do.

19
Montréal
October 1992

It was seven in the evening when Mireille locked the door of the patisserie. She paused for a moment and took a deep breath before helping Mitch take the last of the used crockery and cutlery into the kitchen. "I'll wash, you dry," she said as she donned rubber gloves. "Maybe your idea of getting dishwasher-proof crockery isn't a bad one," she laughed.

Mitch remembered how clumsy he felt when he started working in this mostly female environment. His ungainly hands were at odds with the delicate china, and his brown leather brogues seemed like those of a giant compared to the strappy sandals and high-heeled shoes worn by most of the clientele. He found himself tiptoeing around in an effort not to intrude. Later, he began to appreciate the pristine white paintwork, pale grey walls, lime-washed floorboards, bleached wooden tables and bentwood chairs, in which the flower-strewn mismatched crockery provided a homely touch. Mireille too was a mix of elegance and warmth. Physically, she reminded him of his mother, or how his mother would have looked if she had lived in a land unconstrained by the hardships and shortages of Soviet life.

Now, as he stacked crockery in the glass-fronted armoire, a memory came back to him. His father's face glowed with pride as he entered the cramped apartment in Leningrad. Under his arm a rolled-up rug. That evening, it hung in pride of place on the sitting room wall. Five-year-old Mitch wished his Papa had instead brought home a toy gun like the guns the soldiers carried. Some years later, his mother explained that his father's name had been on a list for two years before he was allowed to buy the rug. Here in Montréal, Mitch was shocked at the still-serviceable items people discarded; items unobtainable for most Russians.

Hardly a day went by now that he wasn't needed in the patisserie. Time flew past in a flurry of serving croissants, beignets, sablés, to name a few of the delicacies Mireille whipped up as if by magic. She had encouraged him to try every item. "How can you describe to customers the taste of sugar-coated beignets if you have never eaten one?" she teased.

But now, the mere thought of sugary concoctions brought a feeling of nausea. "You'll get over it," Mireille prophesied. "You'll soon be yearning for chocolate cake!" He remembered how every day, as a small boy here in Montréal, he begged Maman for a chocolate croissant.

"Do you mind locking up, Mitch?" Mireille asked as he wiped down the last table. "I have to deliver something to a customer."

"Sure," he said, and took the keys from her. "Do you need a hand putting anything in your car?"

"I've already loaded up," she called over her shoulder. "See you tomorrow, early."

He followed her through the back yard and watched as her car disappeared down the laneway. *She seemed in a hurry to get away,* he mused. *Maybe there's a man.* Mireille's husband died some years ago in Vietnam. "He was a freelance journalist. Handsome brute. We were all crazy about him when we were young," Simone had confessed.

* * *

An hour or so later, Mitch climbed the steps to the front door of Simone and Luc's home. As he did every day, he wondered if there would be a note from Vera saying Anja now had his letter. *They must have been able to get it to her by now. It's over two months since I spoke to Vera.* "Sorry I'm late," he called, closing the front door. "Mireille asked me to lock up." He sifted through the mail on the hall table then hung up his coat.

"We're in here," Simone called from the sitting room.

He turned the knob on the door, and was met by a barrage of *"Bonne Fête!* ... Happy Birthday!"

Mitch took a step back. He blinked, for a moment unable to recognise any of the faces. Then, one by one, they came into focus. Micky from the bar where he had worked. Matthieu and his girlfriend, whose name Mitch could never remember. Neighbours. Even the couple from the *dépanneur* where Mitch bought cigarettes.

"S Dnem Rozhdeniya!" Luc pulled him into the room. "I hope that's right. I had to look it up!"

"Your pronunciation needs work!" Mitch laughed.

"Did you think we'd let your thirtieth birthday pass without a party?" Simone hugged him.

"I didn't think anyone knew."

"How could I forget the day I went with my best friend to the hospital?" Simone sounded choked.

"Now you know why I needed to leave before you." Mireille pressed a glass of sparkling wine into Mitch's hand.

"I thought you were going to meet a man!" Mitch quipped.

"If only …"

"What was with the fancy name … Andrei?" Micky gripped Mitch's arm. "Anyone who looks less like an Andrei is hard to imagine," he laughed.

"Sorry about that," Mitch chuckled. "It wasn't my choice." Mitch thought now how much more like his former self he felt since reverting to his given name.

Simone appeared in front of them with a plate of crackers topped with pâté. "It's your favourite," she tempted, handing Mitch and Micky paper plates. Both men put their glasses on a side table and took several crackers. "I'll be back in a minute with shrimp," she promised.

Mitch worked his way around the crowd, thanking everyone for making his birthday special. Apart from bringing a school friend home for a celebratory tea of sandwiches and cake, he had never had a proper birthday party. Even that modest meal must have taken a lot of planning in a country where almost everything was in short supply—at least for those without money to buy on the black market.

As he turned from speaking to one of the neighbours, he spotted Sophia in the corner of the room. *The blonde girl with her? She looks familiar.* She smiled at him across the room. The hair was longer than the last time he saw her, but there was no mistaking those dimples. "What are you doing here?" he asked Lucy as he drew level.

"I couldn't miss your birthday party." There was an impish twinkle in her eyes.

"Seriously?"

She laughed and shook her head. "I'm doing research for a paper I'm working on."

"You're staying here … in this house?"

"No. McGill. I've got a room there for a couple of weeks. Then it's back to Toronto."

"The girl's a genius," Sophia butted in. "Next year she's articling at one of the all-female law firms."

"In Toronto?"

"Yep. Starting in May."

"Where's the birthday boy?" Simone's voice rang out. "Time to cut the cake." She grabbed his arm and led him to the table in the window where a forest of candles glowed on his birthday cake. *Chocolate!* he laughed to himself as he blew the candles out and made a wish. He gulped back the lump in his throat.

"We have to save a piece for your Uncle Yaakov. I went to see him, hoping to persuade him to come, but he said he isn't good in crowds," Simone confided.

"I feel bad I haven't visited him since I picked up the birth certificates."

"I told him Bertrand Langlais is representing you at your citizenship hearing. He remembered him from when he practised. Said you couldn't do better."

At the end of the evening, Mireille offered to give Lucy a lift back to McGill. As Mitch saw them to the door, Mireille suggested Lucy visit them at the patisserie.

"Why don't you?" Mitch urged. "I'd like your advice on law courses."

"I'm a bit pushed for time, but I'll see what I can do," Lucy promised and planted a kiss on both his cheeks.

* * *

Two days later, Mitch was deep in thought as he washed dishes in the kitchen at the patisserie.

"She's here!" Mireille announced, struggling through the doorway with a tray of used crockery. "Your girlfriend's out there." She lowered the tray on to the counter.

Mitch turned towards her, a puzzled look on his face.

"Lucy is here," Mireille enunciated each syllable.

"She isn't my girlfriend," he hissed, and dried his hands.

"Whatever you say. But I think you need to wipe that smear of cream off the front of your shirt first." She dunked the corner of a tea towel into the bowl of soapy water and dabbed at the stain. "Go on. I'll bring coffee and cakes," she promised and pushed him gently towards the doorway.

Mitch found himself walking forward. *Why did you suggest this? You have enough problems without getting involved with someone else.* Lucy turned and smiled. The muscles in his face relaxed.

20
Village Near Omsk, Siberia
January 1993

Anja skipped along the slippery path. She turned her head left then right as she looked into one house then another. There were lights in all the windows, people inside, trees waiting to be dressed, tables laden with food. For weeks, she had found it difficult to contain her excitement.

And now, the day was here at last. *Tonight is Sochelnik,* she thought gleefully. *Christmas Eve. Tonight Ded Moroz and Snegurochka will be here. I wonder what gifts they will bring me. I hope it isn't horrid clothes like last year.*

Tonight we're going inside the church. It belongs to someone called Jesus. Anja didn't know who he was and wondered if he would be there in the church. *Tyotya Yevdokia Marlenova prays to him every day at the krasnyy ugol so he must be important. After the service at the church, we will go home and decorate the tree. Then we can eat all the food Tyotya has prepared.*

"Don't jump around so much, Yelena," Mama cautioned, grabbing one of Anja's gloved hands in hers. Anja hates the name Yelena. *Whatever they say, I will always be Anja.* A few months ago, she heard Mama and Boris arguing. "He's dead. The Boss is dead," Boris said. "You're no longer in danger, so where's the harm in using your real names?"

"We're fine as we are," Mama retorted. "I don't want to be the woman I was when I was Natasha. I shall continue to be Antonina and Anja will be Yelena."

Dyadya Mikhail is dead? Anja had strained to hear more, but they spoke quietly. *If Dyadya is dead, I wonder if my dollhouse is still in his dacha. He said it was mine, nobody else's. Boris can fetch it. There isn't much room in Tyotya's house, but I'll put it in the shed. I'll let Kalisa play with it too.* Anja's daydreaming had been cut short by Tyotya's shrill tones from the kitchen urging her to help prepare the vegetables.

That night, when Mama tucked her into her bed behind the curtain in the kitchen, Anja had whined, "Why can't I be Anja again?"

"Your name is Yelena, and that is the end of it!" Mama said in the horrid voice she used a lot here.

"But I want to be Anja again. I want my real Papa," she wailed. "And my dollhouse." The curtains had swished together at the side of her bed.

Now, Anja craned her neck to check *Tyotya* and her friend Dotnara Vektorova were still behind. Like Anja and her mother, they carried an unlit candle. Boris had set off to visit a friend, bottle under his arm, muttering, "I can't be doing with religion. That stuff's for women."

Snow crackled beneath Anja's boots, and she remembered how Papa used to tell her to listen for the tune the snow made. She listened hard. There it was, the tune carried on the wind. She laughed and began to sing one of the songs Papa made up when they used to tramp through the snow. "Tramp … tramp … tramp …" *Maybe he'll hear me singing.* The thought brought a smile to Anja's face, dimpling her cheeks. *He might be somewhere in the forest. When the deep snow melts, I'll go to look for him. I'll take Kalisa with me, then if Baba Yaga chases us, we can each run in a different direction. That will confuse Baba Yaga.*

"What are you singing, Yelena?"

"Nichego, Mama." Mama had said she was never to mention her Papa again. He did bad things, she said. The wind was quiet now.

"Antonina! Antonina!" A voice pierced the darkness. *"Podozhdite menia!"* Mama's friend Alyona Gavrilova joined them and the three of them picked their way through the ruts in the track leading to the church.

"Have you heard anything from your daughter?" Mama asked.

"Not yet … maybe next week?" Alyona's voice was wistful.

Mama put a comforting arm around her friend. "We'll say a special prayer for her tonight."

Alyona's daughter, Dina, had gone away to work. That was six months ago, and no one had heard from her. Mama had made Anja promise that if anyone told her they would give her lots of roubles, she would run back to Mama as fast as her legs would carry her. Anja peered into the inky-black forest at the side of the track and wondered if Dina was in there. *Maybe I'll find her too, when I look for Papa.*

As they entered Jesus's house, Tyotya hissed, "This is the first time since I was a child that we have had the traditional service." Anja sniffed, trying to smell the cabbages Tyotya said were stored here during the time when religion was forbidden. That was when all the people in the village were forced to work on the *kholkhoz*—the collective farm. Anja sniffed again, wrinkling her nose. *There is a funny smell. Not cabbages. Candles!* Hundreds of candles flickered. She looked around. There were lots of saints—their pictures were on the walls. Tyotya had told her the church was named after St Vladimir; he did good things, but Tyotya couldn't remember what. *If I do good things, will they put my picture on the wall?* Anja wondered. *If I find Dina in the forest, that will be a good thing. I will be Saint Anja. Not Saint Yelena!* she thought crossly. Now that Jesus's house is open again, there will be a feast on St Vladimir's special day in July. Anja loves feasts.

Mama straightened Anja's headscarf, made sure her own was in place, then she and Alyona squeezed in to stand at the end of one of the rows. Anja hurried to the front to join the other children from school, and slipped into a space next to her friend Kalisa.

The chanting began. Anja didn't know the words, but she liked the sound. Then voices soared so loud she thought they would burst through the roof. A man in a long gold dress began to speak; it was like a song. He was very fat. *He looks important. He must be Jesus.* Another man, dressed in white, walked from side to side swinging a long chain with a shiny container at the end. Smoke wafted out of it; it tickled Anja's nose, and she giggled as Kalisa sneezed. The smoke rose all the way to the top of the ceiling. Tyotya had told her that if she prayed hard her prayers would rise up to somewhere called Heaven. Anja closed her eyes and whispered the prayer she said every day in her head. "Oh … and Dina too," she added.

Laryssa Kirillova gathered the children together to sing 'The Carol of the Little Russian Children'. Anja and Kalisa held hands. Mama and Alyona smiled encouragingly as the children's voices rang out, telling the story of a widowed man and his eight-year-old daughter in Siberia, a long, long time ago:

Snow-bound mountains, snow-bound valleys.
Snow-bound plateaus, clad in white.
Fur-robed moujiks, fur-robed children, see the light.

An hour or so passed. There was a constant stream of people crossing themselves in front of the altar. Anja fidgeted. She sighed. Her stomach rumbled at the thought of all that food at home. She hoped Boris and his friends hadn't gone to the house and eaten it all. At last, it was time for everyone to light their candles and lanterns and join the procession around the outside of the church. "Look, Yelena!" Tyotya pointed up to the sky. "The Star of Bethlehem. The star announcing the Christ Child is born."

"S Rozhdestvom Khristovym!" the villagers called to one another.

Anja looked up. The star shone brightly, twinkling down on her. She thought of all the food they were to have … *kutya, Mama's bobal'ki, borscht, sauerkraut. Best of all, pryaniki;* she could already taste the spicy cookies. And chocolates—she could sneak some chocolates to bed with her. As she watched, the star got bigger, brighter. When she was very little, Papa told her that wherever you are in the world, you can see the same stars. *I hope Papa is looking at this star too.*

* * *

Sometime later, Anja helped *Tyotya* pile the empty plates on to the board at the side of the sink. She was sure her stomach would burst but, when no one was looking, she slipped two chocolates into the pocket of her dress. She would put them under her pillow and, when she woke up in the morning, she would eat them. No one would know if she snuggled under the bedclothes first. A shiver of excitement rippled through her body.

"Yelena. It's time for you to go to bed."

"Please Mama. Just a little while longer. I want to see Dotnara Vektorova tell someone's fortune," she pleaded.

"Nyet! Eto slishkom ..." Mama began.

"She's never going to sleep with all this noise going on," Boris cut in.

"Tolko odin," Mama relented. "Then bed!"

Anja exchanged a conspiratorial grin with Boris.

Gertruda Delezhova was first. Dotnara gazed at her friend's hand for so long, Anja thought the two old women had gone to sleep. Dotnara's voice sounded strange as she spoke: "I see a long life. A romance. A man walking up the steps to your house." Gertruda's face lit up.

"I think you've had too much of the vodka, Dotnara Vektorova!" one of Boris's friends called out. His remark was met with laughter.

Anja wondered if she should have her fortune told. *Maybe the man had gone to the wrong house. It could be Papa looking for me.*

Gertruda got up from the chair. Her face looked younger, her eyes shone.

"Yelena! *Nyet* Yelena!" Mama's voice followed Anja as she ran and sat on the chair in front of Dotnara.

Dotnara looked around uncertain what to do. *"Pazhalusta,"* Anja pleaded, first to Dotnara and then to Mama, who was now gripping her daughter's arm. Anja held on to the sides of the chair with all her might.

"Yelena." Dotnara pulled one of Anja's hands away from the chair and gazed at it. "Your hand is much too small. The lines don't tell me anything."

"You must! You must!" Anja cried.

"I tell you what we'll do," Dotnara placated, struggled to her feet and, with help from Boris, lifted a mirror down from the wall and balanced it on the chair in front of Anja. Then she placed a burning candle in front of the mirror. "Now, Yelena. You must stare into the mirror. Stare very hard and you will see someone."

Anja did as she was bid. *Maybe I will see Papa.*

"You will see the likeness of your future husband," Dotnara promised.

Anja leapt to her feet shouting, "I don't want a husband. I want my Papa! My real Papa." She stamped her foot hard and ran to her bed behind the curtain.

Silence descended.

21
Toronto
May 1993

Mitch checked his watch. *Seven-twenty. Where is she?* He picked up the menu but kept one eye on the door as he skimmed the descriptions of dishes. He knew he was in the right restaurant—the waiter had highlighted Lucy's name on the list of reservations. His thoughts drifted back to a day many years ago when he sat in another restaurant waiting for another woman. As time went on, he had convinced himself Natasha wasn't coming, but an hour later she breezed in, arms full of parcels; she had been on a shopping spree with her mother. *If she hadn't turned up, how different my life would have been,* he sighed to himself now. *But there wouldn't be Anja.*

"Penny for your thoughts."

Mitch looked up and met Lucy's amused gaze. "You don't want to know," he laughed, scrambled to his feet and kissed her on both cheeks.

"The darned streetcar broke down, so I had to walk." She flopped onto the chair Mitch pulled out for her. He filled her glass with water from the carafe.

"It's good to see you," he began.

"Mom said to apologise that you couldn't stay at our house." She took a gulp of water then shrugged out of her jacket and draped it over the back of her chair. "My sister, Erin. She's home for a few weeks, otherwise you could have had her room." Lucy went on to explain that Erin is a medical researcher in Sao Paolo, Brazil.

Mitch watched the way she tucked a strand of hair behind an ear. How she gestured with her hands, almost pushing the air to one side. "What's she researching?"

"Oh, something to do with sickle cell anaemia."

"Interesting," he said and picked up his menu, not wanting to confess his ignorance of the strange sounding term.

"I'm starving!" Lucy announced. "Why don't we order straight away?"

"Okay. I'll get some wine while we decide what to eat."

"The house red's pretty good here. Expensive wine's wasted on me."

Not like Natasha. Eating out with her had been a nightmare. She always ordered the most expensive food and wine on the menu—stuff she knew he couldn't afford.

Lucy suggested they share a salad and a bowl of carbonara. "The portions are so big, there'll be more than enough for two." She smiled at the waiter as he poured the wine.

"So, you've decided to apply to law school here," she began after they had ordered.

"I've talked it over with Luc, and he agrees it will give me more options than requalifying in Québec."

"Certainly, if you're going to work on civil cases you don't want to be constrained by Québec's Napoleonic Code," Lucy laughed. "The Québec government's been working on revising the CCQ …" Seeing Mitch's frown, she elaborated: "Civil Code of Québec. Sorry, I talk in jargon!"

"It's okay," he grinned. "Hopefully, I will soon."

"They've been working on revising it for decades. Since before I was born. But it should come into effect soon."

"What will be different?"

"Restatement of judicial interpretation of codal provisions for privacy and personality rights protection, patrimony of affectation …"

"You've lost me already."

Lucy took a gulp of wine. "You'll be sad to leave Simone and Luc, though."

"It'll be a wrench." Mitch had tried not to think about leaving the people he now thought of as family. "But I can't keep depending on them."

Flickering light from the candle danced in Lucy's turquoise eyes. She met his gaze, and he placed a hand on hers.

"Salad." The waiter shifted from one foot to the other at the side of their table. Mitch removed his hand.

While they ate, he told her about his interview at the university the next day. "I hope there won't be a problem. I still haven't got the transcripts and course descriptions from the law school where I studied in Leningrad."

"You didn't bring them with you?"

He shook his head. "I left in a bit of a hurry." He went on to tell her that a friend in Russia was going through his late-father's belongings looking for the documents. Family pictures too.

"What's it like living in a country like that?" she asked.

"Shortages, corruption, lack of freedom … you name it. Like most places, if you have money that sort of thing isn't a problem."

"I guess that's why you left."

He managed to skirt around her further questions as to why he left Russia, telling her instead of the difficulties encountered by people in their everyday lives there.

The waiter poured more wine and cleared the salad dishes.

"Now what's this about you articling at an *all-female* firm?" Mitch asked as they clinked glasses.

"Why not?"

"But why that particular firm?"

"They take the sort of cases I'm interested in. Women's rights. Human rights abuses. I've been working on a case, a young Asian girl who was brought here under false pretences."

Mitch held his breath.

"Usual story. She ended up being forced into prostitution."

Lucy's lips were moving, but her words were lost in the loud booming in his ears. *Oh, God. Please don't let it happen again. Not her.* He shook his head, trying to dislodge the visions that were beginning to penetrate his mind. He could see the room in Leningrad as it was after the *mafiyosa* thugs left. Legal tomes scattered over the floor and, in the corner, the mangled body of the young man. The young man who, minutes before, had pleaded with Mitch and his friend Yuri to help him get his sister away from the brothel in Turkey. His head was twisted to the side, the hair looked wet, congealed into clumps. A trickle of blood ran from the ear down the neck. Now, Mitch's right hand went involuntarily to his own neck. "Timochenko. That was his name."

"What did you say?" Lucy frowned.

"Nothing." He picked up his wine glass, steadying it in both hands.

"Is something the matter?"

Mitch took a gulp of wine then set the glass down carefully. “Lucy.” He met her gaze for a second or two. “You should think very seriously before getting mixed up in that sort of thing. I’ve—”

“Someone has to get mixed up in it,” she cut in. When Mitch didn’t respond, she went on: “All I’m saying is that Canadian law doesn’t specifically prohibit trafficking and, without effective legislation, it’s difficult to prove pimps are living off the avails of prostitution. They’re usually prosecuted using sections of the criminal code and immigration law … lesser crimes with lesser sentences.” She shook her head. “The girls, they’re too scared to testify. You should see them. They come from all over, even Russia, the Ukraine, Georgia.”

“I know.”

“You know?” She looked at him expectantly.

“A friend of mine. His sister. She was taken …” His voice trailed off.

“So? What happened to her?”

“I’d rather not go into it. Not now. Let’s not spoil our dinner.”

She raised her eyebrows.

“All I’m saying, Lucy, is that it’s dangerous. Dangerous to get mixed up in that world.”

“That world? Call it what it is!” She folded her arms across her body. “Human trafficking!”

“Okay.” Mitch sipped his wine. “So … so, what are you going to do about a permanent job? Your career?” he asked in an attempt to change the subject.

“I can’t do anything. Not until my Bar admission.”

“What then?”

“I’m going to lobby for legislation that’ll nail the bastards!”

Mitch bit his lip.

“There’s a great professor at law school,” Lucy went on. “She’s a leading authority on human rights. I spoke to her the other day and she suggested I should work for an NGO.” When Mitch didn’t respond, she leaned across the table towards him. “First of all, the UN … it needs shaking up. I sat in on a meeting of their Human Rights Committee last year. I couldn’t believe that no one challenged the reports the country representatives put forward. Pure fiction! That’s what they were. Denying human rights abuses exist in their countries.” She threw out her arms in despair just as the waiter leaned forward with a big bowl of carbonara. He drew back in mock alarm. “Sorry,” Lucy laughed.

They piled food into individual bowls and ate in silence for a few minutes. "How about you? What will you do when you requalify?" she asked.

Mitch told her he was starting to think he would rather teach law than practise it. "Spending my life in academia has certain attractions," he confessed, twirling pasta onto a fork. "And I would have most of the holidays free to look after my daughter."

"How old is she?"

"Anja? She'll be nine in a few months."

"Do you have a picture?"

Mitch shook his head.

Lucy frowned. "She's here in Canada?"

"She's there, in Russia with her mother. I must get her out of there."

Lucy wiped a smear of sauce from her chin. "Will her mother let her come here? Sophia said you're divorced."

"Anja should be with me." The words came out more sharply than he intended. "Sorry."

He reached out and touched Lucy's arm. "My life's a mess. I don't like to talk about it."

She offered a weak smile. "You'll probably get some teaching experience while you're studying. Someone with your legal background, especially in a system so different from ours, they're sure to want you to teach a course or two."

"I've got to get a place first," Mitch reminded her.

"You will."

Later, Mitch pulled his cigarettes out of his pocket and offered one to Lucy. She shook her head. "Do you mind?" he asked.

"Go ahead. It's your funeral!"

He lit his cigarette and took a drag. "Your parents? What do they do?"

While they sipped coffee, she told him that her father, Donald, is a dentist and her mother, Suzanne, a former teacher. Her father's parents live in England; her mother's used to live next door to Simone and Luc, but died a few years ago. "There's a sixteen-year gap between me and my brother, Greg. I think he was a bit of an accident, although they'll never admit it," she laughed.

"I'm an only child." Those words summed up the loneliness he had felt for most of his life. "My father, he was quite a bit older than my mother."

"Sophia told me your mother met him when he was on a charity mission in Montréal."

"I suppose I was an accident too."

After they left the restaurant, Lucy slipped her arm through Mitch's as they walked to her streetcar stop. A young girl stood awkwardly on the corner, her short skirt barely visible below her jacket. Mitch swallowed hard, his thoughts going back to the girls he saw in London that fateful evening when he had given the information on traffickers to the journalist. He could still visualise them, posed outside nightclubs, in shop doorways, on street corners, hands enticingly placed on hips, painted faces locked in the same frozen smile.

"It happens everywhere, you know," Lucy nodded towards the girl, "some of them are just kids."

Mitch looked down at the sidewalk, willing himself not to look at the girl's face. "A few months ago, I saw this pimp at the bus station in Montréal," he said. "He was trying to entice a young girl away. She couldn't have been more than fourteen."

Lucy stopped walking and turned to look at him. "What did you do?"

"Kicked him on the shin. Missed the place further up I was aiming for!"

"Justice in action!" Lucy's laughter echoed back at them. "What about the girl?"

"She ran off, but I found her. She'd had an argument with her parents and run away."

"That happens so often. Those kids are easy prey for traffickers."

"I bought her a one-way ticket home, put her on the bus and waited until it pulled away. It was all I could do."

"She was lucky."

"It's a drop in the ocean," he said sadly.

"I bet her parents didn't think that." Lucy kissed him on both cheeks. "Thanks for dinner. Let me know how your interview goes," she called as she ran towards the approaching streetcar.

He looked around. The girl was no longer on the street corner.

22
Toronto
October 1993

Mitch tossed and turned in bed in his rented room. His mind raced. Even in the long-ago days of his youth when he was obsessed by Natasha, he hadn't felt like this. *Lucy ... Lucy?* His mind was full of Lucy. She knew what he was thinking, what he was going to do next. Scary, but a comforting sense of belonging. When he wasn't with her, part of him was missing. His thoughts went back to the weekend in June when she stayed in Montréal. She was wearing Simone's apron, rolling out pastry. A smear of flour had transferred itself onto her left cheek. He brushed it off with his fingertips. She turned towards him, holding her dough-encrusted hands to the side.

"Simone and Sophia? They've gone to visit Simone's sister," she said in response to his question. "Luc and Mathieu? They're at some sporting event, I think," she added the instant before his lips met hers. Mitch felt the room tilt. She relaxed a moment in his arms before she pulled away. "They'll be back any minute." The words were no sooner out of her mouth than they heard the front door open. Later, they kissed goodnight outside the room she shared with Sophia. *See you tomorrow,* she mouthed.

Now, late on this Sunday evening he wondered whether, like him, she was reliving the times they made love this weekend. He pictured her as she was this morning, tousled blonde hair spread at odd angles on the pillow. He had propped himself up on an elbow, relishing for a few moments the look of pure innocence on her face in sleep. As he gazed at her, a wave of sadness washed over him. He loved her more than he had ever loved anyone—of that he was sure—but could he give her the happy life she deserved? Was it fair to involve her in his messy life? Lucy had stirred. A smile brushed her face as she looked at him. It was late afternoon when he helped her straighten the bedclothes. Her parents and younger brother were due back from their friends' cottage soon. She held his jacket out to him but, before he could take it, she let it fall to the floor.

She unzipped his pants. "Is that what they call a quickie?" she laughed later as they kissed goodbye. At the end of the street, he looked back; she was still in the doorway.

It's no good. I can't sleep, he sighed now as he hauled himself up in the bed. He flicked on the bedside light, picked up the remote control, turned on the television, and reached for his cigarettes and lighter. Cigarette in mouth, he stared at the picture on the screen. *Tanks? Moscow? What's going on?* He scrambled out of bed and sat on the edge of a chair inches from the TV. *Tanks ... they're firing on the Belyy dom. The White House! What the hell's happening?* He lit the cigarette with trembling hands and watched as smoke billowed out of the top floors of the building.

Over the past weeks, there had been a stand-off between President Yeltsin and the Russian parliament after Yeltsin illegally dissolved parliament and called for the election of a proper legislative body. The Supreme Soviet had stonewalled Yeltsin, refused to leave the parliament building, and their supporters had set up barricades in the streets. *How did it get to this?* The TV reporter was now going over the events of the day. Mitch couldn't believe that, while he and Lucy were ensconced in their own world, armed opponents of Yeltsin successfully stormed the police cordon around the White House.

Clips flashed on the screen: Alexander Ruskoy, the acting president, addressing the crowd earlier from the balcony, urging them to seize the mayor's office and the TV centre at Ostankino. There were reports of pitched battles. And now the Army, which had initially declared its neutrality, had gone over to Yeltsin's side shelling the White House and forcing the Supreme Soviet members out. Mitch got to his feet and paced around. *Please God. Don't let it spread to Siberia and Anja. Please.*

The bangs and flashes on the television filled the room with an unearthly clamour as he berated himself for not trying harder to get his daughter out. He had written several letters—some mailed direct to her, bypassing Vera's contacts—but still hadn't heard anything. Those letters were full of his love for her and promises to come for her as soon as he could. *Empty promises. What sort of father are you?*

He sank down onto the edge of the bed and reached for the framed photograph from the nightstand. He couldn't count the times he had looked at the pictures Vera found in his father's belongings and sent to him with his transcripts from law school. The pictures told of another time. Happy picnics with his parents, Anja wedged in between them on a blanket on the ground; Anja's birthdays; skating in winter. *Why didn't I value those moments more?* He knew the answer: *I spent most of my time worrying about mounting debts.*

He looked at the picture in his hands, remembering it was taken on her fourth birthday. She smiled back at him, dimples in her cheeks, big bow in her hair, long curls tumbling onto her shoulders. She seemed to be trying to tell him something. "*Chto eto, moya dorogaya*?" he whispered and swallowed back the lump in his throat. *I shouldn't have left her there. What was I thinking?*

And now, Anja was to have a new brother or sister, Vera had reported. A year or so ago, he would have been angry that Natasha was carrying another man's child. Not now. *If she has a baby to think about, she may not be so focused on Anja. Maybe she'll let me see her.* But how could he get Anja out of the country? They would need exit visas. He could do what he did before and use Vera's clandestine network. But that would be risky, especially with Anja. *She's almost nine but how would she cope with being spirited away from all she has ever known? And Lucy? Would she accept Anja? What if we have children of our own? How would Anja feel having to share her Papa with others?* Then he remembered: *Anja has another Papa.*

He placed the photograph back on the nightstand as more images flashed on the screen. *Why did the damned place have to erupt again, now when things are going so well for me?* He had successfully proved his eligibility for Canadian citizenship and been accepted into law school in Toronto. There were still several courses and exams to complete before he could obtain a Certificate of Qualification enabling him to apply for admission to the Canadian Bar Association, but he was getting there. Listening to the conversations of other students, most of whom were younger than him, he felt hopeful that a sense of justice still prevailed in the world. In the Soviet Union, the system had suffocated him, moulded him into *Homo Sovieticus*. He had felt a lone voice in the wilderness with his aims of fighting for the underprivileged and bringing to justice those with little regard for human life. Here, when students spoke with fervour of their advocacy for those in need, irrespective of race, creed, or sexual proclivity, he felt a new sense of hope for the future. He had a job on campus and last week when he drew his first pay check, he set money aside. It wasn't a lot, but it was a first step towards renting an apartment and starting a new life with Lucy.

He worried he was becoming detached from that other life … his life with Anja. Days drifted past now when he hardly thought of her. *Is she beginning to forget me too?* A few months ago, that thought would have filled him with dread. But now he had Lucy and the chance to make another life. *If only Papa was still alive. He would make sure Anja was safe, provide a stable home for her … until she can come here.* Mitch lay back on the bed and thought of the times when, as a schoolboy, he waited for his father to come home from work. Best of all were the days he earned a *pyatorka* at school—a five, the highest grade possible. *"Moy umnyy syn,"* his father would exclaim, one hand reaching into his jacket pocket to pull out a *Belochka*, Mitch's favourite chocolate candy. The brown squirrel on the wrapper held a large nut. *I'll probably never know how well Anja is doing at school, her favourite subjects, candies …*

He looked around the room, acknowledging again how inadequate his living arrangements were. Since moving to Toronto, the times when he and Lucy could spend the night together were limited. He couldn't invite her here—they had laughed together imagining the expression on the face of his landlady, Mrs Palmer, at such shenanigans under her respectable roof. The first time he stayed in the home of Lucy's parents, she crept into his room after everyone had settled for the night. They huddled in the narrow bed, every movement causing the bed to creak loudly. At breakfast the next morning, Susan, Lucy's mother, asked Mitch if he had slept okay. He coloured up, causing Susan and Donald to exchange amused glances. The next time he was invited to stay, his overnight bag was placed in Lucy's room. *I wish Maman and Papa could have met Lucy. They would have loved her.* Despite having been brought up in different parts of the world, Mitch and Lucy shared the same values, knew what was right and what was wrong.

He closed his eyes, shutting out the ugly scene playing out on the TV screen. He imagined again the softness of Lucy's breasts, the hardening of her nipples, his tongue exploring her body, his ecstatic release almost as soon as he entered her that first time. She had rolled on top of him, rubbing herself on his body until she came. It was a weekend in July, soon after Mitch received the offer of a place at law school. He was in Toronto to look for somewhere to live, but they spent most of the time in his hotel room. After that first time, they lay side by side, fingers entwined, neither speaking for a few minutes. "That was so good," he breathed, taking her in his arms and kissing her gently. "Only good?" she pouted. "Maybe if we try again, it will be better." Afterwards, they talked into the early hours of the morning, telling of their feelings for each other, tentatively at first, before they both confessed what they felt was love. It was late the next morning when Mitch awoke, his arm draped across Lucy's stomach. A feeling of tenderness rippled through him. He kissed her lips. She stirred. "Time to wake up, sleepy head," he teased as she gazed around. He sucked gently on first one breast then the other. "I give in," she had croaked and curled into his body.

Now, he opened his eyes. The picture on the screen flickered for a moment before he was able to make sense of what was happening in Moscow. The top floors of the White House were blackened. Troops were taking control of the building. *Thank God. A blood bath has been averted!* He checked his watch. It was nearly four in the morning.

* * *

A loud banging on the door roused him from sleep. "Mitch? Are you okay?" Mrs Palmer called. "It's gone nine o'clock. You said you have a lecture this morning."

He scrambled to his feet, wrapped his dressing gown around his body, and opened the door. "I must have forgotten to set my alarm." He rubbed sleep out of his eyes.

"Your breakfast is ready." She looked him up and down. "Come and have it before you take a shower."

Mitch stifled a yawn as he followed her down the narrow staircase and into the small dining room where his breakfast was set out. As he ate, he looked around the immaculately kept room, with its dark furniture, flocked wallpaper, and rose-hued drapes. On top of a glass-fronted cupboard sat a photograph of Mr Palmer dressed in military uniform. "That was in the war. The Second World War, dear," his widow explained to Mitch on the day he moved in. She had been wearing a flower-print dress, and Mitch's thoughts drifted back to Russia, to his old life and to Marta Basilashvili and her two friends in Leningrad. He could see the elderly ladies as if it was yesterday, dressed in identical print dresses pouring tea into cracked cups at Marta's table.

Marta had been a good friend to Mitch when, in order to protect his father, he moved out of Sergei's apartment and into the dilapidated building where

Marta and other illegal tenants lived. The building was due to be demolished, but the genuine warmth of friendship made up for the crumbling surroundings. Mitch hoped Marta and his old professor, Anton Arturovich Nekrassov, had found a home together. Mariya Kornyevskaya and her daughter, Alina, too. So many people had passed in and out of his life.

Back upstairs, he had a quick shower and dressed. Television news reports were now putting the number of dead close to two thousand in Moscow, but the situation seemed to have calmed down. Downstairs, Mitch took his overcoat off the stand in the hallway and called to Mrs Palmer reminding her he would be home late this evening and wouldn't need a meal. He was meeting Lucy after she finished work. "Okay, dear," came the voice from the kitchen.

As he walked along the road towards College Street, his gaze strayed to the glassed-in front porch of a house. It was littered with kids' bicycles, skates hanging by their laces, hockey sticks. He remembered again the hockey stick his father brought home for him one day. *Look, Mitch. You'll be able to play hockey now with the other boys.* Mitch had looked at the battered stick, tape unravelling from its handle, and propped it up in a corner, where it stayed for years until his father gave it to a friend's young son. *Sorry, Papa.*

He glanced again at the porch. *That's the type of family home Lucy and I will have,* he vowed. *Anja too ...?*

23
Western Siberia
March 1994

Pavel gripped the edges of his blanket together around his chest and raised himself from where he had been sitting on the side of Sergei's cot. He had lost track of the hours he spent wiping sweat from his friend's brow, pinning his limbs to the bed when tremors convulsed his body. After the tremors, a period of calm; calm which sent Pavel into paroxysms of fear as he frantically checked Sergei's pulse, telling himself it must be there somewhere. "My friend, you can't leave me," he pleaded. "How could I suffer this place without you?" Then he would grab the jagged piece of mirror—the one that was kept hidden from the guards—and hold it in front of Sergei's mouth. "Thank God!" he breathed and crossed himself as he withdrew the mirror. Never a religious person, Pavel had made many bargains with God during this terrible night when his friend hovered on the brink of death.

Now, he dropped logs into the stove and levered the top back in place. The man in the cot closest to the stove stirred as Pavel made his way silently in the half-light to the small window near his own cot. He scraped ice from the glass and watched as the wind whipped snow into spirals and skimmed them across the white space between the hut and *taiga*. He listened. *The wolves are close tonight.* His mind went back to stories told by old people in his village of the times when wolves circled a house sensing when death was going to strike. As a child, Pavel lived in fear that one day the wolves would choose his house. *It's only the wind howling,* he told himself now.

24
Toronto
May 1995

The streetcar hummed to a stop. Lucy fidgeted in her seat as she rehearsed in her mind the words she would say to Mitch. Passengers got off, their places filled by others. A young woman flopped onto a seat the other side of the aisle, a small child balanced on her lap, shopping bags around her feet. The child pulled off its hat, revealing a mop of black curls, and dropped the hat onto the floor. Lucy leaned over and picked it up. Chubby fingers reached out and grasped the knitted fabric; laughter danced in the deepest black eyes Lucy had ever seen. The hat hit the floor again, but before Lucy could retrieve it, the mother picked it up and tucked it in her coat pocket, admonishing the child as she did so. The two women locked gazes for a second or two. As she often did, Lucy wondered what sort of home awaited the woman and child. Was there a husband? Other children? Grandparents? She hoped it was a happy place.

Her thoughts went back to the case she was working on. That of an eighteen-year-old girl from Edmonton whose mother sold her to a pimp to fund her own drug habit. The girl was fourteen at the time and had been sold on twice, eventually arriving in Toronto, dependent on her pimp for supplies of crystal meth. She had seized a chance to escape and ended up in a safe house, limbs shaking, covered in bruises and open sores, her brain fried by dope. Even if the girl would testify against the pimp, with the current ineffective legislation Lucy doubted whether she could mount a successful case. What was the sense of putting the girl through the agony of a trial, where she would have to face the accused in the dock and formally identify him as the person who kept her captive in a room where a constant stream of men paid to have sex with her? Maybe for this girl, it would be better to help her build a new life for herself. *But what about those other girls still out there? And those to come?*

A year had passed since Lucy was admitted to the Bar, and what had she achieved? One successful prosecution; one pimp behind bars for a minimal sentence. Not much of a record. But now … her heart skipped a beat as she pulled a sheet of paper out of her briefcase. She had read it so many times, she could now recite it word-for-word. A professor at her old law school had emailed it to her yesterday, saying it was just the sort of thing Lucy would be good at and offering to provide a reference. The position was everything she had always wanted: lawyer in an international NGO working to provide safe environments for trafficked victims and lobbying for more effective legislation. She wasn't naïve enough to think she wouldn't run up against roadblocks, but she had to do something so that girls, like the ones she interviewed all too frequently, would have a chance to lead decent lives and see pimps suffer for the damage they had done. The job was based in Toronto, so it wouldn't mean moving out of the duplex she and Mitch were renting in The Beaches. The salary wasn't as much as she currently earned, but Mitch was doing well at the university and would be working on campus in addition to taking extra credits during the summer. She had meant to tell him about the job last night, but he seemed distracted. "A bad headache," he said. That was what he always said. She had to get to the bottom of what was troubling him, shutting her out of part of his life. She guessed it involved his ex-wife and daughter. *Why won't he tell me?* she had asked herself innumerable times. She had tried asking Simone and Sophia. Simone clammed up, saying it was his story to tell; Sophia confided that Mitch came to Canada on a fake passport. In Lucy's view, that could only mean he was running away from something, someone. *His ex-wife? She isn't his ex-? Maybe that's it.* A more sinister thought had run through her mind: *the police ... mobsters?* Surely the Mitch she knew, or thought she knew, couldn't be involved in criminal activities.

Tonight! I have to tell him about the job tonight. She knew he would put obstacles in the way, as he had during their first dinner together in Toronto. The streetscape slipped past as the words she would use ran through her head again and again. As Lucy got to her feet, the child waved a hand. Lucy smiled and returned the wave.

At the liquor store, she bought a bottle of Mitch's favourite red wine, one they usually only drank on special occasions. *Hopefully, it will put him in a good mood.*

"I'm up here," he called as she closed the front door.

She dropped her briefcase in the hall and climbed the stairs. In the den, after planting a kiss on his forehead, she produced the bottle from behind her back. "De Da!"

"What are we celebrating?" he asked, taking her in his arms. "Have you had a pay rise? Promotion?" His eyes lit up in anticipation.

"No hope of that!" she shrugged as he followed her downstairs.

In the kitchen, she handed him the bottle and corkscrew and reached into the cupboard for two glasses. "That smells nice," she remarked, lifting the lid on the pot on the stove. "Goulash. Yumm."

"A peace offering for my bad mood last night," he said as he pulled the cork out of the bottle. "So, what are we celebrating?" The wine glugged in the neck of the bottle as he poured it into the glasses.

"To us," she said as they clinked glasses. She took a deep breath. "And my chance of another job."

"What job? You didn't mention a new job."

"I couldn't." She put down her glass and headed into the hallway. "It's only just been advertised." She retrieved the advertisement from her briefcase and held it against her chest for a few seconds before giving it to him.

As he read, his shoulders tensed. "You're not serious? Tell me …"

"I'm deadly serious," she interjected, startled at the assertiveness in her own voice.

He put the paper face down on the counter. "Lucy! We've been through this before. You can't get involved with these sort of people."

"I'm already involved. Or have you forgotten? I already know what it's like to look into a trafficker's eyes, see the evil there."

"But that's in a court room, with the weight of the law behind you. It's different out on the streets where those gangs operate."

"And how do you think those girls feel? Out there with no one looking out for them? Someone has to try."

Mitch heard his own voice in his head. *Someone has to take a stand. I can't sit by any longer and know all this is going on.* The words he said to his father when he showed him the papers bearing the names of the human traffickers operating in Leningrad. Sergei had raged: *So you're going to write your own death sentence, for the sake of people you don't know?*

Now, Mitch grabbed Lucy's arms and pinned them to her sides. "For God's sake, Lucy! Don't do this!"

"Let go! You're hurting me!" she yelled.

"You can't get involved. The people who traffic those girls are dangerous. They come after anyone who interferes." He choked back a sob. "Please. Don't do this. There will be other opportunities. Other jobs."

She struggled free and pushed him away. "Don't you ever do that again!" she yelled. "It might be okay in Russia, but not here!" She glared at him.

He ran the fingers of both hands through his hair. "I'm sorry. I didn't mean …" He turned his back on her, gripping the edge of the sink.

"I don't want other opportunities, as you so nicely put it." She picked up the job advertisement and held it in the air. "This is what I've always wanted. What I've worked for all these years. Professor Dobrescu thinks I have a good chance, and I'm not going to give it up just because you've got some stupid hang up."

He wheeled around and snapped, "It's not a stupid hang up!"

"What is it then? How can you expect me to understand if you won't tell me?"

"I've seen what happens to people. People who get in their way." He opened his mouth as if to say more, shook his head, strode into the hallway and grabbed his jacket off the hook. He turned to look at her for a moment. Then the front door slammed.

Lucy went into the sitting room and watched him heading up the road struggling to put on his jacket. *Damn you!* she cursed. She was fed up with all this secrecy, his headaches, the way he blew up over the slightest thing. *Why does he go off like that? Is there something in his make-up that makes him walk away every time he's in a tight spot? Is that what happened in Russia? With his wife? His child? Will he walk out on me too?*

In the kitchen, she gulped her wine, going over in her mind what he said: *'I've seen what happens to people. People who get in their way'. Has he been involved with traffickers? His daughter? Is that it? Surely she's too young, but they seem to be going after younger and younger girls. If it was his daughter, he wouldn't have left her there … would he?*

Sometime later, she stared out of the kitchen window. When they moved in just before Christmas, she had imagined the garden filled with spring flowers, she and Mitch sharing a drink after work, talking about what had happened during the day. *Will it ever be like that when I'm shut out of part of his life? We were so happy in those early days, like teenagers having illicit sex. Why has it changed?*

Maybe we should have waited, got to know each other better, she thought to herself as she went into the sitting room again and checked up and down the street. *What if he doesn't come back? He's already walked out on one woman, his child. What is it in his past that still haunts him? Something more than the disappearance of the sister of his friend.* She sank into an armchair.

An hour or so passed as she thought about him, their life together. Although she had had a couple of serious relationships, she had never really loved anyone before. She pictured the way his hair curled at the nape of his neck, how he had saved money to pay for a surprise weekend away for her birthday, of the times he appeared in the doorway of the den with a much-needed tray of coffee and cookies when she was floundering with research she was doing at home. *So why can't he be happy for me over this job?* Tears pricked the corners of her eyes. *I haven't even got it yet!*

She sat up in the chair. *Something's burning!* "The Goulash!" In the kitchen, she grabbed the pan off the stove and gazed at their dinner—now a burnt offering.

She had just finished scouring the pan when she heard his key in the lock. *If he's had too much to drink again…* she resolved, turning from the sink and drying her hands on a towel.

He stood in the doorway. "I'm so sorry, Lucy."

She held back for a moment before going to him. His arms locked around her as though he was hanging on for life. She felt a wetness on her face as tears coursed down his cheeks.

"Come and sit down," she said, guiding him into the sitting room. They sat on the sofa and, for several moments, neither spoke. "Mitch," Lucy began. "If we're going to stay together, be happy, you need to tell me. Tell me what happened in Russia. The real reason you don't want me to apply for this job."

She got to her feet, topped up their wine glasses, and put them on the coffee table. "Is it that bad?"

He pulled a handkerchief out of his pocket and blew his nose. "I don't know where to start," he croaked. "I'm so scared I'm going to lose you, something dreadful will happen to you. People around me seem to be cursed."

"Cursed?"

He shrugged. "Everything I touch goes wrong. Other people suffer because of my stupidity." He took a gulp of wine then ran a hand across his lips.

"I'm sure you're imagining it."

"Slava. He died because of me."

"What are you talking about?"

He leaned forward, an agonising expression on his face.

Lucy knelt before him, her hands resting on his knees. He stared at the floor. "You have to tell me, Mitch. Tell me what happened."

"It's such a mess." His voice was barely audible. He picked up his wine glass then put it back on the table. "I need something stronger." In the kitchen, he poured two glasses of Scotch. "You'll probably need this," he said, handing Lucy the smaller glass, where she was now sitting on the sofa.

She held her breath, twisting the glass around and around in her fingers, steeling herself to hear what he had done.

"The problems started when I was in law school," he began.

Lucy listened to his story, seeing herself in the young Mitch and feeling his frustration at not being able to help those less fortunate in the corrupt society of the former Soviet Union where money and influence count, where supposed justice can be bought. Her heart went out to him as he told her of the young man who sought Mitch and a friend's help in getting his young sister back from the brothel in Turkey where she was being held against her will. How the *vory v zakone* had murdered the young man and beaten up Mitch and his friend as a warning not to get involved. "You should have seen what they did to him. His head …"

"It's okay," she put an arm around him, not wanting to hear what he was finding hard to describe.

"Anja, she was very young. For her sake, I had to ignore what was going on. Do as I was told. Toe the Party line." He took a gulp of his drink. "Natasha, she was running up debts. I couldn't earn enough money. Couldn't risk losing my job."

"You could have left her. Taken Anja."

"It's not like it is here. There, the courts almost always give custody to the mother. I couldn't risk losing her. She was all I had."

Lucy struggled to find words, and it was some time before she asked, "So, what happened with Natasha? Why did you leave Russia?"

Mitch drained his glass then went into the kitchen and refilled it. "Natasha, she was having an affair." He flopped back onto the sofa. "One of the nastiest bastards you could ever imagine. *Vory!*"

Lucy's eyes widened.

"She let him near my Anja."

"They're with him?"

"That scum's dead!" he spat. "It's the only good thing that's come out of this."

"You didn't …?" Lucy hardly breathed.

Mitch shook his head. "Sometimes I wish I had!" There was hatred in his eyes.

"But you can go back there, see Anja. Bring her here."

"I'd need exit permits. Natasha's permission to take her out of the country."

"She can't stop you visiting your daughter."

"It would upset Anja. Unsettle her."

Silence followed his words. "So, you and Natasha, you got a divorce?" Lucy ventured.

"No. She …"

"You're still married!" Lucy gasped.

"No. No. She forged my signature on the divorce papers."

"Forged your signature? But surely you could have taken her to court, proved it wasn't your signature."

"She said that if I let it go she would let me see Anja. One day a week."

"You didn't agree?"

"What was I to do?" he shrugged. "The terms of settlement of the so-called divorce granted her sole custody of Anja. I was shut out of my daughter's life, not allowed to see her at all." His voice was now little more than a croak. "They said she … she preferred to live with Natasha. That's what they said."

"Oh, Mitch. I'm so sorry." She reached for one of his hands. "You could have appealed."

"It was complicated. Natasha, she said she would tell them …" He hesitated, pulled his hand away, then said quickly, "Anja. I couldn't put her through all the questioning. She would have been terrified."

"Wouldn't it have been better if you'd stayed in Russia? You could have seen Anja."

"I had to get out."

He went on to tell her how he risked everything to make public the names of the people running the human trafficking ring in Leningrad. "I'd already planned to go to England and hand the information to an investigative journalist who was writing an article about the girls and the men who controlled them. Then I found out who was heading the ring." He clenched both fists together. "It was him. Yagudin! Her lover!" He spat the words out.

"What happened? The article. Was it published?"

He nodded. "It was, but not in Russia. It was at the time of the coup when Gorbachev was kidnapped. There was a publication ban. I couldn't even get that right." He shook his head then reached out, picked up his glass and took a gulp. "Those bastards! They came after me. Planted a bomb under my car!" His hand shook as he lifted the glass to his lips again and drained it. "The bomb, it was meant for me. But they killed that poor old man, Slava!"

"Slava?" Lucy barely whispered.

"The caretaker at the building where we lived. What harm had that poor old man ever done?" Silence settled around them for a moment. "I can still hear his wife. She was searching the wreckage, calling his name." He covered his mouth and nose with his hand. "The smell of burnt flesh. It keeps coming back to me."

Bile rose in Lucy's throat.

"It should have been me." Mitch's eyes looked haunted as he turned to look at her. "So, now you see. People around me get hurt."

* * *

Later, Lucy looked at him asleep beside her in bed, his long eyelashes fanned out on the patches of dark skin under his eyes. *How has he lived with that? Bottled it up for so long? No wonder he is moody at times.* A lump came to her throat as she stared at him. *It took a lot of courage to do what he did and expose those evil people.* She gripped the bedclothes tight under her chin as Mitch's story ran through her head like a horror movie. But it wasn't a movie. It was real. *That poor old man was blown up. But surely that doesn't mean I should stop trying to help trafficked victims, ensure traffickers are punished. It's different here. Isn't it?* A vision came into her mind of the girl whose case she was dealing with. *I can't just abandon her and the others. There are so many out there. But what if someone dies because of something I do?* She thought of all the people she loved: *Mitch, Mom and Dad, Erin, Greg, Abigail my goddaughter ... friends. And why didn't he tell me before?* She stared at the shadows on the ceiling, remembering the way he had hesitated, looked away from her, as he explained why he hadn't contested the divorce. He had begun to say something. Something else.

25
Toronto
August 1995

On this balmy summer evening, Lucy and Mitch lingered over after-dinner drinks in the garden, glad of the cooling breeze after what had been a scorching day. The old building where Lucy now worked lacked air-conditioning, and several times in the past few days she had thought longingly of the cool office she previously occupied at the law firm on King Street.

Her thoughts drifted back to her final interview in the shabby building on Church Street where the NGO was based. After an hour of probing questions, she had barely contained her excitement. The job was hers. The sidewalk seemed to hum as she walked to the bus stop. She thought of calling Mitch, but knew his reaction to her news would rob her of joy. Instead, she headed to her parents' home. "That's wonderful, darling. Well done," her mother had said, giving Lucy a big hug. "Stay for supper," her father suggested as the three of them sipped celebratory glasses of slightly warm Prosecco. "Call Mitch. Tell him we're all eating here tonight. If he sees we're all behind you, he may come around."

Lucy had demurred and headed home. She was firm, telling Mitch the job was something she had to do: "I feel as you did when you made the decision to expose those people in Leningrad." She had braced herself, waiting for his outrage, but he pulled her into his arms and rocked to and fro as if comforting a baby. If she thought that was the beginning of a thaw, she was mistaken. Since then he had shown little interest in her work. He was still the Mitch she loved, but there was a barrier between them, one both were loath to cross.

Now, Lucy cleared their glasses off the table. "Have you ever taken drugs?" she asked.

"Not me. It's a fool's game." Mitch looked quizzically at her. "Did you?"

“No, but someone told me today that there’s a chronic shortage of hard drugs in the city,” she went on. “Traffickers have a virtual monopoly. They get their victims hooked on them and—”

“I thought we’d agreed,” he cut in. “We don’t talk about your job.”

“This isn’t about my job, it’s about yours.” Lucy paused while he lit a cigarette. “You need to watch for warning signs in your students, particularly the young women. Pimps mingle with youngsters, flirt with them, build emotional dependency, then get them hooked on drugs. And we know where they end up.”

Mitch stared at the cigarette between his fingers. “You never let it drop.”

Lucy sat back down at the table. “Look, Mitch. I’m not asking you to show any interest in my job, but surely part of your work is to watch for changes in behavioural patterns in your students, some of whom are away from home for the first time in their lives.”

“What sort of things?”

“Lack of concentration, not keeping up with course work, dropping out, self-harming, unexplained bruises, expensive jewellery.” When silence followed her words, Lucy sighed. “Have you listened to anything I’ve said?”

He took a long drag on his cigarette. “I’ll bring it up at the faculty meeting at the start of the next semester.”

Lucy got to her feet and squeezed his shoulder. “I’ll bring home some hand-outs.”

26
Village Near Omsk, Siberia
February 1996

"Anja … Anja."

"Mama?" Anja jerked forward in the chair. The book she was reading dropped to the floor. It was so long since her mother had called her by her real name. Everyone in the village now knew that Boris wasn't Anja's father, but Mama insisted she still use the name denoting her as his daughter. "What is it Mama?"

"I need to tell you …" Natasha tried to raise herself in the bed, but sank back.

"Should I get *Tyotya*?" Anja asked, getting up quickly.

Natasha shook her head. "I have to tell you," her breath came in laboured gasps, "before it's too late."

"No, Mama. You mustn't talk like that." Anja knelt at the side of her mother's bed. "The doctor said you just need to rest, then you will be well."

"What does that old man know?" Natasha reached out with one hand and stroked the side of her daughter's face with the tips of her fingers.

Anja blinked back tears. "You must get better, Mama."

"There is something," she took a noisy breath, "something I must tell you."

Anja leaned forward. Then she remembered *Tyotya's* words: *You mustn't tire her out, Yelena.* "Not now, Mama. You can tell me later, when you are feeling better."

Natasha closed her eyes and drifted back to sleep. "You have to get well, Mama," Anja whispered as she got to her feet. They were a family now, Mama, Boris, Anja, and little Timofei. *Tyotya* Yevdokia, too; she looked after Timofei while Mama and Boris were at work. That was before Mama was sick. Timofei was two-years-old now. He was there, in Mama's arms, when Anja rushed home from school on the day she became nine. "He isn't very pretty," she said when she looked at the baby's wrinkled face. Her mother had laughed, telling her that boys weren't supposed to be pretty. "Give him time, Yelena. He'll fill out, you'll see." She patted the bed for Anja to sit down. "Never forget, *moi galubchik.* You were my first born. No one can ever take your place." She tucked a lock of Anja's hair behind an ear, then placed Timofei in her daughter's arms. Anja stiffened, scared she would drop him. After a few minutes, Natasha reached out and took the baby, saying, "*Tyotya* has made you a cake. Go and see." At the doorway, Anja had turned and asked if there was a cake for Timofei too. Her mother shook her head. "He can share mine," Anja said and ran through to the kitchen.

Now, Anja walked across the room to the little bed where Timofei slept. She picked up the rag doll—the one that used to belong to her. She sniffed; the old odour of wood mingled with the sweet smell of her brother. She stroked the place where the doll's eyebrow used to be. Timofei had picked out what was left of the wool and had now started on the other eyebrow. *I'll ask Tyotya if she has any black wool so that we can mend the doll.*

She looked out of the window at the log pile in front of the shed. The log pile Boris said needed replenishing if they were to get through the rest of the winter. The doctor said they must keep Mama warm, feed her nourishing soups, and then when sunshine warms the land, she will begin to get better. They could all have a picnic again in the gardens in Omsk; Mama loved the flowers and fountains there. And Boris promised to take them to the Theatre of Young Spectators. The puppets are Anja's favourites. This time, Timofei will be able to go. *I'll take him on the stage to wave around big butterflies on sticks with the other children. That will be fun. Mama can wear the pretty dress Boris bought her when they went into the city before Christmas. Before the cough came.*

She tiptoed to her mother's bed. Apart from the funny noise which came with each breath, she was sleeping peacefully. Boris had taken Timofei to visit his relatives in Omsk but, if she left the bedroom door open, *Tyotya* and her friend Dotnara would hear if Mama called or started to cough.

"Don't go too far, and be sure to be back before it's dark," *Tyotya* cautioned as Anja wrapped a thick scarf around her head, buttoned her coat and put on boots and gloves.

Outside, she hurried around the side of the house and pulled the sledge out of the shed. The wind had got up, whipping loose flakes of snow into her face. She paused outside her mother's bedroom window, listening. Then she trudged towards the forest, saying the prayer she said many times a day now, sometimes in front of the *krasnyy ugol* when no one was around. The saint still wore his mournful expression, but Anja hoped one day he would smile and Mama would get well. Her prayers used to be for her real Papa—the one she hadn't seen for a long time. She still thought about him, but maybe it was better if he didn't come to find her now. One day soon after Mama got sick, she had cried when Anja asked about her real Papa. Anja hadn't meant to; it just came out.

She shivered as she walked along the path into the forest. It was quiet here, and she peered around checking the *leshii* wasn't waiting to jump out from behind a tree. The *leshii* was the master of the forest and wild animals. Anja had heard he sometimes looked like a big white wolf and carried off young girls and women. One day she asked Mama if the *leshii* had taken Dina, Alyona's missing daughter. Mama shook her head saying, "The *leshii* that took Dina was an evil human being, not of the spirit world."

Now, Anja prised a log out from under the snow and put it on the sledge, remembering how she and Mama laughed when they collected wood together on the way home from the bakery. They would balance the basket containing bread on top of the logs and drag the sledge home, singing all the way. The thought cheered her. *When Mama's well, I will take Timofei to meet her at the bakery. He can collect little sticks for the fire. We'll have to sing one of the songs Timofei knows. He sometimes gets all the words muddled up, but his voice is sweet.* Mama said that, with his blond hair, he must have been an angel in another life. Anja clutched a log to her chest, wondering why she had never seen a picture of an angel with brown hair like hers. She would ask *Tyotya* when she got home. *Tyotya* knew everything about matters of religion, or so Boris said. *Just one brown-haired angel would be nice.* The wind howled through the trees as she dropped the last log on top of the pile on the sledge. She picked up the rope and pulled the sledge back along the path in the gathering dusk.

27
Western Siberia
March 1996

Frost crackled in the light filtering through the pine trees. The rhythm of saws on wood sang in the air. Sergei straightened up, stretching aching limbs. He pulled his hat further down over his frozen ears, and tried not to sway; the dizziness was always with him now. Pavel sawed the end off a log and threw it onto Sergei's small heap. *"Prodolzhay, moi drug,"* he urged. "You can't collapse out here. They'll leave you where you drop."

Sergei took up his saw again and locked its teeth into the bark of the felled tree. As he worked, his mind drifted to winter days long past. Days when Sophia would kiss him goodbye as he left for work. In the icy courtyard, he would look up to see her face at the window. He would think of her smile as he worked on a defence for one client or another—a defence that couldn't be seen as anti-Soviet. He had lived that charade for the sake of his beloved wife and son. *Why didn't I take them away to somewhere we could all have happier, less restricted lives, where Sophia could be true to the traditions and beliefs of her religion?* He had asked himself this many times during the past few years. *Now, they've both* gone, he sighed, as he stared into the light between the trees. On brighter days, he sometimes saw Sophia's face looking down on him, smiling, urging him to stay strong. Today, his head was whirling. He dropped his saw and gripped the felled tree trunk with both hands, steadying himself.

"Prodolzhay," Pavel urged again, not pausing in his own work.

And so another morning passed and an afternoon began in this sleeping land of trees.

As Sergei worked, his head became more muddled. He wondered if his previous life had been a dream. Maybe he had always lived like this and Sophia and Mitch were part of an imagined world to which he escaped to leave this harsh place. For a few minutes, he concentrated on the noise of the saw, watched the dust from the wood accumulate on the ice-encrusted snow covering the forest floor. Another sound intruded. A voice. Not one he recognised. He straightened up and looked around. The words of a new prisoner drifted towards him: "Damn Jews! You can't trust any of them!" Sergei dropped his saw. "There's more and more of them. Every day. More and more on the streets." Sergei picked up his axe. "They've even been allowed to publish the Talmud in Russian!" Sergei lurched towards the man yelling, "*Zatknis'! Zatknis'!*" Pavel dropped his own saw and ran after his friend, grabbed his arm and wrested the axe from his raised hand.

"You must stay calm, take no notice of people like that," Pavel urged as he pulled Sergei away. "Feel sorry for them. They don't know any better."

Sergei caught his breath. "How can I feel sorry for them when they insult my Sophia? Jakob?" A vision of Jakob's body dangling from the tree came into his head. He saw it clearly. It was hanging over Sophia's grave. *How can that be?*

"You must ignore them. Block them out. They're scum, not worth thinking about."

A guard approached, cigarette dangling from his mouth. *"Vozvrashchaysya k rabote,"* he growled, levelling his gun at them.

Pavel handed Sergei his saw. "You must calm down. They'll put you in that freezing hole in the ground."

Sergei stared at him with unseeing eyes.

28
Village Near Omsk, Siberia
March 1996

Anja hurried down the steps of the school building and picked her way between the frozen ruts in the road, eager to get home. Mama had sat up in bed this morning, eaten a bowl of *kasha*, and said she felt much better. *Maybe this afternoon she will get up and eat some of the chocolate Boris brought home last week.* It was Mama's favourite and he hoped it would tempt her to eat. The chocolate was untouched until Anja stole a piece. It stuck in her throat and she spat it into her handkerchief, avoiding the reproachful look the saint in the *krasnyy ugol* shot her way. Boris was happy when he saw some of the chocolate was missing. "*Lyubov' maya.* You are eating again. You will soon be well." Mama had looked at Anja, a faint smile lifting the corners of her mouth. To *Tyotya* Yevdokia, Anja blamed the loss of the chocolate on the *domovoi*, the spirit who lived in the house and played tricks on people when they were lazy. "The *domovoi* … she stole some oats before, so this time she must have fancied chocolate. She tangled my needlework too." *Tyotya* laughed, saying that God forgives children's sins. "As long as they learn from them!" Anja felt sick.

She made many promises to God, and to St Vladimir in his church in the village. "If you will please make Mama well again, I will never steal chocolate, say nasty things to Stepan at school, hide Timofei's toys, or tell lies." And she would go to the church with *Tyotya* every day, not just on the Sabbath; this never happened as by the time she had run to the bakery to pick up bread, and gathered logs on the way home, it was time for school. But now God and St Vladimir had answered her prayers. She skipped along the path.

She waved a gloved hand to Mama's friend, Alyona Gavrilova, who was hurrying along the street towards her. She wondered if Alyona's daughter, Dina, had come home yet. One day, Alyona told Mama she thought they would never see Dina again. "If only I knew she was okay, nobody had hurt her. My brother in Omsk, he went to the employment agency that arranged the job. They said she only stayed there two weeks, then she left. She could be anywhere by now. Turkey? Greece?" Alyona had sobbed. "The girls from the other villages too. No one has heard from any of them." Mama had put her arms around her friend.

Now, Alyona called to Anja as she drew level: "Yelena! Boris … he said you were to come home with me. Just for an hour or so."

"But I have to see how Mama is."

"There is someone at the house with them."

Anja thought Alyona's voice sounded funny. Her eyes were red too. *Maybe she's been crying over Dina again. Mama says she does that a lot.* "Timofei. I always play with him when I get home."

"Timofei is at my house. Dotnara is waiting with him until we get there." Anja looked towards her own home at the end of the street.

"I've made a pot of *Solyanka,*" Alyona tempted. "There's *Syrniki* too … with honey." She rested a hand on Anja's shoulder. "Let's get inside. It's too cold to stand here."

Half an hour or so later, Alyona watched Anja and Timofei mopping the last of the honey from their plates. She choked back tears as she ran a damp cloth around Timofei's mouth. *He is so young. And Anja? How will Boris find the words to tell them?*

Anja licked honey from her fingers. "Can we go home now?" she asked, getting up quickly and tucking her chair under the table.

"Not just yet. Why don't you and Timofei play a game? You could …" Alyona stopped. What was she thinking, asking these two dear children to play a game when their mother has just died? They would never forgive her.

"It's useless playing with him," Anja pouted, flopped down on the rug and threw the cat's toy mouse across the room. The cat scampered after it, closely followed by Timofei.

A shiver ran through Alyona as she imagined the scene in Yevdokia's house. The still body of her friend lying on the bed. The priest was there, giving what comfort he could. This morning, Natasha had seemed so well, but the dying often get strength from somewhere before they go. That's what the old women in the village say. At lunchtime, Yevdokia had come to the place where Alyona worked and told her Natasha was asking for her. "She's coughing up blood. Shivering. We can't keep her warm."

When she got to her friend's bedside, she was shocked at the change in just a few hours. Natasha's eyes were sunken into black holes and her body seemed to have shrunk. "I want you to promise …" Natasha croaked. Alyona leaned closer. "You must promise you will be there for my Anja. Be the mother I can no longer be," Natasha wheezed. Alyona thought she would choke with the ache in her throat as she struggled to tell her friend that she, Natasha, would be there to see Anja grow up. Natasha fluttered a hand in dismissal.

"There is a letter. I wrote it this morning. Promise you will give it to her … on her sixteenth birthday." Natasha lay back on her pillows for several moments, her mouth working trying to force words out. "It has to be then, when she is old enough to understand." She gripped Alyona's hand. "Tell her not to judge me too harshly."

Now, Alyona heard footsteps on the porch. The door opened. Boris came in. His face ashen. Timofei ran towards him. He picked up his son and buried his face in the child.

Anja scrambled to her feet. "Mama? Can we go home to see her now?" Alyona gathered her friend's beloved daughter into her arms.

* * *

Three Days Later

Anja pulled a blanket off her bed, folded it in half and half again, tucked it under her arm, and ran across the kitchen into her mother's bedroom. Timofei was sitting on the floor, rolling his toy tractor up and down an imaginary field. "What you doing, Anja?" he asked, scrambling to his feet.

"I'm going to put this over Mama to keep her warm. She hates to be cold," Anja explained, carefully draping the blanket over her mother's body in the coffin where it rested on a table. Only her face now showed.

"Can I give her this?" Timofei picked up the rag doll. "She'll need toys." Anja lifted him up and he put the doll down the side of the blanket. Anja didn't think Mama would mind the smell. *Tyotya said nothing can harm her now she is living in Heaven.*

The door opened and Boris came in. He nodded his head knowingly when he saw the blanket covering Natasha. "Why don't you two go and put on your coats? The priest and the men will be here soon to take Mama to the church."

"Can't we keep her here a little longer?" Anja's voice was small. "Just one more day?" Boris put a hand on her shoulder, then walked over to the bed and sat down. He leaned forward, hands covering his face, his body wracked with sobs. Timofei tried to look into his father's face; Anja hovered behind her brother. *"Prastite! Prastite!"* Boris murmured after a few moments. Then he took a handkerchief out of his jacket pocket, wiped his eyes, and pulled Anja and Timofei into his arms. "Your Mama, she was so proud of you both. Her two precious angels, she called you."

"Will she have new children up there?" Anja asked, her head tilting upwards.

"*Nyet.* You and Timofei are her special children. She doesn't want any others."

None of them heard *Tyotya* enter the room. "God has asked two angels," she began, "one with brown hair and one blond, to look after Mama in her home in Heaven." *Tyotya* dabbed her eyes with the edge of her apron. "The priest is here, Boris. I'll help the children with their coats and boots." She held her hands out to Anja and Timofei.

A few minutes later, Anja, Boris, and Timofei, followed the four men carrying Natasha's coffin down the steps of the porch, where they carefully lowered the coffin on to the waiting sledge. The priest held a gold cross aloft and walked in front of the procession. Boris, Anja, and Timofei, walked close behind him. Anja threw flowers from a basket as they made their way through the village. They weren't real flowers, but they looked nice. *Mama would like the pink petals.* The streets were quiet; most of the inhabitants followed the procession. As she walked, Anja wished her real Papa was here. *He wouldn't have let Mama die.* She brushed tears away with the back of a glove, thinking she must have done something really bad because everyone she loved died or went away. First there was Babushka Sophia, then Papa, and now Mama. She didn't even know where her other grandparents were. But Anja wished more than anything that Mama was here, walking beside her.

Inside the church, they lit candles from the one the priest now held. Timofei waved his around in the air, and Boris grabbed it and handed it to *Tyotya.* Anja stared at her mother's coffin which rested on a table in front of them. Someone had pulled the blanket back and put a cross into her hands. At the side of the coffin was a smaller table, on top of which was a bowl; *Tyotya* had told her this was the *Kolyva,* the traditional memorial dish of wheat and honey. Anja was glad there was food for Mama—she always liked the *kutya* they had on Christmas

Eve. She started to sob as she thought about Christmas Eve without Mama. *Tyotya* put an arm around Anja's shoulders, and murmured, *"Eto vse budet v poryadke. Eto vse budet v poryadke."* Then the Psalm began. Anja didn't know the words, but *Tyotya* had told her it was the longest Psalm in the Bible. "It will take you half your lifetime to learn it."

Anja's eyes followed a stream of smoke from the censer as it twirled to the roof. She could just make out the paintings around the sides. One day she came here with Mama and some of the other women when they cleaned the church and arranged flowers for a wedding. Mama pointed out the paintings of saints far above, one on each section of the eight-sided roof. During the time of the troubles, the villagers hid the icons in the roofs of their houses. As Anja watched now, the smoke seemed to form into a shape. It looked like a face. Strands wafted around, streaming down either side of the face. She hardly dared breathe. *It's Mama! Mama! She's trying to tell me something.* Anja shifted her gaze to the coffin in front of where she stood. Mama's body was still there. *How can she be so high up in the roof?* She glanced at Boris, *Tyotya*, Dotnara, and Alyona, to see if they had noticed Mama's face hovering above. Their heads were bowed in prayer. When Anja looked up to the roof again, smoke swirled and twisted, but the face had gone.

The rest of the service passed in a blur, as Anja wondered what Mama had been trying to tell her. A few days ago, she said that wherever Anja was in the world, she would always watch over her, make sure she was safe. "Like angels do?" Anja had asked. Mama smiled and told her it would be like having an angel floating above her, keeping her from harm. "Timofei too?" Mama had nodded, her eyes filling with tears. Now, Anja looked down at her brother. He was sitting on the floor playing with the miniature car he insisted on bringing.

"The Prayer of Absolution," *Tyotya* whispered as the priest began to read from a paper.

Then he carefully rolled up the paper and placed it under the cross in Mama's hands.

"Vechnaya ... Pamyat," the choir sang slowly, softly at first. This was the time to give Mama a final kiss. Boris handed his candle to the priest, leaned forward then lifted Timofei. Anja swallowed hard. The voices got louder. She blinked back tears as her candle cast a golden light on her mother's face. *She looks as though she is sleeping peacefully,* Anja thought, then with one hand carefully lifted the edge of the blanket and drew it up under her mother's chin.

When she kissed her forehead, it was as cold as the icicles which hung from the roof in winter. Anja turned and buried her face in *Tyotya's* bosom.

* * *

Six Days Later

Anja stood by her mother's bed and stared hard, hoping she could somehow magic her back to life. She would be beautiful, as she was before she was sick, wearing her white nightdress, the one with embroidery around the neck. *Tyotya* had said, "Sometimes miracles happen, but not this time." Anja stroked the bedcover, listening to *Tyotya*, Dotnara, and Alyona, talking in the kitchen. Yesterday, Alyona had asked whether there was anyone they should try to contact, but Boris shook his head, saying he would handle it when the time was right. "Until then, I'll take care of the children … both of them."

Today they would go to the cemetery again for the *Panikhida* ceremony. Anja had chosen a special tablecloth to spread on Mama's grave, on top of which they would cut bread and sausage. The grown-ups would drink from the bottle Boris had packed in the basket. There were glasses there too. He said the vodka was especially strong—they would need something to warm them. For Anja and Timofei, *Tyotya* had made a special honey drink, the one she usually gave them when they had a cold or chill.

Today, Mama's soul had reached the Throne of God, or so *Tyotya* said, and God would pass judgement on her soul. "There was nothing wrong with her soul," Boris had countered. "She was a good person, a good wife, a good mother." He lifted Timofei onto his lap, patted the seat next to him for Anja to sit on, telling them that if they were only half as good as their mother, they would be fine.

Anja didn't know if she believed in the religious stuff anymore. *If there really is a God and Saints, why didn't they do what I asked and make Mama better? Tyotya* said that it was God's way of testing your faith. But today Anja would go to her mother's grave. *Just in case Mama's soul needs to be saved.*

29
Toronto
Late January 1997

The metal chair creaked as Mitch leaned forward. He gripped his knees and stared, unseeing, at the grey-flecked floor tiles in the waiting room. Words ran through his head—*Lucy. The babies. They'll be okay. They'll be okay*—over and over.

He straightened up, the noises in the corridor a backdrop to his thoughts as his mind went over the past few months. At first, when Lucy told him she was expecting a baby, panic washed through him. He feigned joy. How could he be responsible for another human being when he had failed so badly the child he already had? He felt as though an alien presence had invaded their lives, one which would spoil their new-found happiness. That feeling changed the day they saw the scan of not one but two babies. Mitch's heart went out to the tiny curled-up bodies, the heads, the limbs. He still felt daunted by what was ahead but overlying it all was a feeling of love tinged with a new sense of purpose. He may have failed one child, but these babies would be different, enhancing the love he and Lucy shared. *One day we will all be a family ... with Anja.* As he had stared at the babies' blurry images, he wished they could stay like that forever, safely locked in their warm, watery cocoon, untouched by the harshness of the outside world. But whatever misfortunes befell them, he would be there for them, of this he was sure. He and Lucy decided they didn't want to know the sex of the babies. While he agreed with Lucy that knowing would spoil the sense of anticipation, his real reason was selfish. He didn't want to expose himself to months of anguish as, if one or both were girls, he would always imagine the young Anja in their faces. He would deal with that if it came to it. As time went on, though, he wondered if it would be better to know, give himself time to come to terms with another daughter or daughters.

Lucy had found it more and more difficult to cope with her normal busy schedule, some days scarcely able to drag her swollen body to the streetcar stop. A month ago, she reluctantly agreed to take an extended leave of absence from her job. Mitch secretly hoped she would decide not to go back to the charity—he didn't mind her working, but not at that place.

They planned for Mitch to be present at the birth, and today he gripped her hands and offered words of encouragement as she writhed with each contraction. He was sure he felt her pain himself. It had gone well at first. Then everything stalled. "The babies, they're showing signs of distress," the doctor said. In a flurry of activity, they rushed Lucy into surgery. Mitch ran behind calling her name and telling her he loved her. The swing doors swooshed back and forth in the wake of the gown-clad procession. His voice echoed back as the doors settled into place.

Now, he swallowed hard. *Please God. Keep her safe. I'll do anything,* he promised. *Perhaps I should go down on my hands and knees, prostrate myself?* His father's words from long ago came back to him. It was the first time they entered a Russian Orthodox Church together. The young Mitch had watched the ebb and flow of people, some prostrating themselves in front of the icons. He had tried to wriggle free of his father's grip, saying it would be fun to lie on the floor. "*Nyet.* You don't need to do that, Mitch. As long as your prayers are sincere, God will hear you wherever you are. Be honest with God and he will answer." Over the years, Mitch had made many bargains with God … in vain. *You were wrong, Papa,* he thought now. *I've been honest, but He never answers my prayers. He never sent my Anja back to me. She hasn't even answered my letters.* The worst part was he could no longer imagine what she looked like. She was twelve now, but there was a void where his beloved daughter should be.

He checked his watch, watching seconds tick past. *It's over an hour now since they took her. There must be some news.* A shadow passed the other side of the reeded glass; it moved on.

His shoulders slumped. *God, don't do this to me. Don't let anything happen to her, I beg you ... please.* His forehead and hands were running with sweat, and he pulled a handkerchief out of his jacket pocket and dabbed at his forehead. Tears pricked his eyes as he looked at the handkerchief, still folded in the neat square into which Lucy had ironed it.

After a few minutes, he got up, paced up and down the corridor then went purposefully into the ward. *Someone must know something.* He heard voices, saw feet clad in sensible black shoes—all behind curtains. He retraced his steps back into the corridor, retrieved a quarter out of his jacket pocket and walked towards the telephone alongside the elevators. He would call Lucy's parents. They would be anxious for news. He had to talk to someone.

"Mr Galichin?"

He spun around. A nurse beckoned from a doorway. Her face lit into a smile as he approached. "They've just called from downstairs. You have a son and a daughter."

Mitch stared at her for a moment, mouth open, eyes wide. "Lucy? My wife? My partner?" He scarcely breathed the words.

"She's okay. They're keeping her downstairs for a while until she's recovered properly."

"But she's okay?"

The nurse smiled and nodded her head.

"The babies?"

"They're taking them to the neonatal unit." Seeing the look of alarm on Mitch's face, she touched his arm gently. "It's standard procedure for twins. They're often a little underweight but, with a bit of care in the first few hours, they'll be fine." When Mitch didn't respond, she went on encouragingly: "You can see them, hold them, just the same."

Mitch uncurled his fingers and stared at the quarter which he had been clutching in his fist. "Her parents. I should call them."

"Come back when you've done that and I'll have someone take you to see your son and daughter."

Fifteen minutes later, Mitch looked through the window of the dimly lit neonatal unit. He scanned the array of Perspex cribs, or were they incubators? *Which ones are mine, mine and Lucy's?* He had thought he would know instinctively which babies were theirs but, as far as he could see, they all looked more or less the same. Most had an array of tubes, some more than others. He followed the orderly into a small room with a washbasin and scrubbed his hands until they were raw. After donning the proffered gown and mask, he stepped hesitantly into the room.

The orderly approached a nurse and gestured in Mitch's direction before disappearing back into the corridor.

"Mr Galichin. Congratulations. You have two beautiful babies." Mitch fumbled with the gloves the nurse handed him. His legs felt as if they would give way as he walked behind the pink-clad figure. "The doctor's checked them over. Your son … he has a bit of a breathing problem, but we're giving him oxygen to help," she leaned over an incubator, "and that should sort itself out in a couple of days."

Mitch stared through the Perspex at his new-born son. Tears welled and he swallowed hard trying to get rid of the lump in his throat as he looked at the tubes going into the tiny nostrils, the band-aid across one cheek, the knitted hat on his head. The nurse turned to the adjacent crib. "This little lady's doing fine," she said, putting her hands through two holes in the side of his daughter's incubator. "You can touch her," she urged, stroking the side of the baby's face with a glove-clad finger. She moved out of the way and Mitch stepped closer. His trembling hand hovered over his daughter. "It's always difficult, a bit overwhelming especially with two of them." The nurse glanced at the other crib. "They're your first?"

"No. I have a daughter … another daughter." The words caught in his throat as he stroked his new daughter's arm. Her face screwed up and he pulled his hands away.

"You can bring her in tomorrow to see her new brother and sister."

Mitch didn't trust himself to speak. He closed his eyes for a moment and, when he looked again, his new daughter's face was blurred. It was like the clock had been put back. He was looking at Anja. Anja, the tiny baby who had grown into the sweet, innocent child. The child he left behind on that street in Leningrad.

"Tomorrow, you'll be able to hold them."

Mitch's body started to shake. Sobs rose in his throat.

The nurse guided Mitch to a chair against the wall. "It's always a bit of a shock seeing babies like this," she said. Her words mingled with the beep of machines.

Several minutes later, he looked again at his daughter. Realisation set in. *She doesn't look a bit like baby Anja.* He couldn't really tell who she resembled. *What does it matter? She's here safely and Lucy and I will look after her and her brother.*

The nurse was now repositioning his son in his incubator. The baby wriggled. Mitch smiled a weak smile and stepped back, looking first at his daughter, then his son, marvelling at the pure innocence with which they arrived in the world. *I must have been like that once.* He thought of what his mother had told him about his birth. It was hard for her, a single mother, estranged from her family because she loved, and bore the child of, not only a Russian but a man who wasn't of their strict Hasidic faith. "If only you could see these two, Maman," he whispered. She and his father would have been so proud of these grandchildren, just as they were proud of Anja. And Lucy … she was the daughter-in-law they had always wanted. Then he remembered: *Lucy isn't your wife.*

Later, he sat on the side of Lucy's bed and leaned towards her. Her eyes were closed and there were grey smudges beneath where her eyelashes lay on her cheeks. The nurse said she would be drowsy for a few hours. Mitch gazed at this woman whom he loved, who was more of a wife to him than Natasha had ever been. When Lucy and the babies were safely at home, he would make plans, surprise her with a ring, set a date for their wedding. *If she'll have me.* He had been so obsessed with thinking of Anja, he hadn't appreciated what he had right here. Anja would come later, but now Lucy and their children—their daughter and son—came first.

He felt Lucy's hand on his. She squeezed it gently.

"You okay?" he asked, taking both her hands in his.

"You do like them?" she said in a voice hoarse from the anaesthetic.

"Like them? I love them!" He leaned further forward and kissed her gently on the lips. "How could I not like them?" he laughed softly. "They're beautiful. Our babies are beautiful."

"It doesn't mean you will love her any less … Anja. You can still love her."

As Lucy drifted back to sleep, Mitch lifted her hands to his lips and kissed them.

30
Toronto
Early February 1997

Mitch was up before daylight seeped through, and cleaned the house until it shone. There wasn't a stray newspaper or book to be seen anywhere; no socks or underwear adorned the floor around the laundry hamper. *Lucy will think she's in the wrong house,* he chuckled to himself, trying to settle the quivers in his stomach at the thought that this afternoon he would be bringing Lucy and their daughter, Mariya Sophia (who was to be known as Masha) home. Her brother, Ivor Patrick (or Ivo as they called him), would remain in neonatal care for another week or so until his breathing settled. Both babies were feeding greedily from Lucy, so that was a good sign. A couple of days ago, Mitch had lingered outside the window of the neonatal unit, overcome with love as he watched Lucy feeding Masha. A wave of resentment ran through him as he thought back to Natasha's refusal to feed Anja herself.

This morning, Lucy's mother, Susan, was suitably impressed when at ten o'clock she arrived at the house with the intention of sprucing the place up before her daughter and grandchild arrived home. Mitch left her to put the final touches to the kitchen while he dashed out to buy a bunch of the long-stemmed orange roses Lucy loved. He grabbed two coffees from Second Cup on his way back to his car—or Lucy's parents' car to be precise. That was something they had to sort out as a matter of urgency. They had managed with public transport, or borrowing a car, but now a car was a necessity. He placed the roses carefully on the front passenger seat and put the coffees into the cup holders before casting a satisfied gaze at the two car seats in the back; the seats he had fitted himself and which would keep both babies safe.

Fifteen minutes later, the roses were resplendent in the tall crystal vase Lucy's parents gave them last Christmas. Mitch and Susan sat either side of the kitchen table enjoying their coffees and some of the home-made oatmeal raisin cookies Susan brought with her. "You'd better make the most of these last few hours of peace and quiet," she murmured.

Mitch looked across the table at her, his hand reaching for another cookie. *It's like looking at an older version of Lucy,* he thought, not for the first time. Lucy and her mother shared the same riveting turquoise eyes and flaxen hair—the colour of Susan's hair might be helped along a bit here and there, but Mitch wasn't an expert on that sort of thing. And what did it matter? He felt close to this warm-hearted woman. So different from his feelings for Lena, Natasha's mother. Time after time her barbed comments had wounded him, until eventually he was filled with hatred for her, her husband, and the lavish lifestyle they led. The pity he felt for them after Natasha and Anja disappeared, had long since changed to apathy. When he learnt of Lena and Lyosha's deaths, he felt nothing. The words in the letter from Vera Kishinevskaya seemed as though they were about people he had never met. Strangers. He worried that he had become incapable of feeling any emotion. But then he fell in love with Lucy. And now the twins. They were the first grandchildren for Susan and Donald Bowen, and their arrival was an enormous event for the whole family.

From the moment Mitch first met Lucy's parents, he felt at ease in their presence. Although Donald earned a comfortable living as an Orthodontist, they weren't materialistic. People mattered more to them than possessions. Mitch couldn't help thinking how well they would have got on with his own parents. If only he had met Lucy years ago; but then she would have been too young to be interested in anyone as old as him. *No sense wishing. You have her now ... and our babies.* A ripple of contentment ran through him.

"Susan?" He looked across at the woman he liked to think of as his mother-in-law.

"I was looking at the garden, imagining the twins … sorry, Ivo and Masha," she raised her eyebrows at him, "we'd better get used to using their names or we'll be in big trouble with Lucy, won't we?" She got to her feet and picked up their empty coffee containers. "I was picturing them playing in the garden in the summer. Not this summer, but the next and the ones after that."

"I don't think it will be this garden," Mitch cautioned, as he joined her by the window.

"You're not thinking of moving away are you, Mitch?" A frown creased her forehead.

"Of course not. We wouldn't do that to you. And besides," he laughed, "we need babysitters!"

She gave him a playful dig with an elbow.

"We need more space than we have here." He picked up the plate of cookies and followed her through to the kitchen. "It'll have to be in another part of the city, somewhere cheaper than around here, where we can get a decent-sized house to take all the babies' paraphernalia." He stuffed another cookie into his mouth before putting the plate on the counter.

"We'll always help you with money, Mitch. You only have to say." Susan opened the cupboard under the sink and dropped the coffee containers into the bin.

"Thanks. I really appreciate that." The words seemed inadequate to his own ears. How could he express his appreciation for the quiet support the Bowen family had given him. When he and Lucy first got together, he asked her to explain his circumstances to her parents—at least as much of his circumstances as he had told her. Donald and Susan hadn't pried or asked questions; questions which in those early days might have cracked his fragile state of mind. Even since they heard the news they were to be grandparents, they hadn't once hinted, at least to Mitch, that maybe they should get married. They had supported Lucy in her decision to change her name to his. "It will be easier, especially for the children."

On the day the twins were born, Mitch had gone to their home for a late dinner. They insisted he stay the night, just as his parents had when Anja was born. After a couple of celebratory glasses of wine, Susan went to bed, leaving the two men to enjoy a nightcap. "You know, we really admire what you did there, in Russia," Donald had ventured.

"There's not much to admire in getting an innocent person killed!" Mitch sighed loudly.

"That wasn't your fault. You have to forgive yourself. That's the first thing. If not, it'll destroy you … and Lucy." There was silence between them for a few moments. "You and Lucy have a special relationship. And two beautiful babies." Donald's face broke into a huge grin.

"You haven't seen them yet," Mitch laughed, then took a swig from his glass.

"You've got a bright future. You both have good jobs and …"

"It's Lucy's job that worries me."

"I can see why you were against her doing this job, Mitch. But what she's doing is quite different from what you did."

"It's still dangerous to get involved. And what if …?"

"You can't spend your life thinking like that," Donald cut in. "It's the future that's important now. Hope for the future is all we have. All we need. Any of us."

In bed that night, Mitch had looked around the room that was Lucy's room when she lived here, the room he shared with her a few times. It felt empty now without her warm body to snuggle up to. As he watched shadows flicker across the ceiling, he thought of her and their babies. When he left the hospital, she was sitting up in bed, pillows propped behind her. Her cheeks were flushed, but she said it was just the excitement of the day. He held her tight as he kissed her goodnight. So tight she winced, saying her breasts were painful. He laughed softly, reminding her of how, when they first made love, she apologised that she hardly had any breasts to speak of. "Things have certainly improved since then," he chuckled.

"Be off with you now, Mr Galichin," a nurse had chided good naturedly in her broad Irish brogue. "Your wife needs a good sleep after the day she's had, to be sure."

Now, Mitch watched as Susan put the cookies back in the tin. He checked his watch.

"How about going out for a civilised lunch? There's just about time before I'm due at the hospital."

31
Toronto
February 1997

Mitch hurried along the sidewalk. He had managed to get away from work early, anxious to take over from Lucy with the twins; she badly needed to rest. They both did, but at least he got some respite, even if it was falling asleep on the subway on his way to the university. *I'll make her a cup of tea, and insist she has a nap. If Masha and Ivo sleep too, I'll call Vera in St Petersburg.* He hadn't yet told her of the birth of the twins. *When did I last call her? Did I tell her Lucy was pregnant?* He couldn't remember. *And Anja? When was the last time I asked about her?* A wave of guilt engulfed him.

Some hours later, he tiptoed out of the nursery, leaving the door ajar so that he would hear if the twins awoke. In the bedroom, Lucy was sound asleep. He picked up the mug which held her now-cold tea, closed the door and went silently down the stairs.

He poured himself a drink, sank down into an armchair by the fire and dialled Vera's number, listening for what seemed an age to the once-familiar tinny sound of the ringtone. He looked at his watch. "Christ! It's nearly midnight there!" he muttered, debating whether to end the call. By now, he must have woken them all up in the apartment. "Vera?"

"Ona zdes'. Kto eto?"

"Mitch. Mitch Galichin."

There was a long pause before Vera came on the line. "Mitch? *Chto nay thuk?"*

"There's nothing wrong. I'm sorry to call so late. I'd forgotten what time it is there," Mitch explained before telling her of the arrival of the twins. "They're nearly a month old now. A girl and a boy."

"I'm so pleased for you. You and ..."

"Lucy. Her name's Lucy. And we've called the twins Ivor Patrick and Mariya Sophia."

"Sophia, your mother's name. She would have been so pleased."

Mitch swallowed hard.

"Is there any news of Anja?" His words were met with silence. "Vera? Are you still there?"

"I'm still here."

"What's wrong?"

"There's something … something I should have told you."

"What is it? … Anja? Is she okay?"

"Anja's fine. Natasha! Natasha died!" Vera blurted.

"Died? She can't have." Mitch took a gulp of his drink. "When? When was this?"

"Last winter." Vera's voice was barely audible.

"Last winter, and you're only telling me now?" Mitch snapped.

"Boris. He asked me not to. He thought it was best for Anja."

"Since when has he known what's best for my daughter?" Mitch hissed.

"We knew you would want to come here. It would unsettle her, Mitch."

"Of course I want to be there with her. With Natasha gone …"

"Let her be, Mitch. The child has been through so much."

"She's my daughter, Vera. It's not up to you or Boris to decide what's best for her, for Christ's sake!"

"Let her settle down for a while. Then, when she's older, go there, talk to her. Let her make her own decision."

"She's my child, Vera!"

"Mitch, there's no kind way to say this. Anja has spent over half her life looking upon Boris as her father. She's now lost the most important person … her mother. Boris is the only constant. How do you think she'd feel being taken away from everything and everyone she knows? Her brother, her friends, her home? Are you going to do that to her after all she's been through?"

Mitch paced around the room. "You can't keep me away from my own daughter, Vera."

"No, I can't. I can only tell you what I think is best for Anja."

"I'm the best judge of what's best for her, Vera." He went to the sitting room door and listened before continuing: "If I leave her there with *him*, how do I know he won't revert to his previous life, his old ways? Christ, Vera! If he's still with that scum, Anja could fall prey to traffickers!"

"I told you before, Mitch. He's changed."

"Once a *mafiyosa*, always a *mafiyosa*!"

"That's not so. He's running a legitimate business, paying taxes, and is ..."

"So, paying taxes qualifies him to take care of my daughter?" Mitch cut in, a note of sarcasm in his voice.

"You know that's not what I mean. If you're worried about traffickers, Boris is the best person to protect her. No one will mess with him."

"He's a thug!"

"He isn't like that anymore," Vera persisted.

A wail came from upstairs. "Shit! I have to go, Vera. One of the twins is crying." He barely said goodbye before slamming the receiver down. For a moment, the pounding in his ears blocked out the cries from above.

* * *

Lying in bed early the next morning, Mitch began to absorb the fact that Natasha, the mother Anja loved, was gone, leaving Anja and her half-brother with Boris, the man she now called Papa. *How has it come to this?* He thought back to that long-ago October day when he crept into the ward in the hospital in Leningrad and glimpsed his baby daughter for the first time. How full of plans he had been for his precious child. *Where did it all go wrong? And Natasha? I didn't even ask how she died.* What grieved him now was that he had again failed his daughter when she needed him most. More than once, Lucy had urged him to go there, to Siberia. "See for yourself," she had said. But, with staff shortages, it would have been difficult to get leave from work. And now, how could Lucy cope alone with the twins? He turned his face into the pillow as realisation washed through him: *You always find excuses not to go back to Russia.*

32
Western Siberia
June 1997

A shaft of sunlight pierced the canopy of trees. Sergei squinted following the piercing light as far as he could see. Some days a face beamed down at him. A face which at first looked like his beloved Sophia, then gradually shifted to form the baby-like features of Anja. *But surely Anja doesn't look like that. She's grown up now? Isn't she?* He couldn't remember. Some days, he tried in vain to remember his granddaughter's name, or even his own.

"Eat your rations, my friend," Pavel urged. "It will soon be time to start work again." He picked off ticks seeking to burrow into his bare arms.

"Is it May?"

"*Nyet.* May is over," Pavel picked up a dry biscuit and put it in Sergei's hand, "and most of June."

"It was June when they came to me in Leningrad. All the way from Canada. Sophia and my son." He dipped the biscuit into his mug of water and sucked on it. "I never believed they would come. She was such a beautiful young woman and I … I was a lot older than her. Not the handsome young man she deserved."

"She must have loved you."

"She did. There was never any doubt of that. Her family," he shook his head. "Her family, they cast her out when they knew she was pregnant by a non-believer."

"Difficult. Difficult for her."

"But she brought him here to live with me … my son. Her life was so different in this wretched country." He thought of the many times he had seen that faraway look in Sophia's eyes. He worried that one day he would lose her. He would wake up and she would be gone, taking Mitch with her. But their love was strong, strong enough to sustain them both in bad times. There had been many of those. He remembered now how she tried to get exit permits to visit her mother after her father died. Each morning, she had stood in line. Each evening, she came home with nothing, dejected. To his shame, he had been relieved, as he feared she would not come back to him from Canada. *I should have trusted her. Had faith. Faith in the strength of our love.* Right from the first moment he saw her, he knew. She did too. "My life would have been so much poorer without her."

"You were a lucky man. A wife. A son. What more could you ask?"

"Nothing." There was nothing else in life he wanted. *Now they are both gone.* His gaze followed a Rove Beetle as it foraged among the decaying matter on the forest floor. He envied the freedom it had to go far from here. He picked up a stick and prodded the beetle. It raised the tip of its abdomen, sprayed a foul-smelling mist, and scurried across the ground.

"We must get back to work," Pavel urged, trying not to breathe in the tainted air.

Sergei picked up his saw and trudged silently behind him.

33
Village Near Omsk, Siberia
August 1997

Anja grabbed Timofei's hand and pulled him onto the path at the side of the dirt road which ran through the village. It seemed everything was moving in slow motion as she watched the girl stumble along the middle of the street, swaying from side to side. She clutched a young baby in her arms. A group of women stopped to stare. Anja held her breath, scared the girl would fall and lose her hold on the baby. Timofei pointed a finger in the girl's direction. *"Kto eto?"*

The girl turned and walked slowly towards a house. Anja gasped … Alyona's house. Anja held her breath as the girl climbed the steps onto the porch. "Surely that's not Dina. It can't be," one of the women said. The girl was now trying the door. She banged a fist on it. Then she was still, her forehead resting on the door.

Anja dragged Timofei across the street, calling, "She isn't there. Alyona's at work." The girl sank down; the baby toppled to the side and let out a wail. Anja ran up the steps, picked up the child and yelled to the women, who had now been joined by others: "Fetch Alyona. Tell her to come quickly." Two women turned and hurried along the street towards Alyona's workplace. Anja lowered herself onto the porch next to the girl, indicating to Timofei to sit on the steps. "Are you Dina?" she asked. The girl nodded. Tears dribbled down her cheeks and she bent her head. There were bald patches in her dark hair. "Your mother will be so glad to see you. She talks of you every day. She never gave up hope." The words only succeeded in making Dina sob loudly. Anja realised that the side where she was holding the baby was now warm and wet. Dina looked up, dried her eyes with the back of her hand and took the child. It was then Anja saw the burn marks on her arms.

34
Toronto
September 1997

Mitch leaned back in the armchair. Lucy's voice filtered through the baby monitor on the side table. She was singing softly to the twins. Mitch yawned. *With a bit of luck, they'll go off in a minute and we can have what's left of the evening to ourselves.* The last few days had been busy for both of them. The first semester had begun and Mitch seemed to spend most of his time sorting out problems for the new students. He should be used to it by now, but it never ceased to amaze him that a lot of youngsters seemed incapable of using their own initiative.

Lucy was back at work now after a bout of pneumonia. It had taken her weeks to get over it and, after the traumatic first few weeks, Mitch had enjoyed looking after her, making sure she got enough rest. When she was up and about again, they had spent summer afternoons pushing the twins in their double stroller along the boardwalk. Mitch had wished their lives could go on like that forever. Lucy had tried to persuade him to spend the last couple of weeks of the summer vacation in Russia. "You have to try to see Anja," she had urged. He had prevaricated, saying he didn't want to leave Lucy until she was fully recovered. Deep in his subconscious he knew that wasn't the real reason.

"I think they've gone off now," Lucy said as she came back into the sitting room.

"You look exhausted," Mitch said.

The ghost of a smile drifted across her face as she sank into an armchair. "You certainly know how to charm a girl."

"You know what I mean," he laughed. "Let me get you a drink."

"Maybe just a small one," she said, stifling a yawn. "I wouldn't have believed it was possible to feel so tired."

“I remember when Anja was small.” He poured Scotch into two glasses and handed one to Lucy. “I was still studying, doing a part-time job, and some pro-bono work a friend persuaded me to do.”

“Your wife? Natasha? Was she working?”

He shook his head. “Spending money, that’s what she was doing. Money we didn’t have.”

“Mitch?” Lucy stared at him for a moment. “There’s something … something I think you’re keeping from me.”

“Like what?”

“You never really explained why you and Natasha split up.”

“I told you,” he took a gulp of his drink, “she was having an affair.”

“But surely, if it meant losing Anja, you wouldn’t have left Natasha.”

He flopped down onto the sofa, averting his eyes from Lucy’s steady gaze.

She leaned across and took his hand in hers. “Look at me, Mitch. We’re a family now, and families don’t have secrets.”

He pulled his hand away. “Maybe yours don’t, but Natasha and I spent our lives covering things up, pretending we were happy.”

“I’m not willing to do that … pretend I’m happy. Our relationship has to be based on something stronger.”

Mitch’s shoulders sagged.

“Surely it can’t be that bad,” Lucy coaxed. “I keep imagining awful things.”

“What sort of things?” His voice was barely audible.

Lucy grimaced. “You murdered someone?”

“I nearly did.” Mitch swallowed hard. “Natasha. I nearly killed her.”

“You did what?” Lucy’s face mirrored the horror she felt inside. She took a gulp of her drink. “What … what happened?”

Mitch allowed his mind to go back to that fateful day. “It was a Saturday afternoon. Anja was six.” He reached for his glass and took a swig. “Natasha had gone out, supposedly to see some friends. I didn’t believe her but went along with it. It was easier. You see, I was willing to put up with anything so long as I could be there for Anja. Look after her. Make sure no harm came to her.”

Lucy reached over and took the glass from his trembling hands.

“Anja and I, we’d just come out of a shoe store. She’d cajoled me into buying her a pair of red shoes.” His eyes misted over as he remembered how excited she had been in the store, twisting this way and that, looking at her new shoes. “On the street, she suddenly pointed to the other side of the road and called her mother's name." He shook his head trying to dislodge what he still saw vividly. "There she was … Natasha. The arm of a known member of the *vory v zakone* around her." Mitch's voice rose an octave or two, as he went on: "It's *Dyadya Mikhail,* Anja shouted as she tried to drag me towards them. I couldn't move." Mitch took a sharp intake of breath. In his mind, he was there again on that freezing Leningrad street, staring aghast. Now, he reached for his glass that Lucy was holding and took a mouthful, letting the warmth of the Scotch ease the chill and desolation he was reliving. "It was a shock seeing her with that thug. But, hearing Anja calling him Uncle, I was horrified, unable to take it in."

"What did you do?"

"By the time I'd gathered my wits, they had gone."

"Oh, Mitch. How could she do that to you and Anja?"

"She didn't care. There was only one person that mattered to her." After a moment, he shook his head slowly. "No. That's not fair. She really loved Anja and cared about her. I don't think she'd considered the implications of what she was doing."

"Why didn't you tell me?"

"It was what happened later … when she came home. I was scared you'd think I would do that to you. Hurt you or our children."

Lucy's voice quaked as she asked, "What did you do?"

He put his glass down on the table and took a deep breath. "It was late that night when she eventually came home. Things escalated," he shuddered, the fingers of his hands bent into claws, "I had my hands around her neck. I nearly strangled her."

"Oh, Mitch!"

"The worst part was," he hesitated for a moment, "it felt good. It was as though the tensions of the past few years were there in my fingers, squeezing, punishing her." He sat back in his seat, the stiffness in his hands gradually releasing until he could flex his fingers again. He shook a cigarette out of the packet on the side table. "So now you know what sort of evil person I am."

"You're not evil. You're …" Lucy struggled to find words, "… you're one of the most gentle, caring people I know."

"Maybe that other person is the real me."

35
Toronto
December 1997

"Lucy?" Mitch called up the stairs. "Lucy! Are you coming down?" He listened for a moment then climbed the stairs two at a time. He looked in the bedroom then tried the bathroom door.

"Lucy?" His voice was low. "Are you okay?"

The door opened. "Oh, Mitch," she croaked, and dabbed at her eyes with a Kleenex.

"Whatever's the matter?"

"I don't think I can go through with this," she sobbed.

Blood pulsed through his temples. He reached out and gripped her shoulders.

"I want to, but …" She pulled away from him slightly.

"Is it …" his throat constricted, "… is it what I told you about Natasha? What I did?"

She shook her head. "I told you, I trust you."

"Then what is it?"

"It's okay for you. You've done this before."

"It's different this time." He gathered her into his arms and kissed the top of her blonde hair. "This time it's for keeps."

"But you must have thought that when you married her."

"Deep down I knew," he squeezed Lucy tighter, "I knew it would end."

"What if it doesn't work? What if we end up hating each other?"

"How could I possibly hate you?" He held her away from him and looked straight into her eyes. "We love each other, don't we?" She nodded her head. "But if this isn't what you really want …"

She closed her eyes for a second. "It is. I was being silly."

Mitch took a gulp of air. He had hardly breathed since she opened the door.

She turned and looked in the mirror. "Now look what I've done. My mascara's run."

"You look beautiful." Mitch handed her another Kleenex from the box on the counter.

She wiped grey streaks from her cheeks. "You go down. I'll be there in a minute."

"Are you two all right up there?"

Mitch stepped out onto the landing and called to Susan, Lucy's mother, who was standing at the bottom of the stairs: "The dress. Lucy's dress, it needed a last minute adjustment. The zip."

"Liar," Lucy teased.

"Can I help?" Susan asked.

"It's okay now, Mom. I'll be down in a minute."

"Masha and Ivo, they're getting a bit restless. Masha's yanked the circlet of flowers out of her hair." Susan, who was now half-way up the stairs, added in a theatrical whisper, "And the minister is on his third glass of Scotch!"

"Jesus Christ!" Mitch exclaimed.

"Very appropriate!" Lucy took a big breath and headed into the bedroom. "I'll just put on my shoes."

Five minutes later, conversation in the sitting room hushed as Lucy and Mitch stood before the minister. The rotund, bald-headed man, rambled on in his sing-song voice for what seemed an eternity. He told of his early life in a mining community in South Wales where he learnt true Christian values. "The people, they had very few material possessions but their sense of love and close family and friends, helped them overcome tragedies. Tragedies that were all too frequent as men toiled below the surface in dangerous conditions."

"Get on with it!" Mitch muttered under his breath. He turned and looked at Lucy standing beside him. She was dressed in a knee-length white linen dress, a spray of cream roses pinned on the right shoulder. A wave of tenderness washed through him. He was so lucky to have not only her love but the love and support of her family. His mind wandered back to his previous wedding. Although religious worship was banned in the Soviet Union, Natasha inveigled her doting father into getting a special dispensation from the Party so they could be married in church. Before that, there was the obligatory civil *Brakosochetaniye* ceremony, where they stood before a black-suited official who wore a red sash bearing the emblem of the Russian republic and the legend ‘Proletarians of the World Unite’.

Now, a tug at the right leg of his pants pulled Mitch out of his reverie. He looked down. Masha was hanging on to his leg with one arm and holding her circlet of flowers up to him. He leaned down and picked her up, and she rested her head on his shoulder as he and Lucy exchanged vows.

Some hours and several drinks later, Mitch stood by the corner table which held the small artificial Christmas tree. Lucy had reluctantly agreed to forgo the long-established Bowen family tradition of driving to one of the tree farms which dot the outskirts of the city, where she and her siblings and parents would argue over what each thought was the perfect Christmas tree. “It’s not worth the hassle of extricating these two little monsters from its depths,” she had declared, leaning down and ruffling a child’s hair with each hand. “Our nerves would be more frayed than they are already, and they’ll end up with needles in their little hands and feet.”

Next year, they would bundle the twins into snowsuits and join the rest of the family on their pre-Christmas jaunt. “It’s so much fun, Mitch. We’ll have hot chocolate with marshmallows then ride on the wagon into the forest.” One of the many things he loved about Lucy was her delight in simple things. He hoped Masha and Ivo would grow up with the same values. He remembered how worried he’d been that Anja would be corrupted by her mother’s ideas of what was important in life. *Maybe it’s different in Siberia.*

Now, he looked into the dining room where Lucy was chatting with one of his colleagues from the university. He loved the way she gestured with her hands, pushing the air aside as she emphasised whatever point she was trying to get across. *Better rescue him,* Mitch thought, slipping an arm around Lucy’s waist.

It was almost midnight when Mitch retrieved Lucy’s parents’ coats from the hall closet—they were the last to leave. In the hallway, they spoke in hushed tones, alert for sounds that one or both of the twins had awoken again. After the excitement of the day, it had taken hours to get them settled.

Susan and Donald were putting on their boots when the telephone rang. Lucy grabbed the receiver off the base. “It’s James,” she mouthed to Mitch and, indicating to her parents to wait, headed into the kitchen. It was a minute or two before she came back into the hallway. “James called in at the shelter on his way home. A young girl has been brought in. She’s in a terrible state and they can’t understand what she's saying. James thinks she's Russian and ..." Lucy looked at Mitch.

"And James is wondering whether I can go down there." Mitch sighed.

"She's terrified, Mitch. He thinks it would help if she could talk to someone who understands what she is trying to say."

In the silence that followed, Susan and Donald hovered awkwardly in the hallway.

You can't get involved, Mitch told himself. He had enough bad dreams of girls, girls he didn't know but whose stories were as familiar to him as if he had been in those darkened rooms with them as they cried for the families most would never see again.

Donald peered through the glass in the front door. "Our cab's here."

"We could stay with the children," Susan ventured.

"Mitch? Come with me. Please." Lucy wrapped a scarf around her neck. "You don't have to get involved." She shrugged into the coat her father held out for her then bent to put on her boots.

Mitch took his own coat out of the closet, jammed his feet into his boots, and followed her silently out of the house.

In the cab, he leaned back watching, but not seeing, the streetscape slip past. In his mind, he was in the house in Leningrad, at the bedside of the mother who had not spoken since learning that her only child had been murdered in Cyprus when she tried to escape from the night club where she was forced into prostitution. He remembered how the woman would suddenly start making unintelligible sounds, holding out her arms to the daughter she thought she saw walking down the path, coming home. He had come to know the heartache that mother felt. In the years since he last saw Anja, he imagined he saw her on the street, in the park, in the gaggle of children going to school. It was at that far-off house he finally decided to publicise the details of the people running the trafficking ring in Leningrad—the decision that led to the death of the old man and the loss of his beloved Anja. And now this. *You can't get involved, he told himself,* as the cab lurched to a halt.

Lucy waited on the sidewalk while he paid the driver. Then she punched in a code on the pad set in the wall. The door clicked open and Mitch followed her inside, along a long corridor to the back of the house. James was seated at a large wooden table in the brightly painted kitchen. He got to his feet and helped Lucy off with her coat. They looked out of place, Lucy in her wedding dress, James in white shirt and suit pants, the jacket to which hung over the back of a chair. Mitch shook his head when James offered to take his coat. "Where is she?" Lucy asked.

"She's upstairs. Melody took her up there to see if she would calm down. You know what it's like, Lucy, when they first come here." He turned to Mitch. "They think any moment their pimp is going to break down the door or climb through a window to get at them."

"Where was she found? How did she get here?" Lucy poured two mugs of coffee from the carafe on the coffee maker.

"The Salvation Army. She was at one of their hostels. An older woman was trying to entice her away, back to her pimp. That's what happens in supposedly safe places, Mitch. Not all traffickers are male!" Mitch nodded his head, almost imperceptibly, and tried to block out the conversation. "Luckily, one of the volunteers saw what was going on and made the other woman leave. They guessed the girl wasn't one of the usual homeless people, so they called us and asked if someone could collect her. She can't be more than thirteen, fourteen."

The same age as Anja.

"I'll go and see." Lucy took a gulp of coffee then headed upstairs.

James pulled out a chair for Mitch and pushed the other coffee mug towards him. "I'm sorry. It's not quite how you thought your wedding day would end," he commiserated.

"You can say that again!" Mitch silently cursed himself for not insisting he and Lucy went away somewhere by themselves after the wedding. With the twins' first Christmas coming and the freezing weather, they had decided to postpone their honeymoon for a few months. *If only we'd gone.*

"I can't imagine what that poor child up there is going through," James continued. "It's bad enough for these girls when they can speak the language."

Mitch unbuttoned his overcoat and sank down onto the chair. "I don't know what good it will do, James. Even if you help these girls, what hope is there for them?"

"So you're saying we should ignore them, leave them with people who continually abuse and beat them?"

"I'm not saying that …"

"Sounds like that to me." James took a cigarette out of the packet on the table, lit it and inhaled.

Mitch breathed deeply, imagining the feeling—he was still in the early stages of kicking the habit.

James leaned back in his chair and took another drag.

Mitch twirled his wedding ring around on his finger. "What I was trying to say, James, is there isn't a legal framework here to help them, no criminal code for the offence of human trafficking. At best, victims are given a temporary residence permit. And when that expires, what happens?"

"I know only too well what happens. Most of them are sent back where they came from and fall prey to traffickers again. If they don't co-operate, they put their families in danger."

"Exactly. Don't get me wrong, James. I really admire what you're doing. But, you're only picking up the collateral damage, not attacking the source."

James leaned across the table and looked Mitch in the eyes. "Do you have a better solution?"

Mitch averted his gaze. "I'm not belittling what you're doing, but to cut down on trafficking, governments have to admit what's going on within their borders, make penalties more severe."

"So until that happy day, we sit back and ignore what's happening?" James got to his feet and waved an arm towards the front of the house. "You've only to go out on the street. Open the front door, take a look outside. They're there. The girls. Children, some of them …" His voice trailed off.

"I see them all the time." In truth, Mitch had trained himself to avert his eyes from the mere slips of girls, their painted faces, low-cut tops, short skirts, adopting sexy poses as men looked them up and down. He hated the person he had become—the person who turned his back on their suffering.

"Lucy told me what happened over there, in Russia." James sat down again.

"She shouldn't have. That was between the two of us."

"I know that turned out badly for you and for the man who was blown up in your car."

"Badly!" Mitch scoffed. "That's an understatement, particularly for him." An image of Slava's face flashed through his mind.

"It was tragic, Mitch. But have you ever thought that if you hadn't done what you did, how many girls would have lived abusive lives, met violent ends, at the hands of those you exposed?"

"It didn't make much difference. Another gang took over from them."

“Don’t make light of it, Mitch. It’s a growing global epidemic, and you made people aware of what’s going on. Even if you stopped one girl from being enticed away, don’t you think it was worth it?”

“Worth it? I lost my own daughter because of what I did.”

“So now you’re going to condemn other parents to the same fate.” When Mitch didn’t respond, James continued: “Upstairs, there’s a young girl—not much more than a child—who’s so traumatised by what she’s been through, she cowers in the corner, eyes darting from side to side, alert for danger. She’s like a dog, constantly on the watch for a kick from a boot, a burn from a cigarette end.” He looked at the glowing end of his own cigarette. “That’s what happens if they don’t co-operate.”

“And suppose you set her up with a new identity, find her somewhere to live where her pimp can’t find her, how long is that going to last? How long before she ends up on the streets again while some scum gets rich on the proceeds of her misery?”

“It’s all we can do, Mitch. At least it gives her a chance.”

Mitch leaned back in his chair.

“So, all the things you preach to your students about the importance of protecting human rights, bringing perpetrators to justice … that’s all crap?” James ground the remains of his cigarette in the ashtray.

“You know it isn’t!” Mitch’s eyes blazed. “I really admire what you’re doing, James. What all of you are doing. All I’m saying is that, for a long-term solution, we have to lobby for legislation, make human trafficking a criminal offence with huge penalties. Give foreign victims legal immigration status here.”

“And how can we do that, Mitch? We’re a charity. A small one. Lucy’s doing her best on the legal front, but we can’t afford to pay fancy lawyers to take up the cause.” James met Mitch’s gaze.

“I can’t get involved, James. I’ve spent the past few years making a new life for myself. Trying to forget what happened. And now, with Lucy and the twins …”

“Mitch?” Lucy’s voice came from the doorway. “If you could just find out her name, where she comes from.”

Mitch closed his eyes for a moment, took a deep breath and got to his feet.

“Probably best if you take your coat off,” Lucy advised. “If you look too formal, she’ll think you’re a police officer.”

Mitch took off his coat and dropped it onto the seat of the chair, together with his jacket, the lapel of which was still adorned with a cream rose. He followed Lucy up the stairs, trying to ignore the tight knot gripping his stomach.

"I'll go in first," Lucy murmured, then pushed the door open.

As he followed Lucy into the room, Melody—a short, round-faced young woman with a halo of auburn curls—acknowledged him with a nod of her head. At first, Mitch thought the room was otherwise empty. Then, as his eyes became accustomed to the dim light, he picked out a small figure. The girl was huddled on the floor in the corner of the room, bent legs held tight against her body, shoulders hunched, chin resting on her knees. The only part of her that moved was her eyes, constantly scouring the room. Mitch walked tentatively towards her. She tried to draw back further into the corner.

He raised his hands slowly in a form of surrender and spoke in a soft voice: *"Nikto zdes nay prichinite vam vreda."* The Russian words sounded odd to his ears. He walked carefully to the wall at right angles to where the girl was sitting and lowered himself to the floor. Her eyes followed his every move. *"Vy gavarite pa-ruski?"*

She nodded her head almost imperceptibly.

Mitch thought he saw the fingers clutching her legs relax a bit. It was some moments before he was able to swallow the huge lump that blocked his throat. *"Otkuda vy?"*

Tears streaked down her cheeks as she whispered the word that to her was home. "Novosibirsk."

* * *

Two weeks later, Mitch looked around the room. It was like no other Christmas he had ever known. Lucy's mother had decided they should bring their festive food to the shelter. The whole thing was chaotic as they juggled the turkey in and out of the unfamiliar oven, one minute fearing it was underdone, the next thinking it was overcooked. The roast potatoes and stuffing were finishing off while Susan explained the intricacies of ensuring the brussels sprouts weren't overdone to the gaggle of young women surrounding her. "Nothing worse than an overdone sprout!" James's words brought forth a torrent of playful jibes resulting in him being given the job of carving the bird.

Lucy and the young Russian girl, Nadezhda as she had chosen to be called, were setting the table. Mitch watched; she had come a long way since the evening of his and Lucy's wedding.

She still wouldn't set foot outside the house and ran upstairs when she heard anyone coming in the front door, but at least she was eating now. She seemed happiest when she was playing with Masha and Ivo. The twins adored her, bringing toys with them to give her whenever Mitch and Lucy brought them to the house. Nadezhda told Mitch she had a younger brother and sister.

Apart from that, she had said little of her life in Russia or how she came to be in Toronto. Taking James's advice, Mitch hadn't pursued the subject and, little by little, she was beginning to take an interest in things. Melody, who lived on the premises with her young daughter, said that during the first few nights Nadezhda's screams had awoken everyone, but recently there had only been one incident. That was following a visit by the shelter's doctor, who tried to examine her.

Nadezhda looked up and met Mitch's gaze. Her face lit up with a smile.

If only I could do something ... something to help her. He looked away. *Don't even think about it.*

36
Toronto
October 1998

Mitch wiped a smear of apple purée from Masha's cheek. "It's supposed to go in your mouth, not on your face," he chuckled, guiding the spoon held in his daughter's pudgy hand into her mouth. She laughed, spraying him with food.

"I think she's had enough," Lucy said as she lifted Ivo out of his chair. "Mom said that when she picked them up from daycare, Inga … the young Swedish woman with long blonde hair … she said that Masha cleared her plate at lunch and asked for more."

"You're a growing girl, aren't you?" Mitch said as he picked Masha up and planted a kiss on her dark curls. She pinched his cheek. "Oww! That's naughty!" he said in the firmest voice he could muster. He put her down on the floor and she tottered into the playroom giggling. They were all enjoying having more room in this house, bought in the summer with financial help from Lucy's parents. He thought often of the tiny apartment he, his parents, and paternal grandmother shared in Leningrad; the corridors of the building were an obstacle course, littered with bicycles, prams, and household items that wouldn't fit into overcrowded living spaces.

He went into the kitchen, retrieved a wet cloth, and began to wipe down the children's chairs. "I had a visit from the father of one of my students today," he began.

"Was there a problem?" Lucy stopped what she was doing.

"She hasn't been in class for two weeks, so I asked the admin people to check to see if she was sick."

"And …?"

"She hasn't been home. She said she was staying with a friend."

"Is she a good student?"

“She was. But a few weeks before she disappeared, her marks fell off. According to some of her friends, she has a boyfriend.”

“Older than her?” Lucy’s voice had an ominous tone.

“Apparently.” Mitch put down his cloth. “Two of my students saw her with him at some nightclub. She was wearing jewellery. It looked expensive, they said.”

“Did they talk to her?” Lucy leaned on the table.

“Briefly, but the boyfriend pulled her away. The funny thing is, he called her by a different name, not her own name at all.”

“What happened then?”

“He started yelling at her, grabbed her by an arm and said they had to leave.”

Lucy took a long breath.

“Her father, he went to the police. They said they’d keep a look out for her, but there’s not much they can do.” He slumped down at the table. “He thinks it’s because she’s of native heritage. Ojibwe. The police said girls like that often go off!”

“It makes me sick when they talk like that!” Lucy ran a hand through her hair. “Can you ask her father for a picture? We could circulate it around. Someone might know something.”

“Jesus Christ! You don’t think …?”

37
Village Near Omsk, Siberia
September 1999

Anja stepped out of the way as *Tyotya* Yevdokia hauled another overflowing sack through the front doorway. *We'll never get through all these vegetables,* Anja thought to herself as she bent to pick up a carrot that had fallen out of the sack. It had been going on all day. Sacks of beets, potatoes, and onions. *What is she up to?* "Let me help you," Anja offered as the old woman struggled to open the door to the cellar.

Yevdokia brushed away Anja's hands and bumped the sack down the wooden steps in front of her. "Unbelievers! They'll all perish!" she muttered.

When *Tyotya* came back up the stairs, Anja tempted, "Why don't we make some tea? Alyona brought round a jar of her blackberry jam."

"There's no time to waste drinking tea. The Last Day is coming!" She wagged a finger at Anja before disappearing outside again.

Anja dropped the carrot on to the counter. She spooned dry tea leaves into the small pot from the top of the samovar, mixed it with hot water and stared out of the window as she waited for it to brew. *If only Mama was here. She'd know what to do. Tyotya* had been acting in a strange way the past few weeks, constantly admonishing Timofei and Anja to repent before something called the Apocalypse sweeps down. After school yesterday, she had frightened Timofei, telling him she was going to take him to the river and dunk him under the water. *"Tri raza! Tri raza!"* she yelled after him as he ran out of the house. She had then spent an hour bowing and chanting in front of the *krasnyy ugol,* crossing herself with two fingers extended instead of the three most people used. After she had gone to her room, cursing that the West with all its luxuries is assaulting Russian holiness, Boris explained that *Tyotya* had reverted to the strict Orthodox views of her parents, who had been members of the Old Believers' sect.

"Why did she say she was going to dunk me in the river?" Timofei had asked. "I didn't do anything wrong."

"The baptism," Boris explained, putting a comforting hand on his son's shoulder. "Three full immersions, that's what they believe."

"She's crazy!" Timofei had declared.

"It's what she believes. What her parents believed," Boris responded. "It will pass."

Now, Anja got up, poured a small amount of the thick brew into her glass and diluted it with hot water from the samovar. She was spooning jam into a saucer when the front door burst open and *Tyotya* heaved another sack into the room.

38
Village Near Omsk, Siberia
October 2000

Anja pressed her hands over her ears, muffling the shrieks of *"Prikosnis' ko mne! Prikosnis' ko mne!"* coming from the gang of seven-year-old boys playing a game of 'Wizards' at Timofei's birthday gathering. Boris pulled her hands away and grinned, saying, "Too much for a sixteen-year-old, is it, Annushka?"

"Why do they have to shout?"

"It's what boys do," Boris shrugged.

"I wish Mama was here. She would love to see him happy, having fun."

Boris put an arm around her. "She would be so proud of you. The way you've kept everything together while I've been working."

"We're a family. Isn't that what families do?" Anja secretly worried about what would happen when she had to leave the village to find work, or maybe continue her education. Her teachers said that, with her good marks, in a couple of years she could get into university. But Anja had already decided her immediate future. She would get a job in Omsk, or somewhere close by, so she could live at home and help *Tyotya* Yevdokia with the house and with Timofei. *Tyotya* was becoming more and more distraught, constantly cleaning the house and checking that her stockpile of food was still in the cellar. Timofei was scared of her and wouldn't stay in the house when Anja and Boris weren't home.

Boris worked long hours building up a small engineering business. The collapse of the Rouble two years ago made imports expensive and boosted domestic production. That, combined with higher prices for Russia's oil and gas, stopped the country's economic slide and opened up opportunities for entrepreneurs. Boris had plans, big plans. At the top of his list was a house in Omsk. "We'll put in a courtyard, flowers, a fountain," he mused. "She could never walk past a fountain without dipping her fingers into the water." Whenever he spoke of Natasha, his voice cracked and his eyes clouded over. "Even in winter she would try to poke a hole in the thick layer of ice." Most days, before driving into the city, he stopped at the graveyard. Anja had watched from the pathway as his lips worked, talking to someone. She knew that someone was her mother. Anja did the same, her eyes fixed on the inscription carved into the wooden cross: *Nataliya Alekseevna Galichina.* After Mama died, Boris said that she and Anja should be known by their real names, the ones on their original documents. He explained that, although the danger of discovery was over some time ago, Mama hadn't wanted to take any chances. So, Yelena Borisovna Zubova became Anja Yelena Galichina again. Anja had sighed. *What does a name matter? Mama is dead. She is never coming back. Nothing can change that.* She thought a house in Omsk would be nice, but Anja liked it here where she had friends and could visit her mother every day and tell her what she had been doing. She was careful not to tell her about *Tyotya's* strange behaviour or Timofei's fear of the old woman. Boris said it would pass, so there was no sense worrying Mama.

Recently, Anja was puzzled by strange things that were being said about Boris in the village: "His earlier life is catching up with him. Now he's the one paying protection money to the *vory*." She knew about the *vory*, but what had they to do with Boris? *Tyotya* said it was just gossip from people who were jealous of his success. It puzzled Anja. Surely, her Papa—she now thought of him as her Papa—couldn't be mixed up with the *vory v zakone.* She had heard they were the ones who run prostitution rackets, the type of people who lured Dina away from home, kept her prisoner, threatened her with violence. When Dina came back, Alyona hardly recognised her own daughter. *No! Papa would never get mixed up with people like that.* She had never seen him raise a hand to anyone—even Timofei when he scratched the new truck. He was kind, a good father, a good employer who cared for the people working for him. Recently, he paid for the young son of one of his employees to go abroad for cancer treatment. She remembered that when they lived in Leningrad, he used to drive *Dyadya* Mikhail around. *Dyadya* had been shot, or so she heard Boris telling Mama one day not long after they arrived in the village. Mama cried for two days. Some time ago, Timofei asked Boris what the pictures on his body meant. "They mean I was once stupid and didn't know any better!" Boris replied. *Tyotya* came to his defence, saying, "Your Papa is a good man. Everyone is allowed a mistake or two."

He can't be mixed up in anything illegal, Anja told herself now as she watched Boris shepherd the boys to their places at the table. "There's enough to feed the Army here," he laughed, as *Tyotya* made room for another plate heaped with food.

"The Army? You watch." *Tyotya* wagged a finger. "It will disappear like a Biblical plague of locusts descended!"

Timofei cringed at *Tyotya's* words.

Within twenty minutes, apart from the food that found its way onto the floor, hardly a morsel remained. In past years, Anja and Timofei shared a birthday celebration, but now she and her friends were too old to play 'Cossacks and Robbers', 'Wizards' and other boisterous games Timofei enjoyed. This evening, Alyona had invited Anja and her friends to her home for 'a grown-up party', as she put it. Anja couldn't wait. Alyona was like a mother to her, sorting out problems—real and imagined—that only adolescent girls know about. Anja loved to be with Izabella, Dina's dark-haired, dark-eyed child, taking her for walks in the pram which used to be Timofei's.

Last winter, most early mornings, Anja put Izabella on the sledge and took her to the bakery to collect bread. For some time after her mother died, Anja could feel her presence, see her shadowy figure floating in the dim light of the bakery kitchen where Mama had worked. It both comforted and upset her. But lately, being with young Izabella snapped Anja out of her reverie; they were hardly out of the bakery when the child would smack her lips and hold out a gloved hand for the piece of crust Anja always broke off one of the loaves.

Dina was still suffering the effects of her ordeal in Turkey and, when anyone knocked at the door, she would grab her baby and scurry to her bedroom, the door of which had been fitted with a lock. Some days, she refused to get out of bed and huddled under the covers. She was so thin that to unknowing eyes it appeared the bed was empty. "She'll come around soon," Alyona comforted herself after every attempt to get Dina out of bed failed. Anja hoped Dina would join in the fun this evening.

Tonight, Anja would wear her new dress … the dress she never dreamt would be hers. Some weeks before, she gazed at it in a store window in Omsk. She had never seen anything so beautiful, but knew she would never have enough money to buy it, even if she saved the allowance Boris gave her and the few Roubles Alyona insisted she take for helping with Izabella when Dina took to her bed. *Where would I wear a dress like that?* She had consoled herself as Boris hurried her away from the store. This morning, when she opened the parcel in front of her place at the table, she gasped. She looked around, fixing on familiar things, making sure this wasn't a dream. Then she lifted the turquoise filmy fabric out of the box and held it close. "How did you know?" she gulped.

"When a woman has to be dragged away from a store window, men know," Boris laughed.

Now, in early evening as Anja twirled around in her new dress, Boris told her to stand still and close her eyes. "Your Mama. She wanted you to have this," he said as he draped something around her neck. Anja knew what it was before she opened her eyes: her mother's necklace, the one she wore when they left Leningrad. As she cradled the milky stones in one hand, her thoughts went back to the time long ago when her mother told her the necklace would be hers one day. Now, she swallowed a lump in her throat as she thought back to her life in that other world—the world she and Mama left behind in Leningrad so many years ago. Her real Papa was now only a blurred image. *I wonder if he remembers that today is my birthday. My grandparents too ... do they still think of me?* When Mama died, Boris said he would let people know when the time was right. *When would that be? It seems ungrateful to ask. Maybe when Timofei is a bit older, I'll find them all. Until then, I must take care of him, for Mama's sake.*

Now, Timofei's insistent voice broke her out of her reverie: "Why can't I come to your party? You came to mine."

Anja laughed and planted a kiss on top of her brother's blond head.

He brushed it away with a hand. "Will there be boys there?" He sat back in the armchair and clasped his legs close to his chest.

Boris raised an eyebrow. "Well, Anja?"

Anja's cheeks reddened. Stepan would be there and a couple of other boys from her class.

During the past year, Stepan's antagonism had turned to devotion. He followed her around, ignoring her injunctions to leave her alone. "But, Anja ..." he would say and gaze into her eyes, causing her heart to flutter. Secretly, she enjoyed the way he was always there to lend a hand as she struggled with a heavy book bag or unwieldy parcels from the store. It wasn't just that. His body had filled out, his voice deepened, and he was quite the tallest boy in the school. *Tyotya* said Anja should be glad someone wanted to watch over her. "Many women spend their whole lives longing for that sort of attention." It was nice having someone as handsome as Stepan by her side. Tonight, there would be music, dancing. She put a hand on her stomach, trying to still a quiver of excitement.

* * *

At the end of the evening, Anja and Dina collected the last of the used glasses and put them on the counter in Alyona's kitchen. The music was still playing and, as they worked, they swayed in time to the rhythm. Dina looked different tonight, smiling, wearing the yellow full-skirted dress Alyona had bought her. Her dark hair positively shone.

"I think she's turned the corner," Alyona whispered as Anja sashayed past.

Anja's mind was full of Stepan. The way his tight jeans hugged his body. The glimpse of fine hair on his chest revealed by the open top buttons of his shirt. She could still feel his hand pressed into the small of her back as they danced, their bodies close, blotting out the rest of the world. He had led her out onto the porch, where they stood awkwardly in the darkness. Then they both spoke at the same time. "I wanted to ask …" said he. "Thank you for the bracelet," said she. They laughed. "I could walk you home," he offered and pulled her into his arms.

"Papa. He's coming to collect me." Anja sighed.

"The protective father!" Stepan laughed softly, then cupped her face in his hands and kissed her.

Her body melted. It was some moments before they moved apart. Then they stood awkwardly staring into the dark night. "Maybe some other time?" Stepan ventured.

A shiver ran through her body. "That would be nice," she breathed.

"We'd better get back inside," he murmured, mistaking the tremor for reaction to the cold air.

Now, Anja looked at her watch. It was nearly midnight. *Papa will be here soon.* She picked up a cloth and dried the glasses Dina washed. "It was a lovely party. The best ever. Thank you." She kissed Alyona's cheeks.

"You shouldn't be doing this," Alyona chided and took the cloth out of Anja's hand. "Not on your birthday, and not in that beautiful dress."

Anja twirled around, her mind still going over the events of the evening.

"After the church service tomorrow morning, you must come back here with me," Alyona said. "I have something to give you."

"What is it? You've already given me my birthday gift."

"You'll have to wait until tomorrow. Enough excitement for today." She looked towards the front door. "Sounds as though your Papa's here."

* * *

Next day, it was late in the morning when they got back to Alyona's house. "I thought that service would go on forever!" Alyona grumbled, as Izabella launched herself into her *babushka's* arms. "So cold in there too. Poor Dotnara Vektorova, with her bad legs. I'm glad you found a chair for her, Anja."

"I'll take her for you, if you want to make tea," Anja offered, already reaching for Izabella.

"I've already done it," said Dina, emerging from the kitchen with two steaming glasses on a tray.

Alyona's smile lit up her face from ear to ear.

A few minutes later, reviving hot drinks in hand, Alyona and Anja sat around the stove.

Dina was taking Izabella to see a friend. "Don't be long," Alyona cautioned, as the two went out into the cold morning.

"You said you had something …" Anja began hesitantly.

Alyona got to her feet and retrieved an envelope tucked behind the picture of her late husband in the *krasnyy ugol*. She seemed to be weighing it in her hands and it was some moments before she spoke. "It's a letter … from your mother."

"From Mama? It can't be!"

"She wrote it on the day she died."

"What? Why didn't you give it to me before?"

"She said," Alyona took a noisy breath, "she said I wasn't to give it to you until you were sixteen."

Anja put her glass of tea on the floor. "But, why now? Why not before?"

"She wanted you to be old enough to understand. Not to judge her too harshly."

"Why would she think I would judge her … harshly? She was my mama."

"Things happen in life, Anja. Not everything turns out how we expect."

"I didn't expect her to die. Not when she did."

Alyona sat next to her, took one of Anja's hands in hers and placed the envelope in it. "Your Mama was a good person. You must always remember that. Sometimes people do things out of love. They can't help themselves."

"What did she do?"

"It's explained in her letter."

Anja cradled the envelope in her hands. She looked at her name written in Mama's handwriting and swallowed hard. Tears dribbled down her cheeks and she brushed them away quickly. Then she lifted the envelope to her nose, searching for a trace of the mother who used to be hers. It smelled of jasmine—the *Krasnaya Moskva* perfume Alyona wore on special occasions.

"I kept it in the drawer with my best things," Alyona murmured.

Anja let the envelope rest in her lap, picked up her glass of tea and held it to her lips.

"Aren't you going to open it?"

"Later."

"It might be better if you open it now, while I'm with you." Alyona twisted her hands together in her lap. "In case it upsets you."

"Why would it upset me?" Anja's eyes strayed to the envelope and then to Alyona's face.

"I just thought … but it's up to you."

They sat in silence and sipped their tea.

A few minutes later, Anja looked at her watch. "I'd better go home. Boris will be wondering where I am, and *Tyotya* will have lunch on the table."

"Anja! Listen to me!" Alyona blurted. "I want you to know that I'm here if you need me."

Anja shrugged into her coat, tucked the envelope in her pocket, and donned her hat and scarf. At the door, she bent down and slipped her feet into her *valenki. What can be in the letter? Did Mama do something awful? Nyet!* She dismissed the thought quickly. *Mama was a good person. She wouldn't do anything bad.* Anja kissed Alyona on both cheeks, put on her gloves, and said, "*Spasiba.* Thank you for the tea … for everything."

Alyona stood on the porch and watched until Anja was out of sight.

39
Village Near Omsk, Siberia
October 2000

Anja didn't go home. She ran blindly along the main street and turned onto a path; a path she had walked many times since her mother died. A cold wind blew across the graveyard and whipped flakes of snow into the air. She shielded the exposed part of her face with her hands as she stumbled between graves marked by crosses and frozen flowers. Boris had chosen a plot along the edge. *The trees will shelter her from the winds and keep her safe.* Anja stared at her mother's name carved on the wooden cross. Then she sank down onto the snow-encrusted grave. It was what she always did when she shared tales of what they had been doing. Sometimes she related gossip about the villagers, of newcomers in the area. All the things her mother enjoyed. At first, Anja had imagined her mother's body lying beneath the earth, but *Tyotya* said it was better to think of her as she was. Today, as she stared at the cross, she couldn't remember what her mother looked like … her face, her hair, her voice, her laugh, were gone. She shivered, pulled her hat further down over her ears, tugged off her gloves, took a deep breath, and pulled the envelope out of her pocket.

She opened it. A photograph dropped onto the snow. She gasped. Her father's face stared at her. The face she thought she had forgotten. She picked it up and held it close, shielding it from the wind with the hand that held the envelope. She turned the picture over. In her mother's handwriting, *Mitchell Jakob Galichin. Your Papa.* Memories flooded back. They were walking along the side of the *Neva*, Papa telling her the story of the people marooned on the ice flow, of the helicopter that rescued them. She could hear his voice, feel his hands as he whirled her around and around in the air, imitating the helicopter's rotor blades. Snatches of a song ran through her mind—one of the silly rhymes they sang as they tramped through the snow—*Brodyaga, brodyaga. Nashi sapoga brodyat, brodyagi.* She heard again their laughter as he drove her to kindergarten, telling her funny stories. It was there now. *Where had it been before?*

Biting back tears, she tucked the photograph into the envelope and pulled out the letter.

Maybe it's better not to read it. But Mama wouldn't have left it for me if she didn't want me to.

She hunched her shoulders and unfolded the letter. Two sheets of paper flapped in the wind.

Annushka, moya dorogaya devochka,

I tried many times to tell you this but couldn't bear to see the disappointment I knew would be in your eyes. The last few hours of my life are here. I can't go without making things right. Or as right as I can.

You were old enough to remember when your Papa and I parted. I told you he had done something bad. That was a lie. He was a good person and tried to help young women, young women like Dina who were sold into prostitution by wicked people.

An image came into Anja's mind: Dina stumbling along the road, baby Izabella in her arms.

Your father, this good man, risked his own life to expose the human trafficking ring in Leningrad. To my shame, the trafficking ring was headed by Dyadya Mikhail. His gang planted a bomb under your father's car outside our apartment.

Anja clamped a hand to her mouth. *Papa! Papa's dead?*

It was the old caretaker, Slava, who lost his life when he started up the car.

Anja breathed again. Then a memory came into her mind. *The old man and his wife.* She swallowed hard. *They used to give me candies and little cakes.*

But it could have been your Papa. That day, you at Eugenia's. The blast below your bedroom window. I thank God every day you weren't there, my precious. My involvement with Dyadya Mikhail brought this trouble on us. I offer no excuses. It was only afterwards that I realised it was your Papa, your real Papa, I really loved. Still love.

Anja stared hard at the wooden cross.

Your Papa went to Canada. I never heard from him. Don't know if still there. Papa's father, your Dedushka. Arrested. Fifteen years hard labour. Running a human trafficking ring they said. They lied. Your Dedushka he would never do anything wrong.

Anja choked back a sob, remembering her *Dedushka*, the kind man who always took her for hot chocolate and other treats. *Dedushka! He can't be in one of those horrid camps? He can't be.*

She struggled to read on. It was now difficult to make sense of her mother's words … sentences unfinished, words crossed out.

My sins many, Annushka. Glad brought you to this place where we have simpler life ... you learnt good values which you will take with you wherever you ... Don't make same mistakes me and think money and the things it will buy are important. Stay close home. I watch over. Be careful. Remember your promise. If anyone offers you money, run home fast.

Old woman, Vera Kishinevskaya, Dedushka's friend in Peter. Ask where Papa, Dedushka too. Boris help. Go Dyadya Pyotr. Babushka Lena and Dedushka Lyosha died. I broke their hearts.

Anja gasped.

Should have searched for your Papa. You good like him. Make happy. Brother make sure good. Tell Papa. I sorry. Didn't mean to hurt him.

Anja traced a finger around the shape her mother had drawn at the bottom of the letter. She thought it was a heart. She turned the pages over. There was no more.

The wind howled. Cold crept up her legs. *Why did Mama lie to me? Say Papa was bad? He didn't want me. Made me call Boris Papa.* She got to her feet and stumbled to the shelter of the trees. "Why? Why?" she cried, screwing the letter up in her hands. She wrapped her arms around a tree trunk. "Mama! Mama!" she wailed over and over.

Sometime later, she paced back and forth next to her mother's grave. "If only you had told me!" Tiredness swept over her as she sank down onto the grave and ran her frozen fingertips over her mother's name on the cross. Cloud blotted out the sun. There was an empty void inside her now. *Mama. Boris. They lied. My whole life is a lie.* She shivered, then smoothed the letter out. *I tried many times to tell you this ...*

Anja's thoughts went back to a time before her mother died. *She tried to tell me. She did. 'There is something I must tell you,' Mama had gasped.* But Anja was scared the effort would make Mama worse and had told her she must rest.

You were old enough to remember when your Papa and I parted. I told you he had done something bad. That was a lie. He was a good person...

Anja remembered the awful things she had thought about Papa. She had even imagined he had made Babushka Sophia sick. "Oh, Papa," she wailed as feelings of longing for him ran through her. She pulled the photograph out of the envelope. *I must find him. Tell him I didn't know.* "I never stopped loving you, Papa, even when they made me call Boris Papa."

She looked again at the letter.

... the trafficking ring was headed by Dyadya Mikhail.

Dyadya couldn't have done anything so bad. Could he? He made Mama happy, bought her nice things. Anja thought back to the times she and Mama stayed at *Dyadya's dacha.* The room in the house which was hers alone. The dollhouse he bought especially for her. The birthday party.

Then another image came into her mind: the pictures on *Dyadya's* arms, the backs of his hands. Snakes and horrid things. *Boris has them too.* She heard again the gossip in the village: *"His earlier life is catching up with him. Now he's the one paying protection money to the vory,"* the old women cackled.

She looked again at her mother's letter:

Papa's father, your Dedushka. Arrested. Fifteen years hard labour.

Anja choked back a sob. *They can't have sent Dedushka to a place like that.* She had heard talk of labour camps. Alyona told her of a young man she knew, a healthy, happy, handsome man, who came back from one of those places broken, his body wasted, mind gone. *Why hadn't I known? Why didn't Mama try to find him, help him?* It all went around and around in her head. She saw again her other grandparents, *Babushka Lena and Dedushka Lyosha. What happened to them? Dead. That's what Mama said.*

Why does everyone I love have to die? I must have done something terrible. She crouched lower over the grave, clutching the letter and photograph. *Papa? Is Papa dead too?* The sadness, the longing, the mourning, surfaced. It was all there, as exhaustion overwhelmed her.

Some minutes later, voices approached. "Anja! Anja! What are you doing?" Dina and Alyona rushed towards her. Dina lowered Izabella on to the snow-covered ground at the side of the grave while Alyona lifted Anja into a sitting position, supporting her with an arm around her shoulders. "I knew this is where you would come," the older woman said. "I shouldn't have let you leave."

Izabella edged closer and picked up a handful of snow. "Anja's playing in the snow." She twirled around, laughing, letting the snow fan out around her.

At the sound of Izabella's voice, Anja's eyelids flickered. She tried to move her lips. No sound came out.

"Anja's very cold, Izabella. We must get her home quickly." Dina prised the letter and photograph out of Anja's frozen hand and put them in her own pocket. Then she retrieved the gloves from the snow, forced Anja's hands into them, and turned to her own small daughter.

"Izabella. You have to be a big girl and walk by Mama's side while we help Anja. Hold on to my coat. Can you do that?"

Izabella nodded her head. Her dark eyes shone.

40
Toronto
October 2000

From his seat at the breakfast table, Mitch glanced at the TV on the kitchen counter. "Slow news day, Sunday," he remarked to Lucy, who was loading crockery in the dishwasher.

"You sure you don't mind having the kids today?" she asked.

"No. It'll be nice for you and your mom to have a day together. Treat her to a birthday lunch in St Jacobs." A thought niggled in his brain: *Birthday?* He caught his breath. *Hell! Anja's birthday! It was yesterday! How could I have forgotten?* It was nearly ten years since he last saw his daughter and, in all that time, he had never failed to think of her on her birthday. *Until now,* he sighed. Five years ago, as he had done in other years, he sent her a birthday card. He never heard back from her and, to his shame, had given up writing after that. *She's sixteen now, quite a young lady.* He closed his eyes and tried to picture her. All he saw was the little girl she had once been.

"Mitch? Are you okay?" Lucy's voice penetrated his thoughts.

He opened his eyes and stared unseeing at the litter of dishes on the table. "What?"

"I asked if you would pick up Mom's birthday cake this morning."

"Your dad," he paused, trying to collect his thoughts. "Your dad said we can pick it up on our way back from our walk with the twins."

"Ivo! Look what you've done!" Lucy exclaimed. "He's put jam in his hair." She grabbed a cloth off the counter. "Only babies do things like that. Not three-year-olds," she scolded.

"Me too!" Masha giggled, dipping her fingers in the jam on her toast.

"No you don't!" Mitch grabbed her wrist before the jam made it into her hair. Lucy wiped her daughter's fingers then moved the plate away. Masha pouted and wriggled out of her chair. "Masha! Come back here," Mitch called, pushing his own chair back.

At that moment, a picture flashed on the TV screen. "Lucy! That's her," he yelled. "It's Ash! My student." They both stared open-mouthed at the smiling face on the screen. "What the …?"

"News is just coming in of a fatality at an apartment building in Richmond Hill. Twenty-one-year-old Ashwiyaa Kasabian, also known as Trixie, is thought to have fallen from a balcony. Her body was found early this morning by a passerby."

* * *

Later that morning, Mitch and Lucy pushed their way through the throng of photographers outside the neat Leslieville house where Ash's parents lived. "I'm so sorry to ruin your mom's birthday," he said as they climbed the wooden steps onto the porch.

"It's okay. Mom didn't mind at all. She and Dad are going to take the kids along the boardwalk and then to the playground," Lucy responded. Mitch bent down and called through the letterbox, as arranged by telephone with Ash's father before they left home.

A woman opened the door a crack and they squeezed through. She led them along a corridor, laced with smoke, to the darkened room where the family gathered. The low melodic chanting and mournful drumming were mesmerising.

Later, the woman who had let them in, beckoned them into the kitchen. There, she explained that the soul of Ashwiyaa was on its four-day spiritual journey to a special place. "We will mourn for one year."

"Did the police say anything about what happened at the apartment building?" Mitch asked, still not believing that the vibrant young woman, who he last saw two years ago, was dead.

"There was a party, dancing. It spilled onto the balcony. They say our precious sister she climb on chair, pretend she flying they say. Of course, no one saw what happened to her!"

The beat of drums reverberated in Mitch's head.

41
Toronto
January 2001

Mitch hunkered down further in the car seat. He still had a good view of the nightclub and hopefully the bouncers wouldn't spot him. A few nights ago, they threatened him, but he brazened it out saying he was a private detective watching for his client's husband to come out of the house of his lover. He pointed a finger vaguely in the direction of the adjacent houses. His guts had been tied in knots. The encounter brought back painful memories of brushes with heavies in Russia and made him wonder why he had let himself be drawn into this violent world again.

He reached for his flask of coffee heavily laced with Scotch—to keep out the cold was his excuse. Nearer the truth was that the alcohol gave him much-needed courage. He warmed his hands around the cup of hot liquid, thinking back to the evening some weeks ago when Lucy asked him to look after the twins while she drove downtown to keep vigil outside an apartment building where trafficked victims were known to work. Lucy and James had known he wouldn't let her do that. What self-respecting husband would knowingly expose his wife to danger? He had fallen straight into the trap and, since then, had spent several evenings keeping watch at suspected brothels, waiting for one of the charity's helpers to emerge and to provide a quick getaway if needed. He tried not to think what might happen if things went wrong.

This evening, Nick, one of the volunteers, was in the club posing as a punter looking to have a good time with a girl. His real purpose was to persuade the girl he could help her get away from her pimp. Tonight was a last-ditch attempt with the girl, with whom he had supposedly had sex twice before. Her pimp was becoming suspicious, and Nick was anxious not to expose her to danger.

It was at times like this Mitch longed for a cigarette; even the comfort of holding one between his fingers. It was over three years since he quit smoking but the craving was still there. He picked up his camera, checked the battery, then opened the side window a crack—it wouldn't do for the windows to be fogged-up if he needed to take a photo. Lucy had told him that traffickers move victims frequently, either on public transit or on the network of highways which allow for fast journeys between towns and cities. Last week, one of the volunteers had taken several pictures of girls being herded into a van, but had lost track of the van in heavy traffic. A licence plate search had given them the name of the owner of the vehicle, but they were none the wiser as to where the victims were now incarcerated. By comparing the photos with 'Missing from Home' posters across Canada, they now had two positive identifications, but what was the good of that if they didn't have any idea where the girls were now? It was all too amateurish for Mitch's liking. *We have to do better,* Mitch told himself as realisation set in that, like it or not, he was again involved in the fight against the scum running the rackets.

As he had done before on these late-night vigils, he mulled over the events since that October Sunday when Ashwiyaa was found dead. When the police released her body, her family took Ashwiyaa to their ancestral home on Manitoulin Island. There, in the tradition of her people, she was wrapped in birch bark before burial. Ceremonial drums sent her to the spirit world.

Before Christmas, Ash's father came to the university. An aura of sadness surrounded him as he told Mitch he had spoken to neighbours at the apartment building where his daughter died. "We're scared to go out. There are always men going in and out of that place," one elderly man confessed. "The police, they don't do anything. Not enough manpower they said." A woman told him she saw Ashwiyaa with an older man in the elevator a couple of times. "She say Ashwiyaa she call him daddy. Why she do that?" When Mitch tried to explain, her father cut in: "You say familial loyalty? We are her family!"

After Ashwiyaa's father left, Mitch had sat alone in the classroom, wondering what good he was doing teaching respect for human rights when young girls—even one of his students—were being forced into prostitution and murdered if they became a problem. Why hadn't he seen the warning signs, tried to find Ash, persuaded her to go back home? Was it happening to others, his students, right under his nose? He had failed, not only Ashwiyaa but others like her. The young women living in fear, the families who wait for their lost daughters to come home. How many more of his students would meet the same fate while he pontificated about statistics and what governments could do to prevent the human tragedies behind the statistics? *Are you going to stay on the sidelines forever, covering up your cowardice with a veneer of protecting yourself and those you love?*

On the way home on the streetcar that evening, the noises and movements of the city had reverberated around his fractured thoughts. He saw again another mother and father, the parents of Nadya Nadova who had been found dead in a park in Northern Cyprus. Her grieving parents in Leningrad never recovered from the loss of their only child; her mother spent her remaining days watching for her daughter to come home. It was when he left their home that Mitch had vowed to nail the members of the human trafficking ring in Leningrad. For a time, he convinced himself that his decision to bring the gang to justice was out of concern for girls like Nadya who were easy prey for traffickers. That was before he learnt that the *pakhan*, the boss, was none other than his wife's lover. His altruistic quest turned into a personal vendetta.

Through the window of the streetcar that evening, he had watched an old man bend into the wind, body hunched as he fought his way along the ice-encrusted sidewalk. He remembered another old man, a cheery wave, a toothless grin—Slava as he paused from shovelling snow in the courtyard in Leningrad. The smell of burning flesh was again strong in Mitch's nostrils and he swallowed back bile that rose in his throat.

As the streetcar had jolted to a halt, he asked himself: *Is Slava's death to be in vain? And Ashwiyaa, that beautiful, vibrant young woman, gone forever, while traffickers and pimps live off the profits of misery?* It was then he vowed to find ways to support Lucy and James in their efforts. *It will have to be in the background but my legal knowledge could help them mount prosecutions, lobby for more effective legislation, put proposals together for funding and victim assistance.* A few days before, Lucy had outlined the charity's plans to raise money for a retreat, somewhere outside the city, where girls could be rehabilitated, recover from substance abuse, and learn skills so they could earn a living and not constantly be penalised for the life they had been forced to live.

Lucy and James had already had some success rehabilitating victims who passed through their safe house in Toronto. Among them was Nadezhda, the girl from Novosibirsk who had arrived at the shelter the night of Mitch and Lucy's wedding, and was now settled with a family in another part of Canada on a

Temporary Resident Permit. Although proceedings were dragging on, Lucy was hopeful that Nadezhda's application for permanent residence under the Humanitarian and Compassionate provisions of the Canadian Immigration Act would be successful.

Now, hunkered down in his car, Mitch struggled to keep his eyes open. What he wouldn't give for a good night's sleep. Even three hours of slumber without one or other of the twins waking and calling out. He stretched his aching limbs. It was then he saw it. A car slowed and pulled up outside the club. The headlights faded. Mitch reached for his camera. A man got out and looked around. Mitch did a double-take, then focused the camera and snapped several shots before the man disappeared into the club. *That man? Where have I seen him?* Some minutes later, checking the pictures he had taken, it came to him. He was one of the offenders at the 'John School' program designed to teach clients of prostitutes that their behaviour is exploitative and dangerous. Lucy had attended a session as an observer and arriving early to pick her up, Mitch had stood just inside the door. In a faltering voice, a young girl told how frightened she was of her pimp. "He made me beat one of the other girls. So we wouldn't trust one another." On the way home, Mitch had asked Lucy what would happen to the offenders. "The charges are withdrawn once they've finished the course," she admitted. "It's the best we can do."

Mitch clenched his fists now. *This same man has just gone into the club to violate another young girl.* Although it bore out his argument that letting offenders off their first offence isn't an effective deterrent, he found no comfort in being proved right.

He checked his watch. *Nick should be out by now. Where the hell is he?* Coldness gripped his stomach as he got out of the car and dashed across the street, dodging between vehicles. As he reached the sidewalk, one of the burly men guarding the club door lumbered towards him. Mitch tried to step around him. A hand gripped Mitch's left shoulder and the face came close to his. "If you're looking for your friend, he's in the laneway at the back of the stores!" the man spat in Mitch's face. Mitch wrenched the hand from his shoulder, turned quickly on his heel, and wiped his coat sleeve across his face as he ran. *Christ, Nick! What have they done?* Shouted obscenities followed him down the dark passageway at the side of the building. He slipped on a patch of ice but managed to stay upright as he turned the corner. He stopped. A figure lay beside the garbage bins. He hardly dared breathe as he edged closer.

42
Village Near Omsk, Siberia
September 2001

Izabella's fingers tightened their grip on Anja's hand. "It will be fun. You'll see," Anja comforted. The child glanced from Anja to Dina. Her usually sparkling eyes were dull. Today was her first day at kindergarten. She looked so vulnerable. Her new pink puffy coat failed to mask the thinness of her body. Her stick-like legs ended in the bright red boots of which she was so proud.

Anja met Dina's troubled gaze. This was hard for Dina. Hard too for Alyona, who had excused herself from taking her granddaughter to kindergarten, pleading pressure of work. Anja knew that neither woman could bear the thought that this child, born of tragedy, would be out on her own without their protection.

As they neared the school building, they were joined by other children, some clutching the hands of parents or grandparents, others running ahead or lagging behind. In the schoolyard, Anja bent down level with Izabella and whispered, "Be a brave girl, *moya dragotsennaya.* When you come home, Mama and I will take you to buy *pryaniki*. Would that be good?" Izabella nodded her head; the trace of a smile touched her cheeks. Anja kissed the top of her shining black curls and placed the traditional bunch of flowers in Izabella's hands. She stood back against the fence and watched Dina and Izabella walk slowly across the yard.

When they reached the open doorway, Izabella looked back and fluttered a hand in Anja's direction. Anja turned and headed towards the gate. Splashes of sunlight filtered through the trees on the other side of the wooden fence; the leaves were already turning pink, orange. A woman, head swathed in a scarf, bent low picking mushrooms. Anja looked up at the clear blue sky and prayed that Izabella would be safe. She thought back to her own first day at kindergarten, how she wailed when Mama and Papa left her there. Now Mama was gone … and Papa?

Dina was now hurrying across the schoolyard. When she reached Anja, she turned around and stared at the building. "She'll be fine," Anja said, trying to inject a lightness into her tone.

Dina blew her nose into an already sodden handkerchief. "I know she will. She's a tough little thing." She wiped her eyes with the back of a hand. "She's had to be, with a mother like me!"

"Don't be silly." Anja put an arm around her friend. "You're a good mother."

"You don't know what it was like when I first had her."

"No one can blame you for anything, Dina. You were victims. Both of you."

"That doesn't excuse me."

The two walked in silence for a few minutes, then Anja said, "Come home with me. There's no one else there. *Tyotya* was going into Omsk with Boris after they'd taken Timofei to school."

"I'll be okay on my own. You have to go to work."

"Not today. I switched my day off." She linked an arm through Dina's. "That old dragon of a manager can yell at someone else today," she laughed. For the past couple of months, Anja had been doing menial work in a legal office in Omsk while she decided what she wanted to study at university. Boris was encouraging her to look further afield than the universities and colleges in Omsk. "Your Mama, she wanted you to have a good career, make something of yourself," he urged. Anja wasn't convinced. Mama had wanted her to make sure Timofei didn't get into trouble. Next month, on her seventeenth birthday, Timofei would be eight, and was still getting into mischief. It was nearly a year ago that she read Mama's letter, and what had she done to try to find her papa? Not very much. She was taking English classes with an elderly lady in Omsk, so that if she ever got the chance to go to Canada, she would be better equipped to search for him. She didn't even know if he was still alive, and how could she go to Canada to look for him while trying to make sure that Timofei didn't get into trouble here? She couldn't rely on *Tyotya* to look after him, as the old woman was still obsessed with filling the store room with food. *You either have to study in Omsk or get a proper job and earn money so that you can go to Canada when Timofei is older,* she had told herself many times during the past few weeks.

The house was quiet as she and Dina hung up their coats and shed their *valenki.* Anja loved the house like this … the creak of floorboards, the crackle of the wood stove, warmth wrapping itself around her. In front of the *krasnyy ugol*, she crossed herself—her mother's face smiled back.

They settled at the kitchen table with glasses of tea and generous slices of *Tyotya's Biskvit*, Timofei's favourite sponge cake with cream cheese frosting. "I don't suppose you had any breakfast." She pushed a plate closer to Dina, who picked up a fork and dug it into her cake. Then the fork clattered onto the plate, and she hunched her shoulders, her body wracked with sobs.

"Whatever is it?" Anja asked, getting to her feet and crouching down, her face level with her friend's. "Izabella will be fine. Children always are."

"You don't know how awful I was. What I did." Dina's voice was small.

Anja leaned closer. "Whatever you did, it wasn't your fault. None of it was."

Dina covered her face with her hands, as she tried to stop the gasping noises coming from deep within.

"Come and sit in the chair by the stove. You'll be more comfortable there." Anja guided her to *Tyotya's* favourite chair. She retrieved the glass of tea and put it on a small table at the side. After a minute or two, Dina's breathing eased. She leaned back in the chair and looked up at the ceiling. "Why did I ever go there?"

"You were trying to help, with your father sick and unable to work," Anja said softly. "You weren't to know."

"I should have known. I'd heard enough stories about girls going abroad and never being heard of again. But, like most of them, I thought it wouldn't happen to me."

"You did what you thought was best for your family."

"It was awful, Anja. I've never been able to tell anyone. Not even my mother. The degradation, the sense of abandonment, the squalor. I was made to feel the lowest of the low, that I had brought it all on myself. It was all I was good for. I believed them." She dabbed at her eyes and breathed noisily. "I was a virgin, never been with a man. That first time, the man paid a lot of money for me. He was determined. Determined to get all he paid for. I huddled in the corner of that awful little room." Dina's arm stretched out as if pointing to the place where she had been. "The man. He dragged me to the bed and tore off my clothes. Then he was on me. Like an animal!" She leaned forward in the chair, one arm across her midriff, rocking back and forth.

Anja tried to hide the shudder that ran through her own body. "Don't talk about it. It's too upsetting for you." She moved her chair next to Dina's and placed a hand on her friend's back, rubbing it gently, choking back her own tears.

"I have to! I have to tell someone. It's making me crazy. It's eating me up inside. Don't you see?" She turned pleading eyes towards her friend.

Anja nodded. "Tell me … in your own time."

The story unfolded slowly, as if Dina was retrieving it from a hidden place. She and the other girls with whom she travelled to Turkey were locked in an apartment. "It was in the middle of a city. We didn't know where. Too high up for anyone to hear us call out. They took away our passports and said that if we went outside we would be arrested by the police." She paused. "One girl. She was fourteen. She wouldn't stop screaming: 'Mama! Mama!' I still hear her at night." She swallowed hard. "They beat her in front of us. Burnt her arms with cigarettes. She was the first. The first to be taken by one of the men … the men who came every night, every day." Dina bowed her head as if praying for some inner strength to let the words come.

"Are you sure you want to go on?"

"Let me say it."

"I'm here with you. There's nothing to hurt you," Anja murmured.

"I began to believe I was worthless. It was as if it wasn't my body. It was someone else who was being forced to do the most disgusting things." She shuddered. "They made us put on skimpy skirts, revealing tops. Plaster make-up on our faces. We looked like clowns." She began to laugh, softly at first. Then louder until she became hysterical and gut-wrenching sobs shook her thin frame.

Anja took Dina in her arms, stroking her hair until she quietened. "You poor soul … you poor, poor soul," she comforted over and over again. She thought of Yagudin, who she now knew had been her mother's lover and who she had called *Dyadya* Mikhail. The luxurious *dacha*. The dollhouse he bought for her. She felt hollow inside, ashamed at how much she had loved it. *How many girls like Dina had lived in fear to pay for that?* She pulled her friend closer. *Surely Mama knew what he was doing.*

"I'm sorry, Anja. I didn't mean to upset you." Dina straightened up and reached for Anja's hands. "You've had enough problems of your own."

"Mine were nothing compared to the horror you went through." Anja got to her feet and refreshed both glasses of tea, stirring a spoonful of jam into each.

"The only thing that kept me going through all that, when the men were …" Dina pursed her lips, "… the only thing that kept me going was to think of my mother and father. It was as though I was at home here in the village with them. When I was with a man, I imagined I was walking through my parents' house. It was so clear. The furniture, the pattern on the oilcloth on the kitchen table, flowers in pots in the summer, the smell of my mother's baking."

"Mama used to say that people find a way to cope with whatever happens," Anja comforted.

"After a while, I could no longer sense my father's presence. Papa was dead. I knew." She swallowed hard.

"What happened … when you were pregnant with Izabella? Did you still have to …" Anja couldn't finish her sentence.

"Some men pay more to have sex with a pregnant woman. All the time I hoped what they did would make me lose the baby. I would die too." Her words hung in the air. "Does that shock you?"

"Nyet." Anja avoided looking into Dina's eyes.

"After Izabella was born, I refused to feed her. Wouldn't even give her a name. Every time I looked at her, I tried to imagine which man was her father. Still do, but there were so many of them." She shook her head slowly. "One of the other girls fed her. Her own baby had been taken away. After a week, they made me start work again. I was terrified I would get pregnant again or get some disease. One day, one of the girls whispered to me that the girl who had my baby was planning to make a run for it, taking my baby with her. I watched her and, one day when she was with a man, I took my baby. She stared at me with those dark eyes. I couldn't look away. She was my child. When the girl came back, she tried to wrest the baby from my arms, but I held on." Dina huddled back in the chair, arms across her chest as if still protecting her baby. "She swore at me, saying the traffickers were going to take the baby away, sell her to a childless couple. I knew I had to do something. I kept my baby with me. Hardly slept. Never let her out of my sight."

"How did you get away?"

"One evening when everyone else was working and I was waiting for the next man, I wrapped her in a sheet and knotted the ends around my neck. I opened the window and climbed out, gripping a drainpipe with my hands and feet, and slowly lowered myself down. I was petrified she would fall. There wouldn't have been anything I could do to save her. We would both have plunged to our deaths." She shivered, and Anja lifted the glass of tea to Dina's lips. "The drainpipe. I was scared it would come away from the wall or that someone would see what I was doing. But I made it," she sighed loudly. "As soon as my feet touched the ground, I clutched her to me and ran."

"Where did you go?"

"I didn't know where I was or what I was doing. I just ran as far away as I could. It seemed like I had been running for hours when I came to a forest. I ran further and further into the undergrowth before sitting down and making sure the baby was all right. I put her to my dry breast, cooing to her as she tried to suckle. That moment, when the two of us were entirely alone in the dark forest, was the most precious I have ever experienced. I looked at her, and told her she was to be called Izabella, the name of my *babushka,* my mother's mother."

"How did you get back here without a passport, money?"

"A good woman, she took us in. Looked after us both until I was strong enough to cope with the journey home. Her son, he knew someone who could get me a passport in a false name. They dyed what was left of my hair and took my photograph. He drove me across the border into Armenia. We made out we were husband and wife, a family. He was kind, but I hated being close to him, to any man. Still do." She hunched her shoulders. "We stayed with one of his cousins for a while, and then another member of his family took Izabella and me in his truck into Georgia. From there, we were on our own."

"How did you manage, with a baby as well?"

"It took weeks. I kept away from main roads … I was terrified the traffickers would find us, take us back. And then what would have happened to Izabella?" She twisted her handkerchief around and around in her fingers.

Anja sat in silence. She thought of her own papa, how brave he was to take on the traffickers, to help girls like Dina. "Aren't you scared? Even now, the traffickers may …?" Anja didn't dare put her thoughts into words.

"You're wondering if they might still come after us?"

Anja nodded.

"Boris. He knew someone. He fixed it. Paid them off."

43
Village Near Omsk, Siberia
Late September 2001

Anja gripped Timofei's hand and pulled him behind her as she ran down the path and out through the gateway of the church. Mud squelched beneath their boots as they hurried along the street towards home. They clattered up the steps to the porch and Anja called breathlessly to the man she once called 'Papa': "Boris! Boris! You must come quickly."

Boris rubbed his eyes as he stepped out into the morning light. "What? What's the matter? Is something on fire?"

Anja bent double, trying to summon the breath to tell him.

"It's *Tyotya,*" Timofei began.

"What's she done now?" Boris gave an exasperated sigh.

"She's shouting out in the service. People are getting angry," Anja gabbled, grabbed Boris's arm and began to pull him down the steps. "We have to hurry."

As the three of them got close to the church doorway, *Tyotya's* voice boomed out: "A great war will set father against son. The sun will darken. Blackness will descend on the land!"

Boris cursed loudly as he entered the church.

Tyotya stood in front of the altar. Through a high window, a shaft of sunlight cast a surreal halo around her. "Heathens! Heathens!" she yelled, waving her arms around to encompass the whole congregation. Boris strode towards her; the sound of his footsteps echoed in the church. She pointed an accusing finger at him. "You! You are the worst sinner!"

The *presbyter* took her arm and tried to lead her down the steps. She broke free and grabbed the gold cross which hung on a chain around his neck. "You are not worthy to wear such a thing!" she spat. Boris grabbed her arm and, after a struggle, prised her fingers open. "Repent! Repent!" she shouted as the *presbyter*, cradling his cross in his hand, hurried them towards the door.

Outside, the *presbyter's* words, "She must not come to the church again," set the old woman off on another tirade. Boris led her away.

Alyona, who with Dina and Izabella had followed them out of the church, put an arm around Anja's shoulders. "She'll be okay," she comforted. "It's best if she stays quiet at home for a while. You and Timofei can come and have lunch with us." Izabella slipped her hand into Anja's as they walked slowly along the street.

* * *

Two days later, Anja chopped carrots and onions and tossed them into the pot where the meat was already cooking. The rhythmic thud, thud, of Boris's axe came from outside as he chopped wood. When Anja had arrived home from work an hour or so ago, the house was cold. *Tyotya* was kneeling in front of the *krasnyy ugol*, where she had spent most of her waking hours since the incident in the church. Anja had quickly lit the stove, helped the old woman to her feet and settled her into an armchair, where she was now asleep.

A blast of noise came from the room Timofei shared with Boris: "You can't fool the pitch-black night."

Anja hurried to the doorway. "Turn it down, Timofei! You'll wake *Tyotya!*" she hissed at her brother, who was leaping around the room pretending to play the accompaniment to the tune that his favourite group, Nautilus Pompilius, was belting out. Anja closed the door carefully behind her, stalked across to the CD player and turned the volume down.

"It's Nau!" Timofei retaliated and turned the volume up even higher. "But the river's wide, the river's deep," he sang along.

The door crashed open. *Tyotya* lurched into the room, grabbed the CD player and hurled it onto the floor. Anja and Timofei stared open-mouthed. "Heathen!" *Tyotya* yelled and made a grab at Timofei. He dodged around her and ran into the kitchen, closely pursued by the old woman. Anja tried to grab her, but she ducked and wove as she chased Timofei from one side of the room to the other. Anja quickly hid the knife she had been using under a cloth on the worktop and, grabbing hold of Timofei's arm opened the porch door. *Tyotya's* curses followed them as they ran down the outside steps. From the pathway, they turned and saw that *Tyotya* was now standing by the open door making the sign of the cross.

"What's going on?" Boris appeared around the side of the house.

"She's crazy!" Timofei wailed, pointing to the old woman. "She's smashed my CD player!"

"Anja! Timofei! Get your things together and go to Alyona," Boris ordered.

"Don't hurt her! Don't hurt *Tyotya*!" Anja pleaded, pointing to the axe he held in his hand.

Boris let the axe drop to the ground, walked up the steps and pushed *Tyotya* into the house.

Anja and Timofei crept back in and started collecting together their overnight things. In Timofei's room, Anja pulled out his clean school clothes from the chest of drawers and stuffed them into his bag.

"Tomorrow," Boris began as they emerged into the kitchen, "tomorrow I will take her to the city, to a nursing home, where she will be cared for." He put a hand on Anja's shoulder. "She's lucky. Years ago, heretics were burnt at the stake." His words sent a tremor through Anja's body. She went over to where Yevdokia was lying prostrate in front of the icons and, with one knee bent, kissed the back of her head. Then she turned the stove off and, taking Timofei's hand, walked into the darkness.

44
Toronto
December 2001

Mitch leaned back in his chair. The tilt mechanism squeaked—there was something comforting about the familiar sound. He looked around the empty classroom where balls of screwed-up notepaper littered desks and spilled out of wastepaper bins. He was tempted to unravel a few to see what doodles his students had penned while they were supposed to be concentrating on his examples of inaccuracies in Japan's reports to the United Nations Committee on Racial Discrimination. It wasn't the most riveting subject, so he could hardly blame them for their inattention. Exams were over for this semester and, by the look of some of his students, they had been partying hard.

How different his own young life had been as he tried to keep pace with his legal studies while working at various jobs to earn money to support his wife and baby daughter. His life should have been different. Not only had he missed out on the carefree days of young adulthood but, by marrying Natasha, he had disappointed his parents and hurtled headlong into a never-ending spiral of debt and trouble. His only compensation was Anja. He wouldn't trade his memories of her, although there was no getting away from the uncomfortable fact that he hadn't been a good father. He had cared more for his stupid principles and his own safety. Long ago, he abandoned any pretence that he was waiting for the right moment to go back to Russia to find her. He had finally admitted the truth to himself: *You're scared she will reject you! Who would blame her?*

At least in one area of his life, he had stopped taking the easy way out. Lucy had helped him find the courage to face his demons head on. Today was his last day teaching at the university. He would no longer hide away in a classroom, theorising about the importance of respecting human rights, or cower in darkened cars while others took all the risks. That night in January, Nick was lucky to escape with broken ribs and concussion. As Mitch had paced back and forth in the hospital corridor, he came to a decision. *This is no way to tackle trafficking gangs. The long-term answer is to fight them in the courts where, win or lose, their abuse of young women and the need for effective legislation will be exposed to public view.* He was wasting his life teaching. The summer break this year had seemed endless, his days filled with household chores, breaking up fights between the twins, listening to the conversations of women outside the playgroup building. Much as he loved his children, he needed more than that.

So, in January he would be starting a position with a law firm specialising in cases involving human rights abuses. Mitch was being brought in to concentrate on human trafficking cases and to lobby for effective legislation in the Canadian legal code. *It won't be an easy job but, unlike the corrupt legal system in Russia, at least here both sides get a fair hearing,* he told himself. Leaving his comfortable job in the university wasn't an easy decision, and he had had many sleepless nights since deciding to accept the position, but if he was ever to have any self-respect and earn the respect of others—especially Lucy—it was something he must do.

Now, he looked at his watch. It was nearly six o'clock and he was supposed to be meeting some of his colleagues for a farewell drink. He got to his feet and, as he began loading his remaining belongings into his briefcase, his thoughts drifted back to when he first arrived here—a broken man. He had gradually begun to fit in first as a student and more recently as an associate professor, something of which he knew his late parents would have been proud. And Lucy. He owed her so much. She had given him back his life, his future. A warm feeling rippled through his body as he thought back to the twins' excitement at breakfast this morning when Lucy told them that on Saturday morning they would all be going with her parents to cut a Christmas tree at a farm outside the city. Something his own parents would have loved to do with these soon-to-be-five-year-old 'monsters'.

He wound a scarf around his neck, shrugged into his thick coat, jammed his hat on, pulled his gloves out of his coat pockets, and picked up his briefcase. At the classroom door, he took a last look around. His life would be different from now on. No pausing in his lectures as late-comers tried to sneak in, hurriedly thrown-on clothes draped around their bodies, hair looking as though it hadn't seen a comb in days. *It's been good experience here, but it's time to move on while I'm still young enough to achieve something,* he told himself as he stepped into the corridor.

"Good luck, Professor!"

Mitch turned around. "Thanks. Good luck to you too," he called to the group of students coming towards him. "Remember what I taught you!"

"Oh, we will, sir!" they laughed as they slouched past.

45
Western Siberia
January 2002

"My friend. You must get up. Come!"

Pavel's voice seemed far away, wrapped in mist. Sergei felt pressure on his arms, pulling him up in the cot. The big man's face was close now, his breath warm in the cold air.

"You have to get up. If they know you are sick, they will cast you out on your own." Pavel tried to ignore the gurgle he heard in his friend's lungs as, with one arm around Sergei's upper body and one under his legs, he lifted him out of his cot and carried him to a rickety chair by the woodstove.

"You are a good friend," Sergei wheezed as Pavel guided his arms into his overcoat and jammed his feet into his boots.

"Lean on me as we walk," Pavel urged, hauling him upright and fastening his coat. Outside, they swayed as an icy blast of wind hit them. Sergei stopped, bent double, fighting to control the coughing that wracked his body. "Not far to go," Pavel cajoled as they made their shambling way between the huts. Over the past few years, Pavel had watched in alarm as winter took its toll on the older man. Before, as spring and summer bathed this alien land in warmth, Sergei had seemed to build up his strength again. But not in the past year or so, and Pavel worried that soon the guards would throw his friend out of the camp to fend for himself. It had happened to others, as guards covered up the deteriorating conditions in the camp; better to say they had released one prisoner than for yet another death to blemish their records. Not long ago, a dying man's cries had gone on for most of the night, accompanied by the howling of animals as they circled their prey outside the fence. Then silence.

Inside the mess hut now, Pavel settled Sergei on a bench along a wall then lined up for their meagre rations. *"Schastlivogo Rozhdestva,"* the guard mumbled as he slopped watery *kasha* into tin bowls. Seeing the confused look on Pavel's face, he laughed. "It's Christmas Day. Didn't anyone tell you?" Pavel shrugged, picked up the bowls and shuffled back to Sergei.

"On govorit, chto eto Rozhdestva." Pavel nodded towards the guard as he spooned food into Sergei's mouth.

"Christmas!" Sergei spluttered. A thin line of *kasha* trickled down his chin; Pavel pulled a rag out of his own coat pocket and wiped his friend's face. "I must go. Sophia. She will wonder where I am. We have to go to Anja, take her gifts." Sergei staggered to his feet, swaying as he stared around the room. "Where are they? I must have lost them." He stumbled into the table. *"Ya nay ponimayu. Ya nay ..."*

Pavel grabbed him and settled him back on the bench. "Anja has the gifts. She was here this morning." Pavel continued the charade he had recently begun to play with Sergei. It made him less agitated, calmed him. "She's gone to play with her friends now, to show them the gifts."

"She'll come back later? And Sophia?"

"Yes, they'll be here."

46
Village Near Omsk, Siberia
January 2002

Anja pulled the quilt up to her chin. *Just a few more minutes,* she promised herself as she listened to Boris crashing around in the kitchen. She snuggled further down in the bed trying to recapture the warm feeling that ran through her last night as she gazed at the people around the table set for the traditional Christmas Eve feast—the people who were now her family. She had long ago stopped wondering why she was here, far away from her real family. *What does a blood connection matter? These people have looked after me since Papa abandoned me and Mama died.* But, somewhere deep within, there was an ache which nothing seemed to ease. There was something missing from her life that not even Dina and sweet Izabella could fill.

Dina seems to radiate happiness now. So different from the ghost-like shadow that appeared in the village four or five years ago. Since the day in September when Dina finally opened up, telling Anja the horrific story of her ordeal at the hands of traffickers, she had begun to piece her life back together. She had been accepted at an *uchilishcha* in Omsk, where she would soon begin training to teach music in a school. Anja had been surprised to discover that her friend had a wonderful singing voice. In the early hours of this morning, as they all relaxed after the festive meal, candlelight flickered on Dina and Izabella's faces as they sang the traditional song, *V Lesu Rodilas Yolochka:*

The forest raised a Christmas tree
'Twas silent and serene
In winter and in summer
It was slender and so green

Everyone else joined in. Anja struggled to swallow the lump which clogged her throat as she watched the joyful, innocent look on Izabella's face.

Now, a crash and loud curses from the kitchen disturbed Anja's thoughts. "What's happened?" she asked, poking her head through the gap in the curtains around her bed. A smell of burning wafted towards her.

"I asked him to turn off the stove and he couldn't even do a simple thing like that!" Boris stared at the blackened food in the pan. He turned and shook his head at his son, who was slumped in a chair, earpieces in both ears, as he listened to music on the new portable music player Boris had given him for Christmas. He strode over to Timofei and pulled the earpieces out of his ears. Timofei looked around, a startled expression on his face.

"Let me see to it," Anja said. "We can cut off the burnt pieces." She pulled a thick cardigan over her nightdress. "Timofei! Get the honey out of the cupboard." He fixed her with a sour look, did as she asked, then plugged back into his music.

After breakfast, Timofei dashed off to show his friends his latest acquisition. "You spoil him," Anja admonished as she and Boris lingered over coffee.

He sighed loudly, got to his feet and refilled both glasses. "Anja?" He placed her glass in front of her and nudged the pot of honey towards her. "There's something I have to tell you."

"Is it *Tyotya*? Is something wrong?"

"She's fine."

"I miss her so much."

"She's better where she is. It's not as if she knows one day from another." He paced around the room.

"But I can't bear to think of her there, in that place with strangers. She should be here with us."

"That isn't going to happen, Anja. We can't leave her in the house all day on her own. She'd burn the place down."

"I know."

Boris stopped pacing. His hands gripped the back of a chair. "When you were at Alyona's yesterday, I … I started clearing out *Tyotya's* room. I thought you could move in there."

"I don't know," Anja frowned, "it wouldn't seem right being in her room. She slept there all her life."

"I'll give it a coat of paint, and we can get some new furniture."

"I like her old stuff. She told me stories about everything in the room. Where her bed came from, her cupboard."

"I found some things there … in the cupboard. Things that belong to you."

"What? What did she have of mine?"

Boris went into *Tyotya's* bedroom and brought out a bundle tied with string. "She must have got hold of these before any of us saw them," he said, placing the bundle on the table in front of Anja.

"What are they?"

"Your father. They're from him."

"From Papa? They can't be," Anja blurted as she leaned forward and put a tentative hand on the package. "How? How did *Tyotya* get them?"

"Her friend Dotnara Vektorova. She worked in the mail office, and I assume she gave them to her."

"But why? Why would they take my letters, not give them to me?"

"Maybe she hid them because she didn't want to break up our family, cause more heartache," Boris ventured.

"She had no right!" Anja snapped, then pulled the letters towards her.

"I don't think your mother knew about them. She would have told me."

Anja caught her breath as she undid the string. Blood pulsed noisily in her temples. The handwriting. It was Papa's. She remembered now how he used to put notes in her school bag, notes telling her how much he loved her. *There was usually a funny drawing too.* "What … what does he say? What does he want?"

"I only opened the top one, to see who they were from." Boris hovered at Anja's side. "He's in Canada. Or he was when he sent them."

Anja ran a finger over the stamp on the envelope on top of the pile.

"Aren't you going to open them?"

"Later," Anja barely whispered.

Boris sat on the chair next to her, pulled a handkerchief out of his pocket and wiped tears from her cheeks. "Your Mama and I. We did lots of wrong things, both of us. Maybe it's time to put things right." He kissed Anja's forehead. "Now, why don't you open them and see what he has to say?" When she didn't respond, Boris cajoled: "It looks as though there are cards there too."

Anja thought of her birthdays, Christmas celebrations. The sense of disappointment she felt when nothing came from her father. *Tyotya, she hid the cards from me. His letters. She had them all along. How could she do that?* Cradling the bundle in her arms, Anja got to her feet.

"Anja?" Boris laid a hand on her arm.

"I'll read them later!" she snapped. "Stepan and I, we're going to see his *babushka*. She's …" She choked on the rest of the words.

* * *

Three hours later, Anja pulled her hand out of Stepan's and ran up the steps to the house. She turned and waved. He shrugged his shoulders, thrust his hands in his pockets, and walked away.

For the past year or so, they had been almost inseparable and today, when they left the hospital in Omsk where his *babushka* was recovering from surgery, he had hoped they would spend the rest of the day together. When Anja told him there was something she must do at home, he sulked, asking why he couldn't come with her. "It's something I have to do alone," she said.

Now, as she opened the door to the house, she wondered if the letters were a nasty trick of her imagination. It had happened before. The times she imagined she saw her Papa on the street … in the forest when she was collecting wood. And Mama. For months after she died, Anja ran home from school convinced she would be there preparing their meal. Today, as she kicked off her boots, there was an eerie silence in the house. There was a note from Boris on the table saying he had gone to Omsk. *I've taken Timofei with me. He can help. Will be good for him to do something constructive for a change, and it will give you time on your own.* Anja knew his business wasn't doing well and he was working all the hours he could to try to turn things around.

She hurried to her bedroom alcove and let out a sigh of relief; she hadn't imagined the letters, they were still under her pillows. She clutched them close as, still wrapped in her heavy winter clothing, she sat in the armchair by the stove. *Maybe … maybe it's better if I don't read them.* She threw off her gloves. *What if Mama was right all those years ago when she told me Papa didn't want me. But why would he have written all these letters, cards?* She undid the string and shuffled through the envelopes. The earliest one was at the bottom of the pile. It was addressed to someone in Leningrad. *How did it get here?* She tore the envelope open and pulled out two flimsy sheets. The letter was dated nearly ten years ago. *How can that be? Why didn't Tyotya tell me, or Mama or Boris?* A surge of anger rushed through her. She got to her feet, put the envelopes on the kitchen table, and threw off her coat.

She read letter after letter. The early ones came from Montréal, the place where Papa was born. She remembered he had promised to take her there one day. He related things that happened on his journey to Canada, places he stayed for a while, and of finding *Babushka* Sophia's friend in Montréal. It all sounded so strange, so far away. But, as she read, the sound of his voice came back to her. The voice he used when reading bedtime stories when she was very young. She remembered now how he sometimes made up parts of the story, how they both laughed when she told him the story hadn't been like that before. She touched the side of her forehead, remembering his goodnight kisses. There were four birthday cards, each with 'Daughter' on the front, and under his signature kisses and little drawings like he used to put on the notes he left in her school bag. She blinked back tears.

She read again the letter in which he said *Dedushka* had died. *How can that be? Mama's letter was written much later and she said Dedushka was in one of those camps. Nothing makes sense. Surely Mama would have told me if Dedushka died. Maybe Boris knows.*

The letters all ended with her Papa telling her he loved her and would come for her when he could. *So, why hasn't he? Maybe he thinks I don't love him, have forgotten him. What else was he to think when all his letters went unanswered?* A fresh wave of anger ran through her as she thought of the times she cried herself to sleep, wondering why Papa didn't want her. How *Tyotya* comforted her, saying, "You have us now. You don't need him." *How could she do that?* Anja stared at the array of letters and cards strewn across the table. *How could she have kept them from me?* But, as she thought of the lonely old woman lying in the bed in that horrible place, anger drained away.

She picked up the last of the letters, written over five years ago. It came from an address in Toronto. A shiver ran through her. *Does Papa have a new family? Is that why there are no more letters? Or did Tyotya destroy them? What if something happened to him? He was sick? Dead? "Nyet! Nyet!"* she cried out loud. The anguish she felt so long ago when Mama told her that Papa didn't want her—the hurt that was still there just below the surface—spilled over.

"Papa. Papa," she sobbed as she stumbled blindly towards her bed in the alcove.

"Anja? Wake up. I've brought some tea." Boris's voice was soft.

"What time is it?" she asked, dragging herself up in the bed. It was dark outside the window.

"It's nearly six," Boris replied, putting the glass of tea on the small table at the side of her bed.

"Papa's letters! I left them on the table," Anja said, struggling to get out of bed.

"I put them in here." Boris pulled open a drawer. The envelopes were in a neat pile, tied with string again.

"Timofei? Did he read them?" Anja's voice contained an element of panic.

Boris closed the drawer. "He can't think of anything but his music."

"At least with the earpieces, we don't all have to listen." Anja leaned back against the pillows and took a sip of tea.

"Why don't you write to him … your father?" Boris sat on the side of her bed.

"He probably has another family now." A fresh wave of sadness ran through her as she thought of her father with other children, another wife.

"Did he mention anyone else?"

She shook her head.

"Well then."

Anja's hands started to tremble. "Then why didn't he come to see me? Mama too?"

Boris took the glass and put it back on the table.

"He knew where we were."

"Maybe things got in the way. Time passed, until he thought he'd left it too late."

Anja bit her bottom lip.

"Don't you think you owe him an explanation? Tell him about *Tyotya* and the letters." In the silence that followed his words, Boris leaned forward and pulled her into his arms.

"Whatever you decide, Annushka, you know I'll help you. I've always thought of you as my daughter. So maybe I know a bit of how your real Papa must be feeling. Don't you think?" He held her away from him. "How about a smile?" Anja couldn't help grinning, deepening the dimples in her cheeks. "That's better," Boris laughed. "Now, before you say anything I think you should go there … to Canada … to see him."

"What about Timofei? I can't leave him. I promised Mama."

"She would understand, and Timofei is my problem, not yours."
"But we don't have the money."
"We'll find it."

47
Western Siberia
May 2002

Sergei Galichin … yes, that was his name. He could remember that. He had held on to this name over the years, repeating it many times a day. He was sure it was his. To lose it in the murky recesses of his mind would mean he did not exist. *I must remember.*

It was the first day of May, but Sergei Galichin did not know this. This day had started like any other. Any other he had come to know. Pavel's big, gentle hands rocked him awake on the wooden slats of his cot; his sparse frame had long ago adapted to its rigid resting place. But for many months his sleep had been disturbed, making him look back on the previous years with fondness. Fondness for the ability to sleep, to ignore the bone-chilling cold, or flies feasting on crumbling flesh. Or the days and nights when hunger bellowed in his belly. Now, in the dark hours he would awake drenched in sweat. He lay still, feeling as if he was suspended above his body, watching as it cooled from the dense heat of fever to the chilling cold of the grave. Then the piercing cough would tear his lungs, pushing vile liquid into his mouth to be spat on to the floor. Pavel would always be there, his hands caressing Sergei's forehead. In the times when he slept, he would dream that Pavel had gone. He was never sure whether it was fever or fear that awoke him; they blended into one.

This day in the mess hut, they thrust tin mugs forward to be filled with the bitter liquid with its smoke-tinged taste they had come to know as coffee. They soaked coarse black bread in the hot liquid. The now-soggy bread slid down Sergei's throat, but a moment later he heaved, spewing it down the front of his coat to join other unidentifiable stains. "*Spokoynoy, moy drug*," Pavel comforted.

They shuffled back to their hut, picking their way between the deep ruts that pitted the camp in winter. The land was beginning to thaw and remnants of pine needles would soon find their way through thin soles of boots. Pavel bent to pick up a scrap of paper. He turned it over and over then put it in his overcoat pocket. Sergei paused too, listening to the sighing of the wind through the trees, his face touched with the light of a new dawn. Then his shoulders folded against the red hot heat and searing pain from his lungs.

"Come, my friend," Pavel urged in his thick Ukrainian accent, opening the door to their hut. Inside, Sergei sank down on his cot, his right palm pressed into his chest in an effort to ease his laboured breathing. "They have gone already." Pavel spoke of Trofim and Amazat who shared this fetid hovel. Sergei had worried they would tell of his sickness, but Pavel said, "They won't tell." The two men knew Pavel watched them in the night. He had begun to think that knowing his eyes were on them added to their thrill as their bodies, swaddled in coarse cloth, searched for ways to excite, to please. Pavel thought now of the gentle-faced Trofim, whose slender hands had once moved so delicately, expressively, as he had described his life ... his other life. But now he was part of this life. And part of this life was Amazat, who could dominate the younger man with a piercing look from his almond-shaped eyes or a stern expression on his face—the oriental face of a Tatar—willing Trofim to do his bidding. Pavel shuddered. "Come, Sergei Dmitrievich. It is time to go."

In front of the gates, they joined other men huddling for warmth in the combined mass of bodies. Sergei stood in the shadow of Pavel's towering height, with its promise of protection from the gaze of guards when his search for breath caused his body to convulse. This was the worst part of the day. Time to think of the gruelling work ahead, of the heaving and sawing of logs in the *taiga,* the vast forbidding forest beyond the gates. *You have to do it. You have to keep going,* Sergei told himself. His body told him otherwise.

A guard at the front of the line shouted an order. The prisoners grouped into rows of five.

Over the years, Sergei and Pavel had witnessed a change in the guards' attitude. Once they walked with clipped step, even when the slime of green-streaked mud coated their boots. Now the lethargy which invaded the camp had begun to penetrate their air of authority. When Sergei's mind played tricks on him and hallucinatory images dogged his thoughts, he was convinced that nothing was real here, a nightmare into which he had stumbled.

The men began to mutter amongst themselves and move their feet to keep warm. Sergei stared at Pavel's form in front of him. He looked nowhere else. He had long ago stopped exchanging glances with other prisoners, many of whom were criminals who used their own language and forced others to do their share of work.

"358957. *Shag na front!*"

There was silence. Pavel turned, gripped Sergei's right arm and whispered: "It is you, Seryozha. They want you." Fear rippled through Sergei's flesh. His throat constricted as bodies shifted to make way for him. Pavel's grip tightened, both men rooted to the spot. Sergei looked up, but Pavel's gaze was fixed somewhere above his head. The grip on his arm loosened. Pavel's voice seemed far away: *"Vy dolzhny idti."* Sergei wrapped his arms around his chest, seeking the comfort of his own body. The guard shouted again and Sergei's legs rose and fell, moving forward with each syllable. He stopped and looked over his right shoulder to where Pavel's head, with its grey woollen hat, towered above the other men. He sought Pavel's eyes. His friend nodded his head slowly. Sergei's feet stepped into the void.

A canvas bag was thrown on to the ground in front of him. "You are free to go," the guard snapped. Sergei stared at the bag. It was dark brown and fastened with two knotted pieces of fabric. *"Imbetsil!"* the guard shouted and shoved him hard. He fell to the ground, struggling to breathe as the rasping started in his chest. "Pick it up!" Sergei raised his head. Mucus dribbled from his mouth. He felt hands lifting him to his feet. They held him until he stopped swaying.

"You must go," a soft voice urged. Pavel held out the canvas bag and, taking one of Sergei's hands, wound the strap around his fingers. Sergei's head hung. He stared at his friend's boots. "Go for me if not for yourself," Pavel whispered.

"Nyet ... Moy drug, nyet," Sergei pleaded as Pavel walked slowly back to his place in line.

The gates swung open and, with the blast of a horn, an open-backed truck roared in. Its green paintwork bore the scars of a careless life. The throb of the engine came in surges. Sergei stumbled out of its way and gripped a wooden post outside the guards' hut. Shouts and thuds ran through his head as guards rushed to unload sacks and drums. He moved slowly around the truck, eyes fixed on the line of men shuffling through the gates, each one bending to pick up a rusty saw from the pile the guards had tipped onto the ground. The gates closed and Sergei hurried to the fence, searching until he found a knotted hole in the wood. Through one rheumy eye he watched until Pavel's grey-clad head merged with the forest.

"*Vy!* Get in the back of the truck." Sergei turned around. "I don't have all day!" the driver barked as he opened the door and climbed into the cab. Sergei's feet felt as though they were glued to the ground. The engine spluttered into life as he pushed the bag into the back of the truck and attempted to haul himself up. He wheezed, the top half of his body splayed out on the ridged metal of the rear flap. He twisted sideways as strong hands pushed his legs into the truck. The flap slammed into place. With a blast of the horn the vehicle lurched forward. Sergei rolled around unable to gain a hand- or foothold. The truck stopped and he heard the driver exchange derisory comments with the guard at the gate. Their laughing banter echoed in Sergei's ears as he scrambled to his knees and pulled himself on to a wooden crate. With another lurch, they were through the gates. He drew his coat around his body, his gaze fixed on the wooden palisade around the camp until it was no more than a pinpoint.

The truck bounced along the track for what seemed an eternity. Each bump lifted Sergei's body off the crate. He listened as the engine noise changed with the contours of the land … labouring … racing … labouring. With each steep climb, his fingers locked around the side of the truck and an edge of the crate, his boots unable to grip in the scattering of grains and unidentifiable powdery substances lining the metal floor. He scanned the forest, this side and that. *Where are they taking me? Why have they let me go?* He knew too well that the sick were often turned loose to die outside the camp so their deaths wouldn't be reported. He thought of how Pavel had sought to protect him from that knowledge, and the way his friend had done his best to hide the creeping illness that had taken over Sergei's body. He imagined he could still feel the big man's protective arm around him, hear his gentle voice.

Now the trees were sparse, the ground flattened out. The light was bright and Sergei shielded his eyes with one hand. He thought back to the times in the camp when the first dappled rays of spring sunshine filtered through the trees and he and Pavel basked in unaccustomed warmth.

The truck ground to a halt. "This is where you get off old man," the driver shouted through the open window of the cab.

"Gde eto? Gde ya?" Sergei called as he crawled to the rear of the truck and pushed at the flap. It tumbled open with a clatter, and he slid to the ground dragging the bag behind him. He tried to lift the flap back into place.

“What are you doing there?” The driver flung open the cab door, stomped to the back of the truck, grabbed Sergei by his coat lapels and pushed him to the side of the road.

“Where do I go?” Sergei wheezed as the flap clanged into place.

The man laughed loudly, hoisted himself into the cab and slammed the door. The truck roared away.

48
St Petersburg
May 2002

Anja got out of the car and looked up at the imposing building. She hunched her shoulders. *Everything is so big in the city. Noisy too.* Buildings towered over her, people scurried past, trams clanged, impatient drivers blasted horns. *Is there no end to the mayhem?* So different from her quiet village, where the small houses were made of wood, people she knew stopped to chat on the street, and you could smell the trees and hear the wind sighing. She looked up at the wrought iron balconies of the building. On either side of a balustrade on the second floor, she picked out ornate images of sunflowers. She smiled to herself. Her mother's long ago words ran through her mind: *Those are happy flowers, Annushka.* Every summer since her mother died, Boris brought home a big bunch of sunflowers and the three of them walked together to the cemetery to put them on her grave. Anja caught her breath now. Between the sunflowers on the balcony, an image of a huge spider lurked in an ironwork web.

A now-familiar mixture of fear and excitement rippled through her, much as it had on the day last week when she stepped down from the train onto the platform at Moskovsky Station. A female attendant, resplendent in turquoise coat and black hat, had handed her suitcase to her, and Anja followed the other passengers up the slope, down an escalator, and through marble corridors. Before the exit, she stepped to one side and looked around for *Dyadya* Petya. *He said to wait here, but where is he?* She could hardly remember him, but he said he would find her. "I'd know my only sister's daughter anywhere!" he had laughed when she spoke to him on the telephone from Boris's office.

Then, as she looked around, she saw that everyone from the train had drifted away and, apart from an old man emptying trash bins, she was on her own. *Maybe I should get back on the train and go home.* She still wasn't sure she wanted to be here, even less sure about going to Canada. On the long journey from Omsk, she convinced herself that her father wouldn't want to see her. *Isn't it better to remember him as he was all those years ago when we ran together along the banks of the Neva, or tramped through snow making up silly songs? Maybe Mama was right. Papa doesn't want me. Especially after all these years.*

As she waited in the hallway at Moskovsky Station, her thoughts had drifted back to the scene at the railway station in Omsk. She could still feel Izabella's arms around her neck, her face pressed close as the child whispered: *"Vy vernetes'?"* Anja had choked back tears, telling her she would be back soon. Dina lifted Izabella to the ground. "Be brave, my friend," she called as Boris shepherded Anja onto the train. As the train pulled away, she leaned out of the window trying to etch into her mind the image of her family and friends on the platform. Timofei ran alongside yelling: "Annushka, don't forget! Our Lady Peace! Bring back Our Lady Peace!" Anja waved to him and made a mental note to buy a CD of the Rock Band as soon as she got to Canada. Timofei and the rest of her family faded from sight.

"Anja! It is you!" She had been jolted out of her reverie as a tall man with a shock of dark hair hurried towards her. "I'm so sorry I'm late." *Dyadya* Petya gripped her upper arms. "So much construction. The roads are a mess!" She relaxed as she looked into familiar brown eyes flecked with hazel. Her mother's eyes. "I'd know those dimples anywhere!" he laughed and wrapped his arms around her. "It had to be you." After a few moments, he picked up her suitcase and, with an arm around her shoulders, guided her out of the station. "The rest of them are waiting in the car. We didn't want you to feel overwhelmed."

"The rest of them?" Anja tried to remember the names of her aunt and cousins.

"Well, there's my wife, your *Tyotya* Mila. You must remember her." Anja nodded, trying to drag up a dim memory of her aunt. "Your cousins, Dasha and Gena. And there's Valentin."

"Valentin?"

"He was born after you left. He's nine and a holy terror!"

"Like my brother, Timofei." Anja swallowed hard.

"We were surprised to hear your mother had another child," Petya had remarked as he steered her towards a large silver car. "Next time, you should bring him with you."

Now, *Dyadya* Petya took Anja's arm as they climbed the stone entrance steps of the apartment building. She averted her eyes from the carved fish with gigantic eyeballs gracing either side of the double entrance doors. Inside the hallway, Petya stopped. "If you're uncertain, Anja, you don't have to do this." He squeezed her elbow. "I can go in on my own. Find out what happened. What she promised."

"*Nyet.* I would like to see her. She's my *Dedushka's* friend."

"Let's take the stairs," Petya suggested. "You can't trust these old elevators." They walked in silence up the stairs to the third floor, where they found the apartment for which they were looking. Anja took a deep breath as Petya raised the iron door knocker.

49
St Petersburg
May 2002

Vera Kishinevskaya's hand flew to her mouth.

"I'll let them in." Lyuba hobbled past.

Vera twitched at the blanket covering her legs. She had felt cold all morning. How was she to explain what she had done? How her loyalty to Sergei led to all this deception? Voices came from the hallway; a deep one, which must belong to the man who telephoned a couple of days ago, and a much younger-sounding one, which could only be Mitch's daughter, Sergei's granddaughter. *You have to put the record straight before it's too late,* she told herself as she threw off the blanket and struggled out of the chair.

The young woman walked tentatively into the room. Vera's heart went out to her. She had suffered so much in her young life. Her uncle stood by her side. Vera held her hand out to him. He took it and said, *"Menya zovot Pyotr Alekseevich Lipovsky. Eto moya plemyannitsa, Anja."*

Vera reached out and took one of Anja's hands in hers. The child was trembling, and Vera squeezed the hand gently. "We met years ago, my dear. The first time, you were just a baby." In her mind's eye, Vera saw Mitch cradling his baby daughter carefully in his arms. "Your Papa, he was so proud of you."

Silence settled around them. "I'll bring tea," Lyuba cut in.

Vera let go of Anja's hand and beckoned towards the armchairs opposite her own chair.

For several moments, she sought for words. *Where do I start?* When this man telephoned, telling her that Anja would soon be flying to Canada to find her father—the father who thought his own father was dead—fear had gripped Vera's tongue. Pyotr had gone on to tell her that his own enquiries confirmed Anja's grandfather was still in the labour camp to which he had been sent over ten years ago. "Have you any idea why Mitch thinks his father is dead?" he had asked. "It doesn't make sense."

Choking back tears, Vera had tried to explain. "It was my fault, I should never have promised." When Pyotr asked what she meant, she broke down. How could she confess what a terrible thing she had done? Lyuba had taken the phone from her hand and, after a brief conversation, suggested to the man that he bring Anja here today.

"So why does Mitch think his father is dead?" Petya asked now.

"I told him." Vera stared down at the handkerchief which she was twisting around and around in her fingers. "Sergei, he came here before they arrested him. He knew that when they couldn't find Mitch, they would come after him. *Militsiya, mafiyosa, vory.* Any or all of them." Lyuba bustled into the room, closely followed by Leonid, her husband, carrying a tray laden with glasses of steaming tea and a jar of honey. Vera waited until they had left the room before continuing. "That morning when your grandfather came here, Anja, he was desperate. He made me promise. If he was sent to prison, I would tell your father he had died."

"Why did he want you to do that?" Anja asked.

"People were looking for your father. Dangerous people."

"Was Papa still here?"

"*Nyet.* Your grandfather and I, we got him out of the country. By the time they realised he was gone, he was on a cargo ship heading to Canada. We'd done it before."

"You'd smuggled people out of the country before?" There was an element of disbelief in Petya's voice as he looked at the frail old lady.

Vera nodded, and it was some moments before she spoke again. "Seryozha, he knew … knew that if Mitch came back here, they would have killed him. That's why he made me promise."

"The people who tried to kill Papa before, the ones with the bomb, they were *Dyadya* Mikhail's people, weren't they?" Anja's voice was little more than a whisper.

"They were."

Anja frowned. "But Boris. He was one of them, wasn't he?"

"He was at one time. But then, after he took you and your mother away from harm, he put all that behind him. People I know there in Siberia, they said he turned his life around, helped people when they had problems, tried to make up for all he had done before."

Anja nodded. "He was always very protective of Mama … all of us."

"But your grandfather was right about what would happen. A few hours after he left here, the *militsiya* they came for him. I couldn't find out where they had taken him until, months later, an anonymous note was slipped under our door saying he was to be in court that day. Leonid and I, we went there. It was a farce. He didn't stand a chance. They brought forward a girl who claimed that Sergei had been her pimp, had sold her on to traffickers."

"He wouldn't!" Anja's voice was indignant. "*Dedushka* … he would never do that." An image of Dina flashed into Anja's mind. She choked back tears.

"There was nothing any of us could do. The *militsiya*, the judge, they had all been bought off." Vera shivered now as she pictured Sergei being dragged from the courtroom. "Don't forget your promise! He called out to me as they took him away."

"It must have been terrible for him," Anja said. "For you too."

"I had to do as he asked. I'd promised. So, I wrote to your father saying he had died. It must have broken your Papa's heart after everything …"

"You must have known he would find out some day," Petya cut in.

Vera hung her head.

"And later, when the *mafiyosa* were no longer a threat, you could have told Mitch the truth. He could have tried to help his father."

"I should have." She sighed loudly. "But, as time went on, the magnitude of what I had done seemed to increase. There was no going back. I lost touch with Mitch. My last letter to him came back, saying he was no longer at the address." Vera took a gulp of tea.

"And *Dedushka?* Did you hear from him?"

"I went to see him."

"You went there? To Siberia?" It was Petya who spoke.

"The place where he is. Such a long way from anywhere. Anywhere you would want to be." She sat back in her chair, her eyes glazed over, reliving in her mind that terrible journey … the train … the long car ride. "It was summer. The heat. The insects. It was unbearable."

"You went there on your own?" Petya asked.

"Leonid, he went with me." She stared into the distance. "We waited months for permission to travel there. So far away." Her voice trailed off.

Anja's eyes lit up. "But you saw him? You saw my *Dedushka?*"

The old lady shook her head. "They wouldn't let me in. He wasn't allowed visitors, that's what they said." She gulped back tears. "A couple of days later, we went there again. I tried to bribe the guards, gave them money. Leonid gave them cigarettes, vodka. Everything we had. They made us wait for hours, but they never let us see him. We hung around outside until the men came back to the camp from the *taiga*. They chop wood during the day."

"You saw him?"

"*Nyet.* I don't think he could have been out there that day." How could she tell the child that it was impossible to tell one prisoner from another? They were thin, so thin. All had the same gaunt faces. She and Leonid had called his name, hoping he would hear. The men marched on into the camp.

Vera leaned back in her chair as exhaustion overcame her. "I'm so sorry. Sorry for what I did. What I didn't do..." Her voice broke and she sobbed into her handkerchief.

"I could go there." Excitement crept into Anja's voice. "They might let me see him."

"It's best if you go to Canada, Anja. Find your father first. I'll find out what I can about your grandfather," Petya said, then turned to Vera. "I still don't understand why you didn't tell Mitch later, when the danger had passed."

"He seemed to be getting on with his life, putting it back together. Making a new life for himself in Canada." She wondered whether Anja knew her father had other children. Twins.

Anja's voice cut into her thoughts: "How did you meet *Dedushka*? Was it a long time ago?"

"A very long time ago." Vera dabbed at her eyes. "At the time of the Siege." As she told Anja the story of how she and Seryozha met, of the times they spent together over the years, she felt as if her dearest friend was back here, sitting in the armchair where his granddaughter now sat, listening to the bitter-sweet music of Shostakovich's rendition of *totentanz*. After the memory faded from her mind, she reached into the pocket of her dress and pulled out an envelope. "I want you to give this to your father when you see him, Anja. I've tried to explain ..."

50
Western Siberia
May 2002

Sergei stood in the road clutching the canvas bag to his chest. He watched as the truck turned right at the crossroads. The engine noise dwindled to a murmur, then nothing. He looked back along the track from which he had come, wondering if he should try to get back to Pavel. Maybe he could march into the camp with the others when they finished work. *It's a long way. If you're late, you will have to spend the night in the forest.* He shivered, thinking of the animals whose howls peppered his dreams. *Follow the truck, that's what you must do,* he told himself and took his first hesitant step. He trudged on, his breath laboured, his progress slow. Time passed. Time in which he saw no vehicle or living soul. He thought he was still alive, but perhaps not. *Have I passed into the land above?*

Soon the road ran alongside a river. He skirted around tufts of partially frozen vegetation until he reached the riverbank. Sinking to his knees, he touched the water with the fingers of one hand. It was cold, so cold. He drew wet fingers across cracked lips, leaned back against a rock and opened the bag. There was water and bread. Fatigue weighed on him like a blanket.

When he awoke, he looked around. His eyes followed the movement of an ice flow gliding slowly downstream, its grainy surface touched in places by the almost translucent light from the pale northern sun. He watched the steady dance of small pieces of ice as they moved away from the mother lode, turning in the current, whirling to certain oblivion. His hands reached out as if to touch the frozen mass, but fluttered in the chill air. He stared at his ragged fingerless gloves, turning his hands this way and that, the matted wool welded to his skin. He held them to his face, his breath warm on bent fingers. Jagged fingernails pierced his skin.

Dropping his hands to his lap, he gazed at the far bank of the river. It was so long since he had seen the horizon, he had forgotten it was there. His world had been bounded by the green of trees, damp earth, grey-green lichen, a flicker of light piercing the forest tomb. He looked up now to the high wilderness sky, then quickly averted his eyes from the terrible beauty.

Hours passed. He walked, stopping frequently as another bout of coughing consumed his body. The sound of an engine sent him shuffling into the shelter of trees; trees which stood like sentries along the road. He peered out at the grey body of a car and the bulky figures inside. Then there was silence and he listened to the silky whispering of the wind and the chittering of birds. He sank to the ground, thinking of a garden. It was coming back to him … his grandparents' garden. A delicate song and a birch tree, its foliage home to the tuneful lives of unseen birds. There was an orchard. A foam of white blossom. A woman. His mother. A lock of her hair brushed his cheek as she leaned over to kiss him.

As day faded, he sheltered in the ruins of an *izba,* where a maze of rotting moss-edged timbers shared space with the gnarled roots of a long-dead tree. Inside, he leaned against the crumbling chimney, opened the bag, broke off a piece of dry black bread and forced it between his lips. It lodged between broken teeth in unchanging form until a cough from deep within sent it spewing from his mouth. He closed his eyes and listened to the voice of the wind.

He awoke many times in the night. Sometimes cold penetrated his limbs. At others, sweat dampened his clothes before turning to familiar icy chill. He called out for Pavel. Now, as shafts of light crept across the sky, he thought of his friend. *I should have gone back to him. Told him where I was going. How will he find me?*

He took a sip from the water bottle, clambered to his knees, gripped the sides of the chimney to pull himself up, then walked stiffly back to the road. His pace was painfully slow. Some hours later, a vehicle slowed as it came up behind him. Sergei stepped to the side of the road. The small truck stopped and the driver leaned across to open the passenger door. "Need a ride?" Sergei peered in, nodded his head and threw the bag on to the floor in front of the seat as he clambered in. The driver shifted in his seat as he looked at the figure at his side. *"Vy daleko idete?"*

Sergei scratched his head.

"You need a bath, old man." The driver wound down his window with one hand. Sergei huddled in the seat, eyes fixed on the road ahead.

And so his life continued for several days, riding in trucks, on horse-drawn wagons, ancient tractors. Always he asked the driver to tell Pavel where he was. His words met with blank stares.

Now, in late afternoon, he knocked on the door of a farmhouse and asked if he could sleep in their barn for the night. The old woman who came to the door looked him up and down. With her eyes fixed on his gaping boots, she nodded her agreement. From his bed of sweet-smelling straw, he listened to the clacking of hens in the yard. Then in the barn a man's voice called to him. Sergei sat up, gripping his coat around him. "Mother says you …" The man shifted from one foot to the other. Sergei saw that one hand held a bowl of steaming broth, the other a plate of bread. "Mother says you should have a bath. I've lit the fire to heat the water. It's in the outhouse."

"Spasiba." It was some moments before Sergei could gather his breath to say more. "I appreciate your kindness."

Steam rose from the tin bath in the dimly lit outhouse. Sergei shivered as he shed his coat, his boots, and the rest of his clothes. Remnants of matted wool stuck to his hands as he peeled off his gloves. Gripping both sides of the bath, he climbed in unsteadily and lowered his body into the water. As heat seeped through his aching limbs, he looked at his arms, his legs, and tried to remember the last time he saw them. He slid down further into the bath, letting the water cover his face. It would be easy to let the water take him. Then he spluttered to the surface, gasping as though a knife pierced his lungs. The door creaked open. The woman came in. She picked up the soap and rubbed his hair, sluicing it with water. Then she soaped his arms, his legs, his back. The soap stung the sores on his body, but it was good. She put the soap in his hands and indicated that he should wash the rest of his body. The door closed behind her. He lay back in the water trying to remember the last time he had a bath. At the camp, a quick daily wash was all they were allowed. In winter, sometimes weeks went past before he could face the icy cold water.

As he lay in the now cooling water, he wondered what Pavel was doing. He hoped his friend would soon find him. As they worked in the *taiga*, they had made plans to be together after they were released. The three of them would find an apartment, make their own furniture, fish in the river, grow food. "We must follow the river," Jakob had said. That was before he hung from the tree.

A blast of air came from the doorway. Sergei sat up in the bath. "Mother … she said you could have these." The man put a bundle of clothes on to the chair;

an overcoat and a pair of boots followed. "They were father's." He held out a towel and Sergei rose awkwardly to his feet.

He tossed and turned all night, dust from the straw aggravating his cough. Through a hole in the barn roof, moonlight flickered across the timber walls. It formed shapes. High in the roof, he saw her face. He hardly dared breathe. "Sophia?" His dead wife smiled, her eyes shining brightly through the half-light. As he watched, the soft brown waves framing her face melted.

In the grey light of early morning, he dusted straw from his clothes. As he left the farm a car pulled alongside. The door at the front was thrown open and Sergei got in. The driver was dressed in a dark blue suit, ribbons and medals on his chest. "Going to the parade, are you?" The man's cracked tones ricocheted around the small space.

"Parade?" Sergei stared at the medals, a faint memory stirring in his mind.

The man turned to look at him. "It's Victory Day. The Ninth of May. Everyone's going to the parade."

Victory Day? He remembered now. He was holding a warm young hand, his steady voice was telling his son … he had loved that boy … about the hundreds of thousands of people who had died in the *Blokada.* Nine hundred days it lasted. *Nine hundred days, Mitch, can you believe that? The Red Army was surrounded. There was no heating, no water supply, we hardly had any food.* He and his son stood by the statue of the Motherland at the *Piskariovskoye* Cemetery and watched families walk between memorial stones to lay flowers and wreaths on the graves of long-departed loved ones. Afterwards, he and Mitch hurried along *Prospekt Nepokorionnykh,* stopping to buy a box of Sophia's favourite chocolates.

"Sophia," Sergei breathed softly.

"You okay?" the driver asked.

Sergei nodded his head slowly, trying not to dislodge the memories. He hung on to the door handle as the car wove from one side of the road to the other avoiding deep potholes. Sometime later it picked up speed, the road wider now, the surface smooth. Sergei looked up at tall buildings, their white facades touched by morning light. He caught his breath as a tight band gripped his chest. He wheezed. The driver shifted in his seat, moving further away. They drove past clutches of people walking along the side of the road. "Where are they going?" Sergei asked.

"To the Veterans' Parade. I told you. Everyone's going." A tram clanged past. Sergei shrank back in his seat.

"This is where you get out," the man mumbled and cut across the traffic into a side street.

"Where is this place?" Sergei ventured as the car came to a stop. "Is it Leningrad?"

"Leningrad?" The man shook his head as Sergei clambered out of the car. "It's Ekaterinburg, of course." He leaned forward, picked up Sergei's bag from the floor and threw it after him. "Something wrong with his mind," he muttered as Sergei shut the car door.

Sergei huddled back against a wall as the car pulled away. Two young girls, their shrill voices sounding as one, walked past. Each carried a bunch of scarlet flowers. Behind them, a burly man held the arm of an old woman, her black coat rich against the grey of his overcoat.

Sergei turned into an alleyway and walked until the noises of the city hushed to a murmur. He was in a small square and sat on a wooden bench in the sunshine. An old woman shuffled past. She nodded to him. His stiff cheeks broke into a smile. He watched as she greeted a younger woman. Their faces touched; first one side, then the other, then the other. Arm-in-arm they disappeared around a corner. Sergei touched his cheeks with the fingers of one hand. He had forgotten what it was like to feel soft lips on his skin. He shrank back in the seat as a boy ran past, then another smaller boy. *"Idi syuda!"* a woman called as she ran after the fleeing figures.

She stopped and turned around. *"Spesit!"* she urged, holding out a hand to a small girl.

Sergei's heart missed a beat. "Anja! Anja!" he called.

The woman grabbed the child's hand and they both ran across the square. Sergei stood up, his eyes fixed on the bobbing brown curls. Cascades of red ribbon tumbled on to her shoulders. *It is her ... my Anja!* The words rang joyously in his head. "Anja? Annushka? *Kuda vy sobiraetes?"* His boots clattered on the cobblestones as he pursued the red ribbons. "Anja, wait. Wait for *Deda,*" he sobbed. Sweat found its beady course down his face. He held on to the corner of a wall, bent double, the only sound now the gasp which came with each intake of breath.

51
Ekaterinburg
May 2002

Sergei awoke to the sound of voices. Faces peered down at him. He groaned, hunched his shoulders, shielding his head with his arms. The boys edged away, the thud of their boots like drumbeats as they ran down the alleyway. Sergei rolled to one side and raised himself onto his knees, spewing sputum on the ground as he coughed. He inched his way upwards using the wall for support, the heel of one hand pressed to his chest as he waited for the burning to ease. He looked around, uncertain which way to go, then staggered between the maze of walls towering above him, weaving a haphazard path away from where the boys had gone. It was some time before he looked down at his hands. *The bag? Where is it?* He turned and blinked into the shadows.

Light splashed around him as he emerged into a courtyard and followed a concrete path which hugged the walls of the buildings around the perimeter. A window was thrown open on a floor above and the murmur of voices reached his ears. He stepped off the path, seeking sanctuary under a gnarled tree, his fingers touching rough bark, stripped in places by children or birds.

As he peered between the branches, a shadowy figure moved in front of the brickwork. It floated, changed shape. The ghostly form grew taller, its legs, clothed in grey, stretched into spindly streaks. Sergei stepped out into the sunlight and looked upwards, arm raised towards the figure as it teetered almost out of sight. Then it sank to the ground and a small body with a familiar face took shape. It came towards him. "Mitch!" Sergei reached out. "Is it you?" The face twisted into grotesque shapes until it no longer looked like a face. Sergei shrank back. His arms flailed in front of him as he crashed through the low branches of the tree. He breathed heavily and it was some moments before he garnered the strength to look again. There wasn't anyone there. He leaned his left cheek against the bark of the tree as he tried to get air into his lungs.

"Old man," a voice called. Sergei stiffened and crept around the trunk of the tree. A slight form emerged from a doorway. It tiptoed along the path, coming closer, closer. He saw the face of a boy. Dark rings encircled his eyes. Brown freckles sprinkled the palest skin he had ever seen. The boy wore grey pants, ending half-way up his calves. A dark blue jacket. Sergei couldn't see his hair. *That's strange. He must have hair.* He held his breath. He would wait until the boy passed by. But his throat constricted and the wheezing came. He staggered across the courtyard, bent double. A gut-wrenching cough spilled vile fluid out of his mouth and nose, and he wiped the cuff of his coat across his face. When he looked again, the boy was standing still, hands in his jacket pockets. Red hair flamed around him.

You must get away, find a way out, he told himself. As he looked around, he saw it—a wide passageway at the end of which were steps, a door. Above, a bulbous dome of deepest blue surmounted by a gold cross. He looked again at the boy. He had not moved. As Sergei watched, a bearded priest, the hem of pink robes bright below a black coat, hurried across the courtyard. The boy called out to the holy man in a high-pitched voice. The priest turned, mouthing words Sergei could not hear. Then, with a flash of pink, he climbed the steps, opened the door and disappeared inside.

The priest. He'll protect me. Sergei glanced once more at the boy and edged into the passageway. His boots clattered on the uneven surface. With each step he took, he was pushed back, his coat heavy, dragging against the thrust of his arms and legs. Grey and red cobblestones merged into one and rushed towards him. He hit the ground hard and lay still for a moment struggling to force air into his lungs. His fingers scratched at the polished stones, slippery now with sweat from his palms. Sweat dripped from his forehead as he clambered unsteadily to his feet. A sea of stone steps was all he saw as he staggered upwards.

He grabbed the iron door handle and pulled. It wouldn't budge. He could hear the boy coming closer. Then, with two hands on the handle, Sergei wrenched the door open and staggered into the dusk of candlelight. He breathed heavily as he walked forward. Small steps. He crossed himself and looked upwards, seeking the richly decorated ceiling he knew would be there. Gold glistened in the heights and the muscles in his face relaxed as he gazed at a vision of Heaven. He walked towards the altar. Gilt icons—three rows lit by candles.

He stood still, spellbound by the images of the saints clothed in gold, red, and black. His thoughts drifted back to another icon. The *obraz* of The Mother of God. The blessed figure, surrounded by the purest, palest green, was perched on a pink throne. Tiny pink feet protruded from robes of brown and black. He had stared at her for hours when he had important decisions to make. She had never let him down. *Where was that?* he asked himself now. She was lost in the fog of his mind. Angels floated in front of him as he stumbled towards a chapel in the corner of the church. He must sleep.

Sometime later, a thin voice sang: "I spell you into sleep ..." The voice rose then fell and Sergei felt something stroking the side of his face in time with the haunting words of the *Bayushki Bayu*. In his dreamlike state, he saw Mitch's young face on snow white pillows.

Sergei's own voice, barely audible, whispered the words of the old lullaby. He held his son's hand in his, tucked it carefully under the sheet and crept to the door. He grunted now, the palms of his hands cooled by the cold stone floor as he sat up. He opened his eyes. A face looked at him—pale skin, black circles around deep brown eyes. Red hair.

"It's okay, old man. Don't be frightened," the boy whispered. "I won't hurt you. Here. Some water."

Sergei shuffled his body backwards across the floor. The boy edged towards him, holding out an ornate cup. Sergei hesitated for a few seconds then reached out and took the cup in both hands. He stared at the figure of Christ painted on the side of the cup. The holy figure was depicted in deep ochre with a circlet of gold leaves. Two delicate lines of turquoise framed lettering around the rim. He looked at his own dirt encrusted hands. "I am not worthy to drink from a holy cup," he murmured. The boy pressed the cup to Sergei's lips. The water was cold as it flooded his mouth, ran down his beard. Then the boy grabbed the empty cup and scurried to the side of the church. When he returned, Sergei reached out eagerly and took another gulp of water. Then he sipped it; sweet, so sweet. The boy sat down beside him and grinned, spreading brown freckles across his cheeks.

"Was that you singing?"

"My mother, she used to sing that song to me." The boy lowered his voice. "She had a cough like yours."

Sergei put a tentative hand on the boy's knee. *"Kak vas zovut?"*

"Kolya. What's yours?"

"Sergei Galichin. Yes, that is my name. I must remember." The two sat in silence, broken only by the rustle of the priest's robes. They watched as he bowed his head in front of the icon on its stand in the glass case by the side of the chapel steps. Sergei breathed in the pungent smell of incense. He felt at peace for the first time in many years. "Why were you following me?" he rasped.

"There are gangs of kids in the alleyways. They sniff glue and do bad things. It isn't safe for you." The boy frowned at Sergei. "You are like my *deda*. I used to protect him too." He laughed softly. "But we must go. They will be coming for the service soon." He gestured towards the priest who was now lighting candles in the apse. "He said I was to take you to his house."

Sergei grabbed Kolya's arm. *"Nyet! Nyet!"* His voice echoed around them.

"It's okay. Father Nikolai, he is a good man. You'll like him." Kolya gripped Sergei's wrists, pulling him on to his knees.

Sergei tried to shove the boy out of his way as he struggled to his feet, but Kolya grabbed hold of his overcoat.

"Ah, Kolya. Aren't you going to introduce me to your friend?" the priest's deep voice sang out. He had a large oval face and two bright red spots on his cheekbones shone like beacons above a black beard. He wore the familiar small black hat. Dark blue eyes looked quizzically at Sergei as he grasped his hands in his. Kolya announced Sergei's name and the priest said, "It is a pleasure to meet you, Sergei Galichin." Sergei shifted uncomfortably, trying to move away, but the grip on his hands tightened. "You are hungry." A statement, not a question. "Kolya will take you to my house. There is always a pot of *kasha* on the stove," Father Nikolai tempted. "Olga Pietrovna, my housekeeper, can be a bit fierce but she has a good heart."

Sergei shook his head. "I have to find Pavel. He will be waiting for me."

"You don't have to stay, my friend. Just wait there until I get back," Father Nikolai urged.

A few minutes later, Kolya ushered Sergei down a pathway at the side of the priest's house. He opened a door and called, "Olga Pietrovna?" Then, gripping the arm of Sergei's coat he called again more urgently: "Olga Pietrovna!"

"Who is it?"

"It's me, Kolya. Father Nikolai, he told me to bring my friend here."

"Who have you brought this time?"

Kolya stepped inside the doorway, pulling Sergei with him.

"Father Nikolai … he said you should give him *kasha*."

A thickly set woman, with grey hair pulled back from her face, bustled across the kitchen towards them.

"His name is Sergei Galichin."

"Can't he speak for himself?" Olga Pietrovna looked Sergei up and down, straightened her shoulders, a grimace twisting her face.

Sergei turned away from her, making for the door, but Kolya pulled him back. "If **you** have *kasha*, she'll give me some," he whispered.

"Come in if you're going to." A chair scraped across the floor. "Sit here."

Sergei felt Kolya's hands in the small of his back, urging him towards the chair. He sat down and, within what seemed a few seconds, there was a bowl of steaming *kasha* in front of him. It burnt his mouth, but it was good. He managed half a bowl of it and a few sips of strong coffee before he felt his gut twist. Olga Pietrovna helped him off with his coat and urged him to rest in the chair by the stove for a while. He leaned back, trying to remember when he had last sat in a chair like this, but he gasped for breath as a coughing fit rose from deep within. She handed him a handkerchief and Kolya rubbed his back until the cough subsided and he drifted into exhausted sleep.

When Sergei awoke, Father Nikolai had returned. He leaned over Sergei. "Tomorrow, my friend, you must go to the sanatorium," he said. "They will make you well." Sergei didn't have the strength to protest.

In the early evening, Sergei rested in a chair by the fire listening to the conversation of Father Nikolai, Olga Pietrovna, and Kolya, as they finished their meal at the table. He had tried to eat but the *ukha* lodged in his throat. He looked down at his unfamiliar green check shirt and brown woollen pants which Olga Pietrovna had produced from out of a cupboard. The pants were held up by a length of tape tied around where his waist had been.

"I don't know where Kolya puts all the food," Father Nikolai called to Sergei as the boy reached for another *Pirozhki*. "He must have hollow legs," the priest laughed and got to his feet. "But he should be going soon," he cajoled, his hands now on Kolya's narrow shoulders.

"I'll be back in the morning before school starts." Kolya rose from the table, cramming pastry into his mouth, and put on his jacket. "You will be here?" he asked, looking anxiously at Sergei. Then he grabbed another *Pirozhki* from the plate and bolted for the doorway.

"That boy! I don't know why you put up with him, Father." The faint smile touching the corners of Olga Pietrovna's mouth betrayed her words.

"Where does he live?" Sergei ventured.

"Kolya? He's one of the lucky ones." Father Nikolai scratched his chin through his beard. "He lives with an elderly widow a few streets away from here. He chops her firewood, runs errands and does other jobs around the house. Before that, he was in Perm. Love's Bridge took him in." Seeing the puzzled look on Sergei's face, the priest explained: "Love's Bridge. It's an organisation that looks after kids who live on the street. Before they took him in, he was living in the sewers, sniffing glue and scavenging for food." Father Nikolai sat down in the chair opposite Sergei and leaned forward; the reflection of flames from the fire streaked his face with a burst of orange light. "He goes to school now, has a warm place to sleep, good food, and people who care about him. He's lucky, but he's a good boy." He sat back in his chair. "There are so many of them now. In the old days, the Soviet days, there was at least some kind of social safety net. The problem of homeless children didn't exist."

Sergei was silent. In the camp they heard of the disintegration of the Soviet Union, but it hadn't made any difference to them—the forgotten ones. He thought now of Pavel's rugged face, his gentle hands. *I must find him. He'll be wondering where I am. But where is that place ... the place where he is?*

"And you, Sergei Galichin." Father Nikolai interrupted his thoughts. "Do you have children?"

Sergei gazed at the fire. "I had a son." He gasped and his hand went to his mouth as he remembered: *I mustn't tell anyone.*

"What happened to him?"

"Gone. He has gone."

Later, Sergei stood at the side of a bed. Tonight, it was his bed. A folded white nightshirt lay on a coverlet of muted brown and blue patchwork. He bent down, tracing the seams of the patches with his fingers. He looked at his feet, swaddled as they were now in *tapochki. Sophia always kept tapochki by the front door.*

His gaze strayed to the icon above the bed. The face was gaunt, enshrouded in gold, and he reached out and touched the cracked surface with the tips of his fingers. The long-dead artist had given the Christ figure black eyes, brown robes. The left hand held a book, the pages open, the scriptures to be read, the thumb and second finger of the raised right hand in familiar pose.

Tears dribbled down Sergei's face and on to the floor.

A few minutes later, from the comfort of a soft bed, smooth sheets, Sergei's eyelids began to close. As he drifted into sleep, he thought of Pavel and his own empty cot in the hut. He thought of Sophia. Anja. *They were here in this place. And Mitch. I saw them. But where did they go?*

52
Toronto
May 2002

A light breeze drifted through the open window of Mitch's study. Snatches of conversation floated in from the garden; Masha's high-pitched babble penetrated his thoughts.

"Ivo! Please. It won't take you a minute to put Amelia's head back on. I've tried …"

"Go away! You're a pest!" her brother snapped.

"Please, please," the wheedling voice persisted. "You're so mean!"

Mitch got to his feet and looked out of the window. Masha held the two parts of her injured doll under Ivo's nose, where he squatted on the grass—he put on a good show of reading his comic, as if the doll wasn't obliterating his vision.

Mitch removed the printed sheets from the printer tray and paced around the room reading over his notes on Canada's first anti-trafficking legislation: the Immigration & Refugee Protection Act, currently before parliament. If enacted, Section 118 of the Act would make it an offence to organise the coming into Canada of one or more persons by means of abduction, fraud, deception, or use of threat. It would also criminalise the receipt or harbouring of those persons after their entry into Canada. He could already identify loopholes in the legislation which traffickers would undoubtedly exploit, but it was a start, carrying a maximum penalty of life imprisonment, a fine of $1,000,000, or both. *Whether it will cut down on the flow of victims or make it any easier to press charges remains to be seen*, he thought to himself as he looked out over the rooftops. *How many are out there behind locked doors? Countless numbers in this city alone.*

He heard doors slamming and raised voices trading childish insults. The argument that had been droning on in the garden had moved indoors. "What the hell's going on?" he yelled as he went downstairs. Two startled faces appeared around the edge of the kitchen door.

"Masha took the last cookie. She's a greedy pig!" Ivo pushed his sister into the hallway. Her body was bathed with shafts of coloured light—pink, purple, blue—filtering through the stained-glass panel in the front door.

"Shut up, both of you!"

Masha's bottom lip trembled as she hugged the severed parts of her doll to her chest. "Papa? Could you put Amelia's head back on? She's so sad like this."

Mitch swallowed his anger. "We'll soon have her mended, pumpkin. Don't you worry." He sat on the edge of a stair, pulled his daughter into his arms, remembering another small figure, so frail, so vulnerable.

53
Ekaterinburg
May 2002

The next morning, Sergei awoke with a start. "Pavel?" he rasped, pulling himself up in the bed.

He looked around. *Where am I? Where is this place?* "Pavel? Pavel! Where are you?" he called. *Where is my coat ... my boots?* He looked down at the strange garment he was wearing. The sodden nightshirt clung to his skin. Long ago, he had stopped thinking that the hot sweats would vanish and that the raw feeling in his lungs would go away. They were part of his life. *You must find Pavel,* he told himself now. *He'll know what to do.* He swung his legs over the side of the bed, then bent forward as a spasm of coughing wracked his body. He reached for a bowl on the bedside table, leaned over and spat into it. He no longer looked at the streaks of blood.

If only he knew where he was. Where Pavel was. His head was so muddled. His breathing eased and he got to his feet, gripping the table, waiting for his head to stop spinning. It was then he saw it. The icon on the wall. *The priest's house. The young boy.* Sergei's fingers reached out and touched the body of Christ.

In the narrow passageway, he curled up his toes as the woven floor covering pricked the soles of his swollen feet. Noises came from downstairs; household sounds he had not heard for so long. A warm feeling rushed through him. *Sophia. She is making breakfast.* Then he remembered.

Inside the bathroom, he bent low over the washbasin. As he dried himself with a towel, he saw a strange man in the mirror. The whites of his eyes shone like yellow beacons. Black circles inhabited his eye sockets. His skin was a dirty yellow. Sergei dropped the towel and looked at his hands; they were yellow too.

When he was dressed, he hesitated at the top of the stairs, savouring the smell in his nostrils. It came back to him from long ago. *Bread. Someone is baking bread. The woman?* He walked slowly down the stairs trying to remember her name.

"Dobroye utro ..."

"My God, man! Don't creep up on me like that." Olga Pietrovna turned abruptly to face him, cheeks flushed with heat from the stove. She wafted a cloth in front of her face, and Sergei scurried to the other side of the table and sat on a chair. She reached for a cup from the mismatched assortment hanging from hooks under a shelf, filled it with coffee and set it before him.

"The boy was here earlier." She cut two slices of bread, put them on a plate and slid it across the table. "Help yourself to butter. There should be some of my sour cherry jam in the pot, if the boy hasn't eaten it all!"

"Spasiba." Sergei's fingers caressed the soft bread, still warm from the oven.

"Kolya, he was worried about you. Father Nikolai told him to come back after morning school and he could see you then. He's polished your boots." She shrugged her shoulders. "He did his best."

"Where is the priest?" Sergei scraped the remains of the jam out of the stone container.

"Father Nikolai's gone to visit Zinovy Lurye." She rolled up her sleeves and turned towards the sink. "Sent him home to die, they have. I don't know how his poor wife is going to manage. Five children and none of them able to work yet." She lifted a saucepan out of the sink and began to dry it. "I don't know what the good Lord is thinking," she said, clanging the pan onto the table then crossing herself.

The words had hardly left her mouth when a voice called out from the hallway: "I'm back, Olga Pietrovna."

"How is he, Father?" she called.

"Not good. But he's glad to be home with his family." A moment later the priest put his head around the open door. "Ah, Sergei Galichin. You are with us," he said, rubbing his hands together and walking towards the stove. "Kolya waited, hoping you would wake up. He wasn't very happy when I pushed him out of the door," he laughed, picked up a cloth and lifted the coffee pot from the stove. He topped up Sergei's cup and reached for one for himself.

"If there's nothing else you need, Father, I'll be going to post the parcel to my niece in Chelyabinsk." Olga Pietrovna took off her apron, folded it, and put it on the back of a chair. "I won't be long."

The priest drizzled honey into his coffee and stirred it, pushing the pot of honey and spoon towards Sergei. "Now, Sergei Galichin, what are we going to do with you?" Sergei looked down at his empty plate. "There is a sanatorium on the other side of the city. I have arranged for you to go there this afternoon." The priest raised his eyebrows. "Kolya will come with us."

Sergei shrank back in the chair, the fingers of one hand pulling on his beard. "This place … this sanatorium. What is it like?" he asked hesitantly.

"It is run by the angels themselves. They will take such care of you, you will never want to leave."

Sergei ran a finger along the faded design on his coffee cup. "But … I can leave? If I don't like it?" The cup shook as he lifted it to his mouth with both hands.

"Of course." The priest walked around the table and placed a hand on Sergei's shoulder. "If you don't like it, Kolya and I, we'll bring you back here." He picked up a log from a bucket on the hearth and threw it into the stove. "We should tell your family where you are," he mused.

"I don't have any family." Sergei got to his feet and edged around the table.

"But yesterday, you said you have a son?"

Be careful, Sergei cautioned himself. "He has gone."

"There must be someone else. A friend?"

"Pavel. I have to find Pavel. Jakob too. Or did he go somewhere else?" *Why is everything so muddled?* he asked himself, taking a few steps towards the door.

"Pavel? Jakob? If you tell me where they are, I'll get a message to them."

Sergei shook his head slowly. In his mind's eye, he saw red ribbons floating in the air. He reached out to touch them. "Anja. Wait for *Deda.*"

The priest took Sergei gently by the arm and led him to an armchair. "We'll get you to the sanatorium. The Sisters will make you well, and then we can talk again."

Sergei leaned back and closed his eyes. He heard cupboards opening and closing.

"Here. Drink this." Sergei looked up. Father Nikolai held a small glass towards him. "Our secret," he said, eyes twinkling. Sergei sipped the strong liquid. He gasped, then his muscles relaxed and he began to breathe more easily. "Try to rest. I'll wake you when we're ready to leave." The priest's words whirled around in the fog in Sergei's mind.

* * *

Cocooned in blankets in the back of Father Nikolai's ancient car that afternoon, Sergei listened to Kolya's commentary from the front seat. "Look! Over there!" He pointed to the right. "That's the Order of Lenin. It was given to the city," Kolya paused for a moment, "something to do with the Great Patriotic War, I think."

"Quite the little tour guide, aren't you?" Father Nikolai laughed and ruffled the boy's hair with his right hand.

Sergei looked out of the window at the imposing red sculpted monument, its pinnacles rising to the sky. He shivered.

"And did you know that Tsar Nicholas and his family were murdered here?" Kolya leaned over the front seat to look at Sergei before continuing. "They came for them at midnight! Shot them all! Buried them in the woods!"

"Kolya. I think that's enough," the priest ordered, changing gears noisily as the traffic slowed.

"And the *mafiyosa.* They're here now. They shoot people too! Gunfights on the street!" Sergei's body stiffened and he slid further down in the seat.

"Kolya!" the priest snapped. "If you don't stop this, I'll make you get out and go to school."

Sergei tried to will the stomach cramps to go away. "Will we be there soon?" he asked.

"Not far now. We should be there in ten minutes or so." A tram clanged across the tracks in front of them, and the car jolted and stalled as Father Nikolai jammed on the brakes.

As the car juddered into life again, Kolya spoke: "Did you know this is where Nautilus Pompilius is from?"

"Who?" Sergei and the priest spoke as one.

"Nautilus Pompilius, the rock band." Kolya turned and looked from one to the other.

"You must have heard of them. Apostle Andrei?"

"Apostle who?" Father Nikolai glanced at the boy.

"Apostle Andrei. You must have heard the tune." Kolya tapped his fingers on the dashboard and hummed loudly.

Sergei leaned back in the seat; the pains in his stomach were beginning to ease. He watched as a panorama of commercial buildings drifted past, then large imposing houses gave way to low-rise apartment buildings, their cream-coloured stucco streaked with grime. Soon the road became a dirt track edged by tall trees.

"Here we are." Father Nikolai nudged the snub nose of the car between white gateposts. Kolya stopped humming. Trees gathered around a long driveway, at the end of which a single-story, cream painted building emerged. Tyres crunched on loose gravel as they pulled up at the front entrance. The priest and Kolya jumped out of the car. Sergei unfolded himself awkwardly from the back seat and Father Nikolai linked his arms around Sergei's waist and pulled him to his feet. Sergei squinted at the inscription above the door. It was some moments before he made out the words: 'Sanatorium of The Blessed Xenia of St Petersburg. Do not fear grief, privation, nor the mockery of men, but go where you are needed. Blessed peace and happiness.'

He was whisked away and checked over by white-coated male doctors. One, two, perhaps more—their faces blurred into one. Sometime later, he sank back on plump pillows in a bright, sunny room. He stared at a shiny patch, white against the yellow skin on the back of his hand. As he looked, his hand grew bigger until it was the size of a balloon, the patch a pinprick. He held his breath and closed his eyes, scared his body was going to explode. When he looked again, his hand was as it had always been. *The sun was playing tricks on you,* he told himself as a figure dressed all in white tucked the bedcovers in firmly. Her young pink face gazed into his. "You look better already," she declared. "I'll be back in a minute with something good to drink. The doctor said you were to have lots of fluids."

Who is she? Sergei asked himself. He had seen several of them—or maybe it was the same one—all dressed in long white dresses and veils. They seemed to float, as if walking on air. Each had a crucifix dangling from the cord around her waist. *Perhaps I have died.*

He saw a movement at the door from the garden. Kolya waved a hand and grinned, stroking his chin. "Where's your beard?" he asked, skidding to a halt beside the bed. Sergei fingered his own chin. *Where has it gone?* "There's a lake out there," Kolya continued. "Next time we come, I'll show it to you." Sergei smiled. "They must have a boat. The three of us could take it out," Kolya enthused, shifting from one foot to the other in his excitement. "I can row, and I suppose Father Nikolai can too." A frown crossed the young boy's face. "Are priests allowed to row?"

"I think the robes might be a problem!" A chuckle rose from deep within Sergei's throat.

“What are you two laughing about?” Father Nikolai asked as he came into the room and looked from one to the other. He patted Sergei’s arm gently. “Come, Kolya, we must go. Our friend needs rest.”

“But we will come again. Say we will,” Kolya implored.

“Yes, yes. We’ll come on Monday. After school,” Father Nikolai assured as he leaned forward and took Sergei’s hands in his. “God will give you strength to deal with this.”

* * *

Sergei could not know the heavy burden Father Nikolai carried in his heart on the drive home. Olga Pietrovna had banked up the stove in the kitchen. “I thought it would take the chill out of us,” she said knowingly. “How bad is it?”

He shook his head. “It’s bad.” He leaned forward in the armchair, staring into the flames. “They did lots of tests. They’ll have the results in a few days. But the doctor said he could tell just by looking at him that the TB germs have broken out of the walls of his lungs into his kidneys. It’s pretty far advanced.” He cradled his head in his hands.

“Does he know?”

Father Nikolai met her troubled gaze and shook his head.

“And the boy?”

“I haven’t told him.”

54
Ekaterinburg
May 2002

Late afternoon the following Monday, the pupils of the woman's dark eyes shrank to pinpricks as she stared at Sergei above her white mask. He turned his face into the pillow. Her voice droned on: "I'm only trying to help you. Your family … they'll be worrying about you."

Sergei sat up in bed. His shouted, "*Nyet! Nyet!* I don't have a family! No one!" brought on another coughing fit. It also brought Sister Agatha to his side, her touch cool on his forehead as he spewed blood into a kidney dish. He heard her voice, which never rose above a gentle whisper, telling the woman—whoever she was—that it would be better if she left. Sister Agatha lowered him back on to the pillows, took the kidney dish from his trembling hands, and wiped his lips with a cloth. She tidied the bedclothes into precise order, her eyes following the woman's movements as she gathered her sheaf of papers.

The woman leaned towards him. "When I came in, you were calling in your sleep. Someone called Mitch. Your son? Your grandson?" Sergei shrank away from her. She snapped her briefcase shut. "I'll come back tomorrow." In the corridor, she peered at him through the glass panels as she removed her mask. He turned away. Sister Agatha was busying herself around the room. She stopped and adjusted the pale green curtains. Sunlight coloured her white habit with orange light.

Sergei's mind drifted. He saw a river, its waters streaked deep mauve with the fading light of day. Above, a slender pinnacle touched with gold. His hand reached out, pointing. "Mitch," he murmured. "Look. Over on the far embankment. There! The Peter and Paul Fortress. Do you see?" He waited, but no reply came. The gold-tinged steeple faded, then was gone.

He lay still, silently willing the vision to return. Sweat bathed his body with cloying intensity. A cool hand caressed his forehead. “Sophia,” he breathed. Sister Agatha smiled at him then turned and floated away. Gentle, like her martyred namesake.

He slept. When he awoke, Father Nikolai was sitting in the chair by the side of the bed, head bent in prayer. “How are you today, my friend?” The priest’s voice broke the silence.

“Ya v poryadke.” Sergei avoided meeting the priest’s gaze. He noticed now that Kolya was on the other side of the room examining the plethora of wires coming out of the wall behind a vacant bed.

“Kolya,” Father Nikolai called softly. The boy dropped the wires onto the bed and came towards them. His shabby shoes shone and his grey pants looked as if they had been pressed. His hair was slicked down on his forehead. “Quite the young gentleman,” Sergei quipped. Kolya grinned and started to relate an amusing tale told to him by one of his classmates. His exuberant mood was infectious and it wasn’t long before he had Sister Agatha and Sister Euphrosyne tut-tutting. The shaking of their upper bodies betrayed the laughter they were trying to stifle as they hurried from the room.

“The boy’s a real tonic,” Sergei sighed and lay back on the pillows. “A gift from Heaven.” The flicker of a smile touched his sunken cheeks.

Sister Euphrosyne appeared at the door with two large glasses of fresh lemonade, which she gave to Father Nikolai and Kolya. She was soon back with a glass containing thick liquid.

“Do try to drink some of this,” she urged Sergei. He took a couple of sips then pushed it away. “He isn’t eating, Father.”

Sergei and Kolya chatted companionably. Father Nikolai stole furtive glances at the old man, noticing the way his face contorted from time to time. He left the room and came back with Sister Agatha. She held pills cradled in a small wax paper cup. Sergei put them in his mouth, one at a time, struggling to swallow them with gulps of water from the glass the nun held to his mouth.

“Well, Kolya. I think we should go. Our friend is tired and needs to rest,” Father Nikolai said.

Kolya pursed his lips and slid off the bed. He looked down at his shoes, shoulders shaking.

“Come now, Kolya. I’m sure Father Nikolai will bring you to see me again,” Sergei cajoled. “Won’t you Father?”

Kolya wiped his eyes with the back of his hand and moved closer to Sergei.

He took the boy's hands in his. "Now, Kolya," Sergei's voice seemed to have disappeared somewhere down in his gullet, "you must remember what I am going to tell you." He looked into the boy's eyes.

"What is it?" a small voice asked.

"You must always be true to your parents. Make them proud of you. That is the most important lesson in life. Remember that."

"But …"

"Yes, I know. Your parents are no longer here. Well, I never knew my father. He was killed when I was a few weeks old." Sergei took a gasp of breath. "My mother taught me to live by his high standards and to be true to his memory, make him proud of me. So that is what you must do. Do you promise?" Sergei put his head on one side.

The boy's 'I promise' was barely audible.

"And Father. Thank Olga Pietrovna for the jam, won't you?" He fought to get air into his lungs. "Thank you too. For everything." The two men's eyes met for a few seconds then the priest nodded his head and, with a hand on Kolya's shoulder, guided the boy out of the room.

Later, Sister Agatha moved a jug of bright red and yellow flowers onto the bedside table.

"You can see them better there."

"Kolya, he earned the money for them running errands for Olga Pietrovna. She's Father Nikolai's housekeeper … I think." *Or is she that woman who was here?*

"I'll see you in the morning," the young nun said as she smoothed the bed cover.

"Sister Agatha." Sergei's call stopped her in her tracks at the doorway.

She turned and came closer. "What is it?"

"You must promise me …" He leaned forward as he started to wheeze. "Promise me, you won't let that woman back in here," he spluttered.

"Now, now. It's going to be all right." She rearranged his pillows, then lowered him gently back onto them. "You don't have to see her if you don't want to." Her tone was soft.

"But she said … she said she was coming back," he gasped. "She doesn't understand. No one does."

"God understands." She sat down in the chair; her hands were cool as she held his. "Do you know the story of St Xenia?" Sergei shook his head. "Well, she lived in the time of the Empresses Elizabeth Petrovna and Catherine the Second. Her husband died very young without repenting his sins, and she devoted the rest of her life to atoning for this. She renounced earthly joys and treasures and went wherever she was needed." Sergei's eyelids felt heavy. "Which is why we are here. But the Blessed Xenia had God's gift of clairvoyance. One day she urged her friend to go at once to the Smolensk Cemetery. 'God has given you a son,' she told the startled woman." Sergei's eyes opened wide at the word, *son*. Sister Agatha reached up and stroked his brow with the tips of her fingers. "When her friend got near the cemetery, a crowd gathered by the roadside. Pushing them aside, she saw a new-born baby; the mother dead at its side. She gathered the boy into her arms, took him home and raised him as her own son." The only noise now was Sergei's laboured breathing. "You will know when it is time to take your son into your heart again," the nun whispered.

Sergei did not hear the end of the nun's tale. Exhausted sleep claimed him. He dreamt he was lying on a red and white blanket, his head resting on a cushion, its fabric patterned with splashes of bright red stitches. There was a wicker picnic basket on the far edge of the blanket. He sat up. Looked around. He was surrounded by tall grass. Rising to his feet, he saw a flash of pink weaving around in the grass. He heard Mitch's voice calling: "Anja? Where are you, Anja?" Sergei watched as Mitch swayed towards him as though swimming through the long grass. Then he was gone; the only sound was the rustle of wind through the grass.

"*Nyet! Nyet!* They must not find him." Sergei's own voice jolted him awake. He looked around. The dimmed light in the corridor shone through the glass panels onto the tiled floor.

There was a flicker of movement. *There's someone there! That woman. It's her!* The woman removed her mask. Her mouth moved but he could not hear her words. Her lips were thin and a lizard-like tongue darted in and out of her mouth. He shuddered and pulled the bedclothes over his face, trembling. When he dared to look again, she had gone.

I'll come back tomorrow, that's what she said. Sergei slid his legs over the side of the bed. *I must find Pavel. Kolya. Father Nikolai. They'll stop her.* His feet pattered on the tiles as he walked over to the locker where his clothes were hanging. He shivered as he discarded his nightshirt, put on his pants and shirt before reaching for the sweater on the shelf. He checked over his shoulder; there wasn't anyone in the corridor. *Hurry, before she comes back,* he cautioned himself as he sat on the bed and pulled on the boots. Olga Pietrovna's words ran through his head: "*He's put some polish on your boots." Kolya. I have to find Kolya. And Anja? Pavel? Where are they?* He cried to himself as he tried to unravel the muddle in his mind. They were all in there somewhere, if only he could find them. "I must tell them to watch out for that woman," he muttered, and opened the door to the garden. It was quiet, cold. He breathed in the damp air before shuffling across the wide expanse of grass, holding onto his pants as they started to drift downwards. He reached the line of trees and stood still until his eyes became accustomed to the dark. *The lake. Kolya's gone to the lake. That's where he is. He will help me.*

He didn't find the lake. Eventually, he stumbled out of the woods and found himself on a dirt path at the side of a road. Early-morning light streaked through gaps in the trees as he picked his way around garbage on the path. He stopped now and then, bent double, trying to still the rasping in his lungs. The dirt path became a paved pathway. There were a few people about now. He tried to ask an elderly man if he knew where Pavel was, but he brushed past him. Sergei started to shiver. *If only I could find someone. Anyone. Anja's here somewhere. I saw her.* He called his granddaughter's name and waited.

At a crossroads, he stepped into the road. A blast of a car's horn sent him scurrying back to the pathway. After a while, he sank down onto a wooden bench. His breath came in gasps, his throat on fire. He thought of the bright, sunny room, the pale green curtains, Sister Agatha. He bent his head and stared at the worn pathway. When he looked up, an old woman was standing two or three steps away. Her mouth was open, revealing rotting teeth. Her coat was tied around her waist with string, and she carried a bulging plastic bag in each hand.

"Who are you?" she bellowed. "You're sitting on my seat!"

Sergei got to his feet and backed away from her, his arms hugging his upper body.

"Kolya … I'm looking for Kolya," he whimpered.

"Don't know no Kolya."

"He lives here. With the priest. He'll help me find Anja." Sergei wiped the back of one hand across his lips. He stared at the dark red stain on his skin.

"Don't come near me, old man." The woman backed away.

"I have to find them. I thought they were here." He put a hand to the side of his head. "But it may have been that other place. Jakob told me. Perm. Yes, that's it."

"Perm? Well, you'd best be getting the train. That's the quickest way. You got the fare, old man?"

Sergei searched his pockets.

"Well you best get in the carriage with all the goods. You can hide there. At least it's warm," she cackled, opening her cavernous mouth wide. "Watch they don't catch you."

"Tell me, please," he waved a hand in front of his body, "Where is it … the train?"

"Don't you know nothing?" She pointed an arm back the way he had come, put her bags on the seat and sat down. "Don't you be sitting on my seat again, old man."

55
Toronto
May 2002

Mitch sighed as he loaded the last of the lunchtime crockery into the dishwasher. *Peace reigns at last.* The twins were sitting at the kitchen table, tea towels secured around their upper bodies, Masha moulding clay into something vaguely resembling the shape of a dog while Ivo painted his newly-constructed miniature racing car. Mitch picked up the newspaper and pulled out a stool from under the counter. Before he could sit down, the doorbell rang.

In the hallway, he peered through the stained-glass window. He couldn't see anyone. "Is Mama back?" Masha's voice came from behind him as he opened the door. A young woman stood at the side of the porch. "Yes?" Mitch asked. She stared at him. "Do you want to see my puppy?" Masha asked, holding out the clay figure. Stifling a cry, the young woman turned on her heel and fled.

"Hey! Wait!" Mitch clattered down the porch steps after her. It wasn't unheard of for a girl who had been trafficked to appear on their doorstep. It was something he and Lucy didn't particularly want to happen but, in an emergency, it was sometimes unavoidable. "Don't go. Tell me why you're here." He looked quickly up and down the street, checking she hadn't been followed by a pimp or one of the heavies.

On the sidewalk, she turned slowly around. "Papa?"

Mitch stopped in his tracks and stared at her. *Papa? What does she mean? No. She can't be. This young woman with straight brown hair ... she can't be Anja.* His breath caught in his throat as he noticed the sprinkling of freckles across her nose. "Anja?" he gripped the gate post.

At that moment, Masha grabbed one of Anja's hands and looked up at her. "Will you play with me? You could make your own puppy."

A weak smile drifted across Anja's face. She wiped tears away with the back of her hand.

"Annushka … it is you … isn't it?" Mitch touched her cheeks gently with the fingers of one hand, then pulled his precious daughter into his arms. "*Moya dorogaya devochka.* It really is you." He held her away, for a moment not daring to believe that his beloved daughter was really here. Then he hugged her close again. *"Ya ne mogu v eto poverit'."*

"Papa, *ya nashel tebya. Ya nashel tebya."* Anja sobbed.

Mitch felt her breath warm on his neck. "My darling … you're really here?"

"Can she stay, Papa? Can she stay and play with me?" Masha's insistent tones penetrated the whirling in his brain.

Mitch kissed the side of Anja's face. "I can't believe it!" He gulped back the heartache of the past years.

"Papa!" Masha stamped her foot.

Mitch released his grip on Anja. "This absolute menace is Masha," he croaked, wiping tears away with the backs of his hands. "And this beautiful young lady is your sister, Masha. Her name is Anja." *Am I really saying this?* He reached for the reassuring warmth of his lost daughter's hand.

"My sister?" Masha screwed up her face. "Like Charlotte's sister, Chloë?"

"Charlotte is Masha's friend at school," Mitch explained in Russian. He gripped Anja's hand tighter.

"But she's big!" Masha pouted.

"Some sisters are big," Mitch told her. "Like Mama's sister, your Auntie Erin." He cuffed away tears that were again running down his cheeks.

"I like having a sister," Masha decided. "I've only got Ivo. We were born on the same day, you know. We're twins." Masha pointed to her brother, who was standing on the porch steps. "He's mean sometimes, but I suppose he's all right."

"I … I have a brother too," Anja said. The English words she had painstakingly learnt in Omsk sounded strange to her ears in this unfamiliar place.

"Let's go inside," Mitch suggested, putting an arm around Anja as they walked up the path to the house. How often he had dreamt of this moment.

"She's my sister," Masha boasted to Ivo as she ran ahead.

"No she's not!" Ivo shot back at her.

"She is so. Papa said."

Ivo hunched his shoulders.

"Come on," Mitch said, as he ushered all three of his children inside and closed the door. "When did you get here? Did you fly over on your own? How did you find me?" The questions which were whirling around in his head spilled out as Masha pulled Anja along the hallway and into the kitchen. Ivo trailed behind.

"*Dyadya* Pyotr, Mama's brother …" Anja paused for a moment. Mitch nodded, remembering Natasha's brother, who had been a couple of years ahead at law school. He also remembered Pyotr's warning when he heard Mitch was romantically involved with Natasha: *You can't afford her. How right he was*, Mitch thought now. "He arranged for an exit visa and a letter of invitation from a friend of one of his colleagues who lives in Toronto," Anja explained as she looked around. "Your …? The twins' mother?"

"Lucy. She was called in to work. It happens sometimes." Mitch thought it best not to elaborate about Lucy. There was an awkward silence for a moment, then he suggested, "Have you eaten? I could make you a sandwich."

"I'm not hungry, but maybe a cup of tea …"

"It will have to be English tea," Mitch explained, filling the kettle and switching it on.

After Anja was introduced properly to Ivo, the twins settled back at the table. "I told you she's my sister!" Masha gloated. Ivo stuck his tongue out at her. "Mama says you'll be stuck like that one day!" she told him triumphantly.

"We'll go into the sitting room, Anja. Leave these two brats here." Mitch ruffled Ivo's mop of blond hair.

Mitch and Anja sat side by side on the sofa. He felt strangely tense, not knowing what to say to her. So many years had passed. She was a young woman now, not the little girl whose image he had kept in his mind. How could he put into words how he had longed for this day, confess he had been scared to go to Russia to find her? Scared she would reject him. And now she was here, sitting right beside him on their sofa in Toronto. She met his gaze and smiled, deepening the dimples in her cheeks.

"What happened with your hair?" he ventured. "I still imagined you as that little girl with the mop of brown curls."

"*Tyotya* Mila. She and Dasha, they took me to a hairdresser in St Petersburg. We got it straightened. Now, I have this heated thing so that I can do it at home. It takes forever," she laughed, pulling at a strand of hair.

For Mitch, her laughter brought back so many memories of happy times in Leningrad, times when he would take her for a walk along the banks of the Neva … skating outdoors in the winter … making up silly songs as they tramped through the snow. Times it was painful to think about in the long years since he last saw her. Now, it all came rushing back.

Anja delved into her purse. "I have something for you," she said, and held out an envelope to him. "It's from *Deda's* friend Vera Aleksandrovna Kishinevskaya."

"I haven't heard from her for years," Mitch said as he tore open the envelope. "I thought she was probably dead," he added.

Anja watched as he began to read Vera's letter.

"What? I don't believe it!" His hand went to his mouth. "Papa? She says Papa's alive? She told me he was dead! Buried close to my mother, that's what she said."

Anja gripped his arm. "Believe me, Papa. *Deda* is alive. *Dyadya* Pyotr checked. He's in one of those horrid labour camps, somewhere near Perm. I can't bear to think of him in that sort of place." Anja leaned forward, twisting a handkerchief around and around in her fingers.

"Jesus bloody Christ! Why the hell did that stupid old woman tell me he died? Whatever was …"

"She said she promised *Deda*. He didn't want you to go back to Russia."

"And he's been …" Mitch held the side of his head, as he tried to make sense of the images whirling in his mind. *Papa in one of those terrible places? All these years?* "He's been there all that time. And I didn't know." *Why? Why would they send him there? He hadn't done anything wrong.* He picked up Vera's letter again and read on. "They charged him with human trafficking? They can't have."

"*Dyadya* Pyotr said it was to get back at you. When they couldn't find you, they took him."

"It's all my fault. Everything. I should never have done it. I lost you. Papa." Mitch's voice broke up.

"Vera Alexandrovna, she went there, tried to see him. They wouldn't let her. She and Leonid, they hung around for days hoping to get a glimpse of him, hoping he would see them, so he would know they cared about him."

"If only she'd told me, I could have done something to get him out." Mitch swallowed hard and got to his feet. He shook his head as he paced back and forth in the room, running his fingers through his hair. "I have to go there. Find him."

"Mama, she told me what you did. Those girls …" Anja reached out and grasped her father's hand, pulling him back onto the sofa. "I'm so proud of you, Papa."

Mitch took her hand in both of his then wrapped her in his arms and nestled his head in her hair, breathing in the smell of this daughter whom he had thought was lost to him. "Annushka," he murmured as he pulled away.

Anja smiled at him. "*Dyadya* Pyotr's friend here, he said you are working for a law firm, prosecuting traffickers, lobbying for better legislation to bring people like," she hesitated for a moment, "people like Yagudin to justice."

"I'm trying, but it's an uphill battle, and I seriously wonder if it will have any effect."

"At least you're trying … doing something. Dina, one of my friends in the village, she was trafficked to Turkey. She got away and somehow made her way back, carrying her young baby. She was in a terrible state, but she's gradually getting her life back together."

"I was very worried when I found out that you and your mother were with Boris. Vera assured me he is a reformed character, but—"

"Boris is okay. He was good to us," Anja cut in. "He runs a legitimate business in Omsk now, and it was his idea that I came here to find you. He arranged for an elderly lady there to give me English lessons."

Mitch tried not to let his thoughts drift back to the fateful day on Nevsky Prospekt when he and Anja watched from the other side of the street as Boris held the car door open for Natasha and her lover, Mikhail Yagudin.

Now, Mitch squeezed Anja's hand and got to his feet. "The tea … I'll make the tea."

She walked over to the window. Two young girls were turning a skipping rope in the road while three others jumped in and out of it. Snatches of a song they were singing drifted in through an open window. She could hear Mitch talking to the twins, encouraging them to stay in the kitchen a little longer. She picked up a framed photograph from the bookcase. Her father and a blonde-haired woman who was holding a spray of flowers.

"I brought the milk separately. I didn't know how you take it." *How awful is that, not knowing how my own daughter takes her tea?* he asked himself as he put a tray down onto a low table in the middle of the room. "Sugar? Or maybe you'd like honey?"

"It's fine as it is," Anja smiled. "She's very pretty," she murmured, placing the picture back on the bookcase.

"Sorry we don't have any cookies. Masha ate the last one this morning. We were going to the corner store later to get some more."

"I've done nothing but eat since I arrived here," Anja laughed. "I'm staying with *Dyadya* Pyotr's friends and they seem to think I need fattening up!" She sat back on the sofa and took a sip of her tea.

"You look fine to me, just fine." Although Mitch's words held a touch of pride, it felt strange saying them to his daughter, this young woman he hardly knew any more. He picked up Vera's letter again and shook his head. "I still can't believe she told me that … let me believe he was dead. All these years. How could she? I should have known, though. She'd lied to me before." He threw the letter onto the table and sank down next to Anja on the sofa. "God protect me from meddling old women!"

"She's not the only one." Anja sighed. "Another old woman, she meddled in our lives too."

"What old woman?"

"Your letters, birthday cards. They didn't get to me."

"Did your mother take them?"

"*Nyet.* Mama would never do that!"

Mitch bit back his retort. "To begin with, I sent the letters to Vera. Don't tell me she never forwarded them."

"She sent them on. But," Anja sought for words, "Boris's aunt, *Tyotya* Yevdokia, she had a friend who worked in the village mail office. She must have given them to *Tyotya*. We didn't know anything about them until a few months ago when Boris was clearing out her bedroom. *Tyotya's* in a nursing home in Omsk," she explained. "Boris is sure Mama didn't know about them either."

"When I didn't hear from you or your mother, I assumed you didn't want anything to do with me. I kept writing for a while," Mitch paused, shaking his head, "then I gave up." He picked up his mug of tea and held it in both hands.

Silence washed around them, broken a moment or two later by the ring of the doorbell and the sound of the twins pounding along the hallway. Mitch put his mug down and got to his feet. "It's probably Lucy. She's always forgetting her keys," he said. "Stay there."

Anja straightened her shoulders, steeling herself to meet her father's wife … her stepmother. The woman who had taken her mother's place.

56
Ekaterinburg
May 2002

Sergei gripped a wooden post at the side of a shop doorway. *So much noise. So many people. Where are they all going?* he asked himself. He stood for some minutes trying to quell the uneasiness in his stomach before staggering further along the sidewalk—he felt as if he was floating on air, unable to control the direction in which he was headed. *You must find Kolya. He said he was coming back. Where is he? And Pavel? He was always my friend. Where have they all gone?*

He shielded his eyes from the bright lights as he turned into a square. There were parked cars everywhere, some with people in them, some abandoned. Sunlight bounced off the roofs of a row of pale blue vans standing in front of a building. To one side, trucks were lined up. He heard the rhythmic thud, thud, of mechanical equipment. His body convulsed with each thud as he shuffled closer to the building, weaving around slow-moving vehicles as they sought space to park. People got out, some carrying suitcases, shouting to others. *It must be the station*, he told himself as car doors slammed around him. He followed a line of people past a newsstand and into the station building. The people in front of him stopped to let a crowd of people pass, some loaded down with children and luggage.

Sergei lurched to one side and edged along a wall. He could see the stairs now. He gripped the iron rail. One step, two steps … down … down. He kept his head bowed, glancing from side to side. The crowd coming up the steps was diminishing and he moved as fast as he could, afraid someone would see him. *That woman! She could be here!* He missed his footing and crashed onto the bottom step. Crawling on his knees he sought the shadows by the side of a big luggage cart. He looked around the side of the cart. There was a train. Female attendants, in their turquoise coats and black hats, climbed aboard. Doors slammed and, with a loud clunk, the train shunted forward. *'You best get in the carriage with all the goods,'* the crone's words came back to him. *Where is it?* He asked himself as the train gathered speed and the last carriage rumbled past.

Sergei sat back, his head slumped against his bent knees as he began to wheeze. *Tikhiy,* he cautioned himself, but he could no longer smother the rasping cough that engulfed his body. His legs and arms jerked with each spasm, and sweat dripped from his chin as he fought to get air into his lungs. It felt as though he was breathing through a straw, suffocating. He clawed at his sweater. After a few minutes, exhaustion overtook him and he lay down next to the cart.

Sometime later, he heard voices nearby. Using the metal bars running up the side of the cart, he raised himself slowly to his feet. There were people on the platform. A movement on the other side of the tracks caught his eye. A small girl. Brown curls. She was holding a woman's hand and, as he watched, they turned and walked along the far platform. Sergei saw red ribbons.

"Anja! Anja!" His voice sounded far away. He staggered along the platform, his hands working in front of him as though swimming through fog. He tried to call out again, but each laboured intake of breath produced only an eerie gasping sound. He propelled himself forward, lurching from side to side. The mist was all around him now and he could no longer feel the platform beneath his feet. He held out his arms towards a bright light. "Anja! Wait for me … it's *Deda.*" His words tangled with the noise of wheels grinding on steel, the screech of brakes.

On the opposite platform, the woman stepped quickly in front of the small girl's line of vision. "Come, Darya. We must go home." The child's red ribbons bobbed behind her as they hurried away.

57
Toronto
May 2002

Mitch listened to the hum of voices upstairs as he collected toys and books the twins had left strewn around the sitting room. He picked up Masha's mended doll, forgotten in the events of the day. He held it close for a moment. *Better take it upstairs, or she'll be fretting over it in the night,* he thought, going into the hallway and placing it on the side of one of the stairs. Lucy and Anja were chatting upstairs, settling Anja in the guest room.

Earlier, Mitch had driven Anja to collect her belongings from where she had been staying since arriving in Toronto a few days ago. On the way there, Anja had said, "She's nice, Lucy. I like her." The tenseness in Mitch's shoulders had eased as he responded: "It must have been difficult for you, seeing the twins then Lucy."

"It was at first." She stared out of the car window. "But I should have known, and I'm glad you have someone nice who cares about you." They continued in silence for a while, then Anja spoke: "Mama, she changed when we lived in the village. You wouldn't have recognised her. She never wore make-up, let her hair grow really long. She looked beautiful, even in the plain clothes she wore."

Mitch raised his eyebrows, trying to reconcile what Anja said with his memories of his fashion-conscious ex-wife, the woman who would never set foot outside the door without checking every aspect of her appearance in the mirror. The woman whose expensive tastes had plunged them further and further into debt. "She was always a beautiful woman."

Now, as Mitch put the last of the toys away, he remembered the look Lucy had shot at him when Anja read out part of the letter her mother had written to her on the day she died.

"Papa a message. I'm sorry. Tell him. It was a wicked lie. He would never do such a thing." Anja had paused. "What did she mean … Papa?"

"I don't know," he lied, shaking his head. "Maybe she was delirious, mixed me up with someone else." How could he tell Anja that the mother she loved had threatened that if he challenged the faked signature on the divorce papers, she would accuse him of sexually molesting Anja? He would have to explain to Lucy, though.

As he did every night, Mitch opened the front door to breathe in the last of the day. He walked down the steps to the gate. An aircraft droned overhead and his eyes followed its lights twinkling in the clear night sky. He looked up and down the road. It was quiet now, except for the distant noise of traffic along the Danforth and the occasional staccato burst of sound coming through the open windows of the DiRisio's house next door. Mitch and Lucy had long ago learnt that the raised voices of their neighbours did not mean an argument was in progress. Roseann and Albert's rapid speech rose to fortissimo over the merest trifle.

Mitch leaned back on the gate. His gaze travelled to the streaks of light seeping through the wooden shutters in the guest room. He could still hardly believe that his beloved daughter was really here. After all the years of heartache, they were together again. He walked back to the porch and sank down into the cushioned depths of a wicker chair. His mind flickered over the events of the day, the feeling that ran through him when he realised the young woman really was his Anja. The day he longed for had finally arrived. But, his father? Strangely, his father's death had been easier to accept than the thought of him in that terrible place, the horrors he might have experienced, the sense of degradation. *How could a proud man like Papa cope?* "Oh, Papa? Why did you make that stupid old woman lie to me?"

This evening, Mitch had called the airline and got himself a seat on the same plane as Anja to St Petersburg. Tomorrow, he would sort out a visa. In a week's time, they would be on their way. He was tempted to phone or go to see Vera Kishinevskaya, but he had more important things to do. *Papa! I must get Papa out of that place. Tomorrow, I'll call Pyotr and ask him what is the quickest way to secure his release.* He didn't dare let himself imagine what sort of state Papa would be in. A man of …? *How old is Papa now?* Since Vera told him Sergei had died, he had not allowed himself to imagine him as any different to the man who had reluctantly walked away from him in the Cathedral crypt. He had thought of him so often, he could trace every line on his face. A frisson of excitement ran through his body now at the thought of seeing his beloved father again. *I'll get the best medical attention for him. Take him somewhere to rest and then bring him here to Canada.* He could scarcely contain his excitement at the thought of hearing again the sound of his father's voice, his laugh. *Unbelievable!* he thought, not for the first time since he read Vera's confession. *Papa will be so happy when he hears Anja is safe, that he has two more grandchildren. And Lucy.* He leaned back in the chair, inhaling the smells of spring—sweet lilac, the delicate scent of verbena, a trace of barbeque smoke—as he imagined the day they would all be together here in Canada.

The familiar strains of a tenor voice reached his ears. *"Che gelida manina ... se la lasci riscaldar." Puccini.* He chuckled to himself. Roseann and Albert played that record every night.

He got to his feet and, with an arm wrapped around one of the posts supporting the porch, watched the halo of light enshrouding the city blend from gold into navy blue as it met the night sky.

Glossary of Russian Words and Phrases

(Russian words often have numerous spellings depending on the tense and/or gender)

Archangel Kozulya cookies	Cookies in shape of a deer, goat, or sheep enjoyed during the Christmas season
Baba Yaga	Supernatural being appearing as a deformed or ferocious-looking old woman
Babushka	Grandmother
Bayushki Bayu	Russian lullaby
Belochka	Chocolate candy with a squirrel on wrapper
Biskvit	Sponge cake with cream cheese frosting
Blatniyeh	Lower caste of connected thieves
Blokada	Prolonged military blockade by Nazi Germany against Soviet city of Leningrad during World War II
Blyad!	Whore!
Bobal'ki	Lenten bread
Borscht	Sour beetroot soup
Brakosochetaniye	Marriage
Brodyaga. Brodyaga Nashi sapoga brodyat, brodyagi	Tramp. Tramp. Our boots tramp, tramp
Bulachnaya	Bakery
Chifir	Bitter, concentrated brew of tea
Chto eto, moya dorogaya?	What is it, my darling?
Chto nay thuk?	What's wrong?
Da	Yes
Dacha	Country house / cottage
Da eto	Yes, it is

Ded Moroz	Grandfather Frost—Slavic version of Santa Claus
Deda / Dedushka	Grandfather
Der'mo!	Shit!
Desyat'?	Ten?
Desyat' minut	Ten minutes
Dobroye utro	Good morning
Domovoi	House spirit of Slavic mythology
Dostatochno!	Enough!
Durák	Idiot
Dyadya	Uncle
Eto dla vas	It is for you
Eto moya plemyannitsa	This is my niece
Eto nay	It's not
Eto nepravilno	This is wrong
Eto nevozmozhno	It is not possible
Eto slishkom	It's too much
Eto vse budet v poryadke	It's all going to be okay
Gde eto?	Where is it?
Gde ya?	Where am I?
Govno!	Shit!
Homo Sovieticus	Person uncritically supporting Soviet values / having a Soviet mentality (usually used sarcastically)
Idi syuda!	Come here!
Imbetsil	Imbecile
Izba	House built from square frames of logs
Kafe-konditerskaya	Café / pastry shop
Kak vas zovut?	What is your name?
Kasha	Porridge
Kholkhoz	Collective farm
Kolyva	Traditional wheat berry memorial food
Krasnaya Moskva	Red Moscow (Russian perfume)
Krasnyy ugol	Corner for Christian iconography in the house (akin to a house altar or praying spot)
Kto eto?	Who is this?
Kuda vy sobiraetes?	Where are you going?
Kutya	Porridge made from wheatberries, honey and poppy seeds

Leshii	Tutelary deity of the forests in pagan Slavic mythology
Lyubov' maya	My love
Mafiyosa	Mafia
Menya zovot	My name is
Militsiya	Militia / police
Mne thuck zhal	I'm so sorry
Moi galubchik	My darling
Moujiks	Russian peasants
Moy drug	My friend
Moy umnyy syn	My smart son
Moya dorogaya devochka	My darling girl
Moya dragotsennaya	My precious
Naden' etu grebanuyu odezhdu!	Put the fucking clothes on!
Nevoz	Impossible
Nichego	Nothing
Nikto zdes nay prichinite vam vreda	No one here will hurt you
Nyet	No
Nyet ... Ya ne	No … I don't
O Bozhe!	Oh my God!
Obraz	Image
Ona zdes'	She's here
On govorit, chto eto Rozhdestva	He says it's Christmas
Otkuda vy?	Where are you from?
Pakhan	Mafia boss /godfather
Palach!	Executioner!
Panikhida	Service for the repose of the departed
Pazhalusta	Please
Pelmeni	Dumplings
Pirozhki	Puffed pastries filled with potatoes, meat, cabbage or cheese
Podozhdite menia!	Wait for me!
Pomogi mne!	Help me!
Pozvol'te mne pomoch' vam	Let's help you
Prastite	Pardon / sorry
Presbyter	Priest/leader of congregation in Russian Orthodox Church
Prikosnis' ko mne	Come to me!
Privedi ego s soboy	Bring him in
Prodolzhay, moi drug	Keep going, my friend

Pryaniki	Honey spiced cookies
Pyatorka	The highest grade at school
Samizdat	Dissident underground publication
Sauerkraut	Fermented raw cabbage
Schastlivogo Rozhdestva	Merry Christmas
S Dnem Rozhdeniya!	Happy Birthday to you!
Shag na front!	Step to the front!
Snegurochka	The Snow Maiden
Sochelnik	Christmas Eve—celebrated on January 6
Solyanka	Thick spicy and sour soup
Spasiba	Thank you
Spesit	Hurry up
Spokoynoy nochi	Good night
Spokoynoy, moy drug	Calm, my friend
S Rhozhdestvom Khristovym	With the birth of Christ (Happy Christmas)
Syn	Son
Syrniki	Fried quark pancakes
Taiga	Boreal forest
Tapochki	Slippers
Tikhiy	Quiet
Tolko odin	Just one
Totentanz	Dance of the Dead, composed by Franz Liszt
Tri raza!	Three times!
Troika	Vehicle drawn by three horses
Ty ne spish'?	Are you awake?
Tyotya	Aunt
Ty v poryadke?	Are you okay?
Ublyudok	Bastard
Uchilishcha	School
Ukha	Fish soup with a clear broth
Valenki	Felt boots
Vechnaya pamyat	Eternal memory
Verni menya, pazhalusta	Take me back, please
V lesu rodilas yolochka	A Christmas tree was born in the forest
Vory v zakone	Thieves in law / mobsters
Vozvrashchaysya k rabote	Get back to work
Vy	You
Vy daleko idete?	Are you going far?

Vy dolzhny idti	You have to go
Vy gavarite pa-russky?	You speak Russian?
Vy vernetes'?	You'll come back?
Vyyti!	Get out!
Ya nashel tebya	I found you
Ya nay ponimayu	I don't understand
Ya ne	I don't
Ya ne mogu v eto poverit'	I can't believe it
Ya v poryadke	I am well
Yurist	Lawyer
Zatknis'!	Shut up!
Zakuska	Cold appetisers / hors d'oeuvres